THE LAST ENCHANTMENT

'I told the midwife to take him away, and find me a son I dared to show you. Perhaps I did wrong. I did it to save my name, and your honour. I hated the child. How could I want to bear any man's child but yours? I had hoped it was your son, not his, but it was his. It is true that he was sickly. Let us hope that he is dead, too, by this.' The king said, 'Let us do more than that. Let us make sure.'

THE LAST ENCHANTMENT, Mary Stewart's third magnificent and haunting novel of Dark Age Britain.

'Fully captures the flavour of Arthurian Britain and its rich legends, with larger than life characters who involve the reader in every action and emotion.'

The Bookseller

'Spell-binding.'

Harpers Queen

The Last Enchantment

Mary Stewart

CORONET BOOKS
Hodder and Stoughton

*To one who was dead and is alive again,
who was lost, and is found.*

Copyright © 1979 by Mary Stewart

First published in Great Britain 1979 by
Hodder and Stoughton Limited

Coronet edition 1980

Printed in Canada

ISBN 0 340 25292 8

CONTENTS

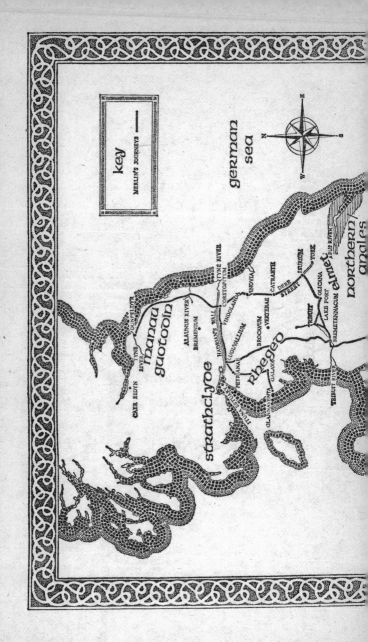

key

MERLIN'S JOURNEYS ——————

german sea

DUNPELDYR

manau guotodin

CAER EIDYN

RIVER TYNE

ALAUNUS RIVER

BREMENIUM

strathclyde

HADRIAN'S WALL

PASS

CORSTOPITUNE RIVER

VINDOLANDA

LUGUVALLIUM

TRIMONTIUM

PETRIANAE

GLANNAVENTA

GALAVA

BROCAVUM

VERTERAE

rheged

VINOVIA

DERE STREET

CATRAETE

ISURIUM

OLICANA

RIBUT

LAKE FORT

BREMETENNACUM

TRIBUT RIVER

YORE

elmet

URE RIVER

northern

angles

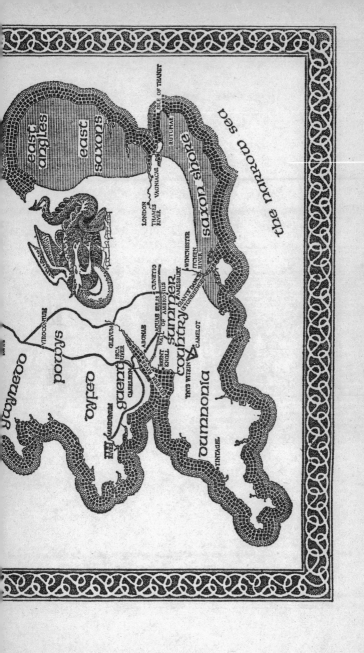

Book 1

DUNPELDYR

CHAPTER 1

Not every king would care to start his reign with the wholesale massacre of children. This is what they whisper of Arthur, even though in other ways he is held up as the type itself of the noble ruler, the protector alike of high and lowly.

It is harder to kill a whisper than even a shouted calumny. Besides, in the minds of simple men, to whom the High King is the ruler of their lives, and the dispenser of all fates, Arthur would be held accountable for all that happened in his realm, evil and good alike, from a re-sounding victory in the battlefield to a bad rain-storm or a barren flock.

So, although a witch plotted the massacre, and another king gave the order for it, and though I myself tried to shoulder the blame, the murmur still persists; that in the first year of his reign, Arthur the High King had his troops seek out and destroy some score of newly-born babies in the hope of catching in that bloody net one single boy-child, his bastard by incest with his half-sister Morgause.

'Calumny', I have called it, and it would be good to be able to declare openly that the story is a lie. But it is not quite that. It is a lie that he ordered the slaughter; but his sin was the first cause of it, and, though it would never have occurred to him to murder innocent children, it is true that he wanted his own child killed. So it is just that some of the blame should rest on him; just, too, that some of it should cling to me; for I, Merlin, who am accounted a man of power and vision, had waited idly by while the dangerous child was engendered, and the tragic term set to the peace and freedom which Arthur could win for his people. I can bear the blame, for now I am beyond men's judgment, but Arthur is still young enough to feel the sting of the story, and be haunted by thoughts of atonement; and when it happened he was younger still, in all the first white-and-golden flush of victory and kingship, held up on the love of the people, the acclamation of the soldiers, and the blaze of mystery that surrounded the drawing of the sword from the stone.

It happened like this. King Uther Pendragon lay with his army at Luguvallium in the northern kingdom of Rheged, where he was to face a massive Saxon attack under the brothers Colgrim and Badulf, grandsons of Hengist. The young Arthur, still little more than a boy, was brought to this, his first field, by his foster-father Count Ector of Galava, who presented him to the King. Arthur had been kept in ignorance of his royal birth and parentage, and Uther, though he had kept himself informed of the boy's growth and progress, had never once seen him since he was born. This because, during the wild night of love when Uther had lain with Ygraine, then the wife of Gorlois, Duke of Cornwall and Uther's most faithful commander, the old Duke himself had been killed. His death, though no fault of Uther's, weighed so heavily on the King that he swore never to claim for his own any child born of that night's guilty love. In due course Arthur had been handed to me to rear, and this I had done, at a far remove from both King and Queen. But there had been no other son born to them, and at last King Uther, who had ailed for some time, and who knew the danger of the Saxon threat he faced at Luguvallium, was forced to send for the boy, to acknowledge him publicly as his heir and present him to the assembled nobles and petty kings.

But before he could do so, the Saxons attacked. Uther, though too sick to ride at the head of the troops, took the field in a litter, with Cador, Duke of Cornwall, in command of the right, and on the left King Coel of Rheged, with Caw of Strathclyde and other leaders from the north. Only Lot, King of Lothian and Orkney, failed to take the

field. King Lot, a powerful king but a doubtful ally, held
his men in reserve, to throw them into the fight where
and when they should be needed. It was said that he held
back deliberately in the hope that Uther's army would be
destroyed, and that in the event the kingdom might fall to
him. If so, his hopes were defeated. When, in the fierce
fighting around the King's litter in the centre of the field,
young Arthur's sword broke in his hand, King Uther
threw to his hand his own royal sword, and with it (as
men understood it) the leadership of the kingdom. After
that he lay back in his litter and watched the boy, ablaze
like some comet of victory, lead an attack that put the
Saxons to rout.

Afterwards, at the victory feast, Lot headed a faction of
rebel lords who opposed Uther's choice of heir. At the
height of the brawling, contentious feast, King Uther
died, leaving the boy, with myself beside him, to face and
win them over.

What happened then has become the stuff of song and
story. Enough here to say that, by his own kingly bearing,
and through the sign sent from the god, Arthur showed
himself undoubted King.

But the evil seed had already been sown. On the previous day, while he was still ignorant of his true parentage,
Arthur had met Morgause, Uther's bastard daughter, and
his own half-sister. She was very lovely, and he was young,
in all the flush of his first victory, so when she sent her
maid for him that night he went eagerly, with no more
thought of what the night's pleasure might bring but the
cooling of his hot blood and the loss of his maidenhood.

Hers, you may be sure, had been lost long ago. Nor was
she innocent in other ways. She knew who Arthur was,
and sinned with him knowingly, in a bid for power.
Marriage, of course, she could not hope for, but a bastard
born of incest might be a powerful weapon in her hand
when the old King, her father, died, and the new young
King took the throne.

When Arthur found what he had done, he might have

added to his sin by killing her, but for my intervention. I
banished her from court, bidding her take horse for York,
where Uther's true-born daughter Morgan was lodged
with her attendants, awaiting her marriage to the King of
Lothian. Morgause, who like everyone else in those days
was afraid of me, obeyed me and went, to practise her
woman's spells and nourish her bastard in exile. Which
she did, as you will hear, at her sister Morgan's expense.

But of that later. It would be better, now, to go back to
the time when, in the breaking of a new and auspicious
day, with Morgause out of mind and on her way to York,
Arthur Pendragon sat in Luguvallium of Rheged to receive homage, and the sun shone.

I was not there. I had already done homage, in the small
hours between moonlight and sunrise, in the forest shrine
where Arthur had lifted the sword of Maximus from the
stone altar, and by that act declared himself the rightful
King. Afterwards, when he, with the other princes and
nobles, had gone in all the pomp and splendour of
triumph, I had stayed alone in the shrine. I had a debt to
pay to the gods of the place.

It was called a chapel now—the Perilous Chapel, Arthur
had named it—but it had been a holy place long before
men had laid stone on stone and raised the altar. It was
sacred first to the gods of the land itself, the small spirits
that haunt hill and stream and forest, together with the
greater gods of air, whose power breathes through cloud
and frost and speaking wind. No one knew for whom the
chapel had first been built. Later, with the Romans, had
come Mithras, the soldiers' god, and an altar was raised to
him within it. But the place was still haunted with all its
ancient holiness; the older gods received their sacrifices,
and the nine-fold lights still burned unquenched by the
open doorway.

All through the years when Arthur had been hidden,
for his own safety, with Count Ector in the Wild Forest, I
had stayed near him, known only as the keeper of the

shrine, the hermit of the Chapel in the Green. Here I had
finally hidden the great sword of Maximus (whom the
Welsh called Macsen), until the boy should come of an
age to lift it, and with it drive the kingdom's enemies out
and destroy them. The Emperor Maximus himself had
done so, a hundred years before, and men thought of the
great sword now as a talisman, a god-sent sword of magic,
to be wielded only for victory, and only by the man who
had the right. I, Merlinus Ambrosius, kin to Macsen, had
lifted it from its long hiding-place in the earth, and had
laid it aside for the one to come who would be greater
than I. I hid it first in a flooded cave below the forest lake,
then, finally, on the chapel altar, locked like carving in
the stone, and shrouded from common sight and touch in
the cold white fire called by my art from heaven.

From this unearthly blaze, to the wonder and terror of
all present, Arthur had raised the sword. Afterwards,
when the new King and his nobles and captains had gone
from the chapel, it could be seen that the wildfire of the
new god had scoured the place of all that had formerly
been held sacred, leaving only the altar, to be freshly
decked for him alone.

I had long known that this god brooked no companions.
He was not mine, nor (I suspected) would he ever be
Arthur's, but throughout the sweet three corners of
Britain he was moving, emptying the ancient shrines, and
changing the face of worship. I had seen with awe, and
with grief, how his fires had swept away the signs of an
older kind of holiness; but he had marked the Perilous
Chapel—and perhaps the sword—as his own, beyond
denying.

So all through that day I worked to make the shrine
clean again and fit for its new tenant. It took a long time;
I was stiff from recent hurts, and from a night of sleepless
vigil; besides, there are things that must be performed
decently and in order. But at length all was done, and
when, shortly before sunset, the servant of the shrine came

back from the town, I took the horse he had brought, and
rode down through the quiet woods.

*   *   *

It was late when I came to the gates, but these were
open, and no one challenged me as I rode in. The place
was still in a roar; the sky was alight with bonfires, the air
throbbed with singing, and through the smoke one could
smell roasting meats and the reek of wine. Even the
presence of the dead King, lying there in the monastery
church with his guards around him, could not put a bridle
on men's tongues. The times were too full of happening,
the town too small: only the very old and the very young
found sleep that night.

I found none, certainly. It was well after midnight when
my servant came in, and after him Ralf.

He ducked his head for the lintel—he was a tall young
man—and waited till the door was shut, regarding me
with a look as wary as any he had ever given me in the
past when he had been my page, and feared my powers.

'You're still up?'

'As you see.' I was sitting in the high-backed chair beside the window. The servant had brought a brazier,
kindled against the chill of the September night. I had
bathed, and looked to my hurts again, and let the servant
put me into a loose bedgown, before I sent him away and
composed myself to rest. After the climax of fire and pain
and glory that had brought Arthur to the kingship, I, who
had lived my life only for that, felt the need for solitude
and silence. Sleep would not come yet, but I sat, content
and passive, with my eyes on the brazier's idle glow.

Ralf, still armed and jewelled as I had seen him that
morning at Arthur's side in the chapel, looked tired and
hollow-eyed himself, but he was young, and the night's
climax was for him a new beginning, rather than an end.
He said, abruptly: 'You should be resting. I gather that
you were attacked last night on the way up to the chapel.

How badly were you hurt?'

'Not mortally, though it feels bad enough! No, no, don't worry, it was bruises rather than wounds, and I've seen to them. But I'm afraid I lamed your horse for you. I'm sorry about that.'

'I've seen him. There's no real damage. It will take a week, no more. But you—you look exhausted, Merlin. You should be given time to rest.'

'And am I not to be?' As he hesitated, I lifted a brow at him. 'Come, out with it. What don't you want to say to me?'

The wary look broke into something like a grin. But his voice, suddenly formal, was quite expressionless, the voice of a courtier who is not quite sure which way, as they say, the deer will run. 'Prince Merlin, the King has desired me to bid you to his apartments. He wants to see you as soon as it is convenient for you.' As he spoke his eye lingered on the door in the wall opposite the window. Until last night Arthur had slept in that annexe of my chamber, and had come and gone at my bidding. Ralf caught my eye, and the grin became real.

'In other words, straight away,' he said. 'I'm sorry, Merlin, but that's the message as it came to me through the chamberlain. They might have left it till morning. I was assuming you would be asleep.'

'Sorry? For what? Kings have to start somewhere. Has he had any rest yet himself?'

'Not a hope. But he's got rid of the crowd at last, and they cleared the royal rooms while we were up at the shrine. He's there now.'

'Attended?'

'Only Bedwyr.'

That, I knew, meant, besides his friend Bedwyr, a small host of chamberers and servants, and possibly, even a few people still waiting in the antechambers.

'Then ask him to excuse me for a few minutes. I'll be there as soon as I've dressed. Will you send Lleu to me, please?'

But this he would not have. The servant was sent with the message, and then, as naturally as he had done in the past when he was a boy. Ralf helped me himself. He took the bedgown from me and folded it, and gently, with care for my stiff limbs, eased me into a day-robe, then knelt to put my sandals on and fasten them.

'Did the day go well?' I asked him.

'Very well. No shadow on it.'

'Lot of Lothian?'

He glanced up, grimly amused. 'Kept his place. The affair of the chapel has left its brand on him ... as it has on all of us.' The last phrase was muttered, as if to himself, as he bent his head to buckle the second sandal.

'On me, too, Ralf,' I said. 'I am not immune from the god's fire, either. As you see. How is Arthur?'

'Still on his own high and burning cloud.' This time the amusement held affection. He got to his feet. 'All the same, I think he's already looking ahead for storms. Now, your girdle. Is this the one?'

'It will do. Thank you. Storms? So soon? I suppose so.' I took the girdle from him and knotted it. 'Do you intend to stay with him, Ralf, and help him weather them, or do you count your duty done?' Ralf had spent the last nine years in Galava of Rheged, the remote corner of the country where Arthur had lived, unknown, as the ward of Count Ector. He had married a northern girl, and had a young family.

'To tell you the truth I've not thought about that yet,' he said. 'Too much has happened, all too quickly.' He laughed. 'One thing, if I stay with him, I can see that I'll look back with longing on the peaceful days when I had nothing to do but ride guard on those young dev— that is, on Bedwyr and the King! And you? You will hardly stay here as the hermit of the Green Chapel now? Will you come out of your fastness, and go with him?'

'I must. I have promised. Besides, it is my place. Not yours, though, unless you wish it. Between us, we made him King, and that is the end of the first part of the story.

You have a choice now. But you'll have plenty of time to make it.' He opened the door for me, and stood aside to let me pass him. I paused. 'We whistled up a strong wind, Ralf. Let us see which way it will blow us.'

'You'd let it?'

I laughed. 'I have a speaking mind that tells me I may have to. Come, let us start by obeying this summons.'

* * *

There were a few people still in the main antechamber to the King's apartments, but these were mostly servants, clearing and bearing away the remains of a meal which the King had apparently just finished. Guards stood woodenly at the door to the inner rooms. On a low bench near a window a young page lay, fast asleep; I remembered seeing him when I had come this way three days ago to talk with the dying Uther. Ulfin, the King's body-servant and chief chamberlain, was absent. I could guess where he was. He would serve the new King with all the devotion he had given to Uther, but tonight he would be found with his old master in the monastery church. The man who waited by Arthur's door was a stranger to me, as were half the servants there; they were men and women who normally served Rheged's own king in his castle, and who were helping with the extra pressure of work brought by the occasion, and by the High King's presence.

But they all knew me. As I entered the antechamber there was a sudden silence, and a complete cessation of movement, as if a spell had been cast. A servant carrying platters balanced along his arm, froze like someone faced with the Gorgon's head, and faces that turned to me were frozen similarly, pale and gape-mouthed, full of awe. I caught Ralf's eye on me, sardonic and affectionate. His brow quirked. 'You see?' it said to me, and I understood more fully his own hesitation when he came to my room with the King's message. As my servant and companion he had been close to me in the past, and had many times, in prophecy, and in what men call magic, watched and felt my power at work; but the power that had blazed and blown through the Perilous Chapel last night had been something of quite a different order. I could only guess at the stories that must have run, swift and changing as the wildfire itself, through Luguvallium: it was certain that the humbler folk had talked of nothing else all day. And like all strange tales, it would grow with the telling.

So they stood staring. As for the awe that frosted the air, like the cold wind that comes before a ghost, I was used to that. I walked through the motionless crowd to the King's door, and the guard moved aside without a challenge, but before the chamberlain could lay a hand to the door it opened, and Bedwyr came out.

Bedwyr was a quiet, dark boy, a month or two younger than Arthur. His father was Ban, the King of Benoic, and a cousin of a king of Brittany. The two boys had been close friends since childhood, when Bedwyr had been sent to Galava to learn the arts of war from Ector's master-at-arms, and to share the lessons I gave 'Emrys' (as Arthur was then called) at the shrine in the Wild Forest. He was already showing himself to be that strange contradiction, a born fighting man who is also a poet, at home equally with action or with the world of fancy and music. Pure Celt, you might say, where Arthur, like my father the High King Ambrosius, was Roman. I might have expected to see in Bedwyr's face the same awe left by the events of the miraculous night as in the faces of the humbler men present, but I could see only the aftermath of joy, a sort of uncomplicated happiness, and a sturdy trust in the future.

He stood aside for me, smiling. 'He's alone now.'

'Where will you sleep?'

'My father is lodging in the west tower.'

'Goodnight, then, Bedwyr.'

But as I moved to pass him he prevented me. He bent quickly and took my hand, then snatched it to him, and kissed it. 'I should have known you would see that it all came right. I was afraid, for a few minutes there in the hall, when Lot and his jackals started that treacherous fracas—'

'Hush,' I said. He had spoken softly, but there were ears to hear. 'That's over for the present. Leave it. And go straight to your father in the west tower. Do you understand?'

The dark eyes glimmered. 'King Lot lodges, they tell me, in the eastern one?'

'Exactly.'

'Don't worry. I've already had the same warning from Emrys. Goodnight, Merlin.'

'Goodnight, and a peaceful sleep to us all. We need it.'

He grinned, sketched a half salute, and went. I nodded to the waiting servant, and went in. The door shut behind me.

The royal rooms had been cleared of the apparatus of sickness, and the great bed stripped of its crimson covers. The floor tiles were freshly scoured and polished, and over the bed lay new unbleached sheets, and a rug of wolfskins. The chair with the red cushion and the dragon worked on the back in gold stood there still, with its footstool and the tall tripod lamp beside it. The windows were open to the cool September night, and the air from them sent the lampflames sideways, and made strange shadows on the painted walls.

Arthur was alone. He was over by a window, one knee on a stool that stood there, his elbows on the sill. The window gave, not on the town, but on the strip of garden that edged the river. He gazed out into the dark, and I thought I could see him drinking, as from another river, deep draughts of the fresh and moving air. His hair was damp, as if he had just washed, but he was still in the clothes he had worn for the day's ceremonies; white and silver, with a belt of Welsh gold set with turquoises and buckled with enamel-work. He had taken off his sword-belt, and the great sword Caliburn hung in its sheath on the wall beyond the bed. The lamplight smouldered in the jewels of the hilt; emerald, topaz, sapphire. It flashed, too, from the ring on the boy's hand; Uther's ring, carved with the Dragon crest.

He heard me, and turned. He looked rarefied and light, as if the winds of the day had blown through him and left him weightless. His skin had the stretched pallor of exhaustion, but his eyes were brilliant and alive. About him, already there and unmistakable, was the mystery that falls like a mantle on a king. It was in his high look, and the turn of his head. Never again would 'Emrys' be able to lurk in shadow. I wondered afresh now, through all those hidden years, we had kept him safe and secret among lesser men.

'You wanted me,' I said.

'I've wanted you all day. You promised to be near me while I went through this business of hatching into a king. Where were you?'

'Within call, if not within reach. I was at the shrine— the chapel—till almost sunset. I though you'd be busy.'

He gave a little crack of laughter. 'You call it that? It felt like being eaten alive. Or perhaps like being born ... and a hard birth, at that. I said "hatching", didn't I? Suddenly to find oneself a prince is hard enough, but even that is as different from being a king as the egg is from the day-old chick.'

'At least make it an eaglet.'

'In time, perhaps. That's been the trouble, of course. Time, there's been no time. One moment to be nobody— someone's unacknowledged bastard, and glad to be given the chance to get within shouting distance of a battle, with maybe a glimpse of the King himself in passing; the next —having drawn a couple of breaths as Prince and royal heir—to be High King myself, and with such a flourish as no king can ever have had before. I still feel as if I'd been kicked up the steps of the throne from a kneeling position right down on the floor.'

I smiled. 'I know how you feel, more or less. I was never kicked half as high, but then I was a great deal lower down to start with. Now, can you slow down sufficiently to get some sleep? Tomorrow will be here soon enough. Do you want a sleeping potion?'

'No, no, when did I ever? I'll sleep as soon as you've gone. Merlin, I'm sorry to ask you to come here at this late hour, but I had to talk to you, and there's been no chance till now. Nor will there be tomorrow.'

He came away from the window as he spoke, and crossed to a table where papers and tablets were lying. He picked up a stilus and, with the blunt end, smoothed the wax. He did it absently, his head bent so that the dark hair swung forward, and the lamplight slid over the line of his cheek and touched the black lashes fringing the lowered lids. My eyes blurred. Time ran back. It was Ambrosius my father who stood there, fidgeting with the stilus, and saying to me: 'If a king had you beside him, he could rule the world . . .'

Well, his dream had come true at last, and the time was now. I blinked memory away, and waited for the day-old king to speak.

'I've been thinking,' he said abruptly. 'The Saxon army was not utterly destroyed, and I have had no firm report yet about Colgrim himself, or Badulf. I think they both got safely away. We may hear within the next day or so that they have taken ship and gone, either home across the sea, or back to the Saxon territories in the south. Or they may simply have taken refuge in the wild lands north of the Wall, and be hoping to regroup when they have gathered strength again.' He looked up. 'I have no need to pretend to you, Merlin. I am not a seasoned warrior, and I've no means of judging how decisive that defeat was, or what the possibilities are of a Saxon recovery. I've taken advice, of course. I called a quick council at sunset, when the other business was concluded. I sent for—that is, I would have liked you to be there, but you were still up at the chapel. Coel couldn't be there, either . . . You'd know he was wounded, of course; you probably saw him yourself? What are his chances?'

'Slight. He's an old man, as you know, and he got a

nasty slash. He bled too much before help got to him.'

'I was afraid of it. I did go to see him, but was told he was unconscious, and they were afraid of inflammation of the lungs ... Well, Prince Urbgen, his heir, came in his stead, with Cador, and Caw of Strathclyde. Ector and Ban of Benoic were there, too. I talked it over with them, and they all say the same thing; someone will have to follow Colgrim up. Caw has to go north again as soon as may be; he has his own frontier to hold. Urbgen must stay here in Rheged, with his father the king at death's door. So the obvious choice would be Lot or Cador. Well, it cannot be Lot, I think you will agree there? For all his oath of fealty, there in the chapel, I won't trust him yet, and certainly not within reach of Colgrim.'

'I agree. You'll send Cador, then? You can surely have no more doubts of him?'

Cador, Duke of Cornwall, was indeed the obvious choice. He was a man in the prime of his strength, a seasoned fighter, and loyal. I had once mistakenly thought him Arthur's enemy, and indeed he had had cause to be; but Cador was a man of sense, judicious and far-sighted, who could see beyond his hatred of Uther to the larger vision of a Britain united against the Saxon Terror. So he had supported Arthur. And Arthur, up there in the Perilous Chapel, had declared Cador and his sons the heirs to the kingdom.

So Arthur said merely: 'How could I?' and scowled for a moment longer at the stilus. Then he dropped it on the table, and straightened. 'The thing is, with my own leadership so new—' He looked up then, and saw me smiling. The frown vanished, to be replaced by a look I knew; eager, impetuous, the look of a boy, but with, behind it, a man's will that would burn its way through any opposition. His eyes danced. 'Yes, you're right, as usual. I'm going myself.'

'And Cador with you?'

'No. I think I must go without him. After what happened, my father's death, and then the'—he hesitated—

'then what happened up in the chapel yonder ... If there is to be more fighting, I must be there myself, to lead the armies, and be seen to finish the work we started.'

He paused, as if still expecting question or protest, but I made none.

'I thought you would try to prevent me.'

'No. Why? I agree with you. You have to prove yourself to be above luck.'

'That's it exactly.' He thought for a moment. 'It's hard to put it into words, but ever since you brought me to Luguvallium and presented me to the King, it has seemed —not like a dream exactly, but as if something were using me, using all of us ...'

'Yes. A strong wind blowing, and carrying us all with it.'

'And now the wind has died down,' he said, soberly, 'and we are left to live life by our own strength only. As if —well, as if it had all been magic and miracles, and now they had gone. Have you noticed, Merlin, that not one man has spoken of what happened up yonder in the shrine? Already it's as if it had happened well in the past, in some song or story.'

'One can see why. The magic was real, and too strong for many of those who witnessed it, but it has burned down into the memories of all who saw it, and into the memory of the folk who make the songs and legends. Well, that is for the future. But we are here, now, and with the work still to do. And one thing is certain; only you can do it. So you must go ahead and do it in your own way.'

The young face relaxed. His hands flattened on the table as he leaned his weight on them. For the first time it could be seen that he was very tired, and that it was a kind of relief to let the weariness sweep over him, and with it the need for sleep.

'I should have known you would understand. So you see why I must go myself, without Cador. He didn't like it, I confess, but he saw the point in the end. And to be

honest, I would have liked him with me ... But this is
something I must do alone. You might say it's as much for
my own reassurance as for the people's. I can say that to
you.'

'Do you need reassurance?'

A hint of a smile. 'Not really. In the morning I shall
probably be able to believe everything that happened on
the battlefield, and know it for real, but now it's still like
being in the edges of a dream. Tell me, Merlin, can I ask
Cador to go south to escort Queen Ygraine, my mother,
from Cornwall?'

'There's no reason why not. He is Duke of Cornwall, so
since Uther's death her home at Tintagel must fall under
his protection. If Cador was able to sink his hatred of
Uther into the common weal, he must long ago have been
able to forgive Ygraine for her betrayal of his father. And
now you have declared his sons your heirs to the High
Kingdom, so all scores are paid. Yes, send Cador.'

He looked relieved. 'Then all's well. I've already sent a
courier to her, of course, with the news. Cador should
meet her on the road. They will be in Amesbury by the
time my father's body arrives there for burial.'

'Do I take it, then, that you want me to escort the body
to Amesbury?'

'If you will. I cannot possibly go myself, as I should,
and it must be royally escorted. Better you, perhaps, who
knew him, than I, who am so recently royal. Besides, if he
is to lie beside Ambrosius in the Dance of the Hanging
Stones, you should be there to see the king-stone shifted
and the grave made. You'll do that?'

'Certainly. It should take us, going in a seemly way,
about nine days.'

'By that time I should be there myself.' A sudden flash.
'With average luck, that is, I'm expecting word soon, about
Colgrim. I'll be going after him in about four hours' time,
as soon as it's full light. Bedwyr goes with me,' he added,
as if that should be a comfort and a reassurance.

'And what of King Lot, since I have gathered he does not go with you?'

At that I got a bland look, and a tone as smooth as any politician's. 'He leaves, too, at first light. Not for his own land ... Not, that is, until I find which way Colgrim went. No, I urged King Lot to go straight to York. I believe Queen Ygraine will go there after the burial, and Lot can receive her. Then, once his marriage with my sister Morgan is celebrated, I suppose I can count him an ally, like it or not. And the rest of the fighting, whatever comes between now and Christmas-time, I can do without him.'

'So, I shall see you in Amesbury. And after that?'

'Caerleon,' he said, without hesitation. 'If the wars allow it, I shall go there. I've never seen it, and from what Cador tells me, it must be my headquarters now.'

'Until the Saxons break the treaty and move in from the south.'

'As of course they will. Until then. God send there will be time to breathe first.'

'And to build another stronghold.'

He looked up quickly. 'Yes. I was thinking of that. You'll be there to do it?' Then, with sudden urgency: 'Merlin, you swear you will always be there?'

'As long as I am needed. Though it seems to me,' I added lightly, 'that the eaglet is fledging fast enough already.' Then, because I knew what lay behind the sudden uncertainty: 'I shall wait for you at Amesbury, and I shall be there to present you to your mother.'

CHAPTER 2

Amesbury is little more than a village, but since Ambrosius' day it has taken some kind of grandeur to itself, as befits his birthplace, and its nearness to the great monument of the Hanging Stones that stand on the windy Sarum plain. This is a linked circle of vast stones, a gigantic Dance, which was raised first in times beyond men's memory. I had (by what folk persisted in seeing as 'magic art') rebuilt the Dance to be Britain's monument of glory, and the burial-place of her kings. Here Uther was to lie beside his brother Ambrosius.

We brought his body without incident to Amesbury, and left it in the monastery there, wrapped in spices and coffined in hollowed oak, under its purple pall before the chapel altar. The King's guard (who had ridden south with his body) stood vigil, and the monks and nuns of Amesbury prayed beside the bier. Queen Ygraine being a Christian, the dead king was to be buried with all the rites and ceremonies of the Christian church, though in life he had barely troubled even to pay lip-service to the Christians' God. Even now he lay with gold coins glinting on his eyelids, to pay the fee of a ferryman who had exacted such toll for centuries longer than Saint Peter of the Gate. The chapel itself had apparently been erected on the site of a Roman shrine; it was little more than an oblong erection of daub and wattle, with wooden shafts holding up a roof of thatch, but it had a floor of fine mosaic work, scrubbed clean and hardly damaged. This, showing scrolls of vine and acanthus, could offend no Christian souls, and a woven rug lay centrally, probably to cover whatever pagan god or goddess floated naked among the grapes.

The monastery reflected something of Amesbury's new prosperity. It was a miscellaneous collection of buildings huddled anyhow around a cobbled yard, but these were in good repair, and the Abbot's house, which had been vacated for the Queen and her train, was well built of stone, with wooden flooring, and a big fireplace at one end with a chimney.

The headman of the village, too, had a good house, which he made haste to offer me for lodging, but, explaining that the King would follow me soon, I left him in an uproar of extra preparation, and betook myself with my servants to the tavern. This was small, with little pretension to comfort, but it was clean, and fires were kept burning high against the autumn chills. The innkeeper remembered me from the time I had lodged there during the rebuilding of the Dance; he still showed the awe that the exploit had raised in him, and made haste to give me the best room, and to promise me fresh poultry and a mutton pie for supper. He showed relief when I told him that I had brought two servants with me, who would serve me in my own chamber, and banished his own staring potboys to their posts at the kitchen burners.

The servants I had brought were two of Arthur's. In recent years, living alone in the Wild Forest, I had cared for myself, and now had none of my own. One was a small, lively man from the hills of Gwynedd; the other was Ulfin, who had been Uther's own servant. The late King had taken him from a rough servitude, and had shown him kindness which Ulfin repaid with devotion. This would now belong to Arthur, but it would have been cruel to deny Ulfin the chance of following his master's body on its last journey, so I had asked for him by name. By my orders he had gone to the chapel with the bier, and I doubted if I would see him before the funeral was over. Meantime the Welshman, Lleu, unpacked my boxes and bespoke hot water, and sent the more intelligent of the landlord's boys across to the monastery with a message from me to be delivered to the Queen on her arrival. In it I bade her welcome, and offered to wait on her as soon as she should be rested enough to send for me. News of the happenings in Luguvallium she had had already; now I added merely that Arthur was not yet in Amesbury, but was expected in time for the burial.

I was not in Amesbury when her party arrived. I rode out to the Giants' Dance to see that all was ready for the ceremony, to be told on my return that the Queen and her escort had arrived shortly after noon, and that Ygraine with her ladies was settled into the Abbot's house. Her summons to me came just as afternoon dimmed into evening.

The sun had gone down in a clouded sky, and when, refusing the offer of an escort, I walked the short distance to the monastery, it was already almost dark. The night was heavy as a pall, a mourning sky, where no stars shone. I remembered the great king-star that had blazed for Ambrosius' death, and my thoughts went again to the king who lay nearby in the chapel, with monks for mourners, and the guards like statues beside the bier. And Ulfin who, alone of all those who saw him die, had wept for him.

A chamberlain met me at the monastery gate. Not the monks' porter; this was one of the Queen's own servants, a royal chamberlain I recognised from Cornwall. He knew who I was, of course, and bowed very low, but I could see that he did not recall our last meeting. It was the same man, grown greyer and more bent, who had admitted me to the Queen's presence some three months before Arthur's birth, when she had promised to confide the child to my care. I had been disguised then, for fear of Uther's enmity, and it was plain that the chamberlain did not recognise, in the tall prince at the gate, the humble, bearded 'doctor' who had called to consult with the Queen.

He led me across the weedy courtyard towards the big, thatched building where the Queen was lodged. Cressets burned outside the door, and here and there along the wall, so that the poverty of the place showed starkly. After the wet summer weeds had sprouted freely between the cobbles, and the corners of the yard were waist high in nettles. Among these the wooden ploughs and mattocks of the working brothers stood, wrapped in sacking. Near one doorway was an anvil, and on a nail driven into the jamb hung a line of horse-shoes. A litter of thin black piglings tumbled squealing out of our way, and were called by a sow's anxious grunting through the broken planks of a half-door. The holy men and women of Amesbury were simple folk. I wondered how the Queen was faring.

I need not have feared for her. Ygraine had always been a lady who knew her own mind, and since her marriage to Uther she had kept a most queenly state, urged to this, possibly, by the very irregularity of that marriage. I remembered the Abbot's house as a humble dwelling, clean and dry, but boasting no comfort. Now in a few short hours the Queen's people had seen to it that it was luxurious. The walls, of undressed stone, had been hidden by hangings of scarlet and green and peacock blue, and one beautiful Eastern carpet that I had brought for her from Byzantium. The wooden floor was scrubbed white, and the benches that stood along the walls were piled with furs and cushions. A great fire of logs burned on the hearth. To one side of this was set a tall chair of gilded wood, cushioned in embroidered wool, with a footstool fringed with gold. Across from this stood another chair with a high back, and arms carved with dragons' heads. The lamp was a five-headed dragon in bronze. The door to the Abbot's austere sleeping-chamber stood open, and beyond it I caught a glimpse of a bed hung with blue, and the sheen of a silver fringe. Three or four women—two of them no more than girls—were busying themselves in the bedchamber, and over the table, which, at the end of the room away from the fire, stood ready for supper. Pages dressed in blue ran with dishes and flagons. Three white greyhounds lay as near to the fire as they dared go.

As I entered, there was a pause in the bustle and chatter. All eyes turned to the doorway. A page bearing a wine-jar, caught within a yard of the door, checked, swerved, and stared, showing the whites of his eyes. Someone at the table dropped a wooden trencher, and the greyhounds pounced on the fallen cakes. The scrabbling of their claws and their munching were the only sounds in the room to be heard through the rustling of the fire.

'Good evening,' I said pleasantly. I answered the women's reverences, watched gravely while a boy picked up the fallen trencher and kicked the dogs out of the way, then allowed myself to be ushered by the chamberlain towards the hearth-place.

'The Queen—' he was beginning, when the eyes turned from me to the inner door, and the greyhounds, arched and wagging, danced to meet the woman who came through it.

But for the hounds, and the curtsying women, a stranger might have thought that here was the Abbess of the place come to greet me. The woman who entered was as much a contrast to the rich room as that room had been to the squalid courtyard. She was dressed from head to foot in black, with a white veil covering her hair, its ends thrown back over her shoulders, and its soft folds pinned to frame her face like a wimple. The sleeves of her gown were lined with some grey silken stuff, and there was a cross of sapphires on her breast, but to the sombre black and white of her mourning there was no other relief.

It was a long time since I had seen Ygraine, and I expected to find her changed, but even so I was shocked at what I saw. Beauty was still there, in the lines of bone and the great dark-blue eyes and the queenly poise of her body; but grace had given way to dignity, and there was a thinness about the wrists and hands that I did not like, and shadows near her eyes almost as blue as the eyes themselves. This, not the ravages of time, was what shocked me.

There were signs everywhere that a doctor could read all too clearly.

But I was here as prince and emissary, not as physician. I returned her smile of greeting, bowed over her hand, and led her to the cushioned chair. At a sign from her the boys ran to collar the greyhounds and take them aside, and she settled herself, smoothing her skirt. One of the girls moved a footstool for her, and then, with lowered eyelids and folded hands, stayed beside her mistress's chair.

The Queen bade me be seated, and I obeyed her. Someone brought wine, and across the cups we exchanged the commonplaces of the meeting. I asked her how she did, but with purely formal courtesy, and I knew she could read nothing of my knowledge in my face.

'And the King?' she asked at length. The word came from her as if forced, with a kind of pain behind it.

'Arthur promised to be here. I expect him tomorrow. There has been no news from the north, so we have no means of knowing if there has been more fighting. The lack of news need not alarm you; it only means that he will be here as soon as any courier he might have sent.'

She nodded, with no sign of anxiety. Either she could not think much beyond her own loss, or she took my tranquil tone as a prophet's reassurance. 'Did he expect more fighting?'

'He stayed as a cautionary measure, no more. The defeat of Colgrim's men was decisive, but Colgrim himself escaped, as I wrote to you. We had no report on where he had gone. Arthur thought it better to make sure that the scattered Saxon forces could not re-form, at least while he came south for his father's burial.'

'He is young,' she said, 'for such a charge.'

I smiled. 'But ready for it, and more than able. Believe me, it was like seeing a young falcon take to the air, or a swan to the water. When I took leave of him, he had not slept for the better part of two nights, and was in high heart and excellent health.'

'I am glad of it.'

She spoke formally, without expression, but I thought it better to qualify. 'The death of his father came as a shock and a grief, but as you will understand, Ygraine, it could not come very near his heart, and there was much to be done that crowded out sorrow.'

'I have not been so fortunate,' she said, very low, and looked down at her hands.

I was silent, understanding. The passion that had driven Uther and this woman together, with a kingdom at stake for it, had not burned out with the years. Uther had been a man who needed women as most men need food and sleep, and when his kingly duties had taken him away from the Queen's bed, his own was rarely empty; but when they were together he had never looked aside, nor given her cause for grief. They had loved each other, King and Queen, in the old high way of love, which had outlasted youth and health and the shifts of compromise and expediency which are the price of kingship. I had come to believe that their son Arthur, deprived as he had been of royal status, and brought up in obscurity, had fared better in his foster-home at Galava than he would have done at his father's court, where, with both King and Queen, he would have come far behind the best.

She looked up at last, her face serene again. 'I had your letter, and Arthur's, but there is so much more that I want to hear. Tell me what happened at Luguvallium. When he left to ride north against Colgrim, I knew he was not fit to do so. He swore he must take the field, even if he had to be carried in a litter. Which, I understand, is what happened?'

For Ygraine, the 'he' of Luguvallium was certainly not her son. What she wanted was the story of Uther's last days, not the tale of Arthur's miraculous coming into his kingdom. I gave it to her.

'Yes. It was a great fight, and he fought it greatly. They carried him to the battlefield in a chair, and all through the fighting his servants kept him there, in the very thick

of the battle. I had Arthur brought down from Galava at
his orders, for him to be publicly acknowledged, but Colgrim attacked suddenly, and the King had to take the
field without making the proclamation. He kept Arthur
near him, and when he saw the boy's sword broken in the
fight, threw him his own. I doubt if Arthur, in the heat of
the battle, saw the gesture for what it was, but everyone
else did who was near. It was a great gesture, made by a
great man.'

She did not speak, but her eyes rewarded me. Ygraine
knew, none better, that Uther and I had never loved one
another. Praise from me was something quite other than
the flattery of the court.

'And afterwards the King sat back in his chair and
watched his son carry the fight through to the enemy, and,
untried as he was, bear his part in the rout of the Saxons.
So later, when he presented the boy at last to the nobles
and the captains, his work was half done. They had seen
the sword of kingship handed over, and they had seen
how worthily it had been used. But there was, in fact,
some opposition . . .'

I hesitated. It was that very opposition that had killed
Uther; only a few hours before time, but as surely as the
blow from an axe. And King Lot, who had led the opposing faction, was contracted to marry Ygraine's daughter
Morgan.

Ygraine said calmly: 'Ah, yes. The King of Lothian. I
heard something of it. Tell me.'

I should have known her. I gave her the whole story,
omitting nothing. The roaring opposition, the treachery,
the sudden, silencing death of the King. I told her of
Arthur's eventual acclamation by the company, though
dwelling lightly on my part in that : ('*If he has indeed
got the sword of Macsen, he got it by God's gift, and if he
has Merlin beside him, then by any god he follows, I follow
him!*') Nor did I dwell on the scene in the chapel, but told
her merely of the oath-taking, of Lot's submission, and
Arthur's declaration of Gorlois' son Cador as his heir.

At this, for the first time, the beautiful eyes lighted, and she smiled. I could see that this was news to her, and must go some way to assuaging the guilt of her own part in Gorlois' death. Apparently Cador, either through delicacy, or because he and Ygraine still held aloof from one another, had not told her himself. She put out her hand for her wine, and sat sipping it while I finished the tale, the smile still on her mouth.

One other thing, one most important thing, would also have been news to her; but of this I said nothing. But the unspoken part of the tale was loud in my own mind, so that when Ygraine spoke next, I must have jumped like a dog to the whip. 'And Morgause?'

'Madam?'

'You have not spoken of her. She must have grieved for her father. It was a fortunate thing that she could be near him. He and I have both had cause to thank God for her skills.'

I said, neutrally: 'She nursed him with devotion. I am sure that she will miss him bitterly.'

'Does she come south with Arthur?'

'No. She has gone to York, to be with her sister Morgan.'

To my relief, she asked no more questions about Morgause, but turned the subject, asking where I was lodged.

'In the tavern,' I told her. 'I know it from the old days, when I was working here. It's a simple kind of place, but they have taken pains to make me comfortable. I shan't be here for long.' I glanced round me at the glowing room. 'For yourself, do you plan a long stay, Madam?'

'A few days only.' If she had noticed my look at the luxury surrounding her, she gave no sign of it. I, who am not normally wise in the ways of women, realised, suddenly, that the richness and beauty of the place was not for Ygraine's own comfort, but had been deliberately contrived as a setting for her first meeting with her son. The scarlet and gold, the scents and waxlights, were this ageing woman's shield and enchanted sword.

'Tell me—' She spoke abruptly, straight out of the preoccupation that, through all else, bound her: 'Does he blame me?'

It was the measure of my respect for Ygraine that I answered her directly, with no pretence that the subject was not uppermost in my mind as well. 'I think you need have no fear of this meeting. When he first knew of his parentage, and of his inheritance, he wondered why you and the King had seen fit to deny him that birthright. He could not be blamed if, at first, he felt himself wronged. He had already begun to suspect that he was royal, but he assumed that—as in my case—the royalty came sideways ... When he knew the truth, with the elation came the wondering. But—and I swear that this is true—he gave no hint of bitterness or anger; he was anxious only to know why. When I had told him the story of his birth and fostering, he said—and I will give you his exact words—"I see it as you say she saw it; that to be a prince one must be ruled always by necessity. She did not give me up for nothing." '

There was a little silence. Through it I heard echoing, unspoken save in my memory, the words with which he had finished: 'I was better in the Wild Forest, thinking myself motherless, and your bastard, Merlin, than waiting yearly in my father's castle for the Queen to bear another child to supplant me.'

Her lips relaxed, and I saw her sigh. The soft underlids of her eyes had a faint tremor, which stilled as if a finger had been laid on a thrumming string. Colour came into her face, and she looked at me as she had looked all those years ago, when she had begged me to take the baby away and hide him from Uther's anger. 'Tell me ... what is he like?'

I smiled slightly. 'Did they not tell you, when they brought you news of the battle?'

'Oh, yes, they told me. He is as tall as an oak tree and as strong as Fionn, and slew nine hundred men with his own hand alone. He is Ambrosius come again, or Maximus himself, with a sword like the lightning, and the witch-light round him in battle like the pictures of the gods at the fall of Troy. And he is Merlin's shadow and spirit, and a great hound follows him everywhere, to whom he speaks as to a familiar.' Her eyes danced. 'You may guess from all this that the messengers were black Cornishmen from Cador's troop. They would always rather sing a poem than state a fact. I want fact.'

She always had. Like her, Arthur had dealt with facts, even as a child; he left the poetry to Bedwyr. I gave her what she wanted. 'The last bit is almost true, but they got it the wrong way round. It is Merlin who is Arthur's shadow and spirit, like the great hound who is real enough; that's Cabal, his dog that his friend Bedwyr gave him. For the rest, what shall I say? You'll see for yourself tomorrow ... He is tall, and favours Uther rather than you, though he has my father's colouring; his eyes and hair are as dark as mine. He is strong, and full of courage and endurance—all the things your Cornishmen told you, brought down to life-size. He has the hot blood and high temper of youth, and he can be impulsive or arrogant, but under it all he has hard sense and a growing power of control, like any good man of his age. And he has what I consider a very great virtue. He is willing to listen to me.'

This won another smile from her, with real warmth in it. 'You mean to jest, but I am with you in counting that a virtue! He is lucky to have you. As a Christian, I am not allowed to believe in your magic—indeed, I do not believe in it as the common folk do; but whatever it is, and wherever it comes from, I have seen your power working, and I know that it is good, and that you are wise. I believe that whatever owns and moves you is what I call God. Stay with my son.'

'I shall stay as long as he needs me.'

Silence fell between us then, while we both looked at the fire. Ygraine's eyes dreamed under their long shadowed lids, and her face grew still once more, and tranquil; but I thought it was the waiting stillness of the forest depth, where overhead the boughs roar in the wind, and the trees feel the storms shaking them to the very root.

A boy came tiptoeing to kneel on the hearth and pile fresh logs on the fire. Flames crept, crackled, leaped into light. I watched them. For me, too, the pause was merely one of waiting; the flames were only flames.

The boy went away quietly. The girl took the goblet from the Queen's relaxed hand, and held her own out, a timid gesture, for my cup. She was a pretty creature, slim as a wand, with grey eyes and light-brown hair. She looked half-scared of me, and was careful, as I gave her the cup, not to touch my hand. She went quickly away with the empty vessels. I said softly: 'Ygraine, is your physician here with you?'

Her eyelids fluttered. She did not look at me, but answered as softly. 'Yes. He travels with me always.'

'Who is it?'

'His name is Melchior. He says he knows you.'

'Melchior? A young man I met in Pergamum when I studied medicine there?'

'The same. Not so young now. He was with me when Morgan was born.'

'He is a good man,' I said, satisfied.

She glanced at me sideways. The girl was still out of hearing, with the rest of the women at the other side of the room. 'I should have known I could hide nothing from you. You won't let my son know?'

I promised readily. That she was mortally ill I had known as soon as I saw her, but Arthur, not knowing her, and having no skill in medicine, might notice nothing. Time enough for that later. Now was for beginnings rather than endings.

The girl came and whispered to the Queen, who nodded and stood up. I rose with her. The chamberlain was advancing with some ceremony, lending the borrowed chamber yet another touch of royalty. The Queen half turned to me, her hand lifting to invite me with her to table; when suddenly the scene was interrupted. From somewhere outside came the distant call of a trumpet;

then another, nearer, and then, all at once, the clash and
excitement of arriving horsemen, somewhere beyond the
monastery walls.

Ygraine's head went up, with something of the old lift
of youth and courage. She stood very still. 'The King?'
Her voice was light and quick. Round the listening room,
like an echo, went the rustle and murmur of the women.
The girl beside the Queen was as taut as a bow string,
and I saw a vivid blush of excitement run up clear from
neck to forehead.

'He is early,' I said. My voice sounded flat and precise. I
was subduing a pulse in my own wrist, which had quickened with the swelling hoof-beats. Fool, I told myself,
fool. He is about his own business now. You loosed him,
and lost him; that is one hawk who will never be hooded
again. Stay back in the shadows, king's prophet; see your
visions and dream your dreams. Leave life to him, and
wait for his need.

A knock at the door, and a servant's quick voice. The
chamberlain went bustling, but before him a boy came
pelting with the message hurriedly relayed, and stripped
of its courtly phrasing:

'With the Queen's leave ... The King is here and wants
Prince Merlin. Now, he says.'

As I went I heard the silent room break into hubbub
behind me, as the pages were sent scurrying to refurbish
the tables, and bring fresh waxlights and scents and wine;
and the women, clucking and crooning like a yardful of
fowl, bustled after the Queen into the bedchamber.

CHAPTER 3

'She's here, they tell me?' Arthur was hindering, rather than helping, a servant drag off his muddied boots. Ulfin had after all come back from the chapel; I could hear him in the adjoining room, directing the servants of the household in the unpacking and bestowing of Arthur's clothes and furnishings. Outside, the town seemed to have burst open with noise and torches and the stamping of horses and the shouting of orders. Now and again one could hear, distinct through the hubbub, the squealing giggle of a girl. Not everyone in Amesbury was in mourning.

The King himself gave little sign of it. He kicked free of his boots at last and shrugged the heavy cloak off his shoulders. His eyes came to me in an exact parody of Ygraine's sidelong look. 'Have you spoken with her?'

'Yes. I've just left her. She was about to give me supper, but now I think she plans to feed you instead. She only got here today, and you'll find her tired, but she has had some rest, and she'll rest again all the better for having seen you. We hardly expected you before morning.'

' "Caesar-speed." ' He grinned, quoting one of my father's phrases; no doubt I, as his teacher, had over-used it rather. 'Only myself and a handful, of course. We pushed ahead. The rest of them will come up later. I trust they will be here in time for the burial.'

'Who is coming?'

'Maelgon of Gwynedd, and his son Maelgon. Urbgen's brother from Rheged—old Coel's third son, his name's Morien, isn't it? Caw couldn't come either, so he's sent Riderch—not Heuil, I'm glad to say, I never could stand that foul-mouthed braggart. Then let me see, Ynyr and

Gwilim, Bors ... and I am told that Ceretic of Elmet is on his way from Loidis.'

He went on to name a few others. It seemed that most of the northern kings had sent sons or substitutes; naturally with the remnant of the Saxon armies still haunting the north they would want to stay watching their own borders. So much, indeed, Arthur was saying through the splashing of the water his servant poured for him to wash himself in. 'Bedwyr's father went home, too. He pleaded some urgency, but between ourselves I think he wanted to keep an eye for me on Lot's movements.'

'And Lot?'

'Headed for York. I took the precaution of having him watched. Sure enough he's on his way. Is Morgan there still, or did she come south to meet the Queen?'

'She's still at York. There is one king you haven't mentioned yet.'

The servant gave him a towel, and Arthur disappeared into it, scrubbing his wet hair dry. His voice came muffled. 'Who?'

'Colgrim,' I said, mildly.

He emerged abruptly from the towel, skin glowing and eyes bright. He looked, I thought, about ten years old. 'Need you ask?' The voice was not ten years old; it was a man's, full of mock arrogance, which under the mischief was real. Well, you gods, I thought, you put him there; you cannot count this as hubris. But I caught myself making the sign.

'No, but I am asking.'

He was serious at once.

'It was tougher work than we'd expected. You might say that the second half of the battle was still to fight. We broke their strength at Luguvallium, and Badulf has died of wounds, but Colgrim was unhurt, and rallied what was left of his forces some way to the east. It wasn't just a case of hunting down fugitives; they had a formidable force there, and a desperate one. If we had gone in any less strength, they might even have turned the tables on us. I

doubt if they would have attacked again—they were
making for the east coast, and home, but we caught them
halfway there, and they made a stand on the Glein river.
Do you know that part of the country?'

'Not well.'

'It's wild and hilly, deep in forest, with river glens winding south out of the uplands. Bad fighting country, but
that was against them as well as us. Colgrim himself got
away again, but there's no chance now that he can pause
and remuster any sort of force in the north. He rode east;
that's one of the reasons that Ban stayed behind, though
he was good enough to let Bedwyr come south with me
again.' He stood still, obedient now to his servant's hands
as he was dressed, a fresh cloak flung over his shoulder
and the pin made fast. 'I'm glad,' he finished, briefly.

'That Bedwyr's here? So I—'

'No. That Colgrim escaped again.'

'Yes?'

'He's a brave man.'

'Nevertheless, you will have to kill him.'

'I know that. Now ...' The servant stepped back, and
the King stood ready. They had dressed him in dark grey,
his cloak collared and lined with rich fur. Ulfin came from
the bedchamber holding a carved casket lined with em-
briodery, where Uther's royal circlet lay. The rubies
caught the light, answering the flash from the jewels at
Arthur's shoulder and breast. But when Ulfin proffered
the box he shook his head. 'Not now, I think.'

Ulfin shut the box, and went from the room, taking the
other man with him. The door latched behind them.
Arthur looked at me, in another echo of Ygraine's own
hesitation. 'Am I to understand that she expects me now?'

'Yes.'

He fidgeted with the brooch at his shoulder, pricked his
finger, and swore. Then, with a half smile at me: 'There's
not much precedent for this sort of thing, is there? How
does one meet the mother who gave one away at birth?'

'How did you greet your father?'

'That's different, you know it is.'

'Yes. Do you want me to present you?'

'I was going to ask you to ... Well, we'd better get on with it. Some situations don't improve with keeping ... Look, you are sure about the supper? I've eaten nothing since dawn.'

'Certain. They were running for fresh meats when I left.'

He took a breath, like a swimmer before a deep dive. 'Then shall we go?'

* * *

She was waiting beside her chair, standing in the light of the fire. Colour had run up into her cheeks, and the glow of the fire pulsed over her skin and made the white wimple rosy. She looked beautiful, with the shadows purged away, and youth lent back by the firelight and the brilliance of her eyes.

Arthur paused on the threshold. I saw the blue flash of Ygraine's sapphire cross as her breast rose and fell. Her lips parted, as if to speak, but she was silent. Arthur paced forward slowly, so dignified and stiff that he looked even younger than his years. I went with him, rehearsing in my mind the right words to say, but in the end there was no need to say anything. Ygraine the Queen, who had weathered worse moments in her time, took the occasion into her hands. She watched him for a moment, staring at him as if she would look right through his soul, then she curtsied to the ground, and said: 'My lord.'

He put a hand out quickly, then both hands, and raised her. He gave her the kiss of greeting, brief and formal, and held her hands for a little longer before he dropped them. He said: 'Mother?' trying it out. It was what he had always called Drusilla, Count Ector's wife. Then, with relief: 'Madam? I am sorry I could not be here in Amesbury to greet you, but there was still danger in the north.

Merlin will have told you? But I came as quickly as I could.'

'You made better speed than we could have hoped for. I trust you prospered? And that the danger from Col-grim's force is over?'

'For the moment. We have time, at least, to breathe ... and to do what is to be done here in Amesbury. I am sorry for your grief and loss, Madam. I—' He hesitated, then spoke with a simplicity that, I could see, comforted her and steadied him: 'I can't pretend to you that I grieve as perhaps I should. I hardly knew him as a father, but all my life I have known him as a king, and a strong one. His people will mourn him, and I, too, mourn him as one of them.'

'You have it in your hands to guard them as he tried to guard them.' A pause, while they measured one another again. She was a fraction the taller of the two. Perhaps the same thought touched her; she motioned him towards the chair where I had been sitting, and herself sank back against the embroidered cushions. A page came running with wine, and there was a general breathing and rustle of movement. The Queen began to speak of tomorrow's ceremony; answering her, he relaxed, and soon they were talking more freely. But still behind the courtly exchanges could be felt all the turmoil of what lay between them un-spoken, the air so charged, their minds so locked on one another, that they had forgotten my presence as com-pletely as if I had been one of the servants waiting by the laden table. I glanced that way, then at the women and girls beside the Queen; all eyes were on Arthur, devour-ing him, the men with curiosity and some awe (the stories had reached them soon enough), the women with some-thing added to the curiosity, and the two girls in a dazzled trance of excitement.

The chamberlain was hovering in a doorway. He caught my eye and looked a question. I nodded. He crossed to the Queen's side and murmured something. She assented with

a kind of relief, and rose to her feet, the King with her. I
noticed that the table was now laid for three, but when
the chamberlain came to my elbow I shook my head.
After supper their talk would be easier, and they could
dismiss the servants. They would be better alone. So I
took my leave, ignoring Arthur's glance almost of entreaty, and made my way back to the tavern to see if my
fellow-guests there had left any of the supper for me.

*   *   *

Next day was bright and sunlit, with the clouds packed
away low on the horizon, and a lark singing somewhere as
if it were spring. Often a bright day at the end of September brings frost with it, and a searching wind—and nowhere can the winds search more keenly than on the
stretches of the Great Plain. But the day of Uther's burial
was a day borrowed from spring; a warm wind and a
bright sky, and the sun golden on the Dance of the Hanging Stones.

The ceremonial by the grave was long, and the colossal
shadows of the Dance moved round with the sun until the
light blazed down full in the centre, and it was easier to
look at the ground, at the grave itself, at the shadows of
clouds massing and moving like armies across the distances, than at the Dance's centre where the priests stood in
their robes, and the nobles in mourning white, with jewels
flashing against the eyes. A pavilion had been erected for
the Queen. She stood in its shade, composed and pale
among her ladies, showing no sign of fatigue or illness.
Arthur, with me beside him, stood at the foot of the grave.

At last it was done. The priests moved off, and after
them the King and the royal party. As we crossed the grass
towards the horses and litters, already behind us could be
heard the soft thudding of earth on wood. Then from
above came another sound to mask it. I looked up. High
in the September sky could be seen a stream of birds, swift
and black and small, gossiping and calling as they went

southwards. The last flock of swallows, taking the summer with them.

'Let us hope,' said Arthur, softly, at my elbow, 'that the Saxons are taking the hint. I could do with the winter's length, both for the men and for myself, before the fighting starts again. Besides, there's Caerleon. I wish I could go today.'

But of course he had to stay, as had we all, as long as the Queen remained in Amesbury. She went straight back to the monastery after the ceremony, and did not appear publicly again, but spent her time resting, or with her son. He was with her as much as his affairs allowed, while her people prepared to make the journey to York as soon as she should feel able to travel.

Arthur hid his impatience, and busied himself with the troops at exercise, or in long hours of talk with his friends and captains. Each day I could see him more and more absorbed in what he was doing, and what he faced. I myself saw little of him or of Ygraine; much of my time was spent out at the Giants' Dance, directing the sinking of the king-stone once more into its bed above the royal grave.

At last, eight days after Uther's burial, the Queen's party set off for the north. Arthur watched them decently out of sight along the road to Cunetio, then gave a great breath of relief, and pulled the fighting men out of Amesbury as neatly and quickly as pulling a stopper from a flask. It was the fifth day of October, and it was raining, and we were bound, as I knew to my cost, for the Severn estuary, and the ferry across to Caerleon, City of Legions.

CHAPTER 4

Where the ferry crosses, the Severn estuary is wide, with big tides that come up fast over thick red mud. Boys watch the cattle night and day, for a whole herd can sink in the tidal mud and be lost. And when the spring and autumn tides meet the river's flow a wave builds up like the wave I have seen in Pergamum after the earthquake. On the south side the estuary is bounded by cliffs; the north shore is marshy, but a bowshot from the tide-mark there is well-drained gravel, lifting gently to open woodland of oak and sweet chestnut.

We pitched camp on the rising ground in the lee of the woods. While this was being done, Arthur, with Ynyr and Gwilim, the kings of Guent and Dyfed, went on a tour of exploration, then after supper he sat in his tent to receive the headmen from the settlements nearby. Numbers of the local folk crowded to see the new young King, even the fisherfolk who have no homes but the cliff caves and their frail-skinned coracles. He spoke with them all, accepting homage and complaint alike. After an hour or two of it, I asked leave with a look, got it, and went out into the air. It was a long time since I had smelled the hills of my own country, and besides, there was a place nearby that I had long wanted to visit.

This was the once-famous shrine of Nodens, who is Nuatha of the Silver Hand, known in my country as Llud, or Bilis, King of the Otherworld, whose gates are the hollow hills. He it was who had guarded the sword after I had raised it from its long grave below the floor of Mithras' temple at Segontium. I had left it in his keeping in the lake cave that was known to be sacred to him, before carrying it finally up to the Green Chapel. To Llud, also, I had a debt to pay.

His shrine by the Severn was far older than Mithras' temple, or the chapel in the forest. Its origins had long been lost, even in song or story. It had been a hill fortress first, with maybe a stone or a spring dedicated to the god who cared for the spirits of dead men. Then iron was found, and all through Roman times the place was mined, and mined richly. It may have been the Romans who first called the place the Hill of the Dwarfs, after the small dark men of the west who worked there. The mine had long since been closed, but the name persisted, and so did the stories, of the Old Ones who were seen lurking in the oak woods, or who came thronging out of the earth's depths on nights of storm and starlight to join the train of the dark king, as he rode from his hollow hill with his wild rout of ghosts and enchanted spirits.

I reached the top of the hill behind the camp, and walked down between the scattered oaks towards the stream at the valley's foot. There was a ripe autumn moon that showed me my way. The chestnut leaves, already loosened and drifting, fell here and there quietly to the grass, but the oaks still held their leaves, so that the air was full of rustling as the dry boughs stirred and whispered. The land, after the rain, smelled rich and soft; ploughing weather, nutting weather, the squirrel-time for winter's coming.

Below me on the shadowed slope something moved. There was a stirring of grasses, a pattering, then, like the sound of a hail-storm sweeping past, a herd of deer went by, as swiftly as swallows flying. They were very near. The moonlight struck the dappled coats and the ivory tips of the tines. So close they were that I even saw the liquid shine of their eyes. There were pied deer and white, ghosts of dapple and silver, scudding as lightly as their own shadows, and as swiftly as a sudden squall of wind. They fled by me, down to the valley foot, between the breasts of the rounded hills and up round a curve of oak trees, and were gone.

They say that a white deer is a magical creature. I believe that this is true. I had seen two such in my life, each one the herald of a marvel. These, too, seen in the moonlight, scudding like clouds into the trees' darkness, seemed things of magic. Perhaps, with the Old Ones, they haunted a hill that still held an open gate to the Otherworld.

I crossed the stream, climbed the next hill, and made my way up towards the ruinous walls that crowned it. I picked my way through the debris of what looked like ancient outworks, then climbed the last steep rise of the path. There was a gate set in a high, creeper-covered wall. It was open. I went in.

I found myself in the precinct, a wide courtyard stretching the full width of the flat hilltop. The moonlight, growing stronger every moment, showed a stretch of broken pavement furred with weeds. Two sides of the precinct were enclosed by high walls with broken tops; on the other two there had once been large buildings, of which some portions were still roofed. The place, in that light, was still impressive, roofs and pillars showing whole in the moonlight. Only an owl, flying silently from an upper window, showed that the place had long been deserted, and was crumbling back into the hill.

There was another building set almost in the middle of the court. The gable of its high roof stood up sharply against the moon, but moonlight fell through empty windows. This, I knew, must be the shrine. The buildings that edged the courtyard were what remained of the guest-houses and dormitories where pilgrims and suppliants had lodged; there were cells, walled in, windowless and private, such as I had known at Pergamum, where people slept, hoping for healing dreams, or visions of divination.

I went softly forward over the broken pavement. I knew what I would find; a shrine full of dust and cold air, like the abdicated temple of Mithras at Segontium. But it was possible, I told myself, as I trod up the steps and between the still massive doorposts of the central *cella*, that the old gods who had sprung, like the oak trees and the grass and the rivers themselves—it was possible that these beings made of the air and earth and water of our sweet land, were harder to dislodge than the visiting gods of Rome. Such a one, I had long believed, was mine. He might still be here, where the night air blew through the empty shrine, filling it with the sound of the trees.

The moonlight, falling through the upper windows and the patches of broken roof, lit the place with a pure, fierce light. Some sapling, rooted high up in the masonry, swayed in the breeze, so that shadow and cold light moved and shifted over the dimness within. It was like being at the bottom of a well-shaft; the air, shadow and light, moved like water against the skin, as pure and as cold. The mosaic underfoot, rippled and uneven where the ground had shifted beneath it, glimmered like the floor of the sea, its strange sea-creatures swimming in the swaying light. From beyond the broken walls came the hiss, like foam breaking, of the rustling trees.

I stood there, quite still and silent, for a long time. Long enough for the owl to sail back on hushed wings, drifting to her perch above the dormitory. Long enough for the small wind to drop again, and the water-shadows to fall still. Long enough for the moon to move behind the gable, and the dolphins under my feet to vanish in darkness.

Nothing moved or spoke. No presence there. I told myself, with humility, that this meant nothing. I, once so powerful an enchanter and prophet, had been swept on a mighty tide to God's very gates, and now was dropping back on the ebb to a barren shore. If there were voices here I would not hear them. I was as mortal as the spectral deer.

I turned to leave the place. And smelled smoke.

Not the smoke of sacrifice; ordinary wood-smoke, and with it the faint smells of cooking. It came from somewhere beyond the ruined guest-house of the precinct's north side. I crossed the courtyard, went in through the remains of a massive archway, and, guided by the smell, and then by faint firelight, found my way to a small chamber, where a dog, waking, began to bark, and the two who had been sleeping by the fire got abruptly to their feet.

It was a man and a boy, father and son by the look of them; poor people, to judge by their worn and shabby clothing, but with some look about them of men who are their own masters. In this I was wrong, as it happened.

They moved with the speed of fear. The dog—it was old and stiff, with a grey muzzle and a white eye—did not attack, but stood its ground growling. The man was on his feet more quickly than the dog, with a long knife in his hand; it was honed and bright and looked like a sacrificial weapon. The boy, squaring up to the stranger with all the bravado of twelve or so, held a heavy billet of firewood.

'Peace to you,' I said, then repeated it in their own tongue. 'I came to say a prayer, but no one answered, so when I smelled the fire I came across to see if the god still kept servants here.'

The knife-point sank, but he gripped it still, and the old dog growled. 'Who are you?' demanded the man.

'Only a stranger who is passing this place. I had often heard of Nodens' famous shrine, and seized the time to visit it. Are you its guardian, sir?'

'I am. Are you looking for a night's lodging?'

'That was not my intention. Why? Do you still offer it?'

'Sometimes.' He was wary. The boy, more trusting, or perhaps seeing that I was unarmed, turned away and placed the billet carefully on the fire. The dog, silent now, edged forward to touch my hand with its greyed muzzle. Its tail moved.

'He's a good dog, and very fierce,' said the man, 'but old, and deaf.' His manner was no longer hostile. At the dog's action the knife had vanished.

'And wise,' I said. I smoothed the upraised head. 'He's one who can see the wind.'

The boy turned, wide-eyed. 'See the wind?' asked the man, staring.

'Have you not heard that of a dog with a white eye? And, old and slow as he is, he can see that I come with no intent to hurt you. My name is Myrddin Emrys, and I live west of here, near Maridunum, in Dyfed. I have been travelling, and am on my way home.' I gave him my Welsh name; like everyone else, he would have heard of Merlin the enchanter, and awe is a bad hearth-friend. 'May I come in and share your fire for a while, and will you tell me about the shrine you guard?'

They made way for me, and the boy pulled a stool out of a corner somewhere. Under my questions, at length, the man relaxed and began to talk. His name was Mog: it is not really a name, meaning, as it does, merely 'a servant', but there was a king once who did not disdain to call himself Mog Nuatha, and the man's son was called, even more grandly, after an emperor. 'Constant will be the servant after me,' said Mog, and went on to talk with pride and longing of the great period of the shrine, when the pagan emperor rebuilt and re-equipped it only half a century before the last of the legions left Britain. From long before this time, he told me, a 'Mog Nuatha' had served the shrine with all his family. But now there were only himself and his son; his wife was from home, having gone down that morning to market, and to spend the night with her ailing sister in the village.

'If there's room left, with all that's there now,' the man grumbled. 'You can see the river from the wall yonder, and when we saw the boats crossing I sent the boy to have a look. The army, he says it is, along with the young King—' He broke off, peering through the firelight at my plain robe and cloak. 'You're no soldier, are you? Are you with them?'

'Yes to the last, and no to the first. As you can see, I am

no soldier, but I am with the King.'

'What are you, then? A secretary?'

'Of a sort.'

He nodded. The boy, listening and absorbed, sat cross-legged beside the dog at my feet. His father asked. 'What's he like, this youngster that they say King Uther handed the sword to?'

'He is young, but a man turned, and a good soldier. He can lead men, and he has enough sense to listen to his elders.'

He nodded again. Not for these folk the tales and hopes of power and glory. They lived all their lives on this secluded hilltop, with this one direction to their days; what happened beyond the oak trees did not concern them. Since the start of time no one had stormed the holy place. He asked the only question that, to these two, mattered: 'Is he a Christian, this young Arthur? Will he knock down the temple, in the name of this new-fangled god, or will he respect what's gone before?'

I answered him tranquilly, and as truly as I knew how: 'He will be crowned by the Christian bishops, and bend his knees to his parents' God. But he is a man of this land, and he knows the gods of this land, and the people who still serve those gods on the hills and by the springs and fording-places.' My eye had caught, on a broad shelf opposite the fire, a crowd of objects, carefully arranged. I had seen similar things in Pergamum and other places of divine healing; they were offerings to the gods; models of parts of the human body, or carved statues of animals or fish, that carried some message of supplication or grati-tude. 'You will find,' I told Mog, 'that his armies will pass by without harm, and that if he ever comes here himself he will say a prayer to the god, and make an offering. As I did, and as I will.'

'That's good talking,' said the boy suddenly, and showed a white-toothed grin.

I smiled at him, and dropped two coins into the outstretched palm. 'For the shrine, and for its servants.'

Mog grunted something, and the boy Constant slid to his feet and went to a cupboard in the corner. He came back with a leather bottle, and a chipped cup for me. Mog lifted his own cup up off the floor and the boy tipped the liquor in. 'Your health,' said Mog. I answered, and we drank. The stuff was mead, sweet and strong.

Mog drank again, and drew his sleeve across his mouth. 'You've been asking about times long past, and we've told you as best we may. Now do you, sir, tell us what's been happening up there in the north. All we heard down here were stories of battles, and kings dying and being made. Is it true the Saxons have gone? Is it true that King Uther Pendragon kept this prince hidden all this time, and brought him out, sudden as a thunderclap, there in the battlefield, and he killed four hundred of the Saxon beasts with a magic sword that sang and drank blood?'

So once more I told the story, while the boy quietly fed the fire, and the flames spat and leaped and shone on the carefully polished offerings ranged on the shelf. The dog slept again, its head on my foot, the fire hot on its rough coat. As I talked the bottle passed and the mead went down in it, and at last the fire dwindled and the logs fell to ash, and I finished my tale with Uther's burial and Arthur's plans to hold Caerleon in readiness for the spring campaigning.

My host upended the bottle, and shook it. 'It's out. And a better night's work it never did. Thank you, sir, for your news. We live our own ways up here, but you'll know, being down in the press of affairs, that even things happening out yonder in Britain' (he spoke of it as if of a foreign land, a hundred miles from his quiet refuge) 'can have their echoes, in pain and trouble sometimes, in the small and lonely places. We'll pray you're right about the new King. You can tell him, if ever you get near enough to have speech with him, that as long as he's loyal to the true land, he has two men here who are his servants, too.'

'I shall tell him.' I rose. 'Thank you for the welcome, and the drink. I'm sorry I disturbed your sleep. I'll go and leave you to it now.'

'Go now? Why, it's getting on for the dawning. They'll have locked you out of your lodging, that's for sure. Or were you in the camp down yonder? Then no sentry'll let you through, without you've got the King's own token. You'd best stay here. No'—as I started some sort of protest—'there's a room still kept, just as it was in the old days, when they came here from far and wide to have the dreams. The bed's good, and the place is kept dry. You'd fare worse in many a tavern. Do us the favour, and stay.'

I hesitated. The boy nodded at me, eyes bright, and the dog, which had risen when I rose, wagged its tail and gave a wide, whining yawn, stretching the stiff forepaws.

'Yes. Stay,' begged the boy.

I could see that it would mean something to them if I complied. To stay would be to bring back some of the ancient sanctity of the place; a guest in the guest-house, so carefully swept and aired and kept for the guests who no longer came.

'I shall be glad to,' I said.

Constant, beaming, thrust a torch into the ashes and held it till it kindled. 'Then come this way.'

As I followed him his father, settling himself once more in his blankets by the hearth, said the time-honoured words of the healing-place.

'Sleep soundly, friend, and may the god send you a dream.'

*   *   *

Whoever sent it, the dream came, and it was a true one.

I dreamed of Morgause, whom I had driven from Uther's court at Luguvallium, with an escort detailed to take her with safe ceremony across the high Pennines, and then south-east to York, where her half-sister Morgan lay.

The dream came fitfully, like those hilltop glimpses one

gets through blowing cloud on a dark day. Which, in the dream, it was. I saw the party first on the evening of a wet and windy day, when fine rain blowing down-wind turned the gravel of the road into a slippery track of mud. They had paused on the bank of a river, swollen by rain. I did not recognise the place. The road led down into the river, in what should have been a shallow ford, but now showed as a racing tumble of white water which broke and foamed round an island that split the flood like a ship sailing. There was no house in sight, not even a cave. Beyond the ford the road twisted eastward among its sodden trees, and up through rolling foothills towards the high fells.

With dusk falling fast, it seemed that the party would have to spend the night here, and wait for the river to go down. The officer in command of the party seemed to be explaining as much to Morgause; I could not hear what was said, but he looked angry, and his horse, tired though it was, kept on the fret. I guessed that the choice of route had not been his: the normal way from Luguvallium is by the high moorland road that leaves the west highway at Brocavum and crosses the mountains by Verterae. This last, kept fortified and in fine repair, would have offered the party a staging post, and would have been the obvious choice for a soldier. Instead, they must have taken the old hill road which branches south-east from the five-way crossing near the camp on the River Lune. I had never been that way. It was not a road that had been kept in any kind of order. It led up the valley of the Dubglas and across the high moors, and thence through the mountains by the pass formed by the Tribuit and the Isara rivers. Men call this pass the Pennine Gap, and in past time the Romans kept it fortified and the roads open and patrolled. It is wild country—and still, among the remote summits and cliffs above the tree line, are caves where the Old Ones live. If this was indeed the road Morgause was taking, I could only wonder why.

Cloud and mist; rain in long grey showers; the swollen river piling its white bow-waves against the driftwood and bending willows of the river island. Then darkness and a gap of time hid the scene from me.

Next time I saw them they were halted, somewhere high in the pass, with tree-hung cliffs to the right of the road, and to the left a wide, falling prospect of forest, with a winding river at the foot of the valley, and hills beyond. They had halted by a milestone near the crest of the pass. Here a track branched off downhill to where, in a distant hollow of the valley, lights showed. Morgause was pointing towards these, and it seemed that there was an argument in progress.

Still I could hear nothing, but the cause of the dispute was obvious. The officer had thrust forward to Morgause's side, and was leaning forward in his saddle, arguing fiercely, pointing first at the milestone and then at the road ahead. A late gleam from the west showed, etched by shadow on the stone, the name OLICANA. I could not see the mileage, but what the officer said was clear; that it would be folly to forgo the known comforts that awaited them in Olicana, for the chance that the distant house (if such it was) could accommodate the party. His men, crowding near, were openly supporting him. Beside her, Morgause's women watched her anxiously, one might have said beseechingly.

After a while, with a resigned gesture, Morgause gave way. The escort reformed. The women closed up beside her, smiling. But before the party had gone ten paces one of the women called out sharply, and then Morgause herself, loosing the reins on her horse's neck, put out a hand delicately into the air, as if groping for support, and swayed in her saddle. Someone cried out again. The women crowded to hold her. The officer, turning back, spurred his horse alongside hers and stretched an arm to support her drooping form. She collapsed against him, and lay inert.

There was nothing for it but to accept defeat. Within minutes the party was slithering and thudding down the track towards the distant light in the valley. Morgause, shrouded fast in her big cloak, lay motionless and fainting in the officer's arms.

But I knew, whom am wary of witches, that within the shelter of the rich furred hood she was awake, and smiling her small triumphant smile, as Arthur's men carried her to the house to which, for her own reasons, she had led them, and where she planned to stay.

When the mists of vision parted next, I saw a bed-chamber finely appointed, with a gilded bed and crimson covers, and a brazier burning red, throwing its light on the woman who lay there against the pillows. Morgause's women were there, the same who had attended her in Luguvallium, the young maid called Lind who had led Arthur to her mistress's bed, and the old women who had slept the night through in a drugged slumber. The girl Lind looked pale and tired; I remembered that Morgause, in her rage with me, had had her whipped. She served her mistress warily, with shut lips and downcast eyes, while the old woman, stiff from the long, damp ride, went slowly about her tasks, grumbling as she went, but with sidelong glances to make sure her mistress did not heed her. As for Morgause, she showed no sign of sickness or even fatigue. I had expected none. She lay back on the crimson pillows, the narrow green-gilt eyes staring out through the chamber walls at something far away and pleasurable, and smiling the same smile I had seen on her lips as Arthur lay beside her sleeping.

I must have woken here, shaken out of the dream by hatred and distress, but the god's hand was still on me, because I went back into sleep and into the same room. It must have been later, after some span of time; days, even; however long it had taken Lot, King of Lothian, to wait through the ceremonies at Luguvallium, then gather his troops together and head south and eastwards, by the same devious route, for York. No doubt his main force had gone directly, but he, with a small party of fast horse-men, had hastened to the meeting place with Morgause.

For that it had been prearranged was now clear. She

must have got a message to him before she herself left the court, then she had forced her escort to ride slowly, taking time, and finally had contrived, by her feigned illness, to seek shelter in the privacy of a friend's house. I thought I saw her plan. Having failed in her bid for power through her seduction of Arthur, she had somehow persuaded Lot to this tryst, and now with her witch's wiles she would be set on winning his favour, to find a position of some sort at the court of her sister, Lot's future queen.

Next moment, as the dream changed, I saw the sort of wiles that she was using; witchcraft of a kind, I suppose, but the kind that any woman knows how to use. There was the bedchamber again, with the brazier dealing out a glow of warmth, and beside it, on a low table, food and wine in silver dishes. Morgause stood beside the brazier, the rosy glow playing on the white gown and creamy skin, and glimmering on the long shining hair that fell to her waist in rivulets of apricot light. Even I, who loathed her, had to admit that she was very lovely. The long green-gold eyes, thickly fringed by their golden lashes, watched the door. She was alone.

The door opened and Lot came in. The King of Lothian was a big dark man, with powerful shoulders and hot eyes. He favoured jewels, and glittered with arm-rings and finger rings and a chain on his breast set with citrine and amethyst. At his shoulder, where the long black hair touched his cloak, was a magnificent pin of garnet and worked gold, in the Saxon style. Fine enough, I thought grimly, to have been a guest-gift from Colgrim himself. There was rain on his hair and cloak.

Morgause was speaking. I could hear nothing. It was a vision of movement and colour only. She made no move of welcome, nor did he seem to expect it. He showed no surprise at seeing her. He spoke once, briefly, then stooped to the table, and, picking up the silver jug, splashed wine from it into a cup with such haste and carelessness that the crimson stuff slopped over the table and on to the floor. Morgause laughed. There was no answering smile from Lot. He drank the wine down, deeply as if he needed it, then threw the cup to the floor, strode past the brazier, and with his big hands, still marked and muddied from the ride, laid hold of the two sides of her gown at the neck, and ripped it apart, baring her body to the navel. Then he had hold of her, and his mouth was on hers, devouring her. He had not troubled to shut the door. I saw it shift wider, and the girl Lind, scared doubtless by the crash of the fallen cup, peer in, white-faced. Like Lot, she showed no surprise at what she saw, but, frightened perhaps by the man's violence, she hesitated, as if about to run to her mistress's aid. But then she saw, as I had seen, the half-naked body melt, clinging, against the man's, and the woman's hands sliding up into the black wet hair. The torn gown slipped down to lie in a huddle on the floor. Morgause said something, and laughed. The man's grip on her shifted. Lind shrank back, and the door closed. Lot swung Morgause up and took four long strides to the bed.

Witch's wiles indeed. Even for a rape it would have been precipitate: for a seduction it was a record. Call me innocent, or stupid, or what you will, but at first I could only think, held there in the clouds of dreaming, that some spell had been at work. I believe I thought hazily of drugged wine, Circe's cup, and men turned into rutting swine. It was not until some time later, when the man reached a hand from the bed-covers and turned up the wick of the lamp, and the woman, dazed with sex and sleep, sat up smiling against the crimson pillows and drew the furs up to cover herself, that I began to suspect the truth. He padded across the floor, through the fallen wreck of his own clothes, poured another cupful of wine, drained it, then refilled it and took it back to Morgause. Then he heaved himself back into the bed beside her, sat back himself against the bed-head, and began to talk. She, half-sitting, half-lying against him, nodded and answered, seriously and at length. As they talked, his hand slid down to fondle her breasts; he did it half absently, as was natural.

enough for a man like Lot, who was used to women. But Morgause, the maiden with the unbound hair and demure little voice? Morgause noticed the gesture no more than the man. Only then, with a jar like an arrow thudding deep into a shield, did I see the truth. They had been here before. They were familiar. Even before she had lain with Arthur, Lot had had her, and many times. They were so used to one another that they could lie twined naked on a bed, and, busily and earnestly, talk ... About what?

Treachery. That was, naturally, my first thought. Treachery against the High King, whom both, for differing reasons, had cause to hate. Morgause, long jealous of the half-sister who must always take precedence of her, had laid siege to Lot and taken him to her bed. There had, it was to be supposed, been other lovers, too. Then came Lot's bid for power at Luguvallium. It failed, and Morgause, not guessing at the strength and clemency that would make Arthur accept him back among his allies, turned to Arthur himself in her own desperate play for power.

And now? She had magic of a kind. It was possible that she knew, as I knew, that in that night's incest with Arthur she had conceived. A husband she must have, and who better than Lot? If he could be persuaded that the child was his, she might cheat the hated young sister of marriage and kingdom, and build a nest where the cuckoo could hatch out in safety.

It looked as if she would succeed. When next I saw through the dream-smoke they were laughing together, and she had freed her body of the covers and was seated high on the furs against the crimson curtains of the bed-head, with the rose-gold hair streaming down behind her shoulders like a mantle of silk. The front of her body was bare, and on her head was Lot's royal circlet of white gold, glimmering with citrines and the milk-blue pearls of the northern rivers. Her eyes shone bright and narrow as a purring cat's, and the man was laughing with her as he lifted the cup and drank what looked like a toast to her.

As he lifted it the cup rocked, and wine slopped over the brim to spill down her breasts like blood. She smiled, not stirring, and the king leaned forward laughing, and sucked it off.

The smoke thickened. I could smell it, as if I was there in the room, close by the brazier. Then mercifully I was awake in the cool and tranquil night, but with the night-mare still crawling like sweat on the skin.

To anyone but me, knowing them as I knew them, the scene would have offered no offence. The girl was lovely, and the man fine enough, and if they were lovers, why, then, she had the right to look towards his crown. There should have been nothing to flinch at in the scene, any more than in a dozen such that one sees on any summer evening along the hedgerows, or in the midnight hall. But about a crown, even such a one as Lot's, there is some-thing sacred; it is a symbol of that mystery, the link be-tween god and king, king and people. So to see the crown on that wanton head, with the king's own head, bared of its royalty, bent below it like a beast's pasturing, was profanity, like spittle on an altar.

So I rose, and plunged my head in water, and washed the sight away.

CHAPTER 5

When we reached Caerleon at noon next day, a bright
October sun was drying the ground, and frost lay indigo-
blue in the lee of walls and buildings. The alders along
the river bank, their black boughs hung with yellow coins
of leaves, looked bright and still, like stitchery against the
background of pale sky. Dead leaves, still rimmed with
frost, crunched and rustled under our horses' hoofs. The
smells of new bread and roasting meat wound through the
air from the camp kitchens, and brought sharply to mind
my visit here with Tremorinus, the master engineer who
had rebuilt the camp for Ambrosius, and included in his
plans the finest kitchens in the country.

I said as much to my companion—it was Caius Valerius,
my friend of old—and he grunted appreciatively.

'Let us hope the King takes due time for a meal before
he starts his inspection.'

'I think we can trust him for that.'

'Oh, aye, he's a growing boy.' It was said with a sort of
indulgent pride, with no faintest hint of patronage. From
Valerius it came well; he was a veteran who had fought
with Ambrosius at Kaerconan and since then with Uther:
he was also one of the captains who had been with Arthur
at the battle on the river Glein. If men of this stamp could
accept the young King with respect, and trust him for
leadership, then my task was indeed done. The thought
came unmixed with any sense of loss or declining, but
with a calm relief that was new to me. I thought: I am
growing old.

I became conscious that Valerius had asked me something. 'I'm sorry. I was thinking. You said?'

Book III

APPLEGARTH

CHAPTER 1

To the east of Caer Camel the land is rolling and wooded, ridges and hills of gentle green, with here and there, among the bushes and ferns of the summits, traces of old dwelling-places or fortifications of past time.

One such place I had noticed before, and now, casting about among the hills and valleys, I looked at it once more, and found it good. It was a solitary spot, in a fold between two hills, where a spring welled from the turf and sent a tiny brook tumbling down to meet a valley stream. A long time ago men had lived there. When the sun fell aright you could see the soft outline of ancient walls beneath the turf. That settlement had vanished long since, but since then some other settler, in harder times, had built himself a tower, the main part of which still stood. It had been built, moreover, with Roman stone taken from Caer Camel. The squared shapes of the chiselled stone showed still clean-edged beneath the encroaching saplings and those stinging ghosts that cluster wherever man has been, the nettles. Even these weeds were not unwelcome; they are sovereign for many ailments, and I intended, as soon as the house was done, to plant a garden, which is the chief of the arts of peace.

And peace we had at last. The news of the victory at Badon reached me even before I had paced out the dimensions of my new home. From the account Arthur sent me of the battle it seemed certain that this must be the final victory of the campaign, and now the King was imposing terms, being set on the decisive fixing of his kingdom's boundaries. There was no reason to suppose, his message ran, that there would be any further attack or even resis-

tance for some time to come. I, not having seen the battle-field, but knowing what I knew, prepared to build for a time of peace, where I might live in the solitude I loved and needed, at due remove from the busy centre where Arthur would be.

Meanwhile it would be wise to get hold of all the masons and craftsmen I should require before Arthur's own great schemes for his city began to burgeon. They came, shook their heads over my plans, then set cheerfully to work to build what I wanted.

This was a small house, a cottage, if you will, set in the hollow of the hillside, and facing south and west, away from Caer Camel, towards the distant swell of the downs. The place was sheltered from north and east, and, by a curve of the hill below, from the few passers-by on the valley road. I had the tower rebuilt on its old pattern, and the new house constructed against this, single storeyed, with behind it a square courtyard or garth in the Roman style. The tower formed a corner of this between my own dwelling and the kitchen quarters. At the side opposite the house were workshops and sheds for storage. On the north side of the garth was a high wall coped with tiles, against which I hoped to set some of the more delicate plants. I had long thought of doing what now the masons shook their heads over; the wall was built double, and the hypocaust led warm air into it. Not only in winter would the vines and peaches be safe, but the whole garth would, I thought, benefit from the warmth, as well as from the sunlight it would catch and hold. This was the first time I had seen such an idea put into practice, but later it was done at Camelot, and at Arthur's other palace at Caerleon. A miniature aqueduct led water from the spring into a well at the garth's centre.

The men, finding it a pleasant change from the years of military building, worked quickly. We had an open winter that year. I rode to Bryn Myrddin to oversee the moving of my books and certain of the medical stores, then spent Christmas at Camelot with Arthur. The car-

penters went into my house early in the New Year, and the work was done and the men free in time to start the permanent building at Camelot in the spring.

I still had no servant of my own, and now had to set myself to find one—not an easy task, for few men can settle happily in the kind of solitude I crave, and my ways have never been those of the ordinary master. The hours I keep are strange ones; I require little food or sleep, and have great need of silence. I could have bought a slave who would have had to put up with whatever I wanted, but I have never liked bought service. But this time, as always before, I was lucky. One of the local masons had an uncle who was a gardener; he had given him, he said, an account of the building of the heated wall, and the uncle had shaken his head and muttered something about new-fangled foreign nonsense, but had since evinced the liveliest curiosity about every stage of the building. His name was Varro. He would be glad to come, said the mason, and his daughter, who could cook and clean, would come with him.

So it was settled. Varro started the clearing and digging straight away, and the girl Mora began to scrub and air, and then, in one of those lucid and lovely spells of early weather, with primroses already showing under the budding hawthorns, and lambs couched warm beside the ewes in the hollows of flowering whin, I stabled my horse and unpacked my big harp, and was home.

* * *

Soon after, Arthur came to see me. I was in the garth, sitting in the sunshine on a bench between the pillars of the miniature colonnade. I was busy sorting seeds collected last summer and packed away in twists of parchment. Beyond the walls I heard the stamp and jingle of the King's escort, but he came in alone. Varro went past with a stare and a salute, carrying his spade. I got to my feet as Arthur raised a hand in greeting.

'It's very small,' were his first words, as he looked about him.

'Enough. It's only for me.'

'Only!' He laughed, then pivoted on his heel. 'Mmm ... if you like dog-kennels, and it seems you do, then I must say it's very pleasant. So that's the famous wall, is it? The masons were telling me about it. What are you planting there?'

I told him, and then took him on a tour of my little garth. Arthur, who knew as much about gardens as I about warfare, but who was always interested in making, looked and touched and questioned; he spent a lot of time at the heated wall, and on the construction of the small aqueduct that fed the well.

'Vervain, Camomile, Comfrey, Marigold ...' He turned over the labelled packets of seed lying on the bench. 'I remember Drusilla used to grow marigolds. She gave me some concoction of them when I had the toothache.' He looked round him again. 'Do you know, there is already something of the same peace here that one had at Galava. If only for my sake, you were right in refusing to live in Camelot. I'll feel I have a refuge here, when things are pressing on me.'

'I hope you will. Well, that's all here. I'll have my flowers here, and an orchard outside. There were a few old trees here already, and they seem to be doing well. Would you like to come in now and see the house?'

'A pleasure,' he said, in a tone so suddenly formal that I glanced at him, to see that his attention was not on me at all, but on Mora, who had come out of a doorway and was shaking a cloth in the breeze. Her gown was blown close against her body, and her hair, which was pretty, flew in a bright tangle round her face. She stopped to push it back, saw Arthur, blushed and giggled, then ran indoors again. I saw a bright eye peep through a crack, then she caught me watching, and withdrew. The door shut. It was apparent that the girl had no idea who the young man was who had eyed her so boldly.

He was grinning at me. 'I am to be married in a month, so you can stop watching me like that. I shall be the most model of married men.'

'I am sure of it. Was I watching you? It's no concern of mine, but I should warn you that the gardener is her father.'

'And a tough fellow he looks. All right, I'll keep my blood cool until May. God knows it's landed me in trouble before, and will again.'

'A model married man?'

'I was talking about my past. You warned me that it would reach into my future.' He said it lightly; the past, I guessed, was well behind him now. I doubted if thoughts of Morgause still troubled his sleep. He followed me into the house and, while I found wine and poured it, went on another of his prowling tours of discovery.

There were only two rooms. The living-chamber took two-thirds of the length of the house, and its full width, with windows both ways, on garth and hill. The doorway opened on the collonnade that edged the garth. Today for the first time the door stood open to the mild air, and sunlight fell warmly across the terracotta tiles of the floor. At the end of the room was the place for the fire, with a wide chimney to take the smoke outside. In Britain we need fires as well as heated floors. The hearthstone was of slate, and the walls, of well finished stone, were hung with rich rugs I had brought back with me from my travels in the East. Table and stools were oak, from the same tree, but the great chair was of elm wood, as also the chest under the window, which held my books. A door at the end of the room led to my bedchamber, which was simply furnished with bed and clothes chest. With some memory, perhaps, of childhood, I had planted a pear tree outside the window.

All this I showed him, then took him to the tower. The door to this led off the collonnade in the corner of the garth. On the ground floor was the workroom or still-room, where the herbs were dried, and medicines made

up. There was no furniture but a big table, and stools and cupboards, and the small brick stove with its oven and charcoal burner. A stone stair against one wall led to the upper room. This was the chamber I meant to use as my private study. Here there was nothing as yet but a work-table and chair, a couple of stools and a cupboard with tablets and the mathematical instruments I had brought from Antioch. A brazier stood in one corner. I had had a window made looking out to the south, and this was covered with neither horn nor curtain. I do not readily feel the cold.

Arthur moved round the tiny room, stooping, peering, opening boxes and cupboards, leaning on his fists to gaze out of the window, filling the small space with his immense vitality, so that even the stout, Roman-built walls seemed barely to contain him.

In the main chamber once more, he took a goblet from me, and raised it. 'To your new home. What will you call it?'

'Applegarth.'

'I like that. It's right. To Applegarth then, and your long life here!'

'Thank you. And to my first guest.'

'Am I? I'm glad. May there be many more, and may they all come in peace.' He drank and set the goblet down, looking about him again. 'Already it is full of peace. Yes, I begin to see why you chose it … but are you sure it is all you want? You know, and I know, that the whole of my kingdom is yours by right, and I do assure you I'd let you have half of it for the asking.'

'I'll let you keep it for the present. It's been too much trouble for me to envy you overmuch. Have you time to sit for a while? Will you eat? The very idea will frighten Mora into an epilepsy, because you can be sure she has been out to ask her father who the young stranger is, but I'm certain she can find something—'

'Thank you, no, I've eaten. Have you just the two servants? Who cooks for you?'

'The girl.'

'Well?'

'Eh? Oh, well enough.'

'Which means you haven't even noticed. For God's sake!' said Arthur. 'Let me send you a cook. I don't like to think of you eating nothing but peasant messes.'

'Please, no. The two of them round me by day are all I want, and even they go to their own home at night. I do very well, I assure you.'

'All right. But I wish you would let me do something, give you something.'

'When I find something I want, be sure I'll ask you for it. Now tell me how the building is going. I'm afraid I've been too occupied with my dog-kennel to pay much attention. Will it be ready for your wedding?'

He shook his head. 'By summer, perhaps, it might be fit to bring a queen to. But for the wedding I'll go back to Caerleon. It will be in May. Will you be there?'

'Unless it's your wish that I should be there, I would prefer to stay here. I begin to feel I've had too much travelling in the past few years.'

'As you wish. No, no more wine, thank you. One thing I wanted to ask you. You remember, when first the idea of my marriage was mooted—the first marriage—you seemed to have some doubts about it. I understood that you had had some sort of presentiment of disaster. If so, you were right. Tell me, please—this time, have you any such doubts?'

They tell me that when I guard my face, no man can read what is in my mind. I met his eyes level. 'None. Need you ask me? Have you any doubts yourself?'

'None.' The flash of a smile. 'At least, not yet. How could I, when I am told that she is perfection itself? They all say she is lovely as a May morning, and they tell me this, that and the other thing. But then, they always do. It will suffice if she has a sweet breath and a compliant temper ... Oh, and a pretty voice. I find that I care about voices. All this granted, it couldn't be a better match. As

a Welshman, Merlin, you ought to agree.'

'Oh, I do. I agree with everything Gwyl said, there in the hall. When do you go to Wales to bring her to Caerleon?'

'I can't go myself; I have to ride north in a week's time. I'm sending Bedwyr again, and Gereint with him, and—to do her honour, since I can't go myself—King Melwas of the Summer Country.'

I nodded, and the conversation turned then on the reasons for his journey north. He was going, I knew, mainly to look at the defensive work in the north-east. Tydwal, Lot's kinsman, held Dunpeldyr now, ostensibly on behalf of Morgause and Lot's eldest son Gawain, though it was doubtful if the queen's family would ever leave Orkney.

'Which suits me very well,' said the King indifferently. 'But it creates certain difficulties in the north-east.'

He went on to explain. The problem lay with Aguisel, who held the strong castle of Bremenium, in a nest of the Northumbrian hills, where Dere Street runs up into High Cheviot. While Lot had ruled to the north, Aguisel had been content to run with him, 'as his jackal,' said Arthur contemptuously, 'along with Tydwal and Urien. But now that Tydwal sits in Lot's chair, Aguisel begins to be ambitious. I've heard a rumour—I have no proof of it—that when last the Angles sent their ships up the Alaunus River, Aguisel met them there, not in war, but to speak with their leader. And Urien follows him still, brother jackals, playing at being lions. They may think they are too far away from me, but I intend to pay them a visit and disillusion them. My excuse is to look at the work that has been done on the Black Dyke. From all I hear, I should like a pretext to remove Aguisel for good and all, but I must do it without rousing Tydwal and Urien to defend him. The last thing I can afford, until I am sure of the West Saxons, is a break-up of the allied kings in the north. If I have to remove Tydwal, it may mean bringing Morgause back to Dunpeldyr. A small

thing, compared with the rest, but the day she sits in a mainland castle again cannot be a good day for me.'

'Then let us hope the day will never come.'

'As you say. I'll do my best to contrive it so.' He looked round him again as he turned to go. 'It's a pleasant place. I'm afraid I shan't have time to see you again before I ride, Merlin. I go before the week is out.'

'Then all the gods go with you, my dear. May they be beside you, too, at your wedding. And some day, come and see me again.'

He went. The room seemed to tremble and grow larger again, and the air to settle back into tranquillity.

CHAPTER 2

And tranquillity was the sum of the months that followed. I went over to Camelot soon after Arthur's departure for the north, to see how the building work was going; then, satisfied, left Derwen to complete it, and retired to my new-made fastness with almost the same feeling of home-coming as I felt at Bryn Myrddin. The rest of that spring I spent about my own affairs, planting my garden, writing to Blaise, and, as the countryside burgeoned, collecting the herbs I needed for a renewal of my stores.

I did not see Arthur again before the wedding. A courier brought me news, which was brief but favourable. Arthur had found proof of Aguisel's villainy and had attacked him in Bremenium. The details I did not know, but the King had taken the place and put Aguisel to death; and this without rousing either Tydwal or Urien, or any of their kinsmen against him. In fact, Tydwal had fought beside Arthur in the final storming of the walls. How the King had achieved this, the report did not say, but with the death of Aguisel the world would be cleaner, and, since he died without sons, a man of Arthur's choos-ing could now hold the castle that commanded the Cheviot pass. Arthur chose Brewyn, a man he could be certain of, then went south to Caerleon well content.

The Lady Guinevere duly arrived in Caerleon, royally escorted by princes—Melwas and Bedwyr and a company of Arthur's knights. Cei had not gone with the party; as Arthur's seneschal his duty lay in the palace at Caerleon, where the wedding was celebrated with great splendour. I heard later that the bride's father had suggested May-Day, and that Arthur, after the briefest hesitation, had

said, 'No,' so flatly that eyebrows were raised. But this was the only shadow. All else seemed set fair. The pair were married late in the month on a glorious day of sunshine, and Arthur took a bride to bed for the second time, with, now, days and nights to spare. They came to Camelot in early summer, and I had my first sight of the second Guinevere.

Queen Guinevere of Northgalis was more than 'well enough and with a sweet breath'; she was a beauty. To describe her, one would have to rob the bards of all their old conventions; hair like golden corn, eyes like summer sky, a flower-fair skin and a lissom body—but add to all this the dazzle of personality, a sort of outgoing gaiety, and a way of communicating joy, and you will have some idea of her fascination. For fascinating she was; on the night she was brought to Camelot I watched her through the feasting, and saw other eyes than the King's fixed on her throughout the evening. It was obvious that she would be Queen, not only of Arthur, but of all the Companions. Except perhaps Bedwyr. His were the only eyes that did not seek hers constantly; he seemed quieter even than usual, lost in his own thoughts, and as for Guinevere, she barely glanced his way. I wondered if something had happened on the journey from Northgalis that stung his memory. But Melwas, who sat near her, hung on her every word, and watched her with the same eyes of worship as the younger men.

That was a beautiful summer, I remember. The sun shone blazing, but from time to time the sweet rains came and the soft wind, so that the fields bore crops such as few men could remember, and the cattle and sheep grew sleek, and the land ripened towards a great harvest. Everywhere, though the bells rang on Sundays in the Christian churches, and crosses were to be seen nowadays where once cairns of stone or statues had stood by the wayside, the countryfolk went about their tasks blessing the young King for giving them, not only the peace in which to grow their crops, but the wealth of the crops

themselves. For them, both wealth and glory stemmed from their young ruler, as, during the last year of the sick Uther's life, the land had lain under the black blight. And the common folk waited confidently—as at Camelot the nobles waited—for the announcement that an heir was begotten. But the summer wore through, and autumn came, and, though the land yielded its great harvest, the Queen, riding out daily with her ladies, was as lissom and slender as ever, and no announcement was made.

And here in Camelot, the memory of the girl who had conceived the heir and died of him troubled no one. All was new and shining and building and making. The palace was completed, and now the carvers and gliders were at work, and women wove and stitched, and wares of pottery and silver and gold came into the new city daily, so that the roads seemed full of coming and going. It was the time of youth and laughter, and building after conquest; the grim years were forgotten. As for the 'white shadow' of my foreboding, I began to wonder if it had indeed been the death of the other pretty Guenever that had cast that shadow across the light, and seemed to linger still in corners like a ghost. But I never saw her, and Arthur, if he once remembered her, said nothing.

So four winters passed, and Camelot's towers shone with new gilding, and the borders were quiet, the harvests good, and the people grew accustomed to peace and safety. Arthur was five and twenty, and rather more silent than of old; he seemed to be away from home more, and each time for longer. Cador's duchess bore him a son, and Arthur rode down into Cornwall to stand sponsor, but Queen Guinevere did not go with him. For a few weeks there was whispered hope that she had a good reason for refusing the journey; but the King and his party went and returned, and then left again, by sea, for Gwynedd, and still the Queen at Camelot rode out and laughed and danced and held court, as slim as a maiden, and, it seemed, as free of care.

Then one raining day of early spring, just as dusk fell,

a horseman came thudding to my gate with a message. The King was still away, and was not looked for yet for perhaps another week. And the Queen had vanished.

* * *

The messenger was Cei the seneschal, Arthur's foster-brother, the son of Ector of Galava. He was a big man, some three years older than the King, florid and broad-shouldered. He was a good fighter and a brave man, though not, like Bedwyr, a natural leader. Cei had neither nerves nor imagination, and, while this makes for bravery in war, it does not make for good leadership. Bedwyr, the poet and dreamer, who suffered ten times over for one grief, was the finer man.

But Cei was staunch, and now, since he was responsible for the ordering of the King's household, had come himself to see me, attended only by one servant. This, though he bore one arm in a rough sling, and looked tired and worried out of his slow mind. He told me the story, sitting in my room with the firelight flickering on the ceiling rafters. He accepted a cup of mulled wine, and talked quickly, while, at my insistence, he removed the sling and let me examine his injured arm.

'Bedwyr sent me to tell you. I was hurt, so he sent me back. No, I didn't see a doctor. Damn it, there hasn't been time! Anything could've happened, wait till I tell you ... She's been gone since daybreak. You remember how fair it was this morning? She went out with her ladies, with only the grooms and a couple of men for escort. That was usual—you know it was.'

'Yes.' It was true. Sometimes one or more of the knights accompanied the Queen, but frequently they were occupied on affairs more important than squiring her on her daily rides. She had troopers and grooms, and nowadays there was no danger, so near Camelot, from the kind of wild outlaw who had frequented lonely places when I was a boy. So Guinevere had risen early on what prom-

ised to be a fine morning, mounted her grey mare, and
set out with two of her ladies, and four men, of whom
two were soldiers. They had ridden south, across a belt
of dry moorland bordered, to the south, by thick forest.
To their right hand lay the marshlands, where the rivers
wound seaward through their deep, reedy channels, and
to the east the land showed rolling and forested towards
the high lift of the downs. The party had found game in
plenty; the little greyhounds had run wild after it, and,
said Cei, the grooms had their hands full riding after
them to bring them back. Meantime, the Queen had flown
her merlin after a hare, and had followed this herself,
straight into the forest.

Cei grunted as my probing fingers found the injured
muscle. 'Well, but I told you that it was nothing much.
Only a sprain, isn't it? A pulled muscle? Will it take
long? Oh, well, it's not my sword arm ... Well, she
galloped the grey mare in, and the women stayed back.
Her maid's no rider, and the other, the Lady Melissa, is
not young. The grooms were coming back with the greyhounds on the saddle, and were still some way off. Nobody was worrying. She's a great horsewoman—you know
she even rode Arthur's white stallion and managed it?—
and besides, she's done it before, just to tease them. So
they took it easy, while the two troopers rode after her.'

The rest was easy to supply. It was true that this had
happened before, with no chance of ill, so the troopers
spurred after the Queen at no more than a hand-gallop.
They could hear her mare thudding through the thick
forest ahead of them, and the swish and crackling of the
bushes and dead stuff underfoot. The forest thickened;
the two soldiers slowed to a canter, ducking the boughs
which still swung from the Queen's passing, and guiding
their horses through the tangle of fallen wood and water-
logged holes that made the forest floor such dangerous
terrain. Half cursing, half laughing, and wholly occupied,
it was some minutes before they realised that they could

no longer hear the Queen's mare. The tangled underbrush showed no trace of a horse's passing. They pulled up to listen. Nothing but the distant scolding of a jay. They shouted, and got no answer. Annoyed, rather than alarmed, they separated, riding one in the direction of the jay's scolding, the other still deeper into the forest.

'I'll spare you the rest,' said Cei. 'You know how it is. After a bit they forgathered, and by then, of course, they were alarmed. They shouted some more, and the grooms heard them, and went in and joined the search. Then after a while they heard the mare again. She was going hard, they said, and they heard her whinnying. They struck their spurs in and went after her.'

'Yes?' I settled the injured arm into the freshly tied sling, and he thanked me.

'That's better. I'm grateful. Well, they found the mare three miles off, lame, and trailing a broken rein, but no sign of the Queen. They sent the women back with one of the grooms, and they went on searching. Bedwyr and I took troops out, and for the rest of the day we've been quartering the forest as best we could, but nothing.' He lifted his good hand. 'You know what that country's like. Where it isn't a tangle of tree and scrub that would stop a fire-breathing dragon, it's marsh where a horse or a man would sink over their heads. And even in the forest there are ditches as deep as a man, and too wide to leap. That's where I came to grief. Dead fir boughs spread over a hole, for all the world like a wolf-trap. I'm lucky to have got away with just this. My horse got a spike in the belly, poor beast. It's doubtful if he'll be good for much again.'

'The mare,' I said. 'Had she fallen? Was she mired?'

'To the eyeballs, but that means nothing. She must have galloped through marsh and mire for an hour. The saddle-cloth was torn, though. I think she must have fallen; I can't see the Queen falling off her, else—unless she was swept off by a bough. Believe me, we must have searched every brake and ditch in the forest. She'll be

lying unconscious somewhere ... if not worse. God, if she had to do such a thing, why couldn't she do it when the King was at home?'

'Of course you have sent to him?'

'Bedwyr sent a rider before we left Camelot. There are more men out there now. It's getting too dark to find her, but if she's been lying unconscious, and comes round, maybe they'll hear her calling. What else can we do? Bedwyr's got men down there now with dragnets. Some of those pools are deep, and there are currents in that river to the west ...' He left it there. His rather stupid blue eyes stared at me, as if begging me to do a miracle. 'After I took my toss he sent me back to you. Merlin, will you come with me now, and show us where to look for the Queen?'

I looked down at my hands, then at the fire, dying now to small flames that licked round a greying log. I had not put my powers to the test since Badon. And how long before that since I had dared to call on the least of them? Nor flames, nor dream, nor even the glimmer of Sight in the crystal or the water-drops: I would not importune God for the smallest breath of the great wind. If he came to me, he came. It was for him to choose the time, and for me to go with it.

'Or even just tell me, now?' Cei's voice cracked, imploring.

Time was, I thought, when I would only have had to look at the fire, like this, to lift a hand, like this ...

The small flames hissed, and leaped a foot high, wrapping the grey log with blazing scarves of light, and throwing out a heat that seared the skin. Sparks jumped, stung, with the old welcome, quickening pain. The light, the fire, the whole living world flowed upwards, bright and dark, flame and smoke and trembling vision, carrying me with it.

A sound from Cei flicked my attention back to him. He was on his feet, backed away from the blaze. Through the ruddy light pouring over him I saw that he had gone

pale. There was sweat on his face. He said hoarsely:
'Merlin—'

He was already fading, drowned in flame and darkness.
I heard myself say: 'Go. Get my horse ready. And wait
for me.'

I did not hear him go. I was already far from the firelit
room, borne on the cool and blazing river that dropped
me, light as a leaf loosened by the wind, in the darkness
at the gates of the Otherworld.

* * *

The caves went on and on for ever, their roofs lost in
darkness, their walls lit with some strange subaqueous
glow that outlined every ridge and boss of rock. From
arches of stone hung stalactites, like moss from ancient
trees, and pillars of rock rose from the stone floor to meet
them. Water fell somewhere, echoing, and the swimming
light rippled, reflecting it.

Then, distant and small, a light showed; the shape of a
pillared doorway, formal and handsome. Beyond it something—someone—moved. In the moment when I wanted
to go forward and see I was there without effort, a leaf on
the wind, a ghost in a stormy night.

The door was the gateway to a great hall lighted as if
for a feast. Whatever I had seen moving was no longer
there; merely the great spaces of blazing light, the coloured pavement of a king's hall, the pillars gilded, the
torches held in dragon-stands of gold. Golden seats I
saw, ranged round the gleaming walls, and silver tables.
On one of these lay a chessboard, of silver, dark and
light, with pieces of silver gilt standing, as if half through
an interrupted game. In the centre of the vast floor stood
a great chair of ivory. In front of this was a golden chessboard, and on it a dozen or so gold chessmen, and one
half-finished, lying with a rod of gold and a file where
someone had been working to carve them.

I knew then that this was no true vision, but a dream

of the legendary hall of Llud-Nuatha, King of the Otherworld. To this palace had they all come, the heroes of
song and story. Here the sword had lain, and here the
grail and the lance might one day be dreamed of and
lifted. Here Macsen had seen his princess, the girl who
in the world above he had married, and on whom he
had begotten the line of rulers whose latest scion was
Arthur...

Like a dream at morning, it had gone. But the great
caves were still there, and in them, now, a throne with a
dark king seated, and by him a queen, half visible in
shadows. Somewhere a thrush was singing, and I saw her
turn her head, and heard her sigh.

Then through it all I knew that I, Merlin, this time of
all the times, did not want to see the truth. Knowing it
already, perhaps, beneath the level of conscious thought,
I had built for myself the palace of Llud, the hall of Dis
and his prisoned Persephone. Behind them both lay the
truth, and, as I was the god's servant and Arthur's, I had
to find it. I looked again.

The sound of water, and a thrush singing. A dim room,
but not lofty, nor furnished with silver and gold; a curtained room, well lighted, where a man and a woman sat
at a little inlaid table and played at chess. She seemed
to be winning. I saw him frown, and the tense set of his
shoulders as he hunched over the board considering his
move. She was laughing. He lifted his hand, hesitating,
but withdrew it again and sat a while, quite still. She
said something, and he glanced aside, then turned to
adjust the wick of one of the lamps near him. As he looked
away from the board, her hand stole out and she moved a
piece, neat as a thief in the market-place. When he looked
back she was sitting, demure, hands in lap. He looked,
stared, then laughed aloud and moved. His knight scooped
her queen from the board. She looked surprised, and
threw up her hands, pretty as a picture, then began to set
the chessmen afresh. But he, suddenly all impatience,
sprang to his feet and, reaching across the board, took

her hands in his own and pulled her towards him. Between them the board fell over, and the chessmen spilled to the floor. I saw the white queen roll near his foot, with the red king over her. The white king lay apart, tumbled face downwards. He looked down, laughed again, and said something in her ear. His arms closed round her. Her robe scattered the chessmen, and his foot came down on the white king. The ivory smashed, splintering.

With it the vision splintered, broke in shadow that wisped, greying, back into lamplight, and the last glimmer from the dying fire.

I got stiffly to my feet. Horses were stamping outside, and somewhere in the garth a thrush was singing. I took my cloak from its hook and wrapped it round me. I went out. Cei was fidgeting by the horses, biting his nails. He hurried to meet me.

'You know?'

'A little. She is alive, and unhurt.'

'Ah! Christ be thanked for this! Where, then?'

'I don't know yet, but I shall. A moment, Cei. Did you find the merlin?'

'What?' blankly.

'The Queen's falcon. The merlin she flew and followed into the forest.'

'Not a sign. Why? Would it have helped?'

'I hardly know. Just a question. Now take me to Bedwyr.'

Mercifully Cei asked no more questions, being fully occupied with his horse as we slithered and bounded, alternately, over the difficult ground. Though, in spite of the rain, there was still sufficient light to see the way, it was not easy to pick a quick and safe route across the tract of water-logged land which was the shortest way between Applegarth and the forest where the Queen had vanished.

For the last part of the way we were guided by distant torchlight, and men's voices, magnified and distorted by water and wind. We found Bedwyr up to the thighs in water, three or four paces out from the bank of a deep, still runnel edged with gnarled alders and the stumps of ancient oaks, some cut long ago for timber, and others blasted with time and storm, and growing again in the welter of smashed branches.

Near one of these the men were gathered. Torches had been tied to the dead boughs, and two other men with torches were out beside Bedwyr in the stream, lighting the work of dragging. On the bank, a short way along from the oak stump, lay a pile of sodden debris running with water, which glinted in the torchlight. Each time, one could guess, the nets would come up heavily weighted from the bottom, and each time all the men present would strain forward under the torchlight to see, with dread, if the net held the drowned body of the Queen.

One such load had just been tipped out as Cei and I approached, our horses slithering to a thankful stop on the very brink of the water. Bedwyr had not seen us. I heard his voice, rough with fatigue, as he showed the net-

men where next to sink the drags. But the men on the bank called out, and he turned, then, seizing a torch from the man beside him, came splashing towards us.

'Cei?' He was too far gone with worry and exhaustion to see me there. 'Did you see him? What did he say? Wait, I'll be with you in a moment.' He turned to shout over his shoulder: 'Carry on, there!'

'No need,' I said. 'Stop the work, Bedwyr. The Queen is safe.'

He was just below the bank. His face, upturned in the torchlight, was swept with such a light of relief and joy that one could have sworn the torches burned suddenly brighter. 'Merlin? Thank the gods for that! You found her, then?'

Someone had led our horses back. All around us now the men crowded, with eager questions. Someone put a hand down to Bedwyr, who came leaping up the bank, and stood there with the muddy water running off him.

'He had a vision.' This was Cei, bluntly. The men went quiet at that, staring, and the questions died to an awed and uneasy muttering. But Bedwyr asked, simply:

'Where is she?'

'I can't tell you that yet, I'm afraid.' I looked around me. To the left the muddy channel wound deeper into the darkness of the forest, but westward, to the right, a space of evening light could be seen through the trees where it opened out into a marshy lake. 'Why were you dragging here? I understood the troopers didn't know where she fell.'

'It's true they neither heard nor saw it, and she must have fallen some time before they got on the track of her mare again. But it looks very much as if the accident happened here. The ground's got trampled over now, so you can't see anything much, but there were signs of a fall, the horse shying, probably, and then bursting away through these branches. Bring the torch nearer, will you? There, Merlin, see? The marks on the boughs and a shred of cloth that must have come from her cloak ... There

was blood, too, smeared on one of the snags. But if you say she's safe ...' He put up a weary hand to push the hair from his eyes. It left a streak of mud right down his cheek. He took no notice.

'The blood must have been the mare's,' said someone, from behind me. 'She was scratched about the legs.'

'Yes, that would be it,' said Bedwyr. 'When we picked her up she was lame, and with a broken rein. Then when we found the marks here on the bank and among the branches, I thought I saw—I was afraid I knew what had happened. I thought the mare had shied and fallen, and thrown the Queen into the water. It's deep here, right under the bank. I reckoned she might have held on to the rein and tried to get the mare to pull her out, but the rein broke, and then the mare bolted. Or else the rein got caught on one of the snags, and it was only some time later that the mare could break loose and bolt. But now ... What did happen?'

'That I can't tell you. What matters now is to find her, and quickly. And for that, we must have King Melwas' help. Is he here, or any of his people?'

'None of his men-at-arms, no. But we fell in with three or four of the marsh-dwellers, good fellows, who showed us some of the ways through the forest.' He raised his voice, turning. 'The Mere men, are they here still?'

It seemed that they were. They came forward, reluctant and over-awed, pushed by their companions. Two men, smallish and broad-shouldered, bearded and unkempt, and with them a stripling boy, the son, I guessed, of the younger man. I spoke to the eldest.

'You come from Mere, in the Summer Country?'

He nodded, his fingers twisting nervously in front of him at a fold of his sodden tunic.

'It was good of you to help the High King's men. You shall not be the losers by it, I promise you. Now, you know who I am?'

Another nod, more twisting of the hands. The boy swallowed, audibly.

'Then don't be afraid, but answer my questions if you can. Do you know where King Melwas is now?'

'Not rightly, my lord, no.' The man spoke slowly, almost like one using a foreign language. These marsh-people are silent folk, and, when about their own business, use a dialect peculiar to themselves. 'But you'll not find him at his palace on the Island, that I do know. Seen him away hunting, we did, two days gone. 'Tis a thing he does, now and again, just him and one of the lords, or maybe two.'

'Hunting? In these forests?'

'Nay, master, he went fowling. Just himself, and one to row the boat.'

'And you saw him go? Which way?'

'South-west again.' The man pointed. 'Down there where the causeway runs into the marsh. The land's dry in places thereabouts, and there be wild geese grazing in plenty. There's a lodge he has, a main beyond, but he won't be there now. It's empty since this winter past, and no servants in it. Besides, the news came up the water this dawning, that the young King was on his way home from Caer-y-n'a Von with a score of sail, so he would be putting in at the island, maybe with the next tide. And our King Melwas, surely, must be there to greet him?'

This was news to me, and, I could see, to Bedwyr. It is a constant mystery how these remote dwellers in the marshes get their news so quickly.

Bedwyr looked at me. 'There was no beacon lighted on the Tor when news came about the Queen. Did you see it, Merlin?'

'No. Nor any other. The sails can't have been sighted yet. We should go now, Bedwyr. We'll ride for the Tor.'

'You mean to speak with Melwas, even before we seek the Queen?'

'I think so. If you would give the orders? And see these men recompensed for their help?'

In the bustle that followed, I touched Bedwyr's arm, and took him aside. 'I can't talk now, Bedwyr. This is a high matter, and dangerous. You and I must go alone to

seek the Queen. Can you manage this without being questioned?'

He frowned, searching my face, but said immediately: 'Of course. But Cei? Will he accept that?'

'He's injured. Besides, if Arthur is due, Cei should be back in Camelot.'

'That's true. And the rest can ride for the Island, to wait for the tide. It'll be dark enough soon for us to slip away from them.' The day's strain hacked abruptly through his voice. 'Are you going to tell me what this is all about?'

'I'll explain as we ride. But I want no one else to hear, not even Cei.'

A few minutes later we were on our way. I rode between Cei and Bedwyr, with the men clattering behind us. They were talking light-heartedly among themselves, wholly reassured, it seemed, by my word that all was well. I myself, though still knowing only what the dream allowed me, felt curiously light and easy, riding at the urgent pace Bedwyr set through the treacherous ground, without thought or care, not even feeling saddle or bridle-rein. It was not a new feeling, but it was many years since it had come to me; the god's will streaming past, and myself going with it, a spark blown between the lasting stars. I did not know what lay ahead of us in that watery dusk, but only that the Queen and her adventure were but a small part of the night's destiny, shadows already blown aside by this great forward surge of power.

My memory of that ride is all confusion now. Cei's party left us, and shortly afterwards we found boats, and Bedwyr embarked half the party by the short route across the Lake. The rest he divided, some by the shore road, others by the causeway that led directly to the wharf. The rain had stopped now, and mist lay everywhere with the night coming; above it the sky was filling with stars, as a net with flashing silver fish. More torches were lit, and the flat ferries crammed with men and horses were poled slowly through misty water that streamed with reflected

light like smoke. As the troops on shore broke and re-formed, their horses shoulder deep in the rolling mist, we saw the glimmer of a distant torch mounting the Tor. Arthur's sails had been sighted.

It was easy then for Bedwyr and myself to slip away. Our horses plunged down from the hard road, cantered heavily through a league of wet meadow-land, and gained the fast going of the road that led south-west.

Soon the lights and sounds of the Island sank behind us and away. Mist curled from the water on either hand. The stars showed the way, but faintly, like lamps along a road for ghosts. Our horses settled into their stride, and soon the way widened, and we could ride knee to knee.

'This lodge to the south-west.' His voice was breathless. 'Is that where we go?'

'I hope so. Do you know it?'

'I can find it. Is that why you needed Melwas' help? Surely, when he knows of the Queen's accident, he'll let our troops search his land from end to end. And if he's not at the lodge now—'

'Let us hope he is not.'

'Is that a riddle?' For the first time since I had known him, his voice was barely civil. 'You said you'd explain. You said you knew where she was, and now you're looking for Melwas. Well, then—'

'Bedwyr, haven't you understood? I think Guinevere is at the lodge. Melwas took her.'

The silence that followed was more stormy than any oath. When he spoke I could hardly hear him. 'I don't have to ask you if you're sure. You always are. And if you did have a vision, I can only accept it. But tell me how, and why?'

'The why is obvious. The how I don't yet know. I suspect he has been planning this for some time. Her habits of riding out are known, and she often goes to the forest that edges the marsh. If she encountered him there, when she was riding ahead of her people, what more natural than that she should stop her mare and speak to him?

That might account for the silence, while the troopers tried to find her at first.'

'Yes ... And if he gripped the rein and tried to seize her, and she spurred her mare on ... That would account for the broken rein and the marks we found by the banks. By all the gods, Merlin! It's rape you're talking about! — And you said he must have been planning this for some time?'

'I can only guess at it,' I said. 'It seems likely that he must have made a few false casts before the chance came; the Queen unattended, and the boat ready nearby.'

I did not pursue my own thoughts further. I was remembering the lamplit room, so carefully prepared for her; the chess game; the Queen's demure composure, and her smiling look. I was thinking, too, of the long hours of daylight and dusk that had passed since she had vanished.

So, obviously, was Bedwyr. 'He must be mad! A petty king like Melwas to risk Arthur's anger? Is he out of his mind?'

'You could say so,' I said drily. 'It has happened before, where women are concerned.'

Another silence, broken at length by a gesture, dimly seen, and a change in his horse's stride. 'Slow here. We leave the roadway soon.'

I obeyed him. Our horses slowed to a trot, a walk, as we peered around us in the mist. Then we saw it, a track leading, apparently, straight off into the marsh.

'This is it?'

'Yes. It's a bad track. We may have to swim the horses.' I caught a glance back at me. 'Will you be all right?'

Memory plucked at me; Bedwyr and Arthur in the Wild Forest, riding necks for sale, as boys will, but always with a care for myself, the poor horseman plodding at heel.

'I can manage.'

'Then down here.' His horse plunged down the narrow twist of mud between the reeds, then took the water like

a boat launching; mine went after it, and we were forging, wet to the thigh, through the smooth water. It was a strange sort of progress, because the mist hid the water; hid, even, our horses' heads. I wondered how Bedwyr could see the way, then glimpsed, myself, far out across the gleam of water and banks of mist, and the black shapes of trees and bushes, the tiny glimmer of light that meant a dwelling. I watched it inching nearer, my mind racing this way and that with the possibilities of what must be done. Arthur, Bedwyr, Melwas, Guinevere ... and all the time, like the deep humming that a harp builds up below an intricate web of music, was that other pressure of power which was driving me towards—what?

The horses heaved out of the water and stood, blowing and dripping, on a ridge of dry land. This stretched for some fifty paces ahead of us, and beyond it, some twenty paces further, was the house, across another channel of water. There was no bridge.

'And no boat, either.' I heard him swear under his breath. 'This is where we swim.'

'Bedwyr, I'll have to let you do this last bit alone. But you—'

'Yes, by God!' His sword whispered loose in its scabbard.

I shot a hand out and gripped his horse's bridle above the bit. '—But you will do exactly as I tell you.'

A silence. Then his voice, gentle and stubborn.

'I shall kill him, of course.'

'You will do no such thing. You will save the High King's name and hers. This is Arthur's business, not yours. Let him deal with it.'

Another silence, a long one. 'Very well. I will be ruled by you.'

'Good.' I turned my horse quietly into the cover of a clump of alder. His, perforce, followed, with me still gripping the bit. 'Now wait. Look yonder.'

I pointed to the north-east, the way we had come. Far away in the night across the flat marshlands a cluster of

lights showed, high up, like stars. Melwas' stronghold, alight with welcome. Unless the king himself was there, home from hunting, it could only mean one thing; Arthur had come back.

Then, the sound so magnified by the water that it made us start, came the click and creak of a door opening nearby, and the soft ripple of a boat moving through the water. The sounds came from behind the house, where something invisible to us took to the water and moved away into the mist. A man's voice spoke once, softly.

Bedwyr moved sharply, and his horse flung up its head against my restraining hand. His voice was strained. 'Melwas. He's seen the lights. Damn it, Merlin, he's taking her—'

'No. Wait. Listen.'

Light still showed from the house. A woman's voice called something. The cry had in it some kind of entreaty, but whether of fear, or longing, or sorrow at being left alone, it was impossible to tell. The boat's sound dwindled. The house door shut.

I still held Bedwyr's bridle. 'Now, go across and bring the Queen, and we will take her home.'

CHAPTER 4

Almost before I had finished speaking he was off his horse,
had dropped his heavy cloak across the saddle, and was
in the water, swimming like an otter for the grassy slope
before the door. He reached it, and began to draw himself up from the water. I saw him check, heard a grunt of
pain, a stifled gasp, an oath.

'What is it?'

He made no reply. He got a knee to the bank, then
pulled himself slowly, with the aid of a hanging willow,
to his feet. He paused only to shake the wet from his
shoulders, then trod up the slippery slope to the house
door. He went slowly, as if with difficulty. I thought he
was limping. As he went, his sword came rasping from
the sheath.

He hammered on the door with the hilt. The sound
echoed, as if from an empty house. There was no movement; no reply. (So much, I thought sourly, for the lady
who waits for rescue.)

Bedwyr hammered again. 'Melwas! Open to Bedwyr of
Benoic! Open in the King's name!'

There was a long pause. It could be felt that someone
within the house was waiting with held breath and beating heart. Then the door opened.

It was opened, not with a slam of defiance or bravery,
but slowly, a crack only, which showed the small light of a
taper, and the shadow of someone peering out. A slight
figure, lissom and straight, with loose hair flowing, and a
long gown of fine stuff with a creamy sheen.

Bedwyr said, and it came strangled: 'Madam? Lady!
Are you safe?'

'Prince Bedwyr.' Her voice was breathless, but low, and apparently composed. 'I thank God for you. When I heard you coming I was afraid ... But then, when I knew it was you ... How did you come here? How did you find me?'

'Merlin guided me.'

I heard the swift intake of her breath clear from where I stood holding the horses. The taper lit the pale shape of her face as she turned her head sharply, and saw me beyond the water. '*Merlin?*' Then her voice was once more soft and steady. 'Then I thank God again for his art. I thought no one would ever come this way.'

That, I thought, I can well believe. I said aloud: 'Can you make ready, Madam? We have come to take you back to the King.'

She did not answer me, but turned to go in, then paused, and said something to Bedwyr, too low for me to catch. He answered, and she pushed the door wide, and gestured him in after her. He went, leaving the door standing open. Inside the room I saw the pulsing ebb and flow of light that meant a fire. The room was softly lit by a lamp, and I caught glimpses through doorway and window of a room more richly furnished than any long-neglected hunting-lodge could have shown, with gilded stools and scarlet cushions, and, through another half-open doorway, the corner of a bed or couch, with a coverlet thrown across a tumble of bed-linen. Melwas had prepared the nest well for her, then. My vision of firelight and supper table and the friendly game of chess had been accurate enough. The words that would tell Arthur moved and raced and re-formed in my brain. The mist smoked up round the house like white ghosts, white shadows ...

Bedwyr emerged from the house. His sword was back in its sheath, and in one hand he carried a lamp; the other held a pole such as marsh-men use to push their flat-bottomed craft through the reeds. He approached the water's edge, moving cautiously. 'Merlin?'

'Yes? Do you want me to swim the horses over?'

'No!' sharply. 'There are knives set below the water. I had forgotten that old trick, and drove a knee straight into them.'

'I thought you were limping. Are you badly hurt?'

'No. Flesh wounds only. My lady has dressed them for me.'

'All the more reason why you can't swim back, then. How do you propose to get her over here? There must be some place where I can land the horses safely. Ask her.'

'I have. She doesn't know. And there's no boat.'

'So?' I said. 'Has Melwas any gear that will float?'

'That's what I was thinking. There's sure to be something we can use; and the costlier the better.' A shadow of amusement lightened the grim voice. But neither of us cared to comment on the situation across twenty feet of echoing water with Guinevere herself within earshot.

'She's dressing herself,' he said shortly, as if in answer to my thought. He set the lamp down at the water's edge. We waited.

'Prince Bedwyr?'

The door opened again. She was in riding dress, and had braided her hair. Her cloak was over her arm.

Bedwyr limped up the bank. He held the cloak for her, and she drew it close and pulled the hood to cover the bright hair. He said something, then vanished indoors to reappear in a short while carrying a table.

I suppose the next few minutes, if anyone had been in the mood to appreciate it, would have been rich in comedy, but as it was, Queen Guinevere on one side of the water, and myself on the other, stood in silence and watched Bedwyr improvising his absurd raft, then, as an afterthought, pitching a couple of cushions into it, and inviting the Queen to board it.

This she did, and they came across, an undignified progress, with the Queen crouched low, holding on to one carved and gilded table leg, while the Prince of Benoic poled the contraption erratically across the channel.

The thing came to the bank, and I caught a leg and held it. Bedwyr scrambled ashore, and turned to help the Queen. She came gracefully enough, with a little gasp of thanks, and stood shaking out her stained and crumpled cloak. Like her riding dress, it had been soaked and roughly dried. I saw that it was torn. Something pale shook from the folds and fell to the muddy turf. I stooped to pick it up. It was a chessman of white ivory. The king, broken.

She had not noticed. Bedwyr pushed the table back into the water, and took his horse's bridle from me. I handed him his cloak and said formally to the Queen, so formally that my voice sounded stiff and cold: 'I am glad to see you well and safe, lady. We have had a bad day, fearing for you.'

'I am sorry.' Her voice was low, her face hidden from me under the hood. 'I took a heavy toss when my mare fell in the forest. I—I don't remember much after that, until I woke here, in this house . . .'

'And King Melwas with you?'

'Yes. Yes. He found me lying, and carried me here. I was fainting, I suppose. I don't remember. His servant tended me.'

'He would have done better, perhaps, to have stayed by you till your own people came. They were searching the forest for you.'

A movement of the hand that held the hood close about her face. I thought it was trembling. 'Yes, I suppose so. But this place was near, just across the water, and he was afraid for me, he said, and indeed, the boat seemed best. I could not have ridden.'

Bedwyr was in the saddle. I took the Queen's arm, to help her up in front of him. With surprise—nothing in that small composed voice had led me to suspect it—I felt her whole body shaking. I abandoned the questioning, and said, merely: 'We'll take this ride easily, then. The King is back, did you know?'

I felt the shudder run through her, like an ague. She

said nothing. Her body was light and slender, like a girl's, as I put her up in front of Bedwyr's saddle.

We went gently on the way back. As we neared the Island, it could be seen that the wharf was ablaze with lights, and milling with horsemen.

We were still some distance off when we saw, lit by their moving torches, a group of horsemen detach themselves from the crowd, and come at the gallop along the causeway. A man on a black horse was in the lead, pointing the way. Then they saw us. There were shouts. Soon they came up with us. In the lead, now, was Arthur, his white stallion black with mud to the withers. Beside him on the black horse, loud with relief and concern for the Queen, rode Melwas, King of the Summer Country.

* * *

I rode home alone. There was nothing to be gained, and too much to be lost, by confronting Arthur and Melwas now. So far, by Melwas' quick thinking in leaving the marsh house by the back way, and being present to greet Arthur as his ships put into the wharf, the affair was saved from scandal, and Arthur would not be forced, whatever his private feelings when he found or guessed at the truth, into a hasty public quarrel with an ally. It was best left for the present. Melwas would take them all into his firelit palace and give them food and wine, and perhaps lodge them for the night, and by morning Guinevere would have told her story—some story—to her husband. I could not begin to guess what the story would be. There were elements in it which she would be hard put to it to explain away; the room so carefully ready for her; the loose robe she had worn; the tumbled bed; her lies to Bedwyr and myself about Melwas. And more than all, the broken chessman and its evidence of a true dream. But all this would have to wait until, at the very least, we were off Melwas' land, and no longer surrounded by his men-at-arms. As for Bedwyr, he had said nothing, and

in the future, whatever his thoughts, his love for Arthur
would keep his mouth shut.

And I? Arthur was High King, and I was his chief
adviser. I owed him a truth. But I would not stay tonight,
to face his questions, and perhaps evade them, or parry
them with lies. Later, I thought wearily, as my tired horse
plodded along the shore of the Lake, I would see more
clearly what to do.

*   *   *

I went home the long way round, without troubling
the ferryman. Even if he were willing to ply so late, I
did not feel equal to his gossip, or that of the troops
who might be making their way back. I wanted silence,
and the night, and the soft veils of the mist.

The horse, scenting home and supper, pricked his ears
and stepped out. Soon we had left the sounds and lights
of the Island behind us, the Tor itself no more than a
black shape of night, with stars behind its shoulder.
Trees loomed, hung with mist, and below them lake
water lapped on the flattened shingle. The smell of water
and reeds and stirred mud, the steady plod of hoofs, the
ripple of the Lake, and through it all, faint and infinitely
distant, but tingling like salt on the tongue, the breath of
the sea-tide, turning to its ebb here at its languid limit.
A bird called hoarsely, splashing somewhere, invisible.
The horse shook his damp neck, and plodded on.

Silence and still air, and the calm of solitude. They
drew a veil, as palpable as the mist, between the stresses
of the day, and the night's tranquillity. The god's hand
had withdrawn. No vision printed itself on the dark.
About tomorrow, and my part in it, I would not think. I
had been led to prevent trespass by a prophetic dream;
but what 'high matters' the sudden renewal of the god's
power in me portended, I could not tell, and was too
weary to guess at. I chirruped to the horse, and he quickened his pace. The moon's edge, above a shaw of elms,

showed the night black and silver. In a short half mile we would leave the Lake shore, and make for home along the gravel of the road.

The horse stopped, so suddenly that I was jerked forward on his neck. If he had not been so far spent, he would have shied, and perhaps thrown me. As it was he balked, both forefeet thrust stiffly in front of him, jarring me to the bone.

Here the way ran along the crest of a bank which skirted the Lake. There was a sheer drop, half the height of a man, down to the water's surface. The mist lay thickly, but some movement of air—perhaps from the tide itself—stirred it faintly, so that it swirled and rose in peaks like cream in a tub, or flowed, itself like water, thickened and slow.

Then I heard a faint splashing, and saw what my horse had seen. A boat, being poled along a little way out from shore, and in it someone standing, balancing as delicately as a bird balances on a rocking twig. Only a glimpse I had, dim and shadow-like, of someone young-seeming and slight, in a cloak-like garment that hung to the thwarts and over the boat's edge to trail in the water. The boy stooped, and straightened again, wringing the stuff out. The mist coiled and broke round the movement, and its pallid drift reflected, briefly, the starlight. I saw his face. I felt shock thud under my heart like an arrow to its target.

'Ninian!'

He started, turned, stopped the boat expertly. The dark eyes looked enormous in the pale face.

'Yes? Who's that?'

'Merlin. Prince Merlin. Do you not remember me?' I caught at myself. Shock had made me stupid. I had forgotten that, when I fell in with the goldsmith and his assistant on the road to Dunpeldyr I had been in disguise. I said quickly: 'You knew me as Emrys; that is my name. Myrddin Emrys from Dyfed. There were reasons why I couldn't travel under my own name. Do you remember now?'

The boat rocked. The mist thickened and hid it, and I knew a moment's blind panic. He had gone again. Then I saw him, still there, head on one side. He thought and then spoke, taking time about it, as always.

'Merlin? The enchanter? That is who you are?'

'Yes. I am sorry if I startled you. It was a shock seeing you like this. I thought you were drowned, that time at the Cor Bridge when you went swimming in the river with the other boys. What happened?'

I thought he hesitated. 'I am a good swimmer, my lord.'

There was some secret here. It did not matter. Nothing mattered. I had found him. This was what the night had been moving towards. This, not the Queen's trespass, was the 'high matter' towards which the power had driven me. Here was the future. The stars flashed and sparkled as once they had flashed and sparkled on the hilt of the great sword.

I leaned forward over the horse's neck, speaking urgently. 'Ninian, listen. If you don't want to answer questions, I'll ask none. All right, so you ran away from slavery; that doesn't matter to me. I can protect you, so don't be afraid. I want you to come to me. As soon as I saw you first, I knew what you were; you're like me, and by the Sight that God has given me, I think you will be capable of the same. You guessed it, too, didn't you? Will you come to me, and let me teach you? It won't be easy; you're young yet; but I was younger still when I went to my master, and you can learn it all, I know. Trust me. Will you come and serve me, and learn as much of my art as I can give you?'

This time there was no hesitation at all. It was as if the question had been asked and answered long ago. As perhaps it had. About some things there is this inevitability; they were in the stars from the last day of the Flood.

'Yes,' he said, 'I'll come. Give me a little time, though. There are things to—to arrange.'

I straightened. My rib-cage hurt from the long breaths I drew. 'You know where I live?'

'Everyone knows.'

'Then come when you can. You will be welcome.' I added, softly, as much to myself as to him: 'By God himself, you will be welcome.'

There was no reply. When I looked again, there was nothing but the white mist with the starlight on it, bitter-white, and from below, the lap of the lake-water on the shore.

* * *

Even so, it took me till I got to my own house to realise the very simple truth.

When I had seen the boy Ninian, and yearned to him as to the one human being I had known who could go with me wherever I had gone, it had been years ago. How many? Nine, ten? And he had been perhaps sixteen. Between a youth of sixteen and a man in his middle twenties there is a world of change and growing: the boy I had just recognised with such a shock of joy, the face I had remembered a score of times with grief—this could not be the same boy, even had he escaped the river all those years ago, and lived.

As I lay that night in bed, wakeful, watching the stars through the black boughs of the pear tree, as I had done when a child, I went through the scene again. The mist, the ghostly mist; the upward starlight; the voice coming as an echo from the hidden water; the face so well remembered, dreamed over these ten years; these, combining suddenly to waken a forgotten and futile hope, had deceived me.

I knew then, with tears, that the boy Ninian was truly dead, and that this encounter in the ghostly dark had only mocked my weariness with a confused and cruel dream.

CHAPTER 5

He did not come, of course. My next visitor was a courier from Arthur, bidding me to Camelot.

Four days had passed. I had half expected to be summoned before this, but, when no word came, assumed that Arthur had not yet decided what move to make, or that he was bent on hushing the affair up, and would not force a public discussion even in council.

Normally a courier passed between us three or four times a week, and any messenger whose commission took him past my house had long since formed the habit of calling at Applegarth to see if I had a letter ready, or to answer my questions. So I had kept myself informed.

I heard that, unbelievably, Guinevere was still on Ynys Witrin, where some of her ladies had joined her as guests of the old queen. Bedwyr, too, was still lodged in Melwas' palace; the knives had been rusty, and a couple of the wounds they made had become inflamed; added to this, he had taken a chill from wet and exposure, and was ill now with fever. Some of his own men were there with him, guests in Melwas' hall. Queen Guinevere herself, so said my informant, visited him daily, and had insisted on helping his nurses.

Another fragment of information I gathered for myself. The Queen's merlin had been found dead, hanging from its jesses in a high tree, near the place where Bedwyr had dragged the channel.

On the fifth day the summons came, a letter bidding me to confer with the High King about the new council hall, which had been finished while he was in Gwynedd. I saddled up and left immediately for Camelot.

Arthur was waiting for me on the western terrace of the palace. This was a wide paved walk, with formal garden beds wherein some of the Queen's roses bloomed, and pansies and the pretty summer flowers. Now, in the chilly spring afternoon, the only colour came from the daffodils, and the pale dwindling heads of the fair-maids.

Arthur stood by the terrace wall, looking out towards the distant, shining line that was the edge of the open sea. He did not turn to greet me, but waited until I was beside him. Then he glanced to make sure that the servant who had brought me to him had gone, and said abruptly:

'You will have guessed that it's nothing to do with the council hall. That was for the secretaries. I want to talk with you privately.'

'Melwas?'

'Of course.' He swung round with his back to the parapet, half leaning against it. He regarded me frowningly. 'You were with Bedwyr when he found the Queen, and when he brought her back to Ynys Witrin. I saw you there, but when I turned to find you, you had gone. I am told, moreover, that it was you who told Bedwyr where to find her. If you knew anything about this affair that I do not, then why did you not wait and speak with me then?'

'There was nothing I could have told you then that would not have stirred up trouble that you could well do without. What was needed was time. Time for the Queen to rest; for you to talk with her; time to allay men's fears, not inflame them. Which you seem to have done. I am told that Bedwyr and the Queen are still on Ynys Witrin.'

'Yes. Bedwyr is ill. He took straight to bed with a chill, and by morning was in a fever.'

'So I heard. I blame myself. I should have stayed to dress those cuts. Have you talked with him?'

'No. He was not fit.'

'And the Queen?'

'Is well.'

'But not yet ready to make the journey home?'

'No,' he said shortly. He turned away again, looking towards the distant gleam of the sea.

'I take it that Melwas must have offered some sort of explanation?' I said at length.

I expected the question to strike some kind of spark, but he merely looked tired, grey in a grey afternoon.

'Oh, yes. I talked with Melwas. He told me what had happened. He was fowling in the marshes, himself with one servant, a man called Berin. They had taken their boat into the edge of the forest, up the river that you saw. He heard the commotion in the forest, and then saw the Queen's mare plunge and slide in the mud of the bank. The Queen was thrown clear into the water. Her own people were nowhere to be seen. The two men rowed to her and pulled her out. She was unconscious as if she had struck her head in the fall. While they were doing this they heard her people go by at some distance, without coming near the river.' A pause. 'No doubt at this point Melwas should have sent his man after them, but he was on foot and they were mounted, and besides, the Queen was drenched and fainting, and very cold, and could hardly have been carried home, except by boat. So Melwas had the servant row to his lodge, and make a fire. He had food there, and wine. He had expected to go there himself to pass the night, so the place was ready.'

'That was fortunate.'

I kept the dryness from my voice, but he gave me a flick of a glance, sharp as a dagger. 'Indeed. After a while she began to recover. He sent the servant with the boat to Ynys Witrin to bring help, and women to tend her, with either horses and a litter, or else a barge that could carry her in comfort. But before he had gone far the man returned to say that my sails were in sight, and that it looked as if I would land with the tide. Melwas judged it best to set off at once himself for the wharf to

meet me, as his duty was, and to give me the news of her safety.'

'Leaving her behind,' I said, neutrally.

'Leaving her behind. The only craft he had was the light skin boat that he used for his fowling trips. It was not fit for her—certainly not in the state she was in. You must have seen that for yourself. When Bedwyr brought her to me, she could do nothing but weep and shiver. I had to let the women take her straight away and put her to bed.'

He pushed himself away from the parapet, and, turning aside, took half a dozen rapid steps away and back again. He broke off a sprig of rosemary, and pulled it to and fro in his hands. I could smell its peppery, pungent scent from where I stood. I said nothing. After a while he stopped pacing and stood, feet apart, watching me, but still pulling the rosemary in and out between his fingers.

'So that is the story.'

'I see.' I regarded him thoughtfully. 'And so you spent the night as Melwas' guest, and Bedwyr is still there, and the Queen is lodged there as well ... until when?'

'I shall send for her tomorrow.'

'And today you sent for me. Why? It seems that the affair is settled, and your decisions have been made.'

'You must know very well why I sent for you.' His voice had a sudden rough edge to it that belied his previous calm. 'What do you know that "would have stirred up trouble" if you had spoken to me that night? If you have something to say to me, Merlin, say it.'

'Very well. But tell me first, have you spoken with the Queen at all?'

A lift of the brows. 'What do you think? A man who has been away from his wife for the best part of a month? And a wife who was in need of comfort?'

'But if she was ill, being nursed by the women—'

'She was not ill. She was tired, and distressed, and she was very frightened.'

I thought of Guinevere's composed, quiet voice, the careful poise, the shaking body.

'Not of my coming.' He spoke sharply, answering what I had not said. 'She feared Melwas, and she fears you. Are you surprised? Most people do. But she does not fear me. Why should she? I love her. But she was afraid that some evil tongue might poison me with lies ... So until I went to her, and listened to her story, she could not rest.'

'She was afraid of Melwas? Why? Was her story not the same as his?'

This time he did answer the implication. He sent the mangled sprig of rosemary spinning out over the terrace wall. 'Merlin.' It came quietly, but with a kind of hard-held finality. 'Merlin, you do not have to tell me that Melwas lied to me, and that this was a rape. If Guinevere had been so badly hurt when she fell, that she lay fainting for most of the day, then she could hardly have ridden home with you, nor been as whole and sound as she was when I lay with her that night. She had sustained no hurt at all. Nothing but fear.'

'She told you that his story was a lie?'

'Yes.'

If Guinevere had told him a different tale, I thought I knew what she had not made clear. I said, slowly: 'When she spoke with Bedwyr and myself, her story was the same as Melwas'. Now you say that *the Queen herself* told you it was a rape?'

'Yes.' His brows twitched together. 'You don't believe either story, do you? Is that what you are trying to tell me? You think—by God, Merlin, just what do you think?'

'I don't yet know the Queen's story. Tell me what she said.'

He was so angry that I thought he would leave me then and there. But after a turn or two along the terrace he came back to where I waited. He had almost the air of a man approaching single combat.

'Very well. You are my counsellor, after all, and it seems I shall be in need of counsel.' He drew in his breath. The story came in brief, expressionless sentences. 'This is what she says. She did not take a fall at all. She saw her falcon stoop, and catch its jesses in a tree. She stopped her mare, and dismounted. Then she saw Melwas, in his boat by the bank. She called to him for help. He came up the bank to her, but did nothing about the merlin. He started to talk to her of love; how he had loved her since the time they had travelled up from Wales together. He would not listen when she tried to stop him, and when she made to mount again he took hold of her, and in the struggle the mare broke free and bolted. The Queen tried to call out for her people, but he put a hand over her mouth, and threw her down into the boat. The servant thrust it off from the bank, and rowed them away. The man was afraid, she says, and made some sort of protest, but he did as Melwas bade him. He took her to the lodge. It was all ready, as if he expected her ... or some other woman. You saw it. Was it not so?'

I thought of the fire, the bed, the rich hangings, the robe Guinevere had worn. 'I saw a little. Yes, it was prepared.'

'He had had her in his mind so long ... He had only been waiting his chance. He had followed her before— it was well known that she had a habit of outriding her people.' There was a film of sweat on his face. He put the heel of his hand up to his brow and wiped it away.

'Did he lie with her, Arthur?'

'No. He held her there all day, pleading with her, she says, begging for her love ... He began with sweet speeches and promises, but when they got him nowhere, he grew crazed, she says, and violent, and began to see his own danger. After he had sent his man away, she thinks he might have forced her, but the servant came quickly back to tell his master that my sails had been sighted, and Melwas left her in panic, and hurried to me to tell his lies. He threatened her that if she spoke the truth to me, he,

Melwas, would say he had lain with her, so that I would kill her as well as him. She was to tell the same story as he would tell. Which you say she did, to you.'

'Yes.'

'And you knew it was not true?'

'Yes.'

'I see.' He was still watching me with that fierce but wary look. I was beginning to realise, but without much surprise, that even I could not keep secrets from him now. 'And you thought she might have lied to me. That was the "trouble" you foresaw?'

'Partly, yes.'

'You thought she would lie to me? To me?' He repeated it as if it were unthinkable.

'If she were afraid, who could blame her for lying? Yes, I know you say she is not afraid of you. But she is only a woman, after all, and she might well be afraid of your anger. Any woman would lie to save herself. It would have been your right to kill her, and him, too.'

'It is still my right to do that, whether there was a rape or not.'

'Well, then—? Could she have known that you would even listen to her, that you would be King and statesman before you allowed yourself to be the vengeful husband? Even I stand amazed, and I thought I knew you.'

A flicker of grim amusement. 'With Bedwyr and the Queen on the Island as hostages, you might say my hands were tied ... I shall kill him, of course. You know that, don't you? But in my own time, and on some other cause, when all this is forgotten, and the Queen's honour cannot suffer from it.' He swung away, and put his two hands on the parapet, looking out again across the darkening stretch of land towards the sea. Somewhere a beam broke through the clouds, and a shaft of dusky light poured down, lighting a distant stretch of water to a piercing gleam.

He spoke slowly, into the distance. 'I've been thinking over the story I shall put about. I shall take a tale midway

between Melwas' lie, and what the Queen told me. She was there all day with him, after all, from dawn till dusking ... I shall let it be given out that she fell from her horse, as Melwas said, and was carried unconscious to the hunting-lodge, and there lay, shaken and fainting, for most of the day. Bedwyr and you must bear this out. If it were known that she was not hurt at all, there are those who would blame her for not trying to escape. This, though the servant had the boat under his eye all day, and even if she could have swum, there were the knives ... She could, of course, have threatened them with my vengeance, but she saw that as the road only to her own end. He could have kept her there, and had his pleasure and then killed her. You know that her people had already accepted the fact of her death. Except you. That was what saved her.'

I said nothing. He turned.

'Yes. Except you. You told them she was alive, and you took Bedwyr to her. Now, tell me how you knew. Was it a "seeing"?'

I bent my head. 'When Cei came for me, I called on the old powers, and they responded. I saw her in the flame, and Melwas too.'

A moment of suddenly sharpening concentration. It was not often that the High King searched me for truth as he was wont to search lesser men. I could feel something of the quality that had made him what he was. He had gone very still. 'Yes. Now we come to it, don't we? Tell me exactly what you saw.'

'I saw a man and a woman in a rich room, and beyond the door a bedchamber, with a bed that had been lain in. They were laughing together, and playing chess. She was clad in a loose robe, as if for night, and her hair was unbraided. When he took her in his arms the chessboard spilled, and the man trod on the pieces.' I held out a hand to him, with the broken chessman. 'When the Queen came out to us, this was caught in the fold of her cloak.'

He took it, and bent his head over it, as if studying it. Then he sent it spinning after the sprig of rosemary. 'So. It was a true dream. She said there was a table, and chessmen of ivory and ebony wood.' To my surprise, he was smiling. 'Is this all?'

'All? It is more than I would ever have told you, had I not owed it to you as your counsellor.'

He nodded, still smiling. All the anger seemed to have gone. He looked out again over the dimming plain with its gleams of brightness and the shaft of wheeling light. 'Merlin, a little while ago you said "She is only a woman". You have told me many times that you know nothing of women. Does it never occur to you that they lead lives of dependence so complete as to breed uncertainty and fear? That their lives are like those of slaves, or of animals that are used by creatures stronger than themselves, and sometimes cruel? Why, even royal ladies are bought and sold, and are bred to lead their lives far from their homes and their people, as the property of men unknown to them.'

I waited, to see his drift. It was a thought I had had before, when I had seen women suffer from the whims of men; even those women who, like Morgause, were stronger and cleverer than most men. They were made, it seemed, for men's use, and suffered by it. The lucky ones found men they could rule, or who loved them. Like the Queen.

'This happened to Guinevere,' he went on. 'You yourself said just now that I must still be stranger to her in some respects. She is not afraid of me, no, but sometimes I think that she is afraid of life itself, and of living. And most certainly she was afraid of Melwas. Don't you see? Your dream was true. She smiled, and spoke him fair, and hid her fear. What would you have had her do? Appeal to the servant? Threaten the two of them with my vengeance? She knew that was the road only to her own end. When he showed her the bedchamber, to let her change her wet clothing (he takes women to that house

sometimes, it seems, out of sight of the old queen, his mother, and clothes are kept there, with things such as ladies like), she thanked him merely, then locked the door on him. Later, when he came to bid her to meat, she pretended faintness, but after a while he grew suspicious, then importunate, and she was afraid he would break the door, so she ate with him, and spoke him fair. And so, through the long day, till dusk. She let him think that, with nightfall, he would have his pleasure, while all the time she hoped for rescue still.'

'And then it came.'

'Against all hope, and thanks to you, it came. Well, that is her story, and I believe it.' That quick turn of the head again. 'Do you?'

I did not answer straight away. He waited, showing neither anger nor impatience—nor any shadow of doubt.

When at length I spoke, it was with certainty. 'Yes. She told the truth. Reason, instinct, "Sight" or blind faith, you can be sure of it. I am sorry I doubted her. You were right to remind me that I don't understand women. I should have known she was afraid, and knowing that, I might have guessed that what poor weapons she had against Melwas, she would use ... And for the rest—her silence until she could speak with you, her care for your honour and the safety of your kingdom—she has my admiration. And so, King, have you.'

I saw him notice the form of address. Through his relief came a glint of laughter. 'Why? Because I did not fly out in a high royal rage, and demand heads? If the Queen, in fear, could play-act for a day, surely I could do it for a few short hours, with her honour and my own at stake? But not for longer. By Hades, not for longer!' The force with which he brought his clenched fist down on the parapet showed just what he had held in check. He added, with an abrupt change of tone: 'Merlin, you must be aware that the people do not—do not love the Queen.'

'I have heard whispers, yes. But this is not for anything

she is, or has done. It is only because they look daily for
an heir, and she has been Queen for four years, without
bearing. It's natural that there should be disappointed
hopes, and some whispering.'

'There will be no heir. She is barren. I am sure of it
now, and so is she.'

'I feared it. I am sorry.'

'If I had not planted other seed here and there,' he said
with a wry smile, 'I might share some of the blame with
her; but there was the child I begot on my first queen,
not to speak of Morgause's bastard by me. So the fault—if
it is that—is known to be the Queen's, and because she
is a queen, her grief at it cannot be kept private. And
there will always be those who start whispers, in the hope
that I will put her away. Which,' he added with a kind of
snap, 'I shall not.'

'It wouldn't occur to me to advise it,' I said mildly.
'What does occur to me is to wonder if this is the shadow
that I saw once lie across your marriage bed ... But
enough of that. What we must do now is bring her back
into the people's love.'

'You make it sound easy. If you know how—'

'I think I do. Your swore just now by Hades, and it
broke a dream I had. Will you let me go to Ynys Witrin,
and bring her back to you myself?'

He started to ask why, then half laughed and shrugged.
'Why not? Maybe to you it is as easy as it sounds ... Go,
then. I'll send word for them to prepare a royal escort.
I'll receive her here. At least it saves me having to see
Melwas again. Will you, with all your wise counsels, try
to stop me from killing him?'

'As effectively as a mother hen calling the young swan
out of the water. You will do as you think fit.' I looked
out across the water-logged plain, towards the Tor and
the low-lying shape of its neighbour island, where the
harbour lay. I added, thoughtfully: 'It's a pity that he
sees fit to charge harbour dues—exorbitant ones at that—
to the war-leader who protects him.'

His eyes widened, speculatively. A smile tugged at his mouth. He said slowly: 'Yes, isn't it? And then there's the matter of the toll on the road along the ridge. If my captains should by any chance refuse to pay, then no doubt Melwas will bring the complaint here himself, and who knows, it may even be the first that comes to the new council chamber? Now, since that is what I told the scribe you were coming for, shall we go and see it? And tomorrow, at the third hour, I'll send the royal escort, to bring her home.'

CHAPTER 6

With Bedwyr still on Ynys Witrin, the royal escort was led by Nentres, one of the western rulers who had fought under Uther, and who now brought his allegiance and that of his sons to Arthur. He was a grizzled veteran, spare of body, and as supple in the saddle as a youth. He left the escort fidgeting under its Dragon banners on the road below my house, and came riding himself up the curving track by the stream, followed by a groom leading a chestnut horse trapped with silver. Horse and trappings alike were burnished to a glitter as bright as Nentres' shield, and jewels winked on the breastband. The saddle-cloth was of murrey, worked with silver thread.

'The King sent this for you,' he said with a grin. 'He reckons your own would look like a dealer's throw-out among the rest. Don't look at him like that, he's much quieter than he appears.'

The groom gave me a hand to mount. The chestnut tossed his head and mouthed the bit, but his stride was smooth and easy. After my stolid old black gelding he was like a sailing-boat after a poled barge.

The morning was cold, in the wake of the north wind that had frozen the fields since mid-March. At dawn that day I had climbed to the hilltop beyond Applegarth, and had felt against my skin that indefinable difference that heralds a change of wind. The hilltop thorns were no more than breaking into bud, but down in the valley one could see the green haze on the distant woods, and the sheltered banks nearby were thick with primroses and wild garlic. Rooks cawed and tumbled about the ivied trees. Spring was here, waiting, but held back by the

cold winds, as the blackthorn flowers were locked in the bud. But still the sky was overcast and heavy, almost as if threatening snow, and I was glad of my cloak with all its regal splendours of fur and scarlet.

All was ready for us at Melwas' hall. The king himself was dressed in rich dark blue, and was, I noticed, fully armed. His handsome face wore a smile, easy and welcoming, but his eyes had a wary look, and there were altogether too many men-at-arms crowded in the hall, besides the full company outside, brought down at readiness from his hilltop fortress, to throng into the orchard-fields that served the palace for garden. Banners and bright trappings gave the welcome a festive air, but it was to be seen that every man wore both sword and dagger.

He had, of course, expected Arthur. When he saw me his look at first lightened with relief, then I saw the wariness deepen, and tight lines draw themselves around his mouth. He greeted me fairly, but very formally, like a man making the first move of a gambit at chess. I replied, with the long, studied speech of Arthur's deputy, then turned to the queen, his mother, who stood beside him at the end of the long hall. She showed no such caution as her son's. She greeted me with easy authority, and made a sign towards a door on the right of the hall. There was a stir as the crowd parted, and Queen Guinevere came in among her ladies.

She, too, had expected Arthur. She hesitated, looking for him in the glitter of the packed hall. Her gaze passed me, unseeing. I wondered what god had moved her to wear green, spring green, with flowers embroidered on the breast of her gown. Her mantle was green, too, with a collar of white marten, which framed her face and gave her a fragile look. She was very pale, but bore herself with rigid composure.

I remembered how, that night, I had found her shaking in my grasp; and on the thought, as if I had been dipped in cold water, I saw that Arthur had been right about her.

She might be a queen in bearing and in courage, but under it all there was a timid girl, and one looking, all the time, for love. The gaiety, the ready laughter and high spirits of youth, had masked an exile's eager search for friendship among the strangers of a court vastly different from the homely hearth-stone of her father's kingdom. I would never, wrapped in Arthur as I had been for twenty years, even have troubled to think about her, except as his people thought; a vessel for his seed, a partner for his pleasure, a glowing pillar of beauty to shine, silver beside his gold, on the hilltop of his glory. Now I saw her as if I had never seen her before. I saw a girl, tender of flesh and simple enough of spirit, who had had the fortune to marry the greatest man of the age. To be Arthur's Queen was no mean burden, with all that it entailed of loneliness, and a life of banishment in an alien country, with, as often as not, no husband near to come between her and the flatterers, the power-hungry schemers, those envious of her rank or beauty, or—perhaps most dangerous of all—the young men ready to worship her. Then there would be those (and you could trust them to be many) who would tell her, over and over again, about the 'other Guinevere', the pretty Queen who had conceived from the King's first bedding of her, and for whom he had grieved so bitterly. It would lose nothing in the telling. But all this would have been nothing, would have passed and been forgotten in the King's love, and her new, exciting power, if only she had been able to conceive a child. That Arthur had not used the Melwas affair to have her put aside, to take a fertile woman to his bed, was proof indeed of his love; but I doubted if she had yet had time to see it so. He had been right when he told me that she was afraid of life, afraid of the people round her, afraid of Melwas; and—I could see it now—more than any of them she was afraid of me.

She had seen me. The blue eyes widened, and her hands moved up to clasp the fur at her throat. Her step checked momentarily, then, once more held in that pale com-

posure, she took her place beside the queen, on the side away from Melwas. Neither she nor the king had glanced at one another.

There was a resounding silence. Someone's robe rustled, and it sounded like a tree in the wind.

I walked forward. As if Guinevere had been the only person there, I bowed low, then straightened.

'Greetings, Madam. It's good to see you recovered. I have come, with others of your friends and servants, to escort you home. The High King is waiting to receive you in your palace of Camelot.'

The colour washed into her face. She only came up as high as my throat. I have seen eyes like hers on a young deer pulled down and waiting for the spear. She murmured something, and fell dumb. To cover it, and give her time, I turned to Melwas and his mother, and went smoothly into a courtly, over-elaborate speech, thanking them for their care of Arthur's Queen. It had become patent, while I was speaking, that Melwas' mother still had no idea that anything might be wrong. While her son watched me with a bold look glossing over that mixture of wariness and bravado, the old queen answered me with equally courtly thanks, messages for Arthur, compliments for Guinevere, and, finally, a pressing offer of hospitality. At that the young Queen looked up, briefly, then her eyelids hid her eyes again. As I declined, I saw her hands relax. I guessed that there had been no chance, since that parting in the marshes, for Melwas to speak with her and try to find out what she had told Arthur. I think, indeed, that he was going to insist on our staying, but something in my eyes stopped him, and then his mother, accepting the decision, came with obvious eagerness to the question that interested her.

'We looked for you that night, Prince Merlin. I understand that you were led by your vision to find the Queen, before even my son got back to the Island with the news. Will you not tell us, my lord, what this vision was?'

Melwas had jerked to attention. His bold look defied me

to elaborate. I smiled, and my gaze bore his down. Without my prompting, the old woman had asked the very question that I wanted. I raised my voice.

'Willingly, lady. It is true that I had a vision, but whether it came from the gods of air and silence who have spoken to me in the past, or from the Mother Goddess to whose worship the shrine beyond those apple trees is sacred, I cannot tell. But I had a vision that led me straight through the marshland like a fledged arrow to its mark. It was a double vision, a bright dream through which the dreamer passes to a darker dream below; a reflection seen in deep water where the surface colour lies like glass over the dark world beneath. The visions were confused, but their meaning was clear. I would have followed them more quickly, but I think the gods willed it otherwise.'

Guinevere's head came up at that, and her eyes widened. Again, in Melwas', that spark of doubt. It was the old queen who asked: 'How otherwise? They did not want the Queen found? What riddle is this, Prince Merlin?'

'I shall tell you. But first I will tell you about the dream that came to me. I saw a king's hall paved with marble, and pillared with silver and gold, where no servants waited, but where the lamps and tapers burned with scented smoke, bright as day ...' I had let my voice take on the rhythm of the bard who sings in hall; its resonance filled the room and carried the words right out through the colonnade to the silent crowds outside. Fingers moved to make the sign against strong magic; even Guinevere's. The old queen listened with evident satisfaction and pleasure; it was to be remembered that she was the chief patroness of the Goddess's sacred shrine. As for Melwas, as I spoke I watched him move from suspicion and apprehension into bewilderment, and, finally, awe.

To everyone there, already, the dream had taken on a familiar pattern, the archetype of every man's journey into the world from which few travellers return.

'... And on the precious table a set of gold chessmen, and nearby a great chair with arms curled like lions' heads, waiting for the King, and a stool of silver with doves' claws, waiting for the Lady. So I knew it for Llud's hall, where the sacred vessel is kept, and where once the great sword hung that now hangs on Arthur's wall in Camelot. And from overhead, in the sky beyond the hollow hill, I heard them galloping, the Wild Hunt, where the knights of the Otherworld course down their prey, and carry them deep, deep, into the jewelled halls of no return. But just as I began to wonder if the god was telling me the Queen was dead, the vision changed ...'

To my right was a window, high in the wall. Outside was a prospect of sky, cloudy above the tops of the orchard trees. The budding apple-boughs showed lighter, in their young sorrel-and-green, than the slaty sky. The poplars stood pale like spears. But there had been that breath of change in the morning; I felt it still; I kept my eye on that indigo cloud, and spoke again, more slowly.

'... And I was in an older hall, a deeper cavern. I was in the Underworld itself, and the dark King was there, who is older even than Llud, and by him sat the pale young Queen who was reft from the bright fields of Enna and carried out of the warm world to be the Queen of Hell; Persephone, daughter of Demeter, the Mother of all that grows on the face of the earth ...'

The cloud was moving slowly, slowly. Beyond the budding boughs I could see the edge of its shadow drawing its veil aside. From somewhere a breeze came wandering to shiver the tall poplars that edged the orchard.

Most of the people there would not know the story, so I told it, to the obvious satisfaction of the old queen, who must, like all devotees of the Mother's cult, be feeling the cold threat of change even here in this, its ancient stronghold. Once, when Melwas, doubting my drift, would have spoken, she silenced him with a gesture, and (herself perhaps with more instinctive understanding) put out a hand and drew the Queen closer to her side. I looked

neither at the dark Melwas, nor at Guinevere, pale and wondering, but watched the high window out of the side of my eye, and told the old tale of Persephone's abduction by Hades, and the long, weary search for her that Demeter, the Mother Goddess, undertook, while the earth, robbed of its spring growth, languished in cold and darkness.

Beyond the window the poplars, brushed with the early light, bloomed suddenly golden.

'And when the vision died I knew what I had been told. Your Queen, your young and lovely Queen, was alive and safe, succoured by the Goddess and waiting only to be carried home. And with her coming, spring will come at last, and the cold rains will cease, and we shall have a land growing rich once again to harvest, in the peace brought by the High King's sword, and the joy brought by the Queen's love for him. This was the dream I had, and which I, Merlin, prince and prophet, interpret to you.' I spoke straight past Melwas to the old queen. 'So I beg you now, Madam, to let me take the Queen home, with honour and with joy.'

And at that moment, the blessed sun came bursting out and laid a shaft of light clear across the floor to the Queen's feet, so that she stood, all gold and white and green, in a pool of sunshine.

*　　*　　*

We rode home through a brilliant day smelling of primroses. The clouds had packed away, and the Lake showed blue and glittering under its golden willows. An early swallow hawked for flies, close over the bright water. And the Spring Queen, refusing the litter we had brought for her, rode beside me.

She spoke only once, and then briefly.

'I lied to you that night. You knew?'

'Yes.'

'You do see, then? You really do? You see all?'

'I see a great deal. If I set out to look, and if God wills it, I see.'

The colour came into her face, and her look lightened, as if something had set her free. Before, I had believed her innocent: now I knew it. 'So you, too, have told my lord the truth. When he did not come for me himself, I was afraid.'

'You have no need to be, now or ever. I think you need never doubt that he loves you. And I can tell you too, Guinevere my cousin, that even if you never bear an heir for Britain, he will not put you aside. Your name will stand alongside his, as long as he is remembered.'

'I will try,' she said, so softly that I could hardly hear it. Then the towers of Camelot came in sight, and she was silent, bracing herself against what was to come.

* * *

So the seeds of legend were sown. During the golden weeks of spring that followed, I was more than once to hear men talking under their breaths of the 'rape' of the Queen, and how she had been taken down almost to the dark halls of Llud, but brought back by Bedwyr, chiefest of Arthur's knights. So the sting of the truth was drawn; no shame attached to Arthur, none even to the Queen; and to Bedwyr was credited the first of his many glories, the story growing, and its hero gaining in stature, as his hurts healed and at last were well.

As for Melwas, in the way these things have, if the 'Dark King' of the Underworld became linked in men's minds with the dark-avised king whose stronghold was the Tor, it was still without blame to Guinevere. What Melwas thought nobody knew. He must have realised that Guinevere had told Arthur the truth. He may have grown tired of being cast as the villain of the story, and of waiting (as everyone was waiting) for the High King to move against him. He may even have cherished hopes,

still, that he might in some dim future come to possess the Queen.

Whatever the case, it was he who made the next move, and by doing so gave Arthur his way. One morning he rode to Camelot, and, perforce leaving his armed escort outside the council hall, took his seat in the Chair of Complaining.

* * *

The council hall had been built on the style of a smaller hall that Arthur had seen on one of the visits paid to the Queen's father in Wales. That had been merely a larger version of the daub-and-wattle round house of the Celts; this in Camelot was a big circular building, impressively built to last, with ribs of dressed stone, and between them walls of narrow Roman brick from the long-abandoned kilns nearby. There were vast double doors of oak, carved with the Dragon, and finely gilded. Inside, the place was open, with a fine floor of tiles laid out from the centre, like a spider's web. And, like the outer ring of a web, the walls were not curved, but sectioned off with flat panelling. These panels were covered with matting of a fine golden straw to keep out the draughts, but in time would be ablaze with needlework; Guinevere already had her maids set to it. Against each of these sections stood a tall chair, with its own footstool, and the King's was no higher than the next man's. This place was to be, he said, a hall for free discussion between the High King and his peers, and a place where any of the King's leaders could bring their problems. The only thing that marked Arthur's chair was the white shield that hung above it; in time, perhaps, the Dragon would shimmer there in gold and scarlet. Some of the other panels already showed the blazons of the Companions. The seat opposite the King's was blank. This was the one taken by anyone with a grievance to be settled by the Court. Arthur had called it the Chair of Complaining.

But in later years I heard it called the Perilous Chair, and I think the name was coined after that day.

* * *

I was not present when Melwas tabled his complaint. Though I had at that time a place in the Round Hall (as it came to be called), I seldom took it. If his peers were equal there to the King, then the King must be seen to match them in knowledge, and to give his judgments without leaning on the advice of a mentor. Any discussions Arthur and I had were held in private.

We had talked over the Melwas affair for many hours before it came to the council table. To begin with Arthur seemed sure that I would try to stop him from fighting Melwas, but here was a case where the cold view and the hot coincided. To Arthur it would be satisfying, and to me expedient that Melwas should suffer publicly for his actions. The lapse of time, and Arthur's silence, with the legend I had invoked, ensured that Guinevere's honour would not be in question: the people had taken her once more into their loves, and wherever she went flowers strewed the way with blessings thrown like petals. She was their Queen—their darling's darling—who had almost been taken from them by death, and had been save by Marlin's magic. So the story went among the common folk. But among the more worldly there were those who looked for the King to move against Melwas, and who would have been quick to despise him had he failed. He owed it to himself, as man and as King. The discipline he had imposed on himself over the Queen's rape had been severe. Now, when he found that I agreed with him, he turned, with a fierce joy, to planning.

He could, of course, have summoned King Melwas to the council hall on a trumped-up excuse, but this he would not do. 'If we harass him until he makes a complaint himself, it comes to much the same thing in the sight of God,' he said drily, 'but in terms of my con-

science—or my pride, if you like—I will not use a false charge in the Round Hall. It must be known as a place where no man need fear to come before me, unless he himself is false.'

So harass him we did. Situated as the Island was, between the High King's stronghold and the sea, it was easy enough to find causes. Somehow or another there came to be constant arguments about harbour dues, rights of free way, levies and taxes arbitrarily imposed and hotly contested. Any of the petty kings would have grown restive under the constant stream of minor vexations, but Melwas was even quicker to protest than most. According to Bedwyr (to whom I owed an account of the council meeting) it was apparent from the start that Melwas guessed he had been deliberately brought before the King to answer the older, more dangerous charge. He seemed eager to do so, but naturally enough allowed no hint of this to come into words: that must have meant his certain death for treason by the vote of the whole Council. So the grievances over dues and taxes, the arguments over the right levies for the protection offered by Camelot, took their long-drawn and tedious course, while the two men watched one another as swordsmen do, and at last came to the heart of the matter.

It was Melwas who suggested single combat. How he was brought towards this was not quite clear; my guess was that he took very little steering. Young, keen-tempered, a good swordsman, knowing himself to be in grave danger, he must have leaped at the chance of a quick, decisive solution that gave him a half-hope of success. He may have counted on more. His challenge came at last, hotly: 'A meeting to settle these matters here and now, and man to man, if we are ever to agree as neighbours again! You are the law, King; then prove it with your sword!'

Uproar followed, arguments flying to and fro across the hall. The older of those present found it unthinkable that

the King should risk himself, but all had by this time some inkling that there was more at stake than harbour dues, and the younger knights were quite frankly eager to see a fight. More than one of them (Bedwyr was the most insistent) offered himself as combatant in Arthur's place, until finally the King, judging his moment, got decisively to his feet. In the sudden silence he strode to the round table at the hall's centre, lifted the tablets where Melwas' grievances were listed, and sent them smashing to the floor.

'Now bring me my sword,' he said.

* * *

It was midday when they faced one another on the level field in the north-east quarter of Caer Camel. The sky was cloudless, but a steady cool breeze tempered the warmth of the day. The light was high and even. The edge of the field was deep in people, the very ramparts furred with folk. At the top of one of Camelot's gilded towers I saw the cluster of azure and green and scarlet where the women had gathered to watch. The Queen, among them, was in white, Arthur's colour. I wondered how she was feeling, and could guess at the still composure with which she would hide her fear. Then the trumpet sounded, and silence fell.

The two combatants were armed with spears and shields, and each man had sword and dagger at his belt. Arthur was not using Caliburn, the royal sword. His armour—a light helmet and leather corselet—showed neither jewel nor device. Melwas' dress was more princely, and he was a shade the taller. He looked fierce and eager, and I saw him cast a look towards the palace tower where the Queen stood. Arthur had not glanced that way. He looked cool and infinitely experienced, listening apparently with grave attention to the herald's formal announcement.

There was a sycamore tree to one side of the field. Bedwyr, beside me in its shade, gave me a long look, and then drew a breath of relief.

'So. You're not worried. Thank God for that!'

'It had to come to this in the end. It's best. But if there had been danger for him, I would have stopped it.'

'All the same, it's folly. Oh, I know that he wanted to, but he should never risk himself so. He should have let me do it.'

'And what sort of showing would you make, do you suppose? You're still lame. You could have been cut down, if not worse, and then the legend would have had to start again. There are still simple folk who think that right is with the strongest sword.'

'As it is today, or you'd not be standing idly by, I know. But I wish ...' He fell silent.

'I know what you wish. I think you will have your wish, not once but many times, before your life's end.'

He glanced sharply at me, started to say something more, but then the pennon fell, and the fight had begun.

For a long time the men circled one another, spears poised for the throw, shields ready. The light advantaged neither. It was Melwas who attacked first. He feinted once, then, with great speed and strength behind the throw, hurled the spear. Arthur's shield flashed up to deflect it. The blade slid screaming past the boss, and the spear buried itself harmlessly in the grass. Melwas, snatching for his sword-hilt, sprang back. But Arthur, in the same moment as he turned the spear aside, flung his own. By doing so he cancelled the advantage that Melwas' first throw had given him; but he did not draw his own sword; he reached for the other's spent spear, upright by him in the turf, pulled it up, and hefted it, just as Melwas, abandoning his sword-hilt, sent the King's spear also whizzing harmlessly from his shield, and turned, swift as a fox, to pick it up in the same way and face spear with spear once more.

But Arthur's weapon, harder flung, and more desper-

ately parried, flew spinning to one side, to bounce level along the turf and skid away from Melwas' hand. There was no hope of snatching it up before Arthur could throw. Melwas, shield at the ready, feinted this way and that, hoping to draw the other's spear and so regain the advantage. He reached the fallen weapon; he stooped for it where it lay, the shaft half-propped to his hand by a clump of thistles. Arthur's arm moved, and the blade of his spear flashed in the light, drawing Melwas' eye. Melwas ducked, throwing his shield up into the line of the cast, at the same time swerving down to grab the fallen weapon. But the King's move had been a false one; in the unguarded moment when Melwas stooped sideways for the other spear, the King's, thrown straight and low, took him in the outstretched arm. Arthur's sword whipped into his hand as he followed the spear.

Melwas staggered. As a great shout hit the walls and echoed round the field he recovered, grabbed the spear, and hurled it straight at the King.

Had he been any less fast, Arthur must have closed with him before he could use the spear. As it was, Melwas' weapon struck true when the King was halfway across the space between them. Arthur caught it on his shield, but at that short range the force was too great to turn. The long shaft whipped in a half circle, checking the King's rush. With the sword still held in his right hand, he tried to tear the spear-point from the leather, but it had gone in close by one of the metal stays, and jammed there, caught by its barbs. He flung the shield aside, spear and all, and ran in on Melwas, with nothing to guard his naked side but the dagger at his left hand.

The rush gave Melwas no time to recover himself and grab a spear for a third cast. With the blood streaming down his arm, he dragged out his sword, and met the King's attack, body to body, with a slithering clash of metal. The exchange had left them still evenly matched, Melwas' wound, and the loss of strength in his sword-arm, against the King's unguarded side. Melwas was a

good swordsman, fast and very strong, and for the first few minutes of the hand-to-hand struggle he aimed every stroke and slash at the King's left. But each one met iron. And step by step the King was pressing him; step by step Melwas was forced to give in front of the attack. The blood ran down, weakening him steadily. Arthur, as far as could be seen, was unhurt. He pressed forward, the ringing blows coming fast and hard, the whining whip and parry of the long dagger chiming between. Behind Melwas lay the fallen spear. Melwas knew it, but dared not glance to see where it lay. The dread of fouling it, and falling, made him slower. He was sweating freely, and beginning to breathe like a hard-ridden horse.

One of those moments came when, breast to breast, weapon to weapon, the men stood locked, totally still. Round the field the crowd was silent now, holding its breath.

The King spoke, softly and coldly. No one could hear what he said. Melwas did not reply. There was a moment's pause, then a swift movement, a sudden pressure, a grunt from Melwas, and some kind of growled answer. Then Arthur disengaged smoothly, and, with another low-spoken sentence, attacked afresh.

Melwas' right hand was a blur of glossy blood. His sword moved more slowly, as if too heavy for him. His breathing laboured, loud as a stag's in rut. With a great, grunting effort he brought his shield smashing down, like an axe, at the King. Arthur dodged, but slipped. The shield's edge took him on the right shoulder, and must have numbed the arm. His sword flew wide. There was a gasp and a great cry from the watching people. Melwas gave a shout, and swung his sword up for the kill.

But Arthur, now armed only with a dagger, did not spring back out of range. Before anyone could draw breath he had jumped forward, straight past the shield, and his long dagger bit into Melwas' throat.

And stayed still, followed only by a trickle of blood. No thrust followed. He spoke again, low and fierce.

Melwas froze where he stood. The sword dropped from his lifted hand. The shield fell to the grass.

The dagger withdrew. The King stepped back. Slowly, in the sight of all that throng, the King's men and his own, and of the Queen watching from her tower, Melwas, King of the Summer Country, knelt on the bloody grass in front of Arthur, and made his surrender.

Now, there was no sound at all.

With a movement so slow as to be almost ceremonial, the King lifted his dagger, and cast it, point down, to quiver in the turf. Then he spoke again, more quietly even than before. This time Melwas, with bent head, answered him. They spoke for some time. Finally the King, still with that ceremony of gesture, reached a hand, and lifted Melwas to his feet. Then he beckoned the defeated man's escort to him, and, as his own people came crowding, turned away among them and walked back towards the palace.

* * *

In later years I heard several stories about this fight. Some said that it was Bedwyr who fought, not Arthur, but that is patently foolish. Others asserted that there was no fight, or Melwas would surely have been slain. Arthur and Melwas, they said, were brought by some mediator in the Council to agree on terms.

That is not true. It happened exactly as I have told it. Later I learned from the King what had passed between the two men on the field of combat; Melwas, expecting death, was brought to admit the truth of the Queen's accusation, and his own guilt. It is true that it would not have served for Arthur to kill him, but Arthur—and this on no advice from me—acted with both wisdom and restraint. It is a fact that after that day, Melwas was loyal to him, and Ynys Witrin was reckoned a jewel in the tally of Arthur's sovereignty.

It is a matter of public record that the King's ships paid no more harbour dues.

CHAPTER 7

So the year went by, and the lovely month came, September, my birth-month, the wind's month, the month of the raven, and of Myrddin himself, that wayfarer between heaven and earth. The apple trees were heavy with fruit, and the herbs were gathered and drying; they hung in sheaves and bunches from the rafters in the outhouses at Applegarth, and the stillroom was full of ranked jars and boxes waiting to be filled. The whole house, garden, tower and living quarters, smelled sweetly of herbs and fruit, and of the honey that welled from the hives; even, at the end of the orchard, from the hollow oak where the wild bees lived. Applegarth, it seemed, reflected within its small boundaries the golden plenty of the kingdom's summer. The Queen's summer, men called it, as harvest followed hay-time, and still the land glowed with the Goddess-given plenty. A golden age, they said. For me, too, a golden age. But now, as never before, I had time to be lonely. And in the evenings, when the wind was in the south-west, I could feel it in my bones, and was grateful for the fire. Those weeks of nakedness and hunger, and exposure to the mountain weather in the Caledonian Forest, had left me a legacy that even a strong body could not shake off, and were pricking me forward into old age.

Another legacy that time had left me; whether as a lingering after-effect of Morgause's poison, or from some other cause, I had, from time to time, brief attacks of something that I might have called the falling sickness, save that this is not a malady that comes in later years if it has not been felt before. The symptoms, besides, were not like those in cases that I had seen or treated. The fit

had come three times in all, and only when I was alone, so
none knew of it but myself. What happened was this:
resting quietly, I had drifted off, it seemed into sleep, only
to wake, cold and stiff and weak with hunger—though not
inclined to eat—many hours later. The first time it was a
matter of twelve hours or so only, but I guessed from the
giddiness, and the light, exhausted feeling, that it had
not been normal sleep. On the second occasion the lapse
of time was two nights and a day, and I was lucky that
the malady had struck me when I was safely in my bed.

I told no one. When the third attack was imminent I
recognised the signs; a light, half-hungry sensation, a slight
giddiness, a wish to rest and be silent. So I sent Mora
home, locked the doors, and took myself to my bedchamber. Afterwards I felt as I sometimes had after a time of
prophecy, borne up like a creature ready for flight, with
senses rinsed and clean as if new made, colours and
sounds coming as fresh and brilliant as they must to a
child. Of course I took to my books for enlightenment,
but, finding no help there, I put the matter aside, accepting it, as I had learned to accept the pains of prophecy,
and their withdrawal, as a touch of the god's hand. Perhaps now the hand was drawing me closer. There was no
fear in the thought. I had done what he had required of
me, and when the time came, would be ready to go.

But he did not, I reckoned, require me to sacrifice my
pride. Let men remember the royal prophet and enchanter
who retired from men's sight and his King's service in his
own time; not a dotard who had waited overlong for his
dismissal.

So I stayed solitary, busying myself with the garden and
my medicine, writing and sending long letters to Blaise
in Northumbria, and being cared for well enough by the
girl Mora, whose cooking was from time to time enriched
by some gift from Arthur's table. Gifts went back from
me, too; a basket of some especially good apples from
one of the young trees; cordials and medicines; perfumes,
even, that I concocted for the Queen's pleasure; herbs for

the King's kitchen. Simple stuff, after the fiery gifts of prophecy and victory, but somehow redolent of peace and the age of gold. Gifts of love and contentment; now, we had time for both. A golden time indeed, untroubled by foreboding; but with the prickling sense I recognised of some change to come; something undreaded, but ineluctable as the fall of the leaves and the coming of winter.

What it was, I would not allow myself to think. I was like a man alone in an empty room, contented enough, but listening for sounds beyond the shut door, and waiting with half a hope for someone to come, though knowing in his heart of hearts that he would not.

But he did.

He came on a golden evening, in about the middle of the month. There was a full moon, which had stolen, like a ghost, into the sky long before sunset. It hung behind the apple boughs like a great misty lantern, its light slowly waxing, as the sky around it darkened, to apricot and gold. I was in the stillroom, crumbling a pile of dried hyssop. The jars stood clean and ready. The room smelled of hyssop and of the racks of apples and plums laid on the shelves to ripen. A few late wasps droned, and a butterfly, snared by the room's warmth, flattened rich wings against the stone of the windowframe. I heard the light step behind me, and turned.

Magician they call me, and it is true. But I neither expected his coming, nor heard him until I saw him standing there in the dusk, lit by the deepening gold of the moon. He might have been a ghost, so did I stand and stare, transfixed. The meeting in the mist on the Island's shore had come back to me frequently, but never as something real; with every effort to recall it became more and more of a dream, something imagined, a hope only.

Now the real boy was here, flushed and breathing, smiling, but not quite at ease, as if unsure of his welcome. He held a bundle which, I supposed, must contain his

goods. He was dressed in grey, with a cloak the colour of beech-buds. He had no ornaments, and no weapons.

He began: 'I don't suppose you remember me, but—'

'Why should I not? You are the boy who is not Ninian.'

'Oh, but I am. I mean, it is one of my names. Truly.'

'I see. So when I called you—'

'Yes. When you spoke first, I thought you must know me; but then—when you said who you were—I knew you were mistaken, and—well, I was afraid. I'm sorry. I should have told you straight away, instead of running away like that. I'm sorry.'

'But when I told you that I wanted to teach you my art, and asked you to come to me, you agreed to do so. Why?'

His hands, white on the bundle, clenched and twisted in the fold of the cloth. He hung still on the threshold, as if poised to run. 'That was ... When you said that he—this other boy—had been the—the kind of person who could learn from you.... You had felt it all along, you said, and he had known it, too. Well'—he swallowed—'I believe that I am, too. I have felt, all my life, that there were doors in the back of the mind that would open on light, if one could only find the key.' He faltered, but his eyes did not waver from mine.

'Yes?' I gave him no help.

'Then when you spoke to me like that, suddenly, out of the mist, it was like a dream come true. Merlin himself, speaking to me by name, and offering me the very key ... Even when I realised that you had mistaken me for someone else, who was dead, I had a wild thought that perhaps I could come to you and take his place ... Then of course I saw how stupid that was, to think I could deceive you, of all people. So I did not dare to come.'

'But now you have dared.'

'I had to.' He spoke simply, stating a fact. 'I have thought of nothing else since that night. I was afraid, because ... I was afraid, but there are things that you have

to do, they won't let you alone, it's as if you were being driven. More than driven, hounded. Do you understand?'

'Very well.' It was hard to keep my voice steady and grave. There must have been some note in it of what my heart felt, because, faint and sweet from the upper room, I heard the answer of my harp.

He had heard nothing. He was still braced, braving me, forcing himself into the role of suppliant. 'Now you know the truth. I'm not the boy you knew. You know nothing about me. Whatever I feel, here in myself'—a hand moved as if to touch his breast, but clenched itself again on the bundle—'you may not think I'm worth teaching I don't expect you to take me in, or spend any time on me. But if you would—if you would only let me stay here, sleep in the stable-place, anything, help you with—well, with work like that'—a glance at the pile of hyssop—'until perhaps you would come to know . . .' His voice wavered again, and this time died. He licked dry lips and stood mute, watching me.

It was my gaze that faltered, not his. I turned aside to hide the joy that I could feel mantling my cheeks. I plunged my hands wrist deep in the fragrant herbs, and rubbed the dry fragments between the fingertips. The scent of hyssop, clean and pungent, rose and steadied me.

I spoke slowly, to the herb jars. 'When I called to you by the Lake, I took you for a boy with whom I travelled north many years ago, and who had a spirit that spoke to mine. He died, and ever since that day I have grieved for his death. When I saw you, I thought I had been mistaken, and that he still lived; but when I had time to think about it, I knew that now he would be a boy no longer, but a grown man. It was, you might say, a stupid error. I do not commonly make such errors, but at the time I told myself it was an error bred of weariness and grief, and of the hope that was still alive in me, that he, or such another spirit, would one day come to me again.'

I paused. He said nothing. The moon had moved beyond the window-frame, and the door where the boy

stood was almost in darkness. I turned back to him.

'I should have known it was no error. It was the hand of the god that crossed your path with mine, and now has driven you to me, in spite of your fear. You are not the boy I knew, but if you had not been just such another, you can be sure I would not have seen you, nor spoken to you. That night was full of strong magic. I should have remembered that, and trusted it.'

He said eagerly: 'I felt it, too. You could feel the stars like frost on the skin. I'd gone out to catch fish ... but I let them be. It was no night for death, even for a fish.' Dimly I saw that he smiled, but when he drew breath, it came unsteadily. 'You mean I may stay? I will do?'

'You will do.' I lifted my fingers from the hyssop, and let it trickle back onto the cloth, dusting my fingertips together. 'Which of us, after this, will dare to ignore the god who drives us? Don't be afraid of me. You are very welcome. No doubt I'll warn you, when I have time to be cautious, of the heavy task you're undertaking, and all the thorns that lie in the way, but just at this moment I dare say nothing that will frighten you away from me again. Come in, and let me see you.'

As he obeyed me, I lifted the unlit lamp from the shelf. The wick caught flame from the air, and flared high.

In full light, I knew that I could never have mistaken him for the goldsmith's boy, but he was very like. He was taller by a thumb's breadth, and his face was not quite so thin in outline. His skin was finer, and his hands, as fine boned and clever-looking as the other boy's, had never done slave's work. His hair was the same, a thick dark mane, roughly cut just short of his shoulders. His mouth was like, so like that I could have been deceived again; it had the gentle, dreaming lines that—I suspected—masked a firmness, even obstinacy of purpose. The boy Ninian had shown a quiet disregard of anything that he did not want to notice; his master's discourses had gone unheeded over his head while he took refuge in his own

thoughts. Here was the same soft stubbornness, and in these eyes, too, the same half absent, dreaming look that could shut the world out as effectively as dropped eyelids. They were grey, the iris rimmed with black, and had the clarity of lake water. I was to find that like lake water they could reflect colour, and look green or blue or black-stormy as the mood came. Now they were watching me with what looked like a mixture of fascination and fear.

'The lamp?' I said. 'You've not seen the fire called before? Well, that's one of the first things you'll learn; it was the first my own master taught me. Or is it the jars? You're looking at them as if you thought I was bottling poison. I was packing the garden herbs for winter's use.'

'Hyssop,' he said. I thought there was a glint of mischief, which in a girl I might have called demure. ' "To be burned with brimstone for inflammations of the throat; or boiled with honey to help pleurisy of the lungs." '

I laughed. 'Galen? Well, it seems we have a flying start. So you can read? Do you know—? No, it must wait till morning. For the present, have you had supper?'

'Yes, thank you.'

'You said that Ninian was "one of your names". What do you like to be called?'

' "Ninian" will do ... that is, unless you would rather not use it. What happened to him, the boy you knew? I think you said he was drowned?'

'Yes. We were at Corstopitum, and he went swimming with some other boys in the river beside the bridge where the Cor flows into the Tyne. They came running back to say he had been swept away.'

'I'm sorry.'

I smiled at him. 'You will have to work very hard to make good his loss. Come, then, Ninian, we must find you a place to sleep.'

●　　●　　●

That was how I acquired my assistant, and the god his

servant. He had had his hand over both of us all that time. It seems to me now that the first Ninian was but a forerunner—a shadow cast before—of the real one who came to me later, from the Lake. From the start it was apparent that instinct had deceived neither of us; Ninian of the Lake, though knowing little of the arts I professed, proved a natural adept. He learned quickly, soaking up both knowledge and art as a cloth soaks up clear water. He could read and write fluently, and though he had not, as I in my youth had had, the gift of languages, he spoke a pure Latin as well as the vernacular, and had picked up enough Greek to be able to read a label or be accurate about a recipe. He had once, he told me, had access to a translation of Galen, but knew nothing of Hippocrates beyond hearsay. I set him to reading in the Latin version I had, and found myself, in some measure, sent back to school by the score of questions he asked, of which I had taken the answers so long for granted that I had forgotten how they were reached. Music he knew nothing of, and would not learn; this was the first time I came face to face with that gentle, immovable stubbornness of his. He would listen, his face full of dreaming light, when I played or sang; but sing himself, or even try to sing, he would not; and after a few attempts to teach him his notes on the big harp, I gave it up. I would have liked it if he had had a voice; I would not have wanted to sit by while another man made music with my harp, but now with age my own voice was not as good as it had once been, and I would have liked to hear a young voice singing the poems I made. But no. He smiled, shook his head, tuned the harp for me (that much he could and would do) and listened.

But in everything else he was eager and quick to learn. Recollecting as best I could the way old Galapas, my master, had inducted me into the skills of magic, I took him, step by step, into the strange and misty halls of art. The Sight he had already in some degree; but where I had surpassed my master from the start, Ninian would

do well if in time he could equal me, and he was still a stranger to the flights of prophecy. If he went half as far as I, I would be content. Like all old men, I could not believe that that young brain and gentle body could withstand the stresses that I myself had withstood many times. I helped him, as Galapas had done me, with certain subtle yet safe drugs, and soon he could see in the fire or the lamp, and wake from the vision afterwards no more than weary, and, at times, disturbed by what he had seen. As yet he could not put truth together with vision. I did not help him to; and indeed, in those peaceful months of his apprenticeship there was little happening of enough moment to set prophecy stirring in the fire. Once or twice he spoke to me, in a kind of confusion, about the Queen, and Melwas and Bedwyr and the King, but I put the visions aside as obscure, and pursued them no further.

He steadfastly refused to tell me about himself or whence he came. He had lived most of his life, he said, on or near the Island, and allowed me to gather that his parents had been poor dwellers in one of the outlying Lake villages. Ninian of the Lake, he called himself, and said it was enough; so as such I accepted him. His past, after all, was nothing; whatever he was going to be, I would make. I did not press him; I had had enough, as a bastard and a child with no known father, of the shame of such questioning; so I respected the boy's silences, and asked no more than he would tell me.

All the practical side of healing, the study of anatomy, and the use of drugs, he was interested in, and good at. He could also, as I never could, draw with real skill. He began, that first winter, for sheer delight in the work, to compile a local herbal of his own, though most of the seeking and identifying of the plants, which is more than half the doctor's art, would have to wait till spring. But there was no hurry for it. He had, he told me, for ever.

So the winter passed in deep happiness, each day too short for all it could be filled with. To be with Ninian was to have everything; my own youth again, eager and

quick to learn, with life unfolding full of bright promise; and at the same time the pleasures of quiet thought and of solitude. He seemed to sense when I needed to be alone, and either withdrew physically from my presence to his own room, or fell silent, and apparently into some deep abstraction, which left my thoughts free of him. He would not share the house with me, preferring, he said, to have rooms of his own where he need not disturb me, so I had Mora get ready the upper rooms that would have housed the servants, had any lived with me. The rooms were above the workshop and storeroom, facing west, and, though small and low under the rafters, were pleasant and airy. I did wonder at first if Mora and he had come to some sort of understanding; they spent a lot of time talking together in the kitchen, or down by the stream where the girl did some of the washing; I would hear them laughing, and could see that they were easy together; but there was no sign of intimacy, and in time I realised that Ninian, from things he let fall in talk, knew as little about love as I myself. Which, from the way the power grew in him, palpably week by week, I took to be only natural. The gods do not give two gifts at once, and they are jealous.

*   *   *

Spring came early the next year, with mild sunny days in March, and the wild geese going overhead daily, towards their nesting sites in the north. I caught some kind of chill, and kept to the house, but then one fine day went outside to sit in the little garth, where the doves were already busy about their love-making. The heated walls made the place as pleasant as a fireside; there were rosy cups of quince against the stone, and winter irises full out at the wall's base. In the gardens beyond the stable buildings I could hear the thud of Varro's spade, and thought idly of the planting I had planned. Nothing was in my mind beyond vague, pleasant plans of a domestic

sort, and the sight of the pink sheen on the breast feathers
of the doves, and the sleepy sound of their cooing ...

Later, looking back, I wondered if for a brief hour my
malady had blanketed me from consciousness of the
present. It would have pleased me to think so. But it
seems probable that the malady that overtook me was
age, and the weakness left by the chill, and the lulling
drug of contentment.

Quick footsteps on a stone stair startled me awake. I
looked up. Ninian came hurrying down from his room,
but with uncertain steps, as if it were he, not I, who was
half-drugged, or even ill. He kept a hand on the stone
wall, as if without its guidance he would have stumbled.
Still unsteadily, he crossed the colonnade, and came out
into the sunshine. He paused there, with a hand to one of
the pillars for support. His face was pale, his eyes enormous, the black pupils swimmingly overspreading the iris.
His lips looked dry, but there was damp on his forehead,
and two sharp lines of pain gouged down between his
brows.

'What is it?' I began, in alarm, to get to my feet, but he
put out a hand to calm me, then came forward. He sank
down on the flags at my feet in the sun.

'I've had a dream,' he said, and even his voice was unlike itself. 'No, I wasn't asleep. I was reading by the
window. There was a spider's web there, still full of
drops from last night's rain. I was watching it as it shook
in the sunlight ...'

I understood then. I put a hand down to his shoulder
and held it steadily. 'Sit quiet for a moment. You will
not forget the dream. Wait here. You can tell me later.'

But as I got to my feet he shot a hand out and grabbed
at my robe. 'You don't understand! It was a warning! I
am sure of that! There's some sort of danger—'

'I understand quite well. But until the headache goes,
you will remember nothing clearly. Now wait. I'll be back
soon.'

I went into the stillroom. As I busied myself mixing the

cordial I had only one thought in my mind. He, sitting reading and thinking, had had vision brought to him in a dewdrop's spark of light: I, waiting idly and with passive mind in full sunlight, had seen nothing. I found that my hand shook a little as I poured the cordial for him; it would take love, I thought, to stand peacefully aside and watch the god lift his wing from over me, and take another into its shadow. No matter that the power had brought pain and men's fear and sometimes hatred; no one who has known power like that has any wish to abdicate it to another. Not to anyone.

I carried the goblet out into the sunlight. Ninian, still curled on the flagstones, had his head down, a fist pressed tightly against his brow. He looked very slight and young. He raised his head at my step, and the grey eyes, swimming with tears of pain, looked at me blindly. I sat down, took his hand in mine, and guided the goblet to his mouth. 'Drink this. It will make you feel better presently. No, don't try to talk yet.'

He drank, then his head went down again, this time against my knee. I laid a hand on his hair. For some time we sat like that, while the doves, disturbed by his coming, flew down again onto the coping of the wall, and once more took up their gentle courtship. Beyond the stables the monotonous sound of Varro's spade went on and on.

Presently Ninian stirred.

I lifted my hand. 'Better?'

He nodded and raised his head. The lines of pain had gone. 'Yes. Yes, it's quite gone. It was more than a headache; it was like a sharp pain right through the brain. I've never felt anything like that before. Am I ill?'

'No. You are merely a seer, an eye and a voice for a most tyrannous god. You have had a waking dream, what men call a vision. Now tell me about it, and we shall see if it is a true one.'

He drew his knees up, clasping them with both hands. He spoke, looking past me at the wall with the black branches and red cups of the quince. His eyes were still

dark, dilated with vision, and his voice was low and even, as if reciting something learned by rote.

'I saw a stretch of grey sea, whipped with storm winds, breaking white over rocks like wolves' fangs. There was a beach of pebbles, grey too, and streaming with rain. The waves came in over the beach, and with them came broken spars and casks and torn sails—pieces of wreckage. And people; drowned bodies of men and women. One of the men's bodies rolled near me, and I saw he had not been drowned; there was a deep wound in his neck, but the blood had all been washed away by the sea. He looked like an animal that has been bled. There were dead children, too, three of them. One was naked, and had been speared. Then I saw, out beyond the breakers, another ship, a whole ship, with sails furled in the wind, and the oars out, holding her steady. She waited there, and I saw that she was low in the water as if heavily laden. She had a high, curved prow, with a pair of antlers fastened to it; I couldn't see if they were real, or carved in wood. I could see her name, though; it was *King Stag*. The men in the ship were watching the bodies tumbling on shore, and they were laughing. They were a long way off across the sea, but I could hear what they said, quite clearly ... Can you believe that?'

'Yes. Go on.'

'They were saying, "You were guided, by God! Who could have told that the old scow was so richly found? Luck like yours, and a fair division of the spoils, and we'll all make our fortunes!" They were speaking to the captain.'

'Did you hear his name?'

'I think so. They called him "Heuil".'

'Was that all?'

'No. There was a sort of darkness, like a mist. Then the *King Stag* had gone, but near me on the shore there were horsemen, and some of them had dismounted and were looking at the bodies. One man lifted a piece of broken planking with something on it that might have been the

name of the wrecked ship, and carried it across to where another was sitting on his horse. He was a dark man, carrying no device that I could see, but he was obviously their leader. He looked angry. He said something, and the others got to their horses again, and they all galloped up off the beach, through the dunes and the long grasses. I was left there, and then even the dead bodies were gone, and the wind was blowing into my eyes and making them water ... That was all. I was looking at the spider's web, and the drops had melted in the sunlight. A fly was caught there, shaking the web. I suppose that was what woke me. Merlin—'

He stopped abruptly, and cocked his head to listen. Now I could catch, from the road below, the sounds of a troop of horsemen, and a distant command to halt. A single rider detached himself, and approached at a rapid canter.

'A messenger from Camelot?' I said, 'Who knows, perhaps this is your vision coming home.'

The horse stopped. There was the jingle of the bridle being thrown to Varro. Arthur came in through the archway.

'Merlin, I'm glad to see you about. They told me you had been ill, and I came to see for myself.' He paused, looking at Ninian. He knew, of course, that the boy was with me, but they had not met before. Ninian had refused to go with me to Camelot, and whenever the King had visited me, had made some excuse and retired to his rooms. I did not press him, knowing the awe that the people of the Lake villages felt for the High King.

I was on my feet, just beginning, 'This is Ninian,' when the boy himself interrupted me. He came to his feet in one swift movement, as fast as a snake uncurling, and cried out:

'That's the man! That's the one! It was a true dream, then, it was true!'

Arthur's brows shot up, not, I knew, at the lack of ceremony, but at the words. He looked from Ninian back

to me. 'A true dream?' He said it softly. He knew the phrase of old.

I heard Ninian gasp, as, through the dregs of the vision, he came back to the present. He stood there blinking, like someone thrust suddenly into bright light. 'It's the King. So it was the King.'

Arthur said, sharply now: 'So what was the King?'

Ninian, flushing, began to stammer. 'Nothing. That is, I was just talking to Merlin. I didn't know you at first. I—'

'Never mind. You know me now. What is this about a true dream?'

Ninian looked appealingly at me. Telling me his dream was one thing; making his first prophecy to the King's face was quite another. I said across him, to the King: 'It seems that an old friend of yours is indulging in piracy, or some villainly uncommonly like it, somewhere in his home waters. Murder and robbery, and peaceful traders looted and then wrecked, and no one left alive to tell the story.'

He frowned. 'An old friend of mine? Who, then?'

'Heuil.'

'*Heuil?*' His face darkened. Then he stood for a few moments in thought. 'Yes, it fits. It fits. I had news a while back from Ector, and he said Caw was failing, and that wild brood of his looking around them like idle dogs for something to tear. Then three days ago I heard from Urbgen, my sister's lord in Rheged, of a village on the coast attacked and looted, and the folk killed or scattered. He was inclined to blame the Irish, but I doubted that; the weather's been too rough for anything but local raiding. Heuil, is it? You don't surprise me. Shall I go?'

'It seems you had better. My guess is that Caw is dead, or dying. I can't believe that Heuil would dare, otherwise, to do anything to provoke Rheged.'

'Your guess?'

'That is all.'

He nodded. 'It seems likely. In any case, it will answer

very well. I had been almost ready to invent some pretext for a foray to the northward. With Caw's grip slackening, and that black dog Heuil collecting a following that could contest his brother's claim to the rulership of Strathclyde, I would like to be there to see things for myself. Piracy, eh? You did not see where?'

I glanced at Ninian. He shook his head. 'No,' I said, 'but you'll find him. You will be there, on the shore, while the wreckage and the bodies still lie there. The raiders' ship is *King Stag*. That's all we know. You should be able to fasten the guilt where it belongs.'

'I'll do that, never fear.' He was grim. 'I'll send north to Urbgen and Ector tonight to expect me, and I'll ride myself in the morning. I'm grateful. I've been looking for an excuse to cut my lord Heuil out of the pack, and now you give me this. It may be just the chance I need to get another agreement ratified between Strathclyde and Rheged, and throw my weight in behind the new king. I don't know how long I shall be away. And you, Merlin? All is really well with you?'

'All is very well.'

He smiled. He had not missed the glance that had gone between Ninian and myself. 'It seems you have someone to share your visions with, at last. Well, Ninian, I am glad to have met you.' He smiled at the boy, and said something kind. Ninian, staring, made some sort of answer. I had been wrong, I saw, about him; he was not awed by the presence of the King. There was a quality in the way he looked at Arthur, something I could not quite put a name to; none of the worship that I was used to seeing in men's eyes, but a steady appraisal. Arthur saw it, looked amused, then dismissed the boy and turned back to me, asking for messages for Morgan and Ector. Then he said his goodbyes and went.

Ninian looked thoughtfully after him. 'Yes, it was a true dream. The dark leader on the white horse, with the white shield shining, and no blazon on it but the light of

the sky. It was Arthur beyond doubt. Who exactly is Heuil, and why does the King want an excuse to cut him down?'

'He's one of the sons of Caw of Strathclyde, who has been king on Dumbarton Rock since almost before I can remember. He's very old, and has sired nineteen sons on various women. There may be daughters, too, but those wild northern men make little of their girls. The youngest of the brood, Gildas, has recently been sent to my old friend Blaise, whom you know of, to learn to read and write. He, at least, will be a man of peace. But Heuil is the wildest of a wild breed. He and Arthur have always disliked one another. They fell out and fought, once, over a girl, when Arthur was a boy in the north country. Since then, with Caw's health failing, the King has seen Heuil as a danger to the balance of peace in the north. He would do anything, I think, to harm Arthur, even ally himself with the Saxons. Or so Arthur believes. But now that Heuil has taken to rapine and murder, he can be hunted down and destroyed, and the greater danger will be averted.'

'And the King takes an army north, just like that, on your word?' There was awe in his face now, but not the awe of kings or their counsels. He was, for the first time, feeling the power in himself.

I smiled. 'No, on yours. If I seemed to take the credit for the seeing I am sorry. But the matter was urgent, and he might not have believed you as readily.'

'Of course not. But you saw it, too?'

'I saw nothing.'

He looked startled. 'But you believed me straight away.'

'Of course. Because I did not share it, it doesn't mean it was not a true dream.'

He looked worried, then rather scared. 'But Merlin, do you mean that you knew nothing about this before I told you my dream? I mean, about Heuil's turning pirate . . . I should say, his intention to turn pirate? That you sent the King off to the north on my word alone?'

'That is what I mean, yes.'

A silence, while worry, apprehension, excitement, and then joy, showed in his face as clearly as the reflection of light and cloud blowing across the waters of his native lake. He was still taking in the implications of power. But when he spoke he surprised me. Like Arthur, he saw straight past those implications to others that were my concern, not his. And his next words were an exact echo of Arthur's. 'Merlin, do you mind?'

I answered him as simply. 'Perhaps. A little, now. But soon, not at all. It's a harsh gift, and perhaps it is time that the god handed it on to you, and left me in peace to sit in the sun and watch the doves on the wall.'

I smiled as I spoke, but there was no answering glimmer in his face. He did a strange thing then. He reached for my hand, lifted it to his cheek, then dropped it and went back upstairs to his room without another word or look. I was left standing there in the sun, remembering another, much younger boy, riding downhill from the cave of Galapas, with the visions swirling in his head, and tears on his face, and all the lonely pain and danger hanging in the clouds ahead of him. Then I went indoors to my own room, and read beside the fire till Mora brought the midday meal.

CHAPTER 8

Arthur rode out next day for the north, and thereafter
we got no more news. Ninian went about the place with a
half dazed look, compounded, I think, of wonder at himself and the 'true vision', and at me for not seeming distressed at the way it had passed me by. For myself, I
admit I was divided; looking back on that day, I knew
that I had been lingering in the edges of the poisoned
dream that was my sickness; but even after Arthur's visit
and acceptance of Ninian's prophecy, nothing had come
to me out of the dark, either of proof or denial. For all
that, I seemed to feel, in the rich quiet of the days, a
tranquil approval. It was like watching a shadow that
slowly, as the distant clouds move, withdraws from one
field or forest, and passes on to shroud the next. I had
been shown, gently enough, where happiness now lay; so
I took it, preparing the boy Ninian to be as I had been,
and myself for some future half seen and guessed at
many times, but now seen more clearly and no longer
dreaded, but moved towards, as a beast moves towards its
winter sleep.

Ninian, more even than before, seemed to withdraw into
himself. On one or two occasions, lying wakeful in the
night, I heard him cross the garth soft-footed, and then
run, like a young thing released, down the valley to the
road. Twice, even, I sought to follow him in vision, but
he must have taken care to cloud himself from me, for I
saw no further than the roadway, then the slight figure
running, running, into the mist that lay between Applegarth and the Island. It did not trouble me that he had
secrets, any more than it troubled me to hear him and

the girl Mora talking—sometimes at great length—in the stillroom or the kitchen. I had never counted myself lively company, and with age tended to be even more withdrawn. It only pleased me that the young people should find common interests, and keep each other contented in my service.

For service it was. I worked the boy harder than any slave. This is the way of love, I find; one longs so fervently for the beloved to achieve the best ends that he is spared nothing. And that I loved Ninian there could no longer be any doubt; the boy was myself, and through him I would go on living. As long as the King should need the vision and the power of a King's Prophet, he would find it, as ready to his hand as the royal sword.

One evening we built the fire up high against the chill wind of April, and sat beside it, watching the flames. Ninian settled straight down in his usual place, on the rug before the hearth, chin on fist, the grey eyes narrowed against the flames. Gradually, on the fine pale skin, the gleam of sweat showed, a film which caught the firelight and limned his face with a pure line, damping the edges of his hair, and fringing the black lashes with rainbows. I, as lately more and more often, found myself watching him, rather than reaching after my own power. It was a mixture of deep contentment, and a cruelly disturbing love that I made no attempt either to check or to understand. I had learned the lessons of the past; I went with the time, believing that I was master enough of myself and my thoughts to do the boy no harm.

There was a change in his face. Something moved there, a reflection of grief or distress or pain, like something seen faintly in a glass. Sweat was running into his eyes, but he neither blinked nor moved.

It was time I went with him. I stopped watching him, and turned my eyes to the fire.

I saw Arthur straight away. He was sitting his big white horse at the edge of the sea. It was a pebbled strand, and I recognised the crag-fast castle above;

Rheged's sea-tower, which commands the Ituna Estuary. It was dusk, and the stormy sky piled indigo clouds behind a grey sea lighter than its own horizon. Foam-filled waves dashed down on the stones and raced hissing up the shore, to die in creamy froth and drag back through hissing pebbles. The white stallion stood fast, with the foam swirling round his fetlocks; his splashed and gleaming flanks, and Arthur's grey cloak blown with his horse's mane, looked part of the scene, as if the King had ridden out of the sea.

A man, a peasant by the look of him, was by Arthur's bridle, talking earnestly, and pointing seawards. The King followed the gesture, then sat straight in the saddle, his hand to his eyes. I saw what he was looking at; a light, far out towards the horizon, tossing with the tossing sea. The King asked a question, and the man pointed again, this time inland. The King nodded, something passed from hand to hand, then he turned his stallion's head and lifted an arm. The white horse went up the sea path at a gallop, and through the thickening mists of the vision I could see the troopers pressing after him. Just before the vision faded I saw, at the head of the cliff, lights pricking out in the tower.

I came back to the firelit room to find that Ninian was there before me. He was kneeling, or rather crouching, on the rug, with his head in his hands.

'Ninian?'

No movement but a slight shake of the head. I gave him a moment or two, then reached for the cordial I kept to hand.

'Come. Drink this.'

He sipped, and his eyes thanked me, but still he did not speak.

I watched him for a few minutes in silence, then said: 'So it seems that the King has reached the shores of the Ituna, and has found out about the pirates. He rests in Rheged's sea-tower, and with morning, I have no doubt, he will be hard on Heuil's tracks. So what is it? Arthur

is safe, your vision was true, and he is doing what he set
out to do.'

Still nothing, but that look of white distress. I said
quickly: 'Come, Ninian, don't take it to heart so. For
Arthur this is a small matter. The only hard thing about
it is that he must punish Heuil without offending his
brothers; and even that won't be too difficult. It's a long
time since Heuil—metaphorically speaking—spat on his
father's hearth-stone and went out to do his mischiefs in
his own way. So even if old Caw is still alive, I doubt if
he'll repine; and as for the elder sons. I've no doubt
Heuil's death would come as a relief.' I added, more
sharply: 'If it was tragedy you saw, or disaster, it's all the
more important to speak of it. Caw's death we expected;
whose, then? Morgan, the King's sister? Or Count Ector?'

'No.' His voice sounded strange, like an instrument
meant for music that is blown through by a gritty wind.
'I did not see the King at all.'

'You mean you saw nothing? Look, Ninian, this happens. You remember that it happened the other day, even
to me. You must not let it distress you. There will be many
times when nothing will come to you. I've told you before,
you must wait for the god. He chooses the time, not you.'

He shook his head. 'It isn't that. I did see. But not the
High King. Something else.'

'Then tell me.'

He gave me a desperate look. 'I can't.'

'Look, my dear, as you do not choose what you are
shown, so neither do you choose what you will tell. There
may come a time when you use your judgment in the
halls of kings, but, with me, you tell me all that you see.'

'I cannot!'

I waited a moment. 'Now. You saw in the flames?'

'Yes.'

'Did what you saw contradict what came before, or
what I think I have just seen?'

'No.'

'Then if you are keeping silent out of fear of me, or

fear that I may be angry for some reason—'

'I have never been afraid of you.'

'Then,' I said patiently, 'there can surely be no reason to keep silent, and every reason to tell me what you think you saw. It may not be the tragedy you so obviously think it is. You may be interpreting it wrongly. Has that not occurred to you?'

A flash of hope, soon shut out. He took a shaky breath, and I thought he would speak, then he bit his lip and remained silent. I wondered if he had foreseen my death.

I leaned forward and took his face in my hands and forced it up towards me. His eyes came reluctantly up to meet mine. 'Ninian. Do you think I cannot go where you have just gone? Will you put me to that trouble and stress, or will you obey me now? What was it that you saw in the flame?'

His tongue came out to wet dry lips, and then he spoke, in a whisper, as if he was afraid of the sound. 'Did you know that Bedwyr is not with the High King? That he stayed behind in Camelot?'

'No, but I could have guessed it. It was obvious that the King must leave one of his chief captains to keep his stronghold and guard the Queen.'

'Yes.' He licked his lips again. 'That's what I saw. Bedwyr in Camelot—with the Queen. They were—I think they are—'

He stopped. I took my hands away, and his eyes fell, how thankfully, away from mine.

There was only one way to interpret his distress. 'Lovers?'

'I think so. Yes. I know they are.' Then, in a rush now: 'Merlin, how could she do this thing? After all that has happened—after all he has done for her! The Melwas affair—everyone knows what happened there! And Bedwyr, how could he so betray the King? The Queen— a woman to look aside from such a man, such a King ... If only I could believe that this was no true dream! But I know it's true!' He stared at me, with eyes still dilated

with the dream. 'And Merlin, in God's name, what must we do?'

I said slowly: 'That I cannot tell you yet. But put it from you if you can. This is one burden that you must not be asked to share with me.'

'Will you tell him?'

'I am his servant. What do you think?'

He bit his lip again, staring into the fire, but this time, I knew, seeing nothing. His face was white and wretched. I remember feeling vaguely surprised that he should, apparently, blame Guinevere more for her weakness than Bedwyr for his treachery. He said at length: 'How could you tell him such a thing?'

'I don't know that yet. Time will show me.'

He lifted his head. 'You're not surprised.' It sounded like an accusation.

'No. I think I knew, that night when he swam across to Melwas' lodge in the Lake. And afterwards, when she nursed him ... And I remember how, when she first came to Caerleon for her wedding, Bedwyr was the only one of the knights who would not look at her, nor she at him. I think they had already felt it, on the journey from Northgalis, before ever she saw the King.' I added: 'And you might say that I was told clearly enough many years ago, when they were still boys together, and no woman had yet come, as women will, to disturb their lives.'

He got abruptly to his feet. 'I'll go to bed,' he said, and left me.

Alone, I went back into the flames. I saw them almost straight away. They were standing on the western terrace, where I had talked with Arthur. Now the palace was in darkness, but for the dispersed sparkle of the stars, and one shaft of lamplight that lay slanting over the tiles between the tubs of budding rose-trees.

They were standing silent and stock-still. Their hands were locked in each other's, and they were staring at one another with a kind of wildness. She looked afraid, and

tears stood on her cheeks; his face was haunted, as if the white shadow sapped his spirit. Whatever kind of love had them in its claws, it was a cruel one, and, I knew, neither of them as yet had dared to let it kill their faithfulness.

I watched, and pitied, then turned from the smoking logs and left them to their privacy.

Eight weeks later the King came home. He had caught up with Heuil, beaten him in fair fight, burned his ships, and levied a fine which would keep him singing small for some time to come.

Once again he had crushed back his instincts in favour of policy. He had been met on his journey north with the tidings that Caw of Strathclyde had died, quietly in his bed. Quietly, that is, for Caw; he had spent the day hunting and half the night feasting, then, when the inevitable penalties struck his ninety-year-old body in the small hours of the dawning, had died, surrounded by such of his sons and their mothers as could get to the death-bed in time. He had also named his heir, the second son Gwarthegydd (the eldest had been badly maimed in fighting some years back). The messenger who brought Arthur the news also carried assurances of Gwarthegydd's friendship. So Arthur, till he had met and spoken with Gwarthegydd, and seen how he stood with his brother Heuil, would not put the friendship at risk.

He need not have been so careful. It was said that when Gwarthegydd heard the news of Heuil's defeat he let out a guffaw almost as hearty as his father's great bellow, and drank down a full horn of mead to Arthur's health. So the King rode north with Urbgen and Ector into Dumbarton and sat down with Gwarthegydd for nine days, and watched him crowned at the end of it. Then, well satisfied, he rode south again. He went by the east road to Elmet, found the Vale and the Saxon lands quiet, then crossed the country by the Pennine Gap to Caerleon. There he stayed for a month, and in the first days of

June came home to Camelot.

It was time. Again and again in the fire I had seen the lovers, tossed between desire and faith, Bedwyr fine-drawn and silent, the Queen with great eyes and nervous hands. They were never again alone: always with them her ladies sat and sewed, or his men rode in attendance. But they would sit or ride a little way apart from the rest, and talk and talk, as if, in speech, and now and again a light and desperate touch, there was comfort to be had.

And they watched day and night for Arthur's coming: Bedwyr, because he could not quit his post of torment without the King's leave; Guinevere with the forebodings of a lonely young woman who is half in awe of her husband, but has to depend on him for protection and comfort and what companionship he has time to give.

He was home in Camelot for ten days or so before he came to see me. It was a soft bright morning in June. I had risen soon after dawn, as was my habit, and went walking across the rolling hilltops above the house. I went alone; there was usually no sign of Ninian until Mora called him to breakfast. I had walked for an hour, thinking, and pausing from time to time to gather the plants I was looking for, when, beyond a fold of the downs, I heard hoof-beats, coming easily. Don't ask me how I knew it was Arthur; one hoof-beat is very like another, and there was no foresight in the air that day; but love has stronger wings than vision, and I merely turned and waited for him, in the lee of one of the groves of thorn that here and there break the pale sweep of the high downlands. The thorn trees crowned the edge of a little valley where ran a track as old as the land itself. Up this, presently, I saw him coming, sitting at ease on a pretty bay mare, and with his young hound, Cabal's successor, at heel.

He lifted a hand to me, turned the mare up the slope, then slid from the saddle, and greeted me with a smile.

'Well, so you were right. As if I had to tell you that! And now I suppose I don't even have to tell you what happened? Have you ever thought, Merlin, what a dull thing it is to have a prophet who knows everything before it has happened? Not only can I never lie to you, but I can hardly even come to you afterwards and boast about it.'

'I'm sorry. But I assure you, this time, your prophet waited for your dispatches just as eagerly as anyone else. Thank you for sending the letters ... How did you find me? Have you been to Applegarth?'

'I was on the way there, but a fellow with an ox cart—one of the sawyers—said he had seen you come this way. Are you going further? I'll walk with you if I may.'

'Of course. I was just going to turn for home ... Your letters were very welcome, but I still want to hear every-thing at first hand. It's strange to think that old Caw has gone at last. He's been sitting on that crag of his at Dumbarton for as long as I can remember. Do you think Gwarthegydd can hold his own now?'

'Against the Irish and the Saxons, yes. I wouldn't doubt him there. How he makes out with the seventeen other claimants to the kingdom is another matter.' He grinned. 'Sixteen, I suppose, since I clipped Heuil's wings for him.'

'Make it fifteen. You can hardly count young Gildas, since he went to serve Blaise as his clerk.'

'That's true. A clever boy, that, and was always Heuil's shadow. I fancy that when Blaise dies he'll be headed for a monastery. Perhaps it's as well. Like his brother, he has never loved me.'

'Then it's to be hoped he can be trusted with his master's papers. You should get some of your own scribes to set your records down.'

He cocked a brow at me. 'What's this? A prophet's warning?'

'Nothing of the kind. A passing thought, merely. So Gwarthegydd is your man? There was a time when he

threw Caw off and wooed the Irish kings.'

'He was younger then, and Caw's hand was heavy. That's over. I think he will be well enough. What really matters at this stage is that he agrees with Urbgen ...'

He talked on, telling me all the burden of the weeks away, while we walked slowly back across the downs, with the mare following, and the great hound coursing, nose down, in widening circles round our path.

In essence, I thought, listening, nothing had changed. Not yet. Less and less did he need to come to me for counsel, but, as always since his boyhood, he needed the chance to talk over—to himself as much as to me—the course of events, and the problems of the newly-built concourse of kingdoms as they arose. Usually, at the end of an hour or two, after a conversation to which I might have contributed much, or sometimes nothing at all, I could both hear and see that the knots were in a fair way to being unravelled. Then he would rise suddenly, stretch, give me farewell, and go; an abrupt disappearance with anyone else, but between us there was no need for more. I was the strong tree on which the eagle alighted in passing, for rest or thought. But now the oak showed a withered bough or two. How long would it take the sapling to be up to his weight?

He had come to the end of his narrative. Then, as if my thoughts had communicated themselves to him, he gave me a long look, with trouble in it. 'Now, about you. How have you been during these last weeks? You look tired. Have you been ill again?'

'No. My health need not trouble you.'

'I've thought more than once about my last visit to you. You said that it was this'—he hesitated over it— 'your assistant who "saw" Heuil and his rabble at their work.'

'Ninian. Yes, it was.'

'And you yourself saw nothing?'

'Yes,' I said. 'Nothing.'

'So you told me. I still find that strange. Don't you?'

'I suppose so. But if you remember, I wasn't well that day. I suppose I had not fully recovered from that chill I caught.'

'He's been with you—how long?'

'He came in September. That makes it, what? Nine months?'

'And you have taught him all you know?'

I smiled. 'Hardly. But I have taught him a good deal. You need never lack a prophet, Arthur.'

He did not smile in response. He was looking deeply troubled. He walked on across the flinty turf, with the mare's nose at his shoulder, and the hound running ahead. It was quartering the acres of furze with their loads of scented yellow blossom. Wherever it went it dislodged the tiny blue butterflies in clouds, and scattered the glossy scarlet of the ladybirds. There had been a plague of them that spring, and the furze bushes held them in their hundreds, like berries on the thorn.

Arthur was silent for a space, frowning at his thoughts. Then he came, apparently, to a sudden decision. 'Do you trust him?'

'Ninian? Of course. Why not?'

'What do you know about him?'

'As much as I need to,' I said, perhaps a little stiffly. 'I told you how he came to me. I was certain then, and I am still certain, that it was the god who drew us together. And I could not have an apter pupil. Everything I have to teach him he is more than eager to learn. I don't have to drive him; I have to hold him back.' I glanced at him. 'Why? I would have thought you had seen the proof of his aptitude. His vision was true.'

'Oh, I don't doubt his aptitude.' He spoke drily. I caught the faintest of emphasis on the last word.

'What then? What are you trying to say?' Even I was not prepared for the degree of cold surprise in my voice.

He said quickly: 'I'm sorry, Merlin. But I have to say this. I doubt his intentions towards you.'

Though he had signalled the blow, it still struck with

paralysing force. I felt the blood leave my heart. I stopped and faced him. Around us the scent of the gorse rose, sweet and strong. With it, unconsciously, I recognised thyme and sorrel and the crushed fescue as the bay mare put her head down and tore at a mouthful of grass.

I am not lightly made angry, least of all with Arthur. It was only a moment or two before I could say, levelly: 'Whatever you have to say, you had certainly better say now. Ninian is more than my assistant, he bids fair to be my second self. If I have ever been a staff to your hand, Arthur, he will be such another when I am dead. Whether or not you like the boy—and why should you not, you hardly know him?—you may have to accept him so. I shall not live for ever, and he has the power. He has power already, and it will grow.'

'I know. That is what troubles me.' He looked away from me again. I could not judge if it was because he could not face me. 'Don't you see, Merlin? He has the power. It was he who had the vision. And you did not. You say you were tired, you had been ill. But when did your god ever take that into account? This was no trivial "seeing"; it was not something that normally you would have missed. Because of it I was already there, on the borders of Rheged, when Caw died, and was able to support Gwarthegydd and prevent God knows how much trouble among those warring princes. So why did no vision come to you?'

'Must I keep repeating it? I—'

'Yes, you were ill. Why?'

Silence. A breeze came across the miles of downland, smelling of honey. Under it, through the immense stillness of the day, the grasses rustled. The mare cropped eagerly; the hound had come back to its master's feet and sat there, tongue lolling. Arthur stirred, and began to speak again, but I forestalled him.

'What are you saying? ... No, don't answer. I know quite well what you are saying. That I have taken in this unknown boy, become infatuated, opened to him

all the secret lore of drugs, and something of magic, and now he schemes to take my place and usurp my power. That he cannot be acquitted of using my own drugs against me. Is that it?'

Something of a smile touched his lips, though without lightening his grim look. 'You never did deal in ambiguities, did you?'

'I never hid the truth, least of all from you.'

'But then, my dear, you do not always see all the truth.'

For some reason the very gentleness of the reply touched me with foreboding. I looked at him, frowning. 'I am willing to accept that. So now, since I hardly imagine that all this springs from some vague suspicion, I must assume that you know something about Ninian that I don't. If that's so, why not tell me, and let me be the judge of its importance?'

'Very well. But—' Some change in his expression made me turn and follow his gaze. He was looking past me, away beyond the shoulder of the down, where a little valley held a stream fringed with birch and willow. Beyond this rose the green hill that sheltered Applegarth. Among the willows I caught a glint of blue, and then saw Ninian, who must have been up early after all, stooping over something at the edge of the stream. He straightened, and I saw that his hands were full of greenstuff. Watercress grew there, and wild mint among the king-cups. He stood for a moment, as if sorting the plants in his hands, then jumped the stream and ran away up the far slope, with his blue cloak flying out behind him like a sail.

'Well?' I said.

'I was going to say, let's go down there. We have to talk, and there must be more comfortable ways of doing it than standing face to face on top of the world. You unnerve me still, you know, Merlin, even when I know I'm right.'

'That wasn't my intention. By all means let us go down.'

He tugged the mare's head up from the grass, and led the way downhill to where the little wood crowded along the stream's edge. The trees were mostly birches, with here and there a twisted trunk of alder, overgrown with bramble and honeysuckle. One birch tree lay newly fallen, clean with silver bark. The King loosed a buckle from the mare's bit, tied one end of the rein to a sapling, then left her to graze, and came back to sit beside me on the birch trunk.

He came straight to the point. 'Has Ninian ever told you anything about his parentage? His home?'

'No. I never pressed him. I suspected base origins, or at any rate bastardy—he hasn't the peasant look or way of speech. But both you and I know how little those questions can be welcomed.'

'I have not had your scruples. I have wondered about him since that day when I met him with you at Applegarth. Since I came home I have asked about him.'

'And found out what?'

'Enough to know that he has been deceiving you from the beginning.' Then, striking a fist to his knee, with a sudden violence of exasperation: 'Merlin, Merlin, are you so blind? I would swear that no man could be so deceived, except that I know you ... Even now, a few minutes ago, watching him down here by the stream, you saw nothing?'

'What should I see? I imagine he had been collecting alder bark. He knew we needed more, and you can see where that tree has been stripped. And he was carrying watercress.'

'You see? Your eyes are good enough for that, but not to see what any other man in the world would have seen —if not straight away, then within days of meeting him! I suspected it in those first few minutes there in your courtyard, while you told me the "true dream", and then when I made inquiries I found that it was true. We both watched the same person running uphill just now. You saw a boy carrying watercress, but what I saw was a girl.'

I cannot recall at what point during his speech I knew what he was going to tell me; before he got halfway it came like a truth already known; the heat before the lightning strikes, the silence after the lightning that is filled with the coming thunder. What the wise enchanter with his god-sent visions had not perceived, the young man, versed in the ways of women, had seen straight away. It was true. I could only marvel, dumbly, that I had been so easy to deceive. Ninian. The dim-seen figure in the mist, so like the lost boy that I had greeted her and put the words 'boy' and 'Ninian' into her head before she could even speak. Told her I was Merlin: offered her the gift of my power and magic, gifts that another girl— the witch Morgause—had tried in vain to prise from me, but which I had hastened eagerly to lay at this stranger's feet.

Small wonder that she had taken time to think, to arrange her affairs, to cut her hair and change her dress and gather her courage, before coming to me at Applegarth. That she had refused to share the house, preferring the rooms off the colonnade with their separate stair; that she had taken no interest in Mora, but that the two of them were so easy together. Mora had guessed, then? I swept the thought aside as others crowded. The speed with which she had learned from me; the power, with all its suffering, already accepted with dread, with resignation, and finally with willing joy. The grave, gentle look, the gestures of a worship carefully offered, and as carefully constrained. The way she had gone from me when I spoke so lightly of women disturbing men's lives. Her swift condemnation of Guinevere, rather than of Bedwyr, for giving way to a hurtful love. Then, with quickening memory, the feel of her dark hair under my hand, the sweet bones of her face, and the grey eyes watching in the firelight, and the disturbing love that had so troubled me, and now need trouble me no more. It came to me, like the sunlight breaking through the birch-trees on the forgotten bluebells of the copse where, long ago, a girl

had offered me love, then mocked me for impotence, that this time no jealous god need come between us. At last I was free to give, along with all the rest of the power and effort and glory, the manhood that until now had been the god's alone. The abdication I had feared, and feared to grudge, would not be a loss, but rather a new joy gained.

I came back to the sunshine and a different birch-wood and the faded bluebells of June, to see Arthur staring.

'You don't even look surprised. Did you guess?'

'No. But I should have done; if not by any of the signs that were obvious to you, then by the way I felt ... and feel now.' I smiled at his look. 'Oh, yes. An old fool if you like. But now I know for certain that my gods are merciful.'

'Because you think you love this girl?'

'Because I love her.'

'I thought you were a wise man,' he said .

'And because I am a wise man, I know too well that love cannot be gainsaid. It's too late, Arthur. Whatever comes of it, it is too late. It has happened. No, listen. It has all come clear now, like sunlight on water. All the prophecies I have made, things in the future that I have foreseen with dread ... I see them approaching me now, and the dread has gone. I have said often enough that prophecy is a two-edged sword; the gods are delphic; their threats, like their promises of fortune, turn in men's hands.' I lifted my head and looked up through the gently moving leaves. 'I told you that I had seen my own end. There was a dream I had once, a vision in the flame. I saw the cave in the Welsh hillside, and the girl my mother, whose name was Niniane, and the young prince my father, lying together. Then through and over the vision I saw myself, grey-haired, and a young girl with a cloud of dark hair, and closed eyes, and I thought that she, too, was Niniane. And so she was. So she is. Do you

see? If she has any part in my end, then it will be merciful.'

He got to his feet so abruptly that the hound, curled there, jumped aside, ridge-backed and looking round for danger. Arthur took three steps away from me, and three back to stand in front of me. He drove one fist into the other palm with such violence that the mare, a dozen paces away, started and then stood, ears erect, trembling. 'How do you expect me to sit here and listen to you talking of your death? You told me once that you would end in a tomb, alive, you thought it would be in Bryn Myrddin. Now, I suppose, you will ask me to let you go back there so that this—this witch can leave you there entombed!'

'Not quite. You have not understood—'

'I understand as well as you do, and I think that I remember more! Have you forgotten Morgause's curse? That women's magic would snare you at the end? And what was promised you once by the Queen Ygraine, my mother? You told me what she said. That if Gorlois of Cornwall died, then she would spend the rest of her life praying to any gods there are that you would die betrayed by a woman.'

'Well?' I said. 'And have I not been snared? And have I not been betrayed? And this is all it is.'

'Are you so sure? Forgive me for reminding you yet again that you don't know women. Remember Morgause. She tried to persuade you to teach her your magic, and when you would not, she took power another way ... the way we know about. Now this girl has succeeded where Morgause failed. Tell me one thing: if she had come to you as herself, as a woman, would you have taken her in and taught her your skills?'

'I can't tell you that. Probably not. But the point is, surely, that she did not? The deception was not hers in the first instance; it was forced on her by my error, and that error in its turn was forced on me by the chance

which led me first to meet and love the boy Ninian who was drowned. If you cannot see the god at work there. I am sorry.'

'Yes, yes'—impatiently—'but you have just reminded me that this is a delphic god. What you see now as a joy may be the very death you have dreaded.'

'No,' I said. 'You must take it the other way. That a fate long dreaded can prove, in the end, merciful, like this "betrayal". My long nightmare of entombment in the dark, alive, may prove to be such another. But whatever it is, I cannot avoid it. What will come, will come. The god chooses the time and the form. After all these years, if I did not trust in him, I would be the fool you think me.'

'So you'll go back to this girl, keep her by you, and go on teaching her your art?'

'Just that. I could hardly stop now. I have sown the seeds of power in her, and, as surely as if it were a tree growing, or a child I had begotten, I cannot stop it. And the other seed has been sown, for good or ill. I love her dearly, and were she ten times an enchantress, I can only thank my god for it, and take her to me more nearly than before.'

'I cannot bear to see you hurt.'

'She will not hurt me.'

'If she does,' he said evenly, 'witch or no witch, lover or no lover, I shall deal with her as she deserves. Well, it seems there is no more to be said. We had better go back. That basket looks heavy. Let me take it for you.'

'No, a moment. There is one more thing.'

'Yes?'

He was standing straight in front of me where I still sat on the birch log. Against the delicate boughs of the birches and the shifting of the leaves in the soft breeze he looked tall and powerful, the jewels at shoulder and belt and sword-hilt glittering as if with their own life. He looked, not young, but full of the richness of life, a man in the flower of his strength; a leader among kings.

His face was contained. There was nothing to tell me what he would say, what he might do, after I had spoken.

I said, slowly: 'Since we have been talking of last things, there is one thing I have to tell you. Another vision, which it is my duty to bring to you. It's something that I have seen, not once, but several times. Bedwyr your friend, and Guinevere your Queen, love one another.'

I had been looking away from him as I spoke, not wanting to see how the wounding stroke went home. I suppose I had expected anger, an outburst of violence, at the very least surprise and furious disbelief. Instead there was silence, a silence so drawn out that at length I looked up, to see in his face nothing of anger or even surprise, but a kind of sternly-held calmness that tempered only compassion and regret.

I said, not believing it: 'You knew?'

'Yes,' he said, quite simply. 'I know.' There was a pause, while I looked for words and found none. He smiled. There was something in the smile that did not speak of youth and power at all, but of a wisdom perhaps greater, because more purely human, than is ascribed to me. 'I do not have vision, Merlin, but I see what is before my eyes. And do you not think that others, who guess and whisper, have not been at pains to tell me? It sometimes seems to me that the only ones who have given no hint by word or look have been Bedwyr and the Queen themselves.'

'How long have you known this?'

'Since the Melwas affair.'

And I had never guessed. His kindness to the Queen, her relief and growing happiness, had told me nothing. 'Then why did you leave Bedwyr with her when you went north?'

'To let them have something, however little.' The sun was in his eyes, making him frown. He spoke slowly. 'You have just been telling me that love cannot be ruled or stopped. If you are prepared to accept love, knowing that

it may well bring you to your death, then how much more should I accept this, knowing that it cannot destroy friendship or faith?'

'You believe that?'

'Why not? Everything else you have ever told me has been true. Think back now over your prophecies about my marriage, the "white shadow" that you saw when Bedwyr and I were boys, the *guenhwyvar* that touched us both. You said then that it would not blur or destroy the faith we had in one another.'

'I remember.'

'Very well. When I married my first Guenever you warned me that the marriage might be unwholesome for me. That little girl "unwholesome"?' He laughed, without mirth. 'Well, now we know the truth of the prophecy. Now we have seen the shadow. And now we see it falling across Bedwyr's life and mine. But if it is not to destroy our faith in one another, what would you have me do? I must give Bedwyr the trust and freedom to which he is entitled. Am I a cottager, with nothing in my life but a woman and a bed I am to be jealous of, like a cock on his dunghill? I am a king, and my life is a king's; she is a queen, and childless, so her life must be less than a woman's. Is she to wait year by year in an empty bed? To walk, to ride, to take her meals with an empty place beside her? She is young, and she has a girl's needs, of companionship and of love. By your god or any god, Merlin, if, during the years of days that my work takes me from court, she is ever to take a man to her bed, should I not be thankful it is Bedwyr? And what would you have me do, or say? Anything I say to Bedwyr would eat at the root of the very trust we have, and it would avail nothing against what has already happened. Love, you tell me, cannot be gainsaid. So I keep silent, and so will you, and by that token will faith and friendship stay unbroken. And we can count her barrenness a mercy.' The smile again. 'So the god works for us both in twisted ways, does he not?'

I got to my feet. The birches moved and the sun poured down. The stream glittered against my eyes, so that they watered.

I said quietly: 'You see? This is the final mercy. You no longer need either my strength or my counsel. Whatever you may need after this of warning or prophecy, you can still find at Applegarth. As for me, let your servant go in peace, back to my own home and my own hills, and whatever waits for me there.' I picked the basket up and handed it to him. 'But in the meantime, will you come back with me to Applegarth, and see her?'

CHAPTER 10

When we reached Applegarth it seemed deserted. It was still very early. Varro had not yet come to start work, and I had seen Mora from a distance, making her way towards the village market, with her basket on her arm.

The mare knew the way to the stables, and trotted off, with a clap on the flank. We went into the house. The girl was there, sitting on her accustomed stool in the window embrasure, reading. Not far from her, on the stone sill, perched a redbreast, picking up the crumbs she had scattered.

She must have heard the horse, and assumed either that I had ridden that morning, instead of walking, or that a messenger had come very early from Camelot. She had obviously not expected the King himself. When I went into the room she looked up, with a smile and a 'Good morning', and then, seeing Arthur's shadow fall across the doorway behind me, got to her feet and let the book roll together between her hands. 'I'll leave you to talk, shall I?' she said, and turned, in no haste, to go.

I started to warn her. 'Ninian—' I began, but then Arthur came quickly past me into the room, and stopped just inside the door, his eyes on her face.

Be sure that I was staring, too.

Now that I knew, I wondered how I had not always known. For eighteen, it was hardly a man's face; an immature eighteen might have had that smooth cheek and sweet mouth, and her body under the shapeless clothing was as slim as a boy's, but the hands were not a young man's hands, nor were the slender feet. I can only think that my own memory of the boy Ninian had kept me,

blindly, to the image of him as he had been at sixteen: my desire to have him had been strong enough to let me re-create him, first in the dimly seen ghost of the Lake, then in this girl, so near to me, so closely watched, and yet not seen, through all the past long months. And then, perhaps (I thought), she had been able to use a little of my own magic against me, to keep me blind—and so to keep herself beside me, until her purposes were served.

She stood straight as a wand, facing us. I suppose it needed no magic for her to tell that we knew. The grey eyes met mine for the fraction of a moment, then she faced the King.

What happened then is difficult to describe. There was the quiet, everyday room, filled with the scents and sounds of the summer morning; sweet briar and early roses and the gillyflowers she had planted outside the window; last night's burned logs (the nights could still have a chill in them, and she had insisted on making a fire for me to sit by); the sweet sub-song of the redbreast as he flew up into the apple boughs outside. A summer room, where, to anyone of normal perceptions, nothing passed at all. Just three people, in a pause of silence.

But to me the air tingled suddenly over the skin, like water when lightning strikes. I felt the flesh creep on my bones, and the small hairs on my arms fur up; my nape stirred like the ruff of a dog in a thunder-storm. I do not think I moved. Neither the King nor the girl seemed to notice anything. She watched him gravely, unalarmed, I might have thought unmoved and barely interested, if I had not been getting these fearsome currents washing over and through my flesh as the tide washes over a rock lying on the shore. Her grey eyes held his; his dark ones bored into her. I could feel the force as the two of them met. The air trembled.

Then he nodded, and put up a hand to loosen the cloak from his shoulder. I saw her mouth move with the shadow of a smile. The message had passed. For my sake, he would accept her. And for my sake, she would stand

the trial. The room steadied, and I said, 'Let me,' and took his cloak from him to lay it down. The girl said: 'Shall I bring you some breakfast? Mora left it ready, but you were late, so she went to market. She says the best things are taken if she is not there early.'

She went. The platters were laid ready on the table, and we took our places. She brought bread, and the crock of honey, and a pitcher of milk along with one of mead. She set the latter down at the King's hand, then without a word took her usual place across from me. She had not looked at me again. When I poured a cup of milk for her she thanked me, but without lifting her eyes. Then she spread honey on her bread, and began to eat.

'Your name,' said the King. 'Is it Niniane?'

'Yes,' she said, 'but I was always called Nimuë.'

'Your parentage?'

'My father was called Dyonas.'

'Yes. King of the River Islands?'

'The same. He is dead now.'

'I know that. He fought beside me at Viroconium. Why did you leave your home?'

'I was sent to the Lady's service, in the Isle of Glass. It was my father's wish.' The glimmer of a smile. 'My mother was a Christian, and when she lay dying she made him promise he would send me to the Island; I know she intended me for the service of the Church there. I was only six years old, but he promised her. He himself had never held with what he called the new God; he was an initiate of Mithras—his own father took him there in the time of Ambrosius. So when the time came for him to keep his promise to my mother, he did indeed take me to the Island, but to the service of the Good Goddess, in the shrine below the Tor.'

'I see.'

So did I. As one of the *ancillae* of the shrine she would have been there on the occasion of Arthur's thanksgiving after Caer Guinnion and Caerleon. Perhaps she had

glimpsed me there, beside the King. She must have known that, for her, there was small chance of coming any nearer to the prince-enchanter, and learning any of the greater arts. Then on that misty night I had put the key into her hand. It had taken courage to grasp it, but God knew she had plenty of that.

The King was still questioning her. 'And you wanted to study magic. Why?'

'Sir, I cannot say why. Why does a singer first want to learn music? Or a bird want to try the air? When I first went to the Island, I found some traces of it; and learned all they had to teach, but still I was hungry. Then one day I saw ...' She hesitated for the first time ... 'I saw Merlin in the shrine. You will remember the day. Later, I heard he had come to live here at Applegarth. I thought, if only I were a man I could go to him. He is wise, he would know that magic is in my blood, and he would teach me.'

'Ah, yes. The day we gave thanks for our victories. But if you were there, how is it that you failed to recognise me, the first time you saw me here?'

She went scarlet. For the first time her gaze dropped from his. 'I did not see you, sir. I told you, I was watching Merlin.'

There was a flat pause of silence, as when a hand is laid across the harp-strings, killing the sound. I saw Arthur's mouth open and shut, then the flash of a vivid laughter in his face. She, looking steadfastly at the table, saw nothing of it. He shot me a look brimful of amusement, then drained his cup and sat back in the chair. His voice never altered, but the challenge had gone; he had lowered his sword.

'But you knew that Merlin was not likely to accept you as a pupil, even if the Lady could be persuaded to let you leave her cloisters.'

'Yes. I knew that. I had no hope. But after that I settled even less easily into the life there among the other women. They seemed, oh, so contented to be penned

there with the small magics and the prayers and spells, and looking backwards always towards the times of legend ... It's hard to explain. If there is something within onself, something burning to be free, one knows of it.' A look straight at him, equal to equal. 'You must have known it. I was still unborn, hammering at the egg, to get out into the air. But the only way I could have escaped from the Island would have been if some man had offered for me, and for that I would not have gone, nor would my father have made me.'

He gave a brief nod of acceptance and, I thought, of understanding. 'So?'

'It wasn't easy, even, to find time to be alone. I would watch and wait my chance, and slip out sometimes, only to be alone with my own thoughts, and with the water and sky ... Then, on the night when Queen Guinevere was missing, and the Island was in uproar, I—I'm afraid all I thought of was my chance to get out without being missed ... There was a boat I sometimes borrowed. I went out. I knew no one would see me in the mist. Then Merlin came along the Lake road, and spoke to me.' She paused. 'I think you must know the rest.'

'Yes. So when chance—the god, you would say, if you are Merlin's pupil—made Merlin mistake you for the boy Ninian, and ask you to come and learn from him, you made the second chance for yourself.'

She bent her head. 'When he spoke first, I was confused. It was like a dream. Afterwards I realised what had happened, that he had mistaken me for some boy he had known.'

'How did you get free of the shrine in the end? What did you tell the Lady?'

'That I had been called for higher service. I did not explain. I let her think I was going back to my father's house. I think she imagined that I had to go back to the River Isles, perhaps to be married to my cousin, who rules there now. She did not ask. She put no rub in my way.'

No, I thought to myself; that imperious lady would be glad to rid herself of an adept who must have bidden fair to outshine her. Among those white-robed girls this young enchantress must have shone out like a diamond in white flax.

Behind me, the redbreast flew back to his perch on the window-sill, and tried a stave of song. I doubt if either Nimuë or Arthur heard it. His questions had changed direction: 'Do you need fire for the vision, or can you see, like Merlin, in the small drops of dew?'

'It was in dew-drops that I saw the vision of Heuil.'

'And that was a true one. So. It seems you already have something of the greater power. Well, there is no fire, but will you look for me again, and tell me now if there is any other warning in the stars?'

'I can see nothing to order.'

I bit my lip. It was my own voice as a young man, confident, perhaps a little pompous. He recognised it, too. He said gravely: 'I am sorry. I should have known.'

He got to his feet then, and reached for the cloak that I had laid across a chair. There was a perceptible flaw in her composure, as she hurried to help him with it. He was saying goodbye to me, but I hardly heard him. My own composure bade fair to be in ruins. I, who was never at a loss, had not had time to think what I must say.

The King was in the doorway. The sun caught him and sent his shadow streaming back between us. The great emeralds on Caliburn's hilt flashed in the light.

'King Arthur!' said Nimuë sharply.

He turned. If he found her tone peremptory he gave no sign of it.

She said: 'If your sister, the Lady Morgan, comes to Camelot, lock up your sword and watch for treachery.'

He looked startled, then said harshly: 'What do you mean by that?'

She hesitated, looking in her turn surprised by what she had said. Then she lifted her palms out, in a gesture like a shrug. 'My lord, I don't know. Only that. I am sorry.'

'Well ...' said Arthur. He looked across at me, lifted his brows, then shrugged in his turn, and went out.

Silence, so long that the robin hopped right into the room and onto the table where the breakfast lay, barely touched.

'Nimuë,' I said.

She looked at me then, and I saw that, although she had stood in no awe of the King, she was afraid to meet my eyes. I smiled at her, and saw to my amazement the grey eyes fill with tears.

I put out both my hands. Hers met them. In the end there was no need of words. We did not hear the King's horse go down the hill, nor, much later, Mora come back from market to find the breakfast still uneaten.

Book IV

BRYN MYRDDIN

CHAPTER 1

So, towards the end of my life, I found a new beginning. A beginning it was in love, for both of us. I had no skill, and she, vowed from childhood to be one of the Lake maidens, had hardly thought of love. But what we had was enough and more than enough: she, for all she was many years younger than I, seemed happy and satisfied; and I, calling myself in private dotard, old fool, wisdom dragged at mockery's chariot wheels, knew that I was none of these: between myself and Nimuë was a bond stronger than any between the best matched pair in the flower of their age and strength. We were the same person. We were part of each other as are night and daylight, dark and dawn, sun and shadow. When we lay together we lay at the edge of life where opposites fuse and make new entities, not of the flesh, but of the spirit, the issue as much of the ceaseless traffic of mind, as of the body's pleasure.

We did not marry. Looking back now, I doubt if either of us even thought of cementing the relationship in this way; it was not clear what rites we could have used, nor what faster bond we could have hoped for. With the passing of the days and nights of that sweet summer, we found ourselves closer and yet more close, as if cast in a common mould: we would wake in the morning and know we had shared the same dream; meet at evening and each know what the other had learned and done that day. And all the time, as I believed, each of us harboured our own private and growing joy; I to watch her trying the wings of power like a strong young bird feeling for the first time the mastery of the air; she to

receive this waxing strength, and to know, with love but without pity, that at the same time the power was leaving me.

So the month of June flew by, and then high summer was with us. The cuckoo vanished from the brakes, the meadowsweet was out with its heavy honey smell, the bees droned all day in the blue borage and the lavender. Nimuë called to Varro to set a saddle on the chestnut—Arthur had made her a present of him—then she kissed me and rode off towards the Lake. It was, of course, known now that the former servant of the Goddess was with Merlin at Applegarth. There must have been speculation and gossip, some of it no doubt malicious—and (I was sure) all of it amazed at the impulse that had taken a young and lovely girl into the ageing enchanter's bed. But the High King had stated publicly, and had moreover made it clear by gifts and visits, that our relationship had his approval; so even the Lady of the shrine had not attempted to close her doors against Nimuë; she had, rather, made her welcome, in the hope (Nimuë suggested with amusement) that the shrine might fall heir to some of Merlin's secrets. Nimuë herself did not often leave Applegarth, either for the Island or the court at Camelot. But she was hardly to be blamed if she was a trifle flown with the power and excitement of these first months, and as a young bride enjoys showing off her new status among her maiden colleagues, so, I guessed, Nimuë was eager to revisit her friends among the Goddess's *ancillae*. She had not yet been to the court of Camelot without me; I guessed what she did not say; that, even with the King's support, she was doubtful of her reception there. But on three occasions she had been back to the Island, and this time, she told me, she would see about the promise of some plants from the garden near the holy well. She would be back at dusk. I saw her off, then checked over my bag of medicines, put on a straw hat against the sun, and set out across the hill to visit the house of a woman who was recovering from a bout of

fever. I went blithely. The day was fine but fresh, and
lark-song poured down from a clear sky like rillets of
bright water. I reached the hilltop and followed the
track between gorse bushes ablaze with flowers. A flock
of goldfinches fluttered and dipped through a patch of
tall, seeding thistles, making the sweet, plaintive call that
the Saxons call 'chirm', or 'charm'. The breeze smelled
of thyme.

That is all I remember. Next—it seemed all in a
moment—the world was dark, and the stars were out, with
that clear sparkle that one can feel pricking down into
the eyes and brain. I was lying on my back, flat on the
turf, staring up at them. The gorse bushes were all round
me, humped and dark, and gradually, as if sense were
coming back from a limitless distance, I felt the stab of
their prickles biting into hands and arms. Starlight
sparked from the dew. Everywhere there was a great
silence, like a held breath. Then above me, high in the
black sky, another point of light began to grow. The
darkness lit. Into this single, waxing point of light the
smaller stars, like metal dust to a lodestone, like a swarm
into the hive, fled, till in all the sky there was no other
light. My eyes dazzled. I could not move, but lay there,
it seemed alone on the curve of the world, watching the
star. Then, intolerably bright, it started from its place,
and swiftly, like a brand flung across the sky, it arched
from the zenith to the earth's edge, trailing behind it a
great train of light shaped like a dragon.

I heard someone call out: 'The Dragon! The Dragon!
See where the Dragon falls!' and knew the voice was my
own.

Then lights, and hands, and Nimuë's face, white in
the lantern light, with Varro behind her, and a youth I
vaguely recognised as the shepherd who watched his
flock on the down. Then voices. 'Is he dead?' 'No. Come,
quickly, cover him. He's cold.' 'He's dead, mistress.' 'No!
Never! I'll never believe it! Do as I say!' Then, with
anguish, 'Merlin, Merlin!' And a man's voice, fearfully,

'Who will tell the King?'

After that a gap of time, and my own bed, and the taste of hot wine with herbs infused in it, and another long gap, this time of sleep.

* * *

Now we come to the part of my chronicle that is the most difficult to tell. Whether or not (as the popular belief went) the falling comet with the dragon's tail betokened the true end of Merlin's greater powers, I know that, looking back at the days and nights—more, the weeks and months—that followed, I cannot tell for certain whether what I remember was reality, or a dream. It was the year of my journeying with Nimuë. Looking back now, I see it, scene after scene, like reflections sliding past a boat, blurred and repeated, and broken, as the oars stir the water's glass. Or like the moments just before sleep, when scene after scene swims up into the mind's eye, the true memories like dreams, and the dreams as real as memory.

I still only have to close my eyes to see Applegarth, serene in the sun, with the silver lichen thick on the old trees, where the green fruit, slowly swelling, shone like lamps, and in the sheltered garth lavender and sage and sweet briar breathed their scent into the air as thickly as smoke. And on the hill behind the tower the thorn trees, those strange thorns that flower in winter and have small flowers with stamens like nails. And the doorway where the girl Nimuë first stood shyly, with the light behind her, like the gentle ghost of the drowned boy who might have been a greater enchanter than she. And the ghost itself; the 'boy Ninian' who still haunts my memories of the garth, alongside the slender girl who sat at my feet in the sun.

For perhaps a week after my falling fit on the hilltop, I spent most of my time sitting on the carved seat in the garth. Not from weakness, but because Nimuë insisted,

and I needed time to think.

Then one evening, in the warm dusk, I called her to me. She nestled down in her old place, on a cushion at my feet. Her head was against my knee, and my hand stroked the thick hair. This was growing now, and had reached her shoulderblades. I wondered daily at my old blindness that had not seen the curves of her body, and the sweet lines of throat and brow and wrist.

'You've been busy this week.'

'Yes,' she said. 'Housewife's jobs. Cutting the herbs and bunching them to dry.'

'Are they done?'

'Just about. Why?'

'I've been idle all this time while you have been working, but I have been thinking.'

'About?'

'Among other things, Bryn Myrddin. You have never been there. So before the summer ends, I think we must leave Applegarth, you and I—'

'Leave Applegarth?' She started away from me, looking up in dismay. 'Do you mean live at Bryn Myrddin again ... both of us live there?'

I laughed. 'No. Somehow I don't see that happening. Do you?'

She subsided against my knee, her head bent. She was silent for a while, then she said, muffled: 'I don't know. I've never glimpsed even a dream of it. But you have told me that you will die there. Is that what you mean?'

I put out a hand again and touched her hair. 'I know I have said that that will happen, but I've had no warning of it yet. I feel very well, better than for many months. But look at it like this: when my life does end, yours must begin. And for that to happen you must do one day as I did, and enter the crystal cave of vision. You know this. We've spoken of it before.'

'Yes, I know.' She did not sound reassured.

'Well,' I told her cheerfully, 'we shall go to Bryn Myrddin, but at the end of our journey. Before we get

there we shall have travelled widely, and seen many
places and many things. I want you to visit the places
where I have passed my life, and see the things I have
seen. I have told you as much as I can; now you must
see as much as I am able to show you. Do you understand?'

'I think so. You are giving me the sum of your life, on
which to build my own.'

'Exactly that. For you, the stones on which to build the
life you want; for me, the crown and harvest.'

'And when I have it all?' she asked, subdued.

'Then we shall see.' Amused, I caressed her hair again.
'Don't look like that, child, take it lightly. It's a wedding
journey, not a funeral procession. Our travels may have
a purpose, but we'll take them for pleasure, that's for
sure. I've had this in mind some time; it wasn't just suggested by this last sick turn of mine. We've been happy
here in Applegarth, and no doubt we shall be happy here
again, but you are too young to fold your wings here
year after year. So we'll go travelling. I have a suspicion
that my real object is just to show you the places I've
known and loved, for no more serious reason than that I
have known and loved them.'

She sat up, looking easier. Her eyes began to sparkle.
She was young. 'A kind of pilgrimage?'

'You could call it that.'

'Tintagel, you mean, and Rheged, and the place where
you found the sword, and the lake where you laid it to
wait for the King?'

'More than that. God help us both, we must sail to
Brittany. My story and the High King's has been bound
up—as yours will be, too—in that great sword of his. I
have to show you where the god himself first came to me,
with the first sign of the sword. Which is why we should
go soon. The seas are calm, but in another month or so
the gales will start.'

She shuddered. 'Then by all means let us go now.' Then,
suddenly, all uncomplicated pleasure, a young woman

setting out on an exciting journey, with no other thought in her head: 'And you'll have to take me to Camelot. I really haven't got anything fit to wear ...'

So next day I spoke with Arthur's courier, and not very long after that Arthur himself came to tell me that escort and ships were ready, and that we could go.

We set sail from the Island at the end of July, and Arthur and the Queen rode down to the harbour to see us on our way. Bedwyr was with us, his face a mixture of relief and misery: he had been sent to escort us across the sea, and he was like a man released from the torment of a drug which he knows will kill him, but for which, night and day, he craves. He was charged with dispatches from Arthur to his cousin King Hoel of Brittany, and would escort us as far as Hoel's court at Kerrec.

When we came to the quay the ship was still loading, but soon all was ready, and Arthur bade us farewell, with an admonition to Nimuë to 'take care of him' which brought forcibly back to me memories of the voyage I had made with Arthur himself a squalling baby in his wet-nurse's arms, and King Hoel's escort scowling at the noise, and trying to give me due greeting through it all. Then he kissed Bedwyr, with nothing apparent in his look save warm affection, and Bedwyr muttered something, holding him, before turning to take his leave of the Queen. Smiling by the King's side, she had command of herself; her light touch of Bedwyr's hand, and the serene 'Godspeed' she wished him showed barely more warmth than that given to Nimuë, and rather less than to me. (Since the Melwas affair, she had shown a pretty gratitude and liking, such as a girl might have for her elderly father.) I said my goodbyes, cast a wary eye at the smooth summer sea, and went on board. Nimuë, already pale, came with me. It needed no prophetic vision to foretell that we would see nothing of one another until the ship docked in the Small Sea.

It is no part of this tale to follow our travels league by league. Indeed, as I have explained, I cannot do so. We

went to Brittany, that I know, and were welcomed there
by King Hoel, and spent the autumn and winter in
Kerrec, and I showed Nimuë the roads through the Perilous Forest, and the humble inn where Ralf, my page,
guarded the child Arthur through the dangerous hidden
years. But here already the memories are confused; as I
write I can see them all, crossing each other like ghosts
that crowd, century by century, into an old dwelling
house. Each is as clear as the others. Arthur as a baby,
asleep in the manger straw. My father watching me in
the lamplight, asking, 'What will come to Britain?' The
druids at their murderous work in Nemet. Myself, a frightened boy, hiding in the cattle-shed. Ralf riding post-haste
through the trees with messages for Hoel to send to me.
Nimuë beside me in the budding woods of April, lying
on green turf in a forest glade. The same glade, with the
white doe fleeing like magic, to draw danger away from
Arthur. And across this, confusedly, other memories or
other dreams; a white stag with ruby eyes; the deer fleeing
through the dusk under the oaks at Nodens' shrine;
magic on magic. But through all, like a torch relit for
another quest, the stars, the smiling god, the sword.

We stayed away till summer, this much I know for
certain. I can even record the day of our arrival back
in Britain. Cador, Duke of Cornwall, died that year, and
we disembarked in a country deep in mourning for a
great soldier and a good duke. What I cannot recall is
which of us—Nimuë or myself—knew that it was time to
be gone, or which harbour to sail for. We landed in a
little bay a league or so from Tintagel, on Dumnonia's
northern coast, two days after Cador's death, to find
Arthur there already, with all his train. Having seen our
sail, he came down to the wharf to meet us, and before
ever we landed we saw the covered shields, the lowered
pennons, and the unadorned white of mourning, and
knew what had brought us home.

Scenes like these swim up, brightly lit with hardly a
shadow. But then comes the candlelit chapel where

Cador's body lay in state, with monks chanting; and the scene dislimns, and once again I am standing at the foot of his father's bier, waiting for the ghost of the man I had betrayed. Even Nimuë, when once I spoke to her of this, could be no help to me. For so long now we had shared thought and dream alike that she herself could not (she told me) separate the sight of Tintagel in the summer, with the gentle wind lifting the sea against the rocks, from my stormy tales of time past. Tintagel mourning for Duke Cador recently dead, seems less real to either of us than the storm-beaten stronghold where Uther, lying with Gorlois' wife Ygraine, begot Arthur for Britain.

And so it was with the rest of the time. After Tintagel we went north. Memory, or dream here in the long darkness, shows me the soft hills of Rheged, the hanging clouds of forest, the lakes ringing with fish, and, reflected in the glass of its own lake, Caer Bannog, where I hid the great sword for Arthur to find. Then the Green Chapel where later, on that legendary night, Arthur lifted it at last into his hand.

So, as I had done in earnest years ago, we lightly followed the sword, but something—some instinct I could no longer be sure was prophetic, or even wise—bade me keep silence about the other quest which, sometimes, I had glimpsed in the shadows. It would not be for me; it would come after me; and the time was not yet. So I said nothing of Segontium, or the place where still, deep in the ground, lay buried the other treasures that had come back with the sword to the West.

At last we came to Galava. It was a happy end to a pleasant journey. We were welcomed by Count Ector, an Ector grown stout with age and good living since the peace, who presented Nimuë to the Lady Drusilla (with a wink at me) as 'Prince Merlin's wife, lass, at long last.' And beside him was my faithful Ralf, flushed with pleasure, proud as a peacock of his pretty wife and four sturdy children, and avid for news of Arthur and the south.

Nimuë and I lay together in the tower room where I had once been carried to recover from Morgause's poison. It was some time after midnight, as we lay watching the moon touch the hilltops beyond the window, that she stirred, turning her cheek into the hollow of my shoulder, and said, softly:

'And what, after this? Bryn Myrddin and the crystal cave?'

'I think so.'

'If your own hills are as beautiful as these, perhaps I shan't mind, after all, deserting Applegarth ...' I heard a smile in her voice ... 'at least in summer.'

'I promised you that it wouldn't come to that. Tell me this: for the last stage of your wedding journey, would you rather travel down the western roads, or take ship from Glannaventa, and go by sea to Maridunum? I'm told the seas are calm.'

There was a short pause. Then she said: 'But why ask me to choose? I thought—'

'You thought?'

Another pause. 'I thought you had something still to show me.'

It seemed that her instinct was as true as my own. I said: 'What, then, my dear?'

'You have told me all the story of the sword, and you have shown me now all that happened to it, this wonderful Caliburn that is the symbol of the King's power, and by which he holds his kingdom. You have shown me the places of vision which led you to find it; where you hid it until Arthur should be ready to raise it, and where at last he did raise it. But you have never told me where you yourself found it. I had thought that this would be the last thing you would show me, before you took me home.'

I did not reply. She raised herself in the bed, and lay on an elbow, looking down at me. The moonlight slid over her, making her a thing of silver and shadow, light-

ing the lovely lines of temple and cheek-bone, throat and breast.

I smiled, tracing the line of her shoulder with a gentle finger. 'How can I think and answer you when you look like that?'

'Easily.' She answered the smile, not moving. 'Why have you never told me? It's because there's something else there, isn't it, that belongs to the future?'

So: instinct or vision, she knew. I said, slowly: 'You spoke of a "last thing". Yes, there is still one mystery, the only one; and yes, it is for the future. I haven't seen it clearly myself, but once, before he was King, I made a prophecy for Arthur. It was between the finding and the raising of the sword, when the future was still hedged around with fire and vision. I remember what I said ...'

'Yes?'

I quoted it. ' "I see a settled and shining land, with corn growing rich in the valleys, and farmers working their fields in peace as they did in the time of the Romans. I see a sword growing idle and discontented, and the days of peace stretching into bickering and division, and the need of a quest for the idle swords and the unfed spirits. Perhaps it was for this that the god took the grail and the spear back from me and hid them in the ground, so that one day you might set out to find the rest of Macsen's treasure. No, not you, but Bedwyr ... it is his spirit, not yours, which will hunger and thirst, and slake itself in the wrong fountains." '

A long silence. I could not see her eyes; they were full of moonlight. Then she whispered: 'The grail and the spear? Macsen's treasure, hidden again in the ground, to be the objects of a quest as great as that of the sword? Where? Tell me where?'

She looked eager; not awed, but eager, like a runner in sight of the goal. When she does see the chalice and the spear, I thought, she will bend her head before their magic. But she is only a child, and still sees the things

of power as weapons in her own hand. I did not say to her: 'It is the same quest, because what use to anyone is the sword of power, without the fulfilment of the spirit? All the kings are now one King. It is time the gods became one God, and there in the grail is the oneness for which men will seek, and die, and dying, live.'

I did not say it, but lay for a while in silence, while she watched me, unmoving. I could feel the power coming from her, my own power, stronger now in her than in my own hands. For myself, I felt nothing but weariness, and a kind of grief.

'Tell me, my darling,' she said, whispering, intent.

So I told her. I smiled at her and said, gently: 'I will do better than tell you. I shall take you there, and what there is to see, I shall show you. What is left of Macsen's treasure lies below the ground in the ruined temple of Mithras at Segontium, that is called Caer-y-n'a Von, below Y Wyddfa. And now that is all that I can give you, my dear, except my love.'

I remember that she said, 'And that would have been enough, even without the rest,' as she stooped to put her mouth on mine.

After she slept I lay watching the moon, full and bright, becalmed, it seemed for hours, full in the centre of the window-frame. And I remembered how, long ago, as a child, I had believed that such a sight would bring me my heart's desire. What that had been in those days— power, prophecy, service, love—I could barely remember. Now all that was past, and my heart's desire lay here, sleeping in my arms. And the night, so full of light, was empty of the future, empty of vision; but still, like breathing ghosts from the past, came the voices.

Morgause's voice, the witch's voice spitting her curse at me: 'Are you so sure you are proof against women's magic, Prince Merlin? It will snare you in the end.'

And across it, Arthur's voice, vigorous, angry, full of love: 'I cannot bear to see you hurt.' And then: 'Witch

or no witch, lover or no lover, I shall deal with her as she deserves.'

I held her young body close against my own, and kissed her sleeping eyelids, very gently. I said, to the ghosts, to the voices, to the empty moonlight: 'It was time. Let me go in peace.' Then, commending myself and my spirit to God who all these years had held me in his hand, I composed myself for sleep.

This was the last thing that I know to be truth, and not a dream in darkness.

CHAPTER 2

When I was a small child at Maridunum I had slept with
my nurse in a room in the servants' wing of my grandfather's palace. It was a ground-floor chamber, and outside the window grew a pear tree, where at evening a
thrush would sing, and then afterwards the stars would
come pricking out into the sky behind the branches,
looking for all the world as if they were lights entangled
in the tree. I used to lie watching them in the quiet of
the night, and straining my ears to hear the music which,
I had been told, the stars make as they move along the
sky.

Now at last, it seemed, I heard it. I was lying, warmly
shrouded, on—I thought—a litter, which must, from
the swaying motion, be being borne along under a night
sky. A great darkness wrapped me in, and far above me
arched a night sky teeming and wheeling with stars,
which rang like small bells as they moved. I was part of
the ground that moved and echoed to my pulses, and a
part of the enormous darkness that I could see above me.
I was not even sure if my eyes were open. My last vision, I
thought, feebly, and my heart's desire. My heart's desire
was always this, to hear, before I died, the music of the
stars...

Then I knew where I was. There must be people near
me; I could hear voices talking softly, but seemingly at
a great distance, like voices when one is sick with fever.
Servants were carrying the litter; their arms brushed me
with warmth, the beat in the ground was the soft tread
of their sandals. This was no vision lighted by the singing
spheres; I was only a sick old man, earth-bound, being

carried home by stages, in the helpless silence of my malady. The music of the stars was no more than the bells on the harness of the mules.

How long it took I cannot tell. At length the litter levelled at the head of a long climb, and an archway of warm firelight met me, and more people, and voices everywhere, and someone weeping, and I knew that somehow, out of another falling-fit of the malady, I had been brought home to Bryn Myrddin.

More confusion after that. Sometimes I thought that Nimuë and I were still on our travels; I was showing her the streets of Byzantium, or walking with her on the heights above Berytus. She brought me the drugs she had made, and held them to my mouth. It was her own mouth that was on mine, tasting of strawberries, and her lips murmured sweet incantations above me, and the cave filled with smoke from handfuls of the precious frankincense. There were candles everywhere: in their mellow wavering light my merlin perched on the ledge by the cave's entrance, waiting for the god's breath on his feathers. Galapas sat by the brazier, drawing my first maps for me in the dust, and beside them, now, knelt the boy Ninian, poring over them with his grave and gentle eyes. Then he looked up, and I saw that it was Arthur, vivid and impatient, and ten years old ... and then Ralf, young and sullen ... and then at last the boy Merlin, going at his master's bidding up into the crystal cave. And so came the visions; I saw them again, the dreams that had first stormed into my child's brain here in this very cave. And this time Nimuë held my hand, and saw them with me, star for star, and held the cordial afterwards to my lips, while Galapas and the child Merlin, and Ralf and Arthur and the boy Ninian, faded and vanished like the ghosts they were. Only the memories remained, and they, now, were locked in her brain as they had been in mine, and would be hers for ever.

Through it all, though I had no sense of it, time was

passing, and the days wore through, and still I lay in that strange limbo of helpless body and vividly working mind, while gradually, as a bee sips the honey from a flower, Nimuë the enchantress took from me, drop by drop, the distillation of all my days.

Then one early dawn, with the sound of birds singing outside, and the warm summer breeze bringing the scent of flowers and summer hay into the cave, I woke from a long sleep, and found that the malady had left me. Dream time was over, I was alive, and fully awake.

I was also alone, in darkness, save where a long quill of sunlight drilled through a gap left where they had pulled the tumble of rocks down across the cave-mouth, and had gone away, leaving me in my tomb.

* * *

I had no way of knowing how long I had lain in the waking death. We had been at Rheged in July, and, it was still apparently high summer. Three weeks, or at most a month ...? If it had been longer, I would surely be weaker. As it was, until the last profound sleep, which must have been taken for death, I had been cared for and fed with my own cordials and medicines, so that, though stiff, and very weak, I had every chance of life. There was no hope of my being able to move any of the stones that sealed my tomb, but there was a good chance that I might be able to attract the attention of someone passing this way. The place had been a shrine, time out of mind, and the folk came regularly up the valley with offerings for the god who watched the sacred spring beside the cave. It was possible, now, that they would hold the place even more holy, knowing that Merlin, who had held the High King in his hand, but who had been their own enchanter, giving his time and skill to tend their hurts and those of their animals, was buried here. They had brought gifts daily, of food and wine, while he

was alive; surely they would come with their offerings, to appease the dead?

So, stifling my fear, I raised myself and tried, through the swirling weakness of my new waking state, to judge what I must do.

They had laid me, not in the crystal cave, which was a small hollow high in the wall of the main cavern, but in the main cavern itself, on my own bed. This had been draped in some stuff that felt rich and stiff, and gave back, to the same probe of light, the glimmer of embroidery and precious gems. I fingered the pall that covered me; it was of some thick material, soft and warm, and beautifully woven. My fingers traced the pattern worked on it; the Dragon. And now I could see, at the four corners of the bed, the tall, heavily wrought candlesticks that gave off the gleam of gold. I had been left, apparently, with pomp and with royal honours. Had the King been here, then? I wished I could remember him. And Nimuë? I supposed I had my own prophecies to thank that this was all the burial they had accorded me, and that they had not given me to the earth, or to the fire. The thought was a shiver over the skin, but it prompted me to action. I looked at the candles. Three of them had burned down almost to lumps of shapeless wax, and then died. The other, blown out perhaps by some chance draught, was still a foot or so tall. I put a finger to the nearest, where the wax had run down; it was still soft. Twelve hours, I calculated, or at most fifteen, since they had been lighted, and I had been left here. The place was still warm. If I was to keep alive, it must be kept that way. I leaned back against the stiff pillow, drew the pall with its golden dragon up over my body, fixed my eyes on the dead candle, and thought: we shall see. The simplest of magics, the first I ever learned here in this very place; let us see if this, too, has been taken from me. The effort sent me, exhausted, back into sleep.

I woke to see the sunlight, dim now and rosy, lighting

a far corner of the cave, but the cave itself was full of light. The candle burned steadily, with a warm golden flame. It glimmered on two gold coins lying on the pall; I remembered, vaguely, the weight of them tumbling from my eyes as I woke and moved. It also showed me something more to the purpose; the ritual cakes and wine that had been left beside the bier as offerings to the dead. I spoke aloud to God who kept me, then, sitting on the bier, with the grave-clothes round me, ate and drank what had been left.

The cakes were dry, but tasted of honey, and the wine was strong, running into me like new life. The candlelight, dealing its own faint warmth, dispelled the last wisps of fear. 'Emrys,' I found myself whispering, 'Emrys, child of the light, beloved of kings ... you were told that you would be buried quick in darkness, your power gone; and look, here it has come to pass, and it is not fearful after all; you are buried, and quick, but you have light and air and—unless they have rifled the place— food and drink and warmth and medicines ...'

I lifted the candle from its heavy sconce and carried it into the inner caves which were the storerooms. Everything was just as I had left it. Stilicho had been a more than faithful steward. I thought of the wine and honey-cakes left beside the 'bier', and wondered if, besides, the caverns had been scoured and garnished, then carefully furnished for the dead. Whatever the reason for leaving things as they were, there, row on row, box on box, were the precious stores, and in their places the flasks and jars of drugs and cordials, all that I had not taken with me to Applegarth. There was a real squirrel's hoard of food, dried fruit and nuts, honeycombs gently seeping into their jars, a barrel of olives in oil. No bread, of course, but in a crock I found, bone-hard, some thick oatcake made long ago by the shepherd's wife and given to me; it was still good, being dry as board, so I broke it up and put some of it to sop in wine. The meal garner was half full, and with oil from the olive-barrel I could make

meal cakes of a sort. Water, of course, I had; soon after I had come to take up residence in the cave I had had my servant lead a pipe of water from the spring outside to fill a tank; this, kept covered, ensured clean water even through frost and storm. The overflow, channelled to run down to a fissured corner of a remote inner chamber, served as a privy. There were candles aplenty in store, and tinder with the flints on the ledge where I had always kept them. There was a sizeable pile of charcoal, but I hesitated, for fear of smoke or fumes, to light the brazier. Besides, I might need the warmth in the time ahead. If my reckoning of time were right, in a short month the summer would be over, and autumn setting in with its chill winds and its killing damp.

So at first, while the warm airs of summer still breathed through the cave, I used light only when I needed to see to prepare my food, and for comfort sometimes, when the hours dragged in darkness. I had no books, all having been taken to Applegarth. But writing materials were to hand, and as the days went by and I gained strength and began to fret in the idleness of captivity, I formed the idea of trying to set down in some kind of order the story of my boyhood and the times I had lived through and helped to mould. Music, too, would have been something to be made in darkness, but the standing harp had gone with my books to Applegarth, and my own small harp had not been brought with the other riches, to furnish the house of the dead.

Be sure that I had given thought to escaping from my grave. But those who had laid me there and given me, in honour, the sacred hill itself, with all that lay within it, had used the hill itself to seal me in; half the mountain-side, seemingly, had been levered down to fall across the cave's entrance. Try as I would I could not shove or scrape a way through. No doubt someone with the right tools might have done it in time, but I had none. We kept spades and axes always in the stable below the cliff.

There was another possibility, which I considered time

and again. As well as the caves which I used, there were other, smaller chambers which opened off one another, branching deep into the hill. One of these inner caves was little more than a chimney, a rounded shaft running up through the rock levels, to reach the air in a little corrie of the hill above. Here a low cliff, many years back, had, under the pressure from tree-roots and storms, split open to let light, and sometimes small rocks and rain water, down into the hollow below. Through this fissure, now, the cave-dwelling bats made their daily flights. In time the pile of fallen stones in the cave had built up into a kind of buttress, reaching perhaps a third of the way up towards the 'lantern', as I might term the hole above. When, hopefully, I looked to see if this rough stair had been extended, I was disappointed: above it, still, lay a sheer pitch three times the height of a man, and above that the same again, sloping at first steeply, and then more gently, to reach the gap of daylight. It was just possible that a fit and agile man could have climbed out unaided, though in places the rock was damp and slimy, and in others manifestly unsafe. But for an ageing man, recently in his sick-bed, it was impossible. The sole comfort of the discovery lay in the fact that here, literally, was a 'chimney'; in the cold days to come I could light the brazier there with safety, and savour warmth and hot food and drink.

I did think, naturally, about making a fire of some kind, in the hope that the smoke might attract the attention of the curious, but there were two things against this. First, the country people who lived within sight of the hill were used to seeing the bats go up daily from the hillside, looking for all the world like plumes of smoke; the second was that I had little to spare of fuel. All I could do was conserve the precious stores I had, and wait for someone to make a way up the valley to visit the holy well.

But nobody came. Twenty days, thirty, forty, were notched on my tally stick. I recognised with reluctance

that where the simple folk had come to pray to the spirit of the well, and offer gifts to the living man who healed them, they were afraid of the enchanter lately dead, and of the new haunting of the hollow hill. Since the valley led nowhere but to the cave and the spring, no travellers used it. Nothing came into the high valley, except the birds (which I heard) and, I supposed, the deer, and once a wolf or a fox that I heard snuffling in the night at the tumble of stones that blocked the cave's entrance.

So the tallied days dragged by, and I stayed alive, and —what was harder—kept fear at bay in every way I knew. I wrote, and wrestled with plans for escape, and did what domestic tasks the days demanded; and I am not ashamed to remember that I drugged the nights— and sometimes the desperate days—with wine, or with opiates that stupefied the senses and dulled time. Despair I would not feel; through all that long life in death, I held to one thing, as to a ladder let down from the light above me: throughout my life I had obeyed my god, had received power from him, and rendered it back again; now I had seen it pass to the young lover who had usurped me; but though my life was apparently done, my body had been kept—I could not tell how or why—from either earth or fire. I was alive, and had regained both strength and will, and, prison or no, this was the hollow hill of the god himself. I could not believe that there was not some purpose still to be fulfilled.

I think it was with this in mind that I nerved myself at length to climb into the crystal cave.

All this while, with my strength at low ebb and the power (I knew) gone from me, I had not been able to face the place of vision. But one evening when, with my store of candles running low, I had sat too long in darkness, I brought myself at last to climb the ledge at the back of the main cavern, and, bent double, to creep into the crystal-lined globe.

I went, I believe, for nothing more than the comfortable memories of past power, and of love. I took no light

with me, and looked for no vision. I simply lay, as I had done when a boy, belly down on the rough crystals of the floor, letting the heavy silence enclose me, and filling it with my thoughts.

What they were I cannot now remember: I suppose I was praying. I do not think I spoke aloud. But in a while I became conscious—as, in a black night, a man realises, rather than sees, the coming dawn—of something that answered to my breathing. Not a sound, only the faintest echo of a breath, as if a ghost was waking, taking life from mine.

My heart began to thud; my breathing sharpened. Within the darkness the other rhythm quickened. The air of the cave hummed. Round the crystal walls ran, echoing, a whisper that I knew.

I felt the easy tears of weakness start into my eyes. I said aloud: 'So, after all, they brought you back to your own place?' And, from the darkness, my harp answered me.

I groped forward towards the sound. My fingers met the live, silken feel of wood. The carved fore-pillar nestled into my hand as I had seen the hilt of the great sword slide into the King's grip. I backed out of the cave, silenced the harp's faint plaining against my breast, and picked my way carefully down again into my prison.

*   *   *

This was the song I made. I called it *Merlin's Song from the Grave.*

> *Where have they gone, the bright ones?*
> *I remember the sunlight*
> *And a great wind blowing;*
> *A god who answered me,*
> *Leaning out from the high stars;*
> *A star that shone for me,*
> *A voice that spoke to me,*

A hawk that guided me,
A shield that sheltered me;
And a clear way to the gate
Where they wait for me,
Where surely they wait for me?

The day wanes,
The wind dies.
They are gone, the bright ones.
Only I remain.

What use to call to me
Who have neither shield nor star?
What use to kneel to me
Who am only the shadow
Of his shadow,
Only the shadow
Of a star that fell
Long ago.

* * *

No song comes brand-fire-new and finished from the first playing, so that now I cannot recall just on which occasion, as I was singing it, I became conscious of an unusual sound that had been, as it were, tapping at the door of my brain for several staves. I let the chords die, laid a hand along the strings, and listened.

The beating of my heart sounded loud in the still, dead air of the cave. Below it went another throbbing, a distant beat coming seemingly from the heart of the hill. I can hardly be blamed, shut as I had been for too long from the ordinary traffic of the world, if the first thoughts that came crowding were winged with instinct born of ancient beliefs—Llud of the Otherworld, the horses of the Wild Hunt, all the shadows dwelling in the hollow hills ... Death for me at long last, on this still evening at the

end of summer? Then, in less time than it takes for two short breaths, I had arrived at the truth—and it was already too late.

It was the traveller I had waited for, and at length despaired of; he had ridden up above the cave, and halted by the cliff where the 'lantern' opened on the air, and had heard the music. There was a pause, broken only by the sharp strike of nervous hoofs on stone as the horse fretted, held and sidling. Then a man's voice, calling out:

'Is there anyone there?'

I had already laid the harp aside and, with what speed I could, was scrambling through the half dark towards the cave below him. As I went I tried to call out, but it was a moment or so before my thudding heart and dry throat would let me answer. Then I cried out:

'It is I, Merlin! Don't be afraid, I'm no ghost. I'm alive, and trapped here. Break a way out for me, in the King's name!'

My voice was drowned by the sudden confusion of noise from above. I could guess what had happened. The horse, sensing, as beasts do, some strangeness—a man below ground, the unnatural sounds coming apparently from the fissure in the cliff, even my anxiety—gave a long, pealing whinny, and plunged, scattering stones and small gravel and setting other echoes rattling. I shouted again, but either the rider did not hear, or he took the horse's fear for an instinct truer than his own; there was another sharp clatter of hoofs and cascading stones, then the beating gallop retreated, faster than it had come. I could not blame the rider, whoever he was; even if he did not know whose tomb lay beneath him, he must have known the hill was sacred, and to hear music from the ground, at dusk, on the crest of such a hill ...

I went back to pick up the harp. It was undamaged. I put it aside, and with it the hope of rescue, then set myself grimly to prepare what could, for want of a worse word, be called my supper.

CHAPTER 3

It was perhaps two nights after this, or maybe three, when something woke me in the night. I opened my eyes on total darkness, wondering what had disturbed me. Then I heard the sound. Stealthy scrapings, rattlings of stone, the patter of earth falling. They came from the 'lantern', high in the inner cave. Some beast, I thought, badger or fox or even wolf, scratching its way towards the smell of food. I drew the covers round me, and turned over and shut my eyes again.

But the sounds went on, stealthy, persistent, and now impatient, a fierce scrabbling among the stones that spoke of more than animal purpose. I sat up again, taut with sudden hope. Perhaps the horseman had come back? Or he had told his story, and some other, braver soul had come to investigate? I took breath to shout, then paused. I did not want to scare this one away like the first. I would wait for him to speak to me.

He did not; he was intent merely on scraping his way in through the opening in the cliff. More stuff fell, and I heard the chink of a crowbar, and then, unmistakably, a smothered curse. A man's voice, rough-spoken. There was a pause, as if he was listening, then once again the sounds began, and this time he was using some sort of heavy tool, a mattock or a spade, to dig his way in.

Not for worlds would I have shouted now. No one bent simply on investigating a strange story would do so in such stealthy secrecy; the obvious thing to do would be what the horseman had done, to call out first, or to wait quietly and listen, before attempting to force a way into the lantern. What was more, no innocent man would

have come, for choice, alone and at night.

A few moments' reflection brought me the probable truth. This was a grave-robber; some outlaw, perhaps, who had heard rumours of a royal grave in Merlin's Hill, and who had doubtless had a look at the cave-mouth, decided it was too thoroughly blocked, and had settled on the shaft as being the easier and less conspicuous way of entry. Or perhaps a local man who had watched the rich procession pass, and who had known for years of the cliff and its precarious entry to the hill. Or even a soldier—one of those who, after the ceremonies, had helped to block the cave-mouth, and who had been haunted since by recollections of the riches there entombed.

Whoever he was, he must be a man of few nerves. He would be fully prepared to find a corpse laid here; to brave the stench and sight of a body some weeks dead; even to lay hands on it and rob it of its jewels before he tumbled it from the gem-encrusted pall and gold-fringed pillow. And if he should find, instead of a corpse, a living man? An old man, weakened by these long days underground; a man, moreover, whom the world believed to be dead? The answer was simple. He would kill me, and still rob my tomb. And I, stripped of my power, had no defences.

I rose silently from the bed, and made my way through to the shaft. The digging sounds went on, steadily now, and through the widened opening at the top of the shaft I could see light. He had some sort of lantern there, which dealt him light enough. It would also prevent him from noticing the faint glimmer of a rush-light from below. I went back to the main chamber, kindled a light carefully behind a screen, then set about the only preparations I could make.

If I lay in wait for him with a knife (I had no dagger, but there were knives for preparing food) or with some heavy implement, it was by no means certain that I would be quick enough, or powerful enough, to stun him; and

such an attack would make my own end certain. I had
to find another way. I considered it, coldly. The only
weapon I had was one that in times past I had found to
be more powerful than either dagger or cudgel. The
man's own fear.

I took the blankets off the bed and folded them out
of sight. I spread the jewelled pall over, smoothed it, and
set the velvet pillow in place. The gold candlesticks still
stood where they had been put, at the four corners of the
bed. Beside the bed I set the gold goblet that had held
the wine, and the silver platter studded with garnets. I
took the gold coins, the ferryman's fee, from where I had
laid them, wrapped myself in the king's mantle that they
had left for me, blew out the light, and lay down on the
pall.

A rending sound from the shaft, a scatter of rubble
onto the cavern floor, and with it a rush of fresh night
air, told me that he was through. I shut my eyes, placed
the gold coins on the lids, smoothed the long folds of my
mantle, then crossed my arms on my breast, controlled my
breathing as best I could, and waited.

It was perhaps the hardest thing I have ever done.
Often before I had faced danger, but never without knowing one way or the other what the risks were. Always
before, in times of stress or terror—the fight with Brithael,
the ambush in the Wild Forest—I had known there was
pain to face, but in the end victory and safety and a cause
won; now, I knew nothing. This stealthy murder in the
dark, for a few jewels, might indeed be the ignominious
end which the gods, with their sidelong smiles, had
showed me in the stars as my 'burial quick in the tomb'.
It was as they willed. But, I thought (not coolly at all), if
I have ever served you, God my god, let me smell the
sweet air once more before I die.

There was a soft thud as he landed in the shaft. He must
have a rope with him, tied to one of the trees that grew
from the cliff. I had been right; he was alone. Faintly,
under the weight of the gold on my eyelids, I could see

the warming of the dark that meant he had brought his
lantern with him. Now he was feeling his way, carefully,
across the uneven floor towards the chamber where I
lay. I could smell his sweat, and the reek of the cheap
lantern; which meant, I thought with satisfaction, that
he would not catch the lingering odours of food and
wine, or the smell of the recently doused rushlight. And
his breathing gave him away; with even greater satisfaction I knew that, bravado or no, he was afraid.

He saw me, and stopped in his tracks. I heard his
breath go in as harshly as a death-rattle. He had nerved
himself, one would guess, to face a decaying corpse, but
here was a body like that of a living, or newly-dead man.
For seconds he stood, hesitating, breathing hard, then,
remembering perhaps what he had heard of the embalm-
ers' art, he cursed again softly under his breath, and tip-
toed forward. The light shook and swung in his hand.

With the smell and sound of his fear my own calmness
grew. I breathed smoothly and shallowly, trusting to the
wavering of his lantern and its smoking light not to let
him see that the corpse moved. For an age, it seemed, he
stood there, but at last, with another sharp rattle of
breath and an abrupt movement like a horse under the
spur, he forced himself forward to my side. A hand, unsteady and damp with cold sweat, plucked the gold coins
off my eyelids.

I opened my eyes.

In that one brief flash, before movement or blink or
breath, I took it all in; the dark Celtic face lit by the
horn lantern, the coarse clothing of some peasant levy,
the pitted skin slithering with sweat, the greedy slack
mouth and the stupid eyes, the knife in his belt, razor-
sharp.

I said, calmly: 'Welcome to the hall of the dead,
soldier.'

And from its dark corner, at the sound of my voice, the
harp whispered something, on a sweet, fading note.

The gold coins fell, ringing, and rolled away into dark-

ness. The lantern followed, to be smashed into smoking oil on the floor. He let out a yell of fear such as I have not often heard in my long life, and once again, from the darkness, came the mockery of the harp. Yelling again, he took to his heels and ran, stumbling blindly out of the cave and making for the shaft. He must have made a first vain attempt to climb his rope; he cried out again as he fell heavily back to the rock-strewn floor. Then fear lent him strength; I heard the sobbing breaths of effort receding upwards as he swarmed to the top. His footsteps ran and slipped down the hillside. Then the sounds died, and I was alone again, and safe.

Safe, in my grave. He had taken the rope. In fear, perhaps, that the enchanter's ghost could swarm after him and follow, he had dragged it up after him. The gap he had made showed a ragged window of sky, where a star shone, remote and pure and indifferent. Cool air blew in, and the cold, unmistakable smell of dawn coming. I heard a thrush from the cliff-top.

God had answered me. I had smelled the sweet air again, and heard the sweet bird. And life was as far from me as before.

I went back into the inner chamber and, as if nothing had happened, began my preparations for another day.

* * *

And another. And a third. On the third day, having eaten and rested and written and calmed my mind as far as I could, I once more examined the chimney shaft. The wretched grave-robber had left me a shred of new hope; the pile of fallen stones was higher by almost three feet, and, though he had pulled his rope up after him, he had left me another, which I found lying, loosely coiled, at the base of the shaft. But the hopes that this raised were soon proved false; the rope was of poor quality, a cord no more than four or five cubits in length. I could only assume that he had intended to tie his spoils together— he could never have hoped to carry even one of the

candlesticks out with him on his climb—fasten them to the main rope's end, draw them after him. I calculated that, even to bear away the four candlesticks, the thief would have had to make four journeys up and down the shaft. The cord would never, even had it been long enough to throw and loop over some rocky projection, have been strong enough to bear my weight. Nor could I—scanning yet again the damp and crumbling side of the chimney—see any such safe projection or foothold. It was possible that a young man or an agile boy might have managed the climb, but although I had been a strong man all my life, with a strong man's endurance, I had never been an athlete, and now, with age and illness and privation, the climb was quite beyond me.

One other thing the thief had done: where, before, I would have had to reach the high lantern and then set to work to dig and scrabble a way through—an impossible task without tools and ladder—now the way lay open. All I had to do was get to it. And I had a length of good cord. It would come hard, I thought, if I could not contrive some kind of scaffolding which would take me as far as the sloping section of the chimney, and from there, perhaps, I might be able to rig some kind of makeshift ladder. Much of the cave's furnishing had gone, but there was still the bed, a stool or two, and a table, the casks, and a stout bench forgotten in a corner. If I could find some way to break them up, fasten the pieces together with cord, or with torn strips of blanket, wedge them with sherds from the storage jars ...

All the rest of that day, and the next following, working directly under the light thrown down from above, I toiled at my makeshift scaffold, bearing a wry thought for Tremorinus, my father's chief engineer, who had first taught me my craft. He would have laughed to see the great Merlin, the engineer-artificer who had outpaced his master, and had lifted the Hanging Stones of the Giants' Dance, cobbling together a structure of which the sorriest apprentice would have been ashamed. All I

needed to do, he would have said, was to take my harp
like Orpheus, and play to the fragments of the broken
furniture, and watch it build itself like the walls of
Troy. This had been his theory, stoutly held in public,
about the way I had managed the lifting of the great
trilithons of the Dance.

By nightfall of the second day I had rigged a sort of
rough scaffolding roofed with the stout plank of the
bench, which might serve as a base for a ladder. It was
nine feet high, and fixed firmly enough with a pile of
stones holding it in place. I had only, I reckoned, another
twenty-five feet to build.

I worked until dusk, then lighted the lantern and
made my wretched meal. Then, as a man turns to the
comfort of a lover, I lifted the harp into my arms and,
without thoughts of Orpheus or Troy, played until my
eyelids drooped, and a false chord warned me that it
was time to sleep. Tomorrow would be another day.

*   *   *

Who could have guessed what kind of day? Tired from
my labours, I slept deeply, and woke later than usual to
the light of a bright thread of sunshine, and the sound
of someone calling my name.

For a moment I lay still, thinking myself still caught
in the mists of a dream that had mocked me so often
before, but then I came fully awake to the discomfort of
the cavern floor (I had broken my bed up for use) and
the voice again. It came from the lantern, a man's voice,
overpitched with nerves, but with something familiar
about the queerly accented Latin.

'My lord? My lord Merlin? Are you there, my lord?'
'*Here! Coming!*'

In spite of aching joints, I was on my feet as swiftly as
any boy, and ran to the foot of the shaft.

Sunshine was pouring down from above. I picked my
way, stumbling, to the foot of the rude structure that

almost filled the base of the shaft. I craned upwards.

Framed in the gap of brilliant sky was a man's head and shoulders. At first I could distinguish little against the brightness. Me, he must be able to see clearly, unkempt, bearded, no doubt pale as the ghost he must have feared to see. I heard his shivering gasp of breath, and the head drew back.

I cried out: 'Stay for me, for God's sake! I'm no ghost! Stay! Help me out of here! Stilicho, stay!'

Almost without thinking, I had identified his accent, and him with it. My old servant, the Sicilian, Stilicho, who had married Mai, the miller's daughter, and kept the mill on the Tywy at the valley's foot. I knew his kind, credulous, superstitious, easily afraid of what they did not understand. I leaned against the upright of the scaffolding, gripped it with shaking hands, and fought for a composure that would reassure him. His head came cautiously back. I saw the black eyes staring, the sallow pallor of his face, the open mouth. With a self-control that shook me with another wave of weakness I spoke in his own language, slowly and with apparent calm:

'Don't be afraid, Stilicho. I was not dead when they left me here in error, and all these weeks I have been trapped here in the hill. I am not a ghost, boy; it truly is Merlin, alive, and very much in need of your help.'

He leaned nearer. 'Then the King—all those others who were here—?' He stopped, swallowing painfully.

'Do you think that a ghost could have built this scaffolding?' I asked him. 'I hadn't despaired of escaping. I've lived here in hope, all through these weeks, but by the God of all gods, Stilicho, if you leave me now without helping me from here, I swear I shall be dead before the day is out.' I stopped, ashamed.

He cleared his throat. He sounded shaken, as well he might, but scared no longer. 'Then it really is you, lord? They said you were dead and buried, and we have been mourning you ... but we should have known that your magic would keep you from death.'

I shook my head. I forced myself to go on talking, knowing that with every word he was coming nearer to accepting my survival as true, and nerving himself to approach the tomb and its living ghost.

'Not magic,' I said, 'it was the malady that deceived you all. I am no longer an enchanter, Stilicho, but I have God to thank that I am still a strong man. Otherwise these weeks below the earth would surely have killed me. Now, my dear, can you get me out? Later we can talk, and decide what's to be done, but now, for God's sake, help me out of here and into the air . . .'

It was a grim business, and it took a long time, not least because, when he would have left me to go for help, I begged him, in terms of which I am now ashamed, not to leave me. He did not argue, but set himself to knotting the long, stout rope which he had found still attached to an ash sapling in the rock above the lantern. He finished it with a loop for my foot, then lowered it carefully. It reached the platform, with some length to spare. Then he let himself down into the shaft, and in a short space of time was beside me at the foot of the scaffolding. I think he would have gone on his knees, as his habit had been, to kiss my hands, but I gripped him so tightly that instead he held me, supporting me with his young strength, and then helped me back into the main cavern.

He found the one remaining stool for me, then lit the lantern and brought me wine, and after a while I was able to say, with a smile: 'So now you know that I am a solid body, and no ghost? It was brave of you to come at all, and braver still to stay. What on earth brought you to this place? You're the last person who I'd have thought would go visiting a tomb.'

'I wouldn't have come at all,' he said frankly, 'but that something I heard made me wonder if you were not dead after all, but living here alone. I knew you were a great magician, and thought that perhaps your magic would not let you die like other men.'

'Something you heard? What was that?'

'You know the man I have to help me at the mill, Bran, he's called? Well, he was in the town yesterday, and brought home some tale of a fellow who'd drunk himself silly in one of the taverns, and the story was going about that he had been up to Bryn Myrddin, and that the enchanter had come out of the tomb and spoken to him. People were standing him drinks and asking for more, and of course the tale as he told it was plainly lies, but there was enough to make me wonder ...' He hesitated. 'What did happen, lord? I knew someone had been here, because of the rope on the tree.'

'It happened twice,' I told him. 'The first time it was a horseman riding over the hill ... you can see how long ago, I marked it on the tally yonder. He must have heard me playing; the sound would carry up through the hole in the cliff. The second time was four—five?—days since, when some ruffian came to rob the tomb, and opened the cliff as you saw it, and let himself down with the rope.' I told him what had happened. 'He must have been too scared to stop and untie his rope. It's a mercy you heard his story, and came up before he got his courage back, and came back for it—and perhaps dared the tomb again.'

He gave me a sidelong, shamefaced look. 'I'll not pretend to you, lord. It's not right you praising me for courage. I came up yesterday evening. I didn't want to come alone, but I was ashamed to bring Bran, and Mai wouldn't go within a mile of the place ... Well, I saw the mouth of the cave was just as it had been, and then I heard the harp. I—I turned and ran home. I'm sorry.'

I said, gently: 'But you came back.'

'Yes. I couldn't sleep all night. You remember when you left me once to guard the cave, and you showed me your harp, and how it played sometimes by itself, just with the air moving? And how you gave me courage, and showed me the crystal cave and told me I would be safe there? Well, I thought of all that, and I thought of the times you were good to me, how you took me out of slavery and gave me freedom and the life I have now. And

I thought, even if it is my lord's ghost, or the harp playing by magic, alone in the hollow hill, he would never harm me ... So I came again, but this time I came by daylight. I thought, if it is a ghost, then in sunlight it will be sleeping.'

'And so I was.' The thought touched me, like a cold dagger's point, that if I had drugged myself last night, as I had done so often done, I might have heard nothing.

He was going on: 'I walked over the hill this time, and I saw the new broken stone showing white in the corrie where the little air-shaft comes out. I went to look. I saw the rope then, tied to the ash tree, and the big gap in the cliff, and when I looked down the shaft, I saw the' —he hesitated—'the thing you built there.'

I had not thought to feel amusement ever again. 'That is a builder's scaffold, Stilicho.'

'Yes, of course. Well, I thought, no ghost made that. So I shouted. That's all.'

'Stilicho,' I said, 'if ever I did anything for you, be sure you have paid me a thousand times over. In fact, you have saved me twice over. Not only today; if you hadn't left the place the way I found it, I should have died weeks back, from starvation and cold. I shall not forget it.'

'We've got to get you out of here now. But how?' He looked around him at the stripped cave and the broken furnishings. 'Now we've spoken, and you're feeling stronger, lord, shall I not go and bring men and tools, and open the doorway for you? It would be the best way, truly it would.'

'I know that, but I think not. I've had time now to consider. Until I know how things stand in the kingdoms, I can't suddenly "come to life". That is how the common people will see it, if Prince Merlin comes back from the tomb. No part of the story must be told until the King knows. So, until we can get a private message to him—'

'He's gone to Brittany, they say.'

'So?' I thought for a moment. 'Who is Regent?'

'The Queen, with Bedwyr.'

A pause, while I looked down at my hands. Stilicho was sitting cross-legged on the floor. In the lantern's light he looked still much like the boy I had known. The dark Byzantine eyes watched me.

I wetted my lips. 'The Lady Nimuë? Do you know who I mean? She—'

'Oh, yes, all the world knows her. She has magic, as you used to—as you have, lord. She is always near the King. She lives near Camelot.'

'Yes,' I said. 'Well, I am sorry, my dear, but I cannot have it known before the King comes back from Brittany. Somehow, between us, we shall have to get me out of the shaft. I have no doubt that, if you will bring the tools up out of the stable, we'll manage something.'

And so we did. He was back in something under half an hour with nails and tools and the small stock of timber that had been left in the stable. It was a bad half hour for me: I had no doubts that he would return, but the reaction was so intense that, left alone again, I sat there on the stool, sweating and shaking like a fool. But by the time the stuff was pitched down the shaft, with himself following it, I had myself in hand, and we set to work, and, with me sitting idly on the stool watching and directing, he put together a ladder of a sort and fixed it to the platform I had made. This reached the sloping section of the chimney. Here, as an adjunct to the knotted rope, he cut pieces of wood which, with the help of cracks and protuberances of rock he wedged at intervals against the side of the chimney to act, if not as steps, then as resting-places where one could set a knee.

When all was done he tested it, and while he did so I wrapped the harp in the remaining blanket, and with it my manuscripts and a few of the drugs that I might need to restore my strength fully. He climbed out with them. Finally I took a knife and cut the best of the jewels off the pall, and dropped them, together with the gold coins,

into a leather bag which had held herbs. I slipped the thong of the bag over my wrist, and was waiting at the scaffold's foot when at last Stilicho reappeared at the top, laid hold of the rope, and called for me to begin my climb.

CHAPTER 4

I stayed a month with Stilicho at the mill. Mai, who had held me formerly in trembling awe, once she saw that this was no terrifying wizard, but a man sick and in need of care, looked after me devotedly. I saw no one beside these two. I kept to the upper chamber they gave me—it was their own, the best, they would hear of nothing else. The hired man slept out in the granary sheds, and knew only that some ageing relative of the miller's was staying there. The children were told the same, and accepted me without question, as children will.

At first I kept to my bed. The reaction from the recent weeks was a severe one; I found daylight trying, and the noises of every day hard to bear—the men's voices in the yard as the grain barges came in to the wharf, hoofs on the roadway, the shouts of the children playing. At first the very act of talking to Mai or Stilicho came hard, but they showed all the gentleness and understanding of simple folk, so things gradually became easier, and I began to feel myself again. Soon I left my bed, and began to spend time with my writing, and, calling the elder of the children to me, began to teach them their letters. In time I even came to welcome Stilicho's ebullience, and questioned him eagerly about what had happened since I had been shut away.

Of Nimuë he knew little beyond what he had already told me. I gathered that her reputation for magic, in the weeks since my going, had grown so quickly that the mantle of the King's enchanter had fallen naturally upon her shoulders. She spent some of her time at Applegarth, but since the Lady's death had gone back to the Island

shrine, to be accepted without question as the new Lady of the place. One rumour seemed to indicate that the status of the Lady would change with her; she did not remain on the Island, a maiden among maidens: she paid frequent visits to the court at Camelot, and there was talk of a probable marriage. Stilicho could not tell me who the man was said to be. 'But of course,' he said, 'he will be a king.'

With this I had to be content. There was little other news. Most of the men who came up-river to the mill were simple workmen, or barge-masters, whose knowledge was only local, and who cared for little beyond getting a good price for the goods they carried. All I could gather was that the times were still prosperous; the kingdom was at peace; the Saxons kept to their treaties. And the High King, in consequence, had felt free to go abroad.

Why, Stilicho did not know. And this did not, for the moment, matter to me, except that it must mean my own continued secrecy. I thought the matter over again, after my return to health, and the conclusions I came to were the same. No purpose could be served by my public return to affairs. Even the 'miracle' of a return from the grave would do no more for the kingdom and its High King than my 'death' and the transfer of power had done. I had no power or vision to bring him; it would be wrong to indulge in a return that would tend to discredit Nimuë as my successor, without bringing anything fresh or even valid to Arthur's service. I had made my farewells, and my legend, such as it was, had already begun to gather way. So much I could understand from the tales that, according to Stilicho, had already added themselves to the grave-robber's tale of the enchanter's ghost.

As for Nimuë, the same arguments applied. With what wisdom I could command in the matter, I saw that the love we had had together was already a thing of the past. I could not go back, expecting to claim again the place I had had with her, and to tie jesses to the feet of a falcon already in flight. Something else held me back,

something I would not recognise in daylight, but which mocked me in dreams with old prophecies buzzing around like stinging flies. What did I know of women, even now? When I remembered the steady draining of my power, the last, desperate weakness, the trance-like state in which I had lain before the final desertion in darkness, I asked myself what that love had been but the bond that held me to her, and bade me give her all I owned? And even when I recalled her sweetness, her generous worship, her words of love, I knew (and it took no vision to do so) that she would not lay her power down now, even to have me back again.

It was hard to make Stilicho understand my reluctance to reappear, but he did accept my desire to wait for Arthur's return before making plans. From his references to Nimuë he was obviously not yet aware that she had been more to me than a pupil who had taken up the master's charge.

At length, feeling myself again, and not wanting to impose any longer on Stilicho's little household, I prepared to set off for Northumbria, and set Stilicho to make arrangements for me. I decided to go north by sea. A sea voyage is something I never willingly undertake, but by road it would be a long, hard journey, with no guarantee of continued fine weather, and besides, I could hardly have gone alone; Stilicho would have insisted upon accompanying me, even though at this time of year he could ill be spared from the mill. Indeed, he tried to insist on going with me by ship, but in the end let himself be overruled; this not only by expedience, but because I think he believed me still to be the 'great enchanter' whom he had served in the past with such awe and pride. In the end I had my way, and one morning early I went quietly downstream on one of the barges, and embarked at Maridunum on a north-bound coastal ship.

I had sent no message to Blaise in Northumbria, because there was no courier I could trust with the news

of 'Merlin's return from the dead'. I would think of some way to prepare him when I came near the place. It was even possible that he had not yet heard news of my death; he lived so retired from the world—held to the times only by my dispatches—that it was conceivable that he had only just unrolled my last letter from Applegarth.

This, as it turned out, was the fact; but I did not find out yet for a while. I did not get to Northumbria, but travelled no further north than Segontium.

The ship put in there, on a fine, still morning. The little town sunned itself at the edge of the shining strait, its clustered houses dwarfed by the great walls of the Roman-built fortress that had been the headquarters of the Emperor Maximus. Across the strait the fields of Mona's Isle showed golden in the sun. Behind the town, a little way beyond the fortress walls, stood the remains of the tower that was known as Macsen's Tower. Near by was the site of the ruined temple of Mithras, where years ago I had found the King's sword of Britain, and where, deep under the rubble of the floor and the ruined altar of the god, I had left the rest of Macsen's treasure, the lance and the grail. This was the place I had promised to show Nimuë on our way home from Galava. Beyond the tower the great Snow Hill, Y Wyddfa, reared against the sky. The first white of winter was on its crest, and its cloud-haunted sides, even on that golden day, showed purple-black with scree and dead heather.

We nosed in to the wharf. There were goods to unload, and this would take time, so I went thankfully ashore, and, after a word at the harbour-master's office, made for the wharfside inn. There I could have a meal, and watch the loading and unloading of my ship.

I was hungry, and likely to get hungrier. My idea of any sea voyage, however calm, is to get below and stay below, without food or drink, until it is over. The harbour-master had told me that the ship would not sail before the evening tide, so there was ample time to rest

and make ready for the next dreaded stage of the journey. It did cross my mind to wish I might have time to make my way up once again to the temple of Mithras, but I put the thought aside. Even if I were to revisit the place, I would not disturb the treasure. It was not for me. Besides, the privations of the journey had tired me, and I needed food. I made for the inn.

This was built round three sides of a court, the fourth being open to the wharf, for the convenience, I suppose, of carrying goods straight from the ships into the inn's storerooms, which served as warehouses for the town. There were benches and stout wooden tables under the overhanging eaves of the open courtyard, but, fine though the weather was, it was not warm enough to persuade me to eat out of doors. I found my way into the main room, where a log fire burned, and ordered food and wine. (I had paid my passage with—appropriately—one of the gold coins which had been the 'ferryman's fee'; this had left me change besides, and caused the ship's master to accord me a respect which my apparent style hardly called for.) Now, the servant hastened to serve me with a good meal, of mutton and fresh bread, with a flask of rough red wine such as seamen like, then left me in peace to enjoy the warmth of the fire and watch through the open door the scene at the quay-side.

The day wore through. I was more tired than I had realised. I dozed, then woke, and dozed again. Over at the wharf the work went on, with creak of windlass and rattle of chain and straining of ropes as the cranes swung the bales and sacks inboard. Overhead the gulls wheeled and cried. Now and again an ox-cart creaked by on clumsy wheels.

There was little coming and going in the inn itself. Once, a woman crossed the courtyard with a basket of washing on her head, and a boy hurried through with a batch of bread. There was another party staying, it seemed, in chambers to the right of the court. A fellow in slave's dress hurried in from the town, carrying a flat

basket covered with a linen cloth. He vanished through a doorway, and a short while later some children came running out, boys, well dressed but noisy, and with some kind of outlandish accent I could not place. Two of them—twins by their look—settled down on the sunlit flagstones for a game of knucklebones, while the other two, though ill matched for age and size, started some kind of mock fight with sticks for swords, and old box-lids for shields. Presently a decent-looking woman, whom I took to be their nurse, came out of the same doorway and sat down on a bench in the sun to watch them. From the way the boys, now and then, ran to gaze towards the wharf, I guessed that their party was perhaps waiting to join my ship, or continue its voyage on another vessel that was tied up a few lengths away along the quay.

From where I was sitting I could see the master of my ship, and at his elbow some sort of tallyman with stilus and wax. The latter had written nothing for some time, and on board the activity seemed to have ceased. It would soon be time to get back to my uneasy bed below decks, and wait miserably until the light breezes carried us northward on the next stage of the journey.

I got to my feet. As I did so I saw the master raise his head, with a movement like that of a dog sniffing the air. Then he swung round to look upwards at the inn roof. Straight above my head I heard the long creak of the weather vane swinging round, then whining to and fro in small uneasy arcs as the suddenly rising breeze of evening caught it. To and fro it went, then settled into silence in front of a steady wind. The wind went across the harbour like a grey shadow over the water, and in its wake the moored ships swayed, and ropes sang and rattled against the masts like drumsticks. Beside me the fire flickered and then roared up the open chimney. The master, with a gesture of impatient anger, strode for the ship's gangway, calling out orders. Mingled with my own annoyance was relief; the seas would roughen quickly in this wind, but I would not be on them. With the

fickle violence of autumn, the wind had veered. The ship could not sail. The fresh wind was blowing straight from the north.

I walked across to speak to the master, who, watching the sailors stow and rope the cargo against the new weather, glumly confirmed that there was no question of sailing until the wind blew our way again. I sent a boy to bring up my gear, and went back to bespeak a room at the inn. That there would be one vacant I knew, for the ill wind had apparently blown good for the other lodgers in the place. I could see sailors making ready on the other ship, and back at the inn there was a rush and bustle of preparation. The children had vanished from the courtyard, and presently reappeared, cloaked and warmly shod, the smallest boy holding his nurse's hand, the others frolicking around her, lively and noisy and obviously excited at the prospect of the voyage. They waited, skipping with impatience, while the slave I had seen, with another to help him, came out loaded with baggage, followed by a man in the livery of a chamber-groom, sharp-voiced and authoritative. They must be people of consequence, in spite of their strange speech. About the tallest of the boys, I thought, there was something vaguely familiar. I stood in the shadow of the inn's main doorway, watching them. The innkeeper had bustled up now, to be paid by the chamber-groom, and then a woman, his wife, perhaps, came running with a package. I heard the word 'laundry', then the two of them backed away from the doorway with bow and curtsy, as the principal guest at length emerged from the chamber.

It was a woman, cloaked from head to foot in green. She was slightly built, but bore herself proudly. I caught the gleam of gold at her wrist, and there were jewels at her throat. Her cloak was lined and edged with red fox fur, deep and rich, and the hood, too. This was thrown back on her shoulders, but I could not see her face; she was turned away, speakng to someone behind her in the room.

Another woman came out carefully, carrying a box. This was wrapped in linen, and seemed heavy. She was plainly dressed, like a waiting woman. If the box contained her mistress's jewels, these were persons of consequence indeed.

Then the lady turned, and I knew her. It was Morgause, Queen of Lothian and Orkney. There could be no mistake. The lovely hair had lost its rose-gold glimmer, and had darkened to rose-brown, and her body had thickened with child-bearing, but the voice was the same, and the long slant of the eyes, and the pretty, folded mouth. So the four sturdy boys, ruddy and clamorous with the outlandish accent of the north, were her children by Lot of Lothian, Arthur's enemy.

I had no eyes for them now. I was watching the doorway. I wondered if, at last, I was going to see her eldest son, her child by Arthur himself.

He came swiftly out of the doorway. He was taller than his mother, a slim youth who, though I had never seen him before, I would have known anywhere. *Dark hair, dark eyes, and the body of a dancer.* Someone had once said that of me, and he was like me, was Arthur's son Mordred. He paused beside Morgause, saying something to her. His voice was light and pleasant, an echo of his mother's. I caught the words 'ship' and 'reckoning', and saw her nod. She laid her pretty hand on his, and the party started to move off. Mordred glanced at the sky, and spoke again, with what looked like a hint of anxiety. They went by within feet of where I was standing.

I drew back. The movement must have caught her attention, for she glanced up, and for the merest fraction of a moment, her eyes met mine. There was no recognition in them. But as she turned to hurry for the ship I saw her shiver, and draw the furred cloak about her as if she felt the wind suddenly cold.

The train of servants followed, and Lot's children; Gawain, Agravaine, Gaheris, Gareth. They trod over the

gang-plank of the waiting ship.

They were going south, all of them. What Morgause purposed there I could not guess at, but it could be nothing but evil. And I was powerless to stop them, or even to send a message ahead of them, for who would believe a message from the dead?

Then the innkeeper and his wife were beside me, wanting to know my pleasure.

I did not, after all, ask to sleep in the rooms that the Queen of Orkney and her train had just vacated.

* * *

The wind still blew from the north next day, cold, strong, and steady. There was no question of my own ship's continuing north. I thought again of sending some message of warning to Camelot, but Morgause's ship would easily outpace a horseman, and to whom, in any case, could I send? To Nimuë? To Bedwyr or the Queen? I could do nothing until the High King was back in Britain. And, by the same token, while Arthur was stiil abroad, Morgause could do him no evil. I thought about it as I made my way out of the town, and set off along the track that led below the fortress walls towards Macsen's Tower. It would be an ill wind indeed if I could get no good of it at all. Yesterday's rest had refreshed me, and I had the day in hand. So I would use it.

When I had last been in Segontium, that great military city built and fortified by Maximus whom the Welsh call Macsen, it had been all but a ruin. Since then, Cador of Cornwall had repaired and re-fortified it against attackers from Ireland. That had been many years ago, but more recently Arthur had seen to it that Maelgon, his commander in the West, kept it in repair. I was interested to see what had been done, and how; and this, as much as anything else, took me along the valley track. Soon I was well above the town. It was a day of sunshine and chilly wind, and the city lay bright and washed with

colour below me in the arm of the dark-blue sea. Beside the track the fortress walls rose stout and well-kept, and within them I could hear the clash and bustle of an alert and well-maintained garrison. As if I had still been Arthur's engineer, proposing to report to him, I marked all that I saw. Then I came to the south side of the fortress, where ruin and the four winds had been allowed their way, and paused to look up the valley slope towards Macsen's Tower.

There was the track, once trodden by the faithful legionaries, but probably now only used by sheep or goats and their herds. It led up the steep hillside to the swell of stony turf that hid the ancient, underground shrine of Mithras. For more than a hundred years the place had been ruinous, but when I had been there before, the steps that led down to the entrance had still been passable, and the temple itself, though patently unsafe, still recognisable. I started slowly up the track, wondering why, after all, I had come to see it again.

I need not have wondered. It was not there. There was no sign, either of the mound that had hidden the roof, or of the steps that had led downwards. I did not need to look far to find the cause. At the head of the slope where the temple had lain, the restorers of Segontium, levering away the great stones of the fortress wall for their rebuilding, and quarrying here and there for smaller metal, had set half the hillside rolling in a long slope of scree. In this had seeded and grown half a hundred small trees— thorn and ash and blackberry—so that even the track of the fallen scree was hard to trace. And everywhere, like the weft of a loom, the narrow sheep-trods, white with summer dust, criss-crossed the hillside.

I seemed to hear again, faintly, the receding voice of the god.

'Throw down my altar. It is time to throw it down.'

Altar, shrine and all, had vanished into the locked depths of the hill.

* * *

There is something not quite believable about any change of this kind. I stood there for some time, casting about for the bearings I knew. There was no question of the accuracy of my memory; a line straight from Macsen's Tower on the hill above, to the south-west corner of the old fortress, and another, from the Commandant's house to the distant peak of Y Wyddfa, would intersect one another right over the site of the shrine. Now, they intersected one another right in the middle of the scree. I could see where, almost at that very point, the bushes were sparse, and the boulders showed gaps between, as of a space below.

'Lost something?' asked a voice.

I looked round. A boy was sitting perched above me, on a fallen block of stone. He was very young, perhaps ten years old, and very dirty. He was tousled and half-naked, and was chewing a hunk of barley bread. A hazel stick lay near him, and his sheep grazed placidly a little way up the hill.

'A treasure, it seems,' I said.

'What kind of treasure? Gold?'

'It might be. Why?'

He swallowed the last bit of bread. 'What's it worth to you?'

'Oh, half my kingdom. Were you going to help me find it?'

'I've found gold here before.'

'You have?'

'Aye. And once a silver penny. And once a belt buckle. Bronze, that was.'

'It seems your pasture is richer than it looks,' I said, smiling. This had once been a busy road between fortress and temple. The place must be full of such trove. I looked at the boy. His eyes were clear and lively in the dirty face. 'Well,' I added, 'I don't actually want to dig for gold, but if you can help me with some information, there's a copper penny in this for you. Tell me, have you lived here all your life?'

'Aye.'

'Keep sheep in this valley?'

'Aye. Used to come with my brother. Then he got sold to a trader and went on a ship. I keep the sheep now. They're not mine. Master's a big man over to the hill.'

'Do you remember—' I asked it without hope; some of the saplings were surely ten years grown—'do you remember when this landslide came? When they were rebuilding the fort, perhaps?'

A shake of the tousled head. 'It's always been like this.'

'No. It wasn't always like this. When I was here before, many years ago, there was a good track along the hillside here, and deep in the side of the hill, just over yonder, was an underground building. It had once been a temple. In old times the soldiers used to worship Mithras there. Have you never heard tell of it?'

Another shake.

'From your father, perhaps?'

He grinned. 'Tell me who that is, I'll tell you what he said.'

'Your master, then?'

'No. But if it's under there,' a jerk of the head towards the scree, 'I know where. There's water under. Where the water is, that'll be the place, surely?'

'There was no water when I—' I stopped. A prickling ran over my flesh, like a cold draught. 'Water under where?'

'Under the stones. There. Way under. Twice a man's height, by the feel of it.'

I took in the small dirty figure, the bright grey eyes, the hazel stick at his feet. 'You can find water under the ground? With the hazel?'

'It's easiest wi' that. But I get the feeling sometimes, just the same, on my own.'

'And metal? Is that the way you found gold here before?'

'Once. It was a nice bit of a statue or something. A dog, sort of. The master took it off me. If I found some more

now I wouldn't tell him. But mostly it's copper, copper coins. Up there in the old buildings.'

'I see.' I was thinking that when I found the shrine it had already been a deserted ruin for a century or more. But when it was built, no doubt it would have been beside a spring. 'If you will show me where the water lies below the stones, there will be silver in it for you.'

He did not move. I thought he looked wary. 'That's where it is, this treasure you're looking for?'

'I hope so.' I smiled at him. 'But it's nothing that you could find for yourself, child. It would take men with crowbars to shift those stones, and even if you led them to the place, you would get nothing of what they found. If you show me now, I promise that you will be paid.'

He sat still for a moment or two, scuffling his bare feet in the dirt. Then, groping inside the skin kilt that was his only garment, he produced, flat on a dirty palm, a silver coin. 'I was paid, master. There's others knew about the treasure. How was I to know it was yours? I showed them where to dig, and they lifted the stones and took the box away.'

Silence. Here in the lee of the hill the wind had no way. The bright world seemed to spin far away, then steady, and come back. I sat down on a boulder.

'Master?' The boy slipped from his perch and padded downhill. He stopped near me, peering, but still poised warily, as if for flight. 'Master? If I did wrong—'

'You did no wrong. How could you know? No, stay, please, and tell me about it. I shan't hurt you. How could I? Who were they, and how long ago did they take the box away?'

He gave me another doubtful look, then appeared to take me at my word. He spoke eagerly. 'Only two days since. It was two men, I don't know them, slaves they were, and they came with the lady.'

'*The lady?*'

At something in my face he stepped back half a pace, then stood his ground. 'Aye. Came two days ago, she

did. She must have had magic, I think. Went straight to it, like a bitch to the porridge-pot. Pointed almost to the very place, and said "Try there". The two fellows started shifting the rocks. I was sitting up there. When they'd been at it for a bit, they were moving the wrong way, so I went down. Told her what I told you, that I could find things. "Well," she says, "there's metal hid somewhere hereabout. I've lost the map," she says, "but I know it's here. The owner sent me. If you can show us where to dig, there's a silver coin in it for you." So I found it. Metal! It took the hazel clean from my hand, like a big dog snatching a bone. A powerful kind of gold there must have been there?'

'Indeed,' I said. 'You saw them find it?'

'Aye. I waited for my pay, see?'

'Of course. What was it like?'

'A box, so by so.' Gestures sketched the size. 'It looked heavy. They never opened it. She made them lay it down, then she laid her hands right across it, like this. I told you she had magic. She looked right up there, right into Y Wyddfa, as if she was talking to the spirit. You know, the one that lives there. It made a sword once, they say. The King has it now. Merlin got it for him from the King of the hills.'

'Yes,' I said. 'Then?'

'They took it away.'

'Did you see where they went?'

'Well, yes. Down towards the town.' He shuffled his toes in the dirt, regarding me with clouded eyes. 'She did say the owner sent her. Was that a lie? She was very sweet spoken, and the slaves had badges with a crown on. I thought she was a queen.'

'So she was,' I said. I straightened my back .'Don't look like that, child, you have done nothing wrong. In fact, you have done more than most men would have done in your place; you told me the truth. You could have earned another silver coin if you had kept your mouth shut, showed me the place, and gone on your way. So I shall

pay you, as I promised. Here.'

'But this is silver, master. And for nothing.'

'Not for nothing. You gave me news that must be worth half the kingdom, or even more. A king's ransom, don't they call it?' I got to my feet. 'Don't try to understand me. Stay here in peace, and watch your sheep and find your fortune, and the gods be with you.'

'And with you too, master,' said he, staring.

'It may be,' I said, 'that they still are. All they have to do now is to send another ship in the wake of the first one, and take me south.'

I left him looking wonderingly after me, with the silver coin clutched tightly in the dirty hand.

A south-bound ship docked next day at noon, and sailed again with the evening tide. I was on board, and stayed prostrate and suffering until she came, five days later, safely into the Severn Channel.

CHAPTER 5

The winds stayed strong, but variable. By the time we reached the Channel, the weather had settled to fair, so we did not put in at Maridunum, but held straight on up the estuary.

Enquiries had told me that the *Orc*, Morgause's ship, had been bound for Ynys Witrin, putting in at least twice on the way. It was possible, since by good luck mine was a fast ship, that Morgause and her party might not be too far ahead of me. I suppose I might have bribed the master of my ship to put in at the Island also, but nothing could have saved me there from recognition, with the consequent uproar that I had striven to avoid. Had I known when I saw Morgause that she had the things of power with her from the Mithraeum, and had still (since the boy's judgment seemed good) some magic in her hands, I would have felt bound, whatever the risks, to sail with her in the *Orc*, though I might never have survived the voyage.

I had no means of knowing when Arthur was expected home, and, if I had to stay in hiding until he came, Morgause would probably be able to reach him before I did. What I was hoping for, as I travelled south so closely in her wake, was that I could somehow reach Nimuë. I had faced what might be the result of that. A return from the dead is rarely a success. It was very possible that she might herself want to stop me from reaching Arthur again, and reclaiming my place in his affection and his service. But she had my power. The grail was for the future, and the future was hers. Warn her I must, that another witch was on the way. The rape of Macsen's

treasure had sounded some note of danger which I could not ignore.

To my relief my ship passed the mouth of the estuary that led to the Island's harbour, and held on up into the narrowing Severn channel. We put in at length at a small wharf at the mouth of the Frome River, from which there is a good road leading straight to Aquae Sulis in the Summer Country. I had paid my passage this time with one of the jewels from my grave-clothes, and with the change from this I bought myself a good horse, filled the saddle-bags with food and a change of clothing, and set off at once along the road towards the city.

Except in those places where I was very well known, I thought there was small chance now of my being recognised. I had grown thinner since my entombment, my hair was now quite grey, and I had not shaved my beard. For all that, I planned to skirt towns and villages if I could, and lie at country taverns. I could not lie out; the weather was turning colder every day, and, not much to my surprise, I found the ride exhausting. By the evening of the first day I was ready to rest, and put up thankfully at a small, decent-looking tavern still four or five miles short of Aquae Sulis.

Before I even asked for food, I sought news, and was told that Arthur was home, and at Camelot. When I spoke of Nimuë they answered readily, but more vaguely. 'Merlin's lady', they called her, 'the King's enchantress', and elaborated with one or two fanciful tales, but they were not sure of her movements. One man said she was at Camelot with the King, but another was sure she had left the place a month back; there had been, he said, some trouble in Rheged; some tale about Queen Morgan, and the King's great sword.

So Nimuë, it seemed, was out of touch; and Arthur was home. Even if Morgause did land on the Island, she might not hasten straight to confront the King. If I made all haste, I might reach him before she did. I hurried with my meal, then paid my shot, had them saddle up once

more, and took again to the road. Though I was tired, I had come a scant ten miles, and my good horse was still fresh. If I did not press him, I knew that he could go all night.

There was a moon, and the road was in repair, so we made good time, reaching Aquae Sulis well before midnight. The gates were locked, so I skirted the walls. I was stopped twice, once by a gate guard calling to know my business, and once by a troop of soldiers wearing Melwas' badge. Each time I showed my brooch with its Dragon jewel, and said curtly, 'King's business', and each time the brooch, or my assurance, told, and they let me by. A mile or so after that the road forked, and I turned south by south-east.

The sun came up, small and red in an icy sky. Ahead, the road led straight across the bleak hill land, where the limestone shows white as bone, and the trees are all racked north-eastwards away from the gales. My horse dropped to a walk, then to a plod. Myself, I was riding in a dream, gone in exhaustion beyond either stiffness or soreness. Out of mercy to both weary animals, I drew rein by the next water-trough we passed, tossed hay down from the net that hung at the saddle bow, and myself sat down on the trough's edge and took out my breakfast of raisins and black bread and mead.

The light broadened, flashing on the frosty grass. It was very cold. I broke the cat-ice on the trough, and laved my face and hands. It refreshed me, but made me shiver. If the horse and I were to stay alive we must soon move on. Presently I bitted up again, and led him to where I might mount from the edge of the trough. The horse threw up his head and pricked his ears, and then I heard it, too; hoofs approaching from the direction of the city, and at a fast gallop. Someone who had left the city as soon as the gates had opened, and was coming in a hurry, on a fresh horse.

He came in sight; a young man riding hard, on a big blue roan. When he was a hundred paces off, I recognised

the insignia of the royal courier, and, clambering stiffly down from the trough's edge, moved into the road and held up a hand.

He would not have stopped for me, but here the road was edged on the one side by a low ridge of rock, and on the other by a steep drop, with the trough blocking the narrow verge. And I had turned my horse so that he stood across the way.

The rider drew rein, holding the restless roan, and saying impatiently: 'What is it? If you're fain for company, my good man, I can't provide it. Can't you see who I am?'

'A King's messenger. Yes. Where are you bound?'

'Camelot.' He was young, with russet hair and a high colour, and (as his kind have) a kind of prideful arrogance in his calling. But he spoke civilly enough. 'The King's there, and I must be there myself tomorrow. What is it, old man, is your horse gone lame? Your best plan is—'

'No. I shall manage. Thank you. I would not have stopped you for a triviality, but this is important. I want you to take a message for me. It is to go to the King.'

He stared, then laughed, his breath like a cloud on the icy air. 'For the King, he says! Good sir, forgive me, but a King's messenger has better things to do than take tales from every passer-by. If it's a petition, then I suggest you trot back to Caerleon yourself. The King's to be there for Christmas, and you might get there in time, if you hurry.' His heels moved as if he would set spurs to his horse, and ride on. 'So by your leave, stand aside and let me by.'

I did not move. I said, quietly: 'You would do well to listen, I think.'

He swung back, angry now, and shook his whip free. I thought he would ride over me. Then he met my eyes. He bit back what he had been going to say. The roan, anticipating the whip, bounded forward, and was curbed sharply. It subsided, fretting, its breath puffing white like a dragon's. The man cleared his throat, looked me up

and down doubtfully, then fixed his eyes on my face again. I saw his doubt growing. He made a concession and a face-saver at the same time.

'Well—sir—I can listen. And be sure I'll take any message that seems up to my weight. But we're not supposed to act as common carriers, and I have a schedule to keep.'

'I know. I would not trouble you, except that it is urgent that I reach the King, and as you have pointed out, you will get there rather more quickly than I. The message is this: that you met an old man on the road who gave you a token, and told you that he is on his way to Camelot to see the King. But he can only make his way slowly, so if the King wishes to see him he must come to him by the way. Tell him which road I am taking, and say that I paid you with the ferryman's guerdon. Repeat it, please.'

These men are practised at remembering word for word. Often the messages they take are from men who cannot write. He began to obey me, without thought: 'I met an old man on the road who gave me a token, and told me that he is on his way to Camelot to see the King. But he can only make his way slowly, so if the King wishes to see him, he must—hey, now, what sort of a message is that? Are you out of your mind? The way you put it, it sounds as if you're sending for the King, just like that.'

I smiled. 'I suppose it does. Perhaps I might phrase it better, if it will make a more comfortable message to deliver? In any case, I suggest you deliver it in private.'

'I'll say it had better be in private! Look, I don't know who you are, sir—and it's my guess you're somebody, in spite of, well, not looking it—but by the god of going, it had better be a powerful token, and a good guerdon, too, if I'm to take a summons to King Arthur, however privately.'

'Oh, it is.' I had wrapped my Dragon brooch in linen, and fastened it into a small package. I handed him this,

and with it the second of the gold coins that had sealed my eyelids in the tomb. He stared at the gold coin, then at me, then turned the package over in his hand, eyeing it. He said, doubtfully: 'What's in it?'

'Only the token I spoke of. And let me repeat, this is important, and it's urgent that you should give it to the King in private. If Bedwyr is there with him, no matter, but no other person. Do you understand?'

'Ye-es, but ...' With a movement of knees and wrist he wheeled the roan horse half away from me, and with another movement too fast for me to prevent, he broke open the package. My brooch, with the royal Dragon glinting on the gold ground, fell into his hand. 'This? This is the royal cypher.'

'Yes.'

He said, abruptly: 'Who are you?'

'I am the King's cousin. So have no fear of delivering the message.'

'The King has no cousin, other than Hoel of Brittany. And Hoel doesn't rate the Dragon. Only the ...' His voice trailed away. I saw the blood begin to drain from his face.

'The King will know who I am,' I said. 'Don't think I blame you for doubting me, or for opening the package. The King is well served. I shall tell him so.'

'You're Merlin.' It came out in a whisper. He had to lick his lips and try twice before he could make a sound.

'Yes. Now you see why you must see the King alone. It will be a shock to him, too. Don't be afraid of me.'

'But ... Merlin died and was buried.' He was perfectly white now. The reins ran slack through his fingers, and the roan, deciding to take advantage of the respite, lowered its head and began to graze.

I said quickly: 'Don't drop the brooch. Look, man, I'm no ghost. It is not every grave that is the gate of death.'

I had meant that as a reassurance, but he went, if possible, more ashen than before. 'My lord, we thought ... Everybody knew ...'

'It was thought that I had died, yes.' I spoke briskly,

keeping it matter-of-fact. 'But all that happened was that I fell into a sickness like death, and I recovered. That is all. Now I am well, and will re-enter the King's service ... but secretly. No one must know until the King himself has had the news, and spoken with me. I would have told no one but one of the King's own couriers. Do you understand?'

This had the effect, as I had hoped, of bringing back his self-assurance. The red came back into his cheeks, and he straightened his back, 'Yes, my lord. The King will be— very happy, my lord. When you died—that is, when you— well, when it happened, he shut himself up alone for three days, and would speak to no one, not even to Prince Bedwyr. Or so they say.'

His voice came back to normal while he was speaking, warming, I could see, with pleasurable excitement at the thought of the good news he would have to carry to the King. Gold was the least of it. As he came to an end of telling me how Merlin had been missed and mourned 'the length and breadth of the kingdom, I promise you, sir,' he pulled the roan's head up from the frosty grass, and set it dancing. The colour was back bright in his face, and he looked excited and eager. 'Then I'll be on my way.'

'When do you expect to reach Camelot?'

'Tomorrow noon, with good fortune, and a good change of horses. More probably, tomorrow at lamplighting. You couldn't give my horse a pair of wings while you're about it, could you?'

I laughed. 'I should have to recover a little further before I could manage that. One moment more, before you go .... There's another message that should go straight to the King. Perhaps you bear it already? Did you get any news in Aquae Sulis of the Queen of Orkney? I heard that she was travelling south by ship to Ynys Witrin, no doubt on her way to court.'

'Yes, it's true. She's arrived. Landed, I mean, and on her way now to Camelot. There were those who said she wouldn't obey the summons—'

'Summons? Do you mean that the High King *sent* for her?'

'Yes, sir. That's common knowledge, so I'm not talking out of turn. As a matter of fact I won a small wager on it: they were saying she wouldn't come, even with the safe conduct for the boys. I said she would. With Tydwal sitting tight in Lot's other castle, and Arthur's sworn man, where could she look for refuge if the High King chose to smoke her out?'

'Where, indeed?' I said it absently, almost blankly. This, I had not foreseen, and could not understand. 'Forgive me for detaining you, but I have been a long time without news. Can you tell me why the High King should summon her—and apparently under threat?'

He opened his lips, shut them again, then, obviously deciding that telling the King's cousin and erstwhile chief adviser was no breach of his code, nodded. 'I understand it's a matter of the boys, sir. One in particular, the eldest of the five. The queen was to bring them all to Camelot.'

The eldest of the five. So Nimuë had found Mordred for him ... where I had failed. Nimuë, who had gone north on 'some business for the King'.

I thanked the man, and stood back, moving my horse out of his way. 'Now, on your way, Bellerophon, as best you can, and 'ware dragons.'

'I've got all the dragons I need, thanks.' He gathered the reins, and raised a hand in salute. 'But that's not my name.'

'What is it, then?'

'Perseus,' he said, and looked puzzled when I laughed. Then he laughed with me, flourished his whip, and sent the roan past me at a gallop.

CHAPTER 6

The need for hurry was over. It was likely that Morgause would reach Arthur before the courier, but about that I could do nothing. Though it still disturbed me to know that she had with her the things of power, the sharpest of my worries was gone: Arthur was forearmed; she was there by his orders, and her hostages with her. It was also probable that I myself would be able to see and talk with him before he had dealt with Morgause and Mordred. I had no doubt at all that Arthur, the moment he saw my token and heard the message, would be on the road to find me. Meeting the courier had been a stroke of excellent fortune; even in my prime I could not have ridden as these men ride.

Nor was it urgent, now, that I should get in touch with Nimuë. Of this, in an obscure way, I was glad. There are some tests that one shrinks from making, and some truths that one would rather not hear. I think that if I could have concealed my existence from her I would have done so. I wanted to remember her words of love and grief at my passing, not see in fresh daylight her face of dismay when she saw me living.

For the rest of that day I went slowly, and, well before sunset on a still, cold afternoon, came to a wayside inn, and stopped there. There were no other travellers staying, for which I was glad. I saw my horse stabled and fed, then ate the good supper provided by the innkeeper's wife, and went early to bed, and a dreamless sleep.

All the next day I stayed indoors, glad of the rest. One or two folk passed that way; a drover with his flock, a farmer with his wife on their way home from market, a

courier going north-west. But again, at nightfall, I was the only guest, and had the fire to myself. After supper, when the host and his wife withdrew to their own place, I was left alone in the small, raftered room, with my pallet of straw drawn near the fire, and a stack of logs nearby to keep the place warm.

That night I made no attempt to seek sleep. Once the inn was sunk in silence, I pulled a chair near to the hearth and fed fresh wood to the flames. The goodwife had left a pot of water simmering at the edge of the fire, so I mixed hot water with the remains of the supper's wine, and drank it, while around me the small sounds of the night took over; the settling of the logs in the fire, the rustle of the flames, the scuttle of rats in the thatch, the sound, far away, of an owl hunting in the icy night. Then I set the wine aside and closed my eyes. How long I sat there I have no idea, nor what form the prayers took that brought the sweat to my skin and set the night noises whirling and receding into a limitless and stinging silence. Then at last, the light of the flames against my eyeballs, and through the light the darkness, and through the darkness, light ...

*   *   *

It was a long time since I had seen the great hall at Camelot. Now it was lit against the dark of an autumn evening. An extravagance of waxlight glittered on the gay dresses of the women, and the jewels and weapons of the men. Supper was just over. Guinevere sat in her place at the centre of the high table, lovely in her gold-backed chair. Bedwyr was on her left. They looked happier, I thought, high of heart and smiling. On the Queen's right, the King's great chair was empty.

But just as the chill had touched me, of not seeing him who was all I desired to see, I saw him. He was walking down the hall, pausing here and there to speak to a man as he passed. He was calm, and smiling, and once or

twice set them laughing. A page led him; some message, then, had been sent up to the high table, and the King was answering it himself. He reached the great door, and, with a word to the sentries, dismissed the boy and stepped outside. Two soldiers—guards from the gatehouse—waited for him there, with, between them, a man I had seen before; Morgause's chamber-groom.

The latter started forward as soon as the King appeared, then stopped, apparently disconcerted. It was obvious that he had not expected to see Arthur himself. Then, mastering his surprise, he went down on a knee. He started to speak, in that strange northern accent, but Arthur cut across it.

'Where are they?'

'Why, at the gate, my lord. Your lady sister sent me to beg an audience of you tonight, there in the hall.'

'My orders were that she should come tomorrow to the Round Hall. Did she not receive the message?'

'Indeed, my lord. But she has travelled far, and is weary, and in some anxiety of mind about your summons. She and her children cannot rest until she knows your will. She has brought them—all—with her tonight, and begs you of your grace that you and the Queen will receive them—'

'I will receive them, yes, but not in the hall. At the gate. Go back and tell her to wait there.'

'But, my lord—' Against the King's silence, the man's protests died. He got to his feet with a kind of dignity, bowed to Arthur, then withdrew into the darkness with the two guards. More slowly, Arthur followed them.

The night was dry and still, and frost furred the small clipped trees that lined the terraces. The King's robe brushed them as he passed. He was walking slowly, head down, frowning as he had not let himself frown in the hall full of men and women. No one was about except the guards. A sergeant saluted him and asked a question. He shook his head. So, with neither escort nor company, he walked alone through the palace gardens, past the

chapel wall, and down the steps by the silent fountain. Then through another gate with its saluting sentries, and on to the roadway which led down through the fortress to the south-west gate.

And, sitting by the blaze in the faraway tavern, with the vision driving its nails of pain through my eyes, I cried out to him with a warning as plain as I could make it:

Arthur. Arthur. This is the fate you begot on that night at Luguvallium. This is the woman who took your seed to make your enemy. Destroy them. Destroy them now. They are your fate. She has in her hand the things of power, and I am afraid. Destroy them now. They are in your hand.

He had stopped in the middle of the way. He raised his head as if he could hear something in the night sky. A lantern hanging from a pole threw light on his face. I scarcely knew it. It was sombre, hard, cold, the face of a judge, or an executioner. He stood for a few minutes, quite still, then moved as suddenly as a horse under the spur, and strode down towards the main gate of the fortress.

They were there, the whole party. They had changed and robed themselves, and their horses were fresh and richly caparisoned. Torchlight showed the glint of gold tassels and green and scarlet harness. Morgause wore white, a robe trimmed with silver and small pearls, and a long scarlet cloak lined with white fur. The four younger boys were to the rear, with a pair of servants, but Mordred was beside his mother, on a handsome black horse, its bridle ringing with silver. He was looking around him curiously. He does not know, I thought; she has not told him. The black brows, tipped like wings, were smooth; the mouth, a still mouth, folded like Morgause's, kept its secrets. The eyes were Arthur's, and my own.

Morgause sat her mare, still and upright, waiting. Her hood was thrown back, and the light caught her face. It was expressionless and rather pale; but the eyes glittered

green under the long lids, and I saw the kitten's teeth savaging her underlip. I knew that, under the cool exterior, she was disconcerted, even afraid. She had ignored Arthur's messenger, and deliberately brought her little train to Camelot at this late hour, when all would be assembled in the great hall. She must have reckoned on bringing her royal brood to the steps of the high throne, and perhaps even presenting Arthur's son in public, so forcing the King's hand before his Queen and all the assembled nobles and their ladies. These, she could be sure, would have stood the allies of a lonely queen with a brood of innocents. But she had been stopped at the gate, and now, against all precedent, the King had come out alone to see her, with no witness but his soldiers.

He came down now under the torchlight. He stopped a few paces away, full in the light, and said to the guards: 'Let them come.'

Mordred slid from his horse's back, and handed his mother down. The servants took the horses and withdrew to the gatehouse. Then Morgause, with a boy to either side of her, and the three younger ones behind, went forward to meet the King.

It was the first time they had met since the night in Luguvallium when she sent her maid to lead him to her bed. Then he had been a stripling, a prince after his first battle, gay and young and full of fire; the woman had been twenty years old, subtle and experienced, with her double web of sex and magic to entrance the boy. Now, in spite of the years of child-bearing, there was still something left of whatever had drawn men's eyes and sent them mad for her. But she was not now facing a green and eager boy; this was a man in the flower of his strength, with the judgment that makes a King, and the power to enforce it, and with it all something formidable, dangerous, like a fire banked down that needs only a breath of air to set it blazing.

Morgause went down to the frosty ground in front of him, not in the deep curtsy that one might have expected

from a suppliant who had need of his forgiveness and grace; but kneeling. Her right hand went out and forced the young Mordred, likewise, to his knees. Gawain, on her other side, stood, with the other children, looking wonderingly from his mother to the King. She left them so; they were Lot's, self-confessed, big boned and high-coloured, with the fair skin and hair bequeathed by their mother. Whatever Lot had done in the past, Arthur would visit none of it on his children. But the other, the changeling with the thin face and the dark eyes that had come down through the royal house from Macsen himself . . . she forced him to his knees, where he stayed, but with his head up, and those dark eyes darting round him, looking, it seemed, all ways at once.

Morgause was speaking, in the light, pretty voice that had not changed. I could not catch what she said. Arthur stood like stone. I doubt if he heard a word. He had hardly glanced at her; his eyes were all for his son. Her voice took an edge of urgency. I caught the word 'brother', and then 'son'. Arthur listened, still-faced, but I could feel the words flying like darts between them. Then he took a step forward, and put out a hand. She laid hers in it, and he raised her. I saw among the boys, and in the men who waited at the gate, a subtle relaxation. Her servants' hands did not drop from their hilts—they had studiously not been near them—but the effect was the same. The two older boys, Gawain and Mordred, exchanged a look as their mother rose, and I saw Mordred smile. They waited now for the King to give her the kiss of peace and friendship.

He did not give it. He raised her, and said something, then, turning, led her a little way aside. I saw Mordred's head go round like a hunting dog's. Then the King spoke to the boys:

'Be welcome here. Now go back to the gatehouse, and wait.'

They went, Mordred with a backward look at his mother. For a moment I saw terror in her face, then the

mask of calm came down again. Some message must have passed, for now the chamber-groom came forward, in a hurry, from the gatehouse, bearing in his hands the box that they had brought from Segontium. The things of power ... unbelievably, she had brought them for the King. Unbelievably, she hoped to buy her way to his favour with the treasure of Macsen ...

The man knelt at the King's feet. He opened the box. The light shone down on the treasure that lay within. I saw it all, as clearly as if it lay at my feet. Silver, all silver; cups and bracelets, and a necklet made of silver plaques, designed with those fluid and interlocking lines with which the northern silversmiths invoke their magic. There was no sign of Macsen's emblems of power, no grail studded with emeralds, no lance-head, no dish crusted with sapphire and amethyst. Arthur gave it barely a glance. As the chamber-groom scuttled back into the shelter of the gatehouse, the King turned again to Morgause, leaving the gift lying on the frosty ground. And as he had ignored the gift, so he ignored all that, until now, she had been saying. I heard his voice quite clearly.

'I sent for you, Morgause, for reasons which may not be clear to you. You were wise to obey me. One of my reasons concerns your children; you must have guessed this; but you need not fear for them. I promised you that none of them should be harmed, and I shall keep my promise. But for yourself, no such promise was made. You do well to kneel and sue for mercy. And what mercy can you expect? You killed Merlin. It was you who fed him the poison that in the end brought him to his death.'

She had not expected this. I saw her gasp. The white hands fluttered, as if she would have put them to her throat. But she held them still. 'Who has told you this lie?'

'It is no lie. When he lay dying, he himself accused you.'

'He was always my enemy!' she cried.

'And who is to say he was wrong? You know what you

have done. Do you deny it?'

'Of course I deny it! He hated me, always! And you know why. He wanted no one to have power over you but himself. We sinned, yes, you and I, but we sinned in innocence—'

'If you are wise, you will not speak of that.' His voice was dry and icy. 'You know, as well as I do, what sins were committed, and why. If you hope for any mercy now, or ever, you will not speak of it.'

She bowed her head. Her fingers twisted together. Her pose was humble. When she spoke, she spoke quietly. 'You are right, my lord. I should not have spoken so. I will not encumber you with memories. I have obeyed you, and brought your son to you, and I leave your heart and conscience to deal rightly with him. You will not deny that *he* is innocent.'

He said nothing. She tried again, with the hint of her old sideways, glinting look.

'For myself, I admit that I stand accused of folly. I come to you, Arthur, as a sister, who—'

'I have two sisters,' he said stonily. 'The other one has just now tried to betray me. Do not speak to me of sisters.'

Her head went up. The thin disguise of suppliant was shed. She faced him, a queen to his king. 'Then what can I say, except that I come to you as the mother of your son?'

'You have come to me as the murderer of the man who was more to me than my own father. And as nothing else. You are no more to me, and no less. This is why I sent for you, and what I shall judge you for.'

'He would have killed me. He would have had you kill your own son.'

'That is not true,' said the King. 'He prevented me from killing you both. Yes, I see that shakes you. When I heard of the child's birth, my first thought was to send someone up to kill him. But, if you remember, Lot was before me ... And Merlin, of all men, would have saved

the child, because he is mine.' For the first time passion showed through a crack in his composure. 'But he is not here now, Morgause. He will not protect you again. Why do you think I refused to receive you in the open hall tonight, in the presence of the Queen and the knights? That is what you hoped for, is it not? You, with your pretty face and voice, your four fine boys by Lot, and this youth here with those dark eyes, and the look of his royal kindred ...'

'He has done you no harm!' she cried.

'No, he has done me no harm. Now listen to me. Your four sons by Lot I will take from you, and have them trained here at Camelot. I will not have them left in your care, to be brought up as traitors, to hate their King. As for Mordred, he has done me no wrong, though I have wronged him sorely, and so have you. I will not add sin to sin. I have been warned of him, but a man must do right, even to his own hurt. And who can read the gods accurately? You will leave him with me also.'

'And have you murder him as soon as I am gone?'

'And if I do, what choice have you but to let me?'

'You've changed, brother,' she said, spitefully.

For the first time, something like a smile touched his mouth. 'You might say so. For what comfort it is to you now, I shall not kill him. But you, Morgause, because you slew Merlin, who was the best man in all this realm—'

He was interrupted. From the gatehouse came a clatter of hoofs, the quick challenge from the sentries, a breathless word, then the creak and crash of the gates opening. A horse, tagged with foam, clattered through, and came to a halt beside the King and stood. Its head went down to its knees. Its limbs trembled. The courier slid down from the saddle, grabbed at the girth to keep his own limbs from folding under him, then went carefully on one knee, and saluted the King.

It was hardly a comfortable interruption. Arthur faced about, his brows drawn, and anger in his face. 'Well?' he asked. His voice was even. He knew that no courier would

have got through to him at such a moment, and in such a state, unless his business drove him. 'Wait, I remember you, don't I? Perseus, is it not? What news can you possibly bring from Glevum that makes it worth your while to kill a good horse, and break in on my private councils?'

'My lord—' The man cleared his throat, with a glance at Morgause. 'My lord, it is urgent news, most urgent, that I must deliver privately. Forgive me.' This half to Morgause, who was standing like a statue, hands to her throat. Some wisp of forgotten magic, trailing, may have warned her what the news might be.

The King regarded him in silence for a moment, then nodded. He called out an order, and two of the guards came forward, halting one on either side of Morgause. Then he turned, with a sign to the courier, and walked back up the roadway with the man following him.

At the foot of the palace steps he paused and turned. 'Your message?'

Perseus held out the package I had given him. 'I met an old man on the road who gave me this token, and told me that he is on his way to Camelot to see the King. But he can only make his way slowly, so if the King wishes to see him, he must come to him. He is travelling by the road that runs over the hills between Aquae Sulis and Camelot. He told me—'

'*He gave you this?*' The brooch lay in the King's hand. The Dragon winked and glittered. Arthur looked up from it, his face colourless.

'Yes, my lord.' The clipped recital hurried. 'I was to tell you that he paid me for my service with the ferryman's guerdon.' He held out his hand with the gold coin in the palm.

The King took it like a man in a dream, glanced at it, and handed it back. In his other hand he was turning the brooch this way and that, so that the Dragon flashed in the torchlight. 'You know what this is?'

'Indeed, my lord. It's the Dragon. When I saw it first

I asked what his right to it was, but then I knew him. My lord, yes ...' The King, his face quite bloodless now, was staring. The man licked his lips, and somehow got the rest of the message out. 'When he stopped me, yesterday, he was near the thirteenth milestone. He—he didn't look too good, my lord. If you do ride to meet him, it's my guess he won't have got much beyond the next inn. It stands back from the road, on the south side, and the sign's a bush of holly.'

'A bush of holly.' Arthur repeated it with no expression at all, like a man talking in his sleep. Then, suddenly, the trance that held him shattered. Colour flooded his face. He threw the brooch up in the air, flashing and turning, and caught it again. He laughed aloud. 'I might have known! I might have known ... This is real, at any rate!'

'He told me,' said Perseus, 'he told me he was no ghost. And that it wasn't every tomb that was the gate of death.'

'Even his ghost,' said Arthur. 'Even his ghost ...' He whirled and shouted. Men came running. Orders were flung at them. 'My grey stallion. My cloak and sword. I give you four minutes.' He put out a hand to the courier. 'You will stay here in Camelot till my return. You have done more than well, Perseus. I'll remember it. Now go and rest ... Ah, Ulfin. Tell Bedwyr to bring twenty of the knights and follow me. This man will direct them. Give him food, and tend his horse and keep him till I come again.'

'And the lady?' asked someone.

'Who?' It was plain that the King had forgotten all about Morgause. He said, indifferently: 'Hold her until I have time for her, and let her speak to no one. No one, do you understand me?'

The stallion was brought, with two grooms clinging to the bit. Someone came running with cloak and sword. The gates crashed open. Arthur was in the saddle. The grey stallion screamed and climbed the torchlit air, then

leaped forward under the spur, and was out of the gate with the speed of a thrown spear. It went down the steep, winding causeway as if it had been a level plain in daylight. It was the way the boy Arthur had once ridden through the Wild Forest, and to the same assignation . . .

Morgause, her virgin white spattered with thrown turf and sods, stood stiffly between her guards, as men-at-arms clattered past her. The boys were in their midst, and Mordred among them. They vanished towards the palace without a backward look.

For the first time since I had known her, I saw her, no more than a frightened woman, making the sign against strong enchantment.

CHAPTER 7

Next morning the innkeeper and his wife, to their alarm
and distress, found me lying on the cooling hearth,
apparently in a faint. They got me into bed, wrapped
winter-stones to warm me, piled blankets around me, and
got the fire going once more. When, in time, I wakened,
the good folk looked after me with the anxious care they
might have accorded their own father. I was not much
the worse. Moments of vision have always to be paid for;
first with the pain of the vision itself, then afterwards
in the long trance of exhausted sleep.

Reckoning out the distances, I let myself rest quietly
for the remainder of that day, then next morning, putting
my hosts' protests aside, had them saddle my horse. They
were reassured when I told them I would not ride far,
but only a mile or so down the road, where a friend could
be expected to meet me. I further allayed their fears by
asking them to prepare a dinner 'for myself and my
friend'.

'For,' I said, 'he loves good food, and the goodwife's
cooking is as tasty as any, I'll swear, at the King's court
of Camelot.'

At that the innkeeper's wife laughed and bridled, and
began to talk of capons, so I left money to pay for the
food, and went my way.

After the spell of hard frost, the weather had slack-
ened. The sun was up, and dealing some warmth. The air
was mild enough, but still everywhere was the hint of
winter's coming; in the bare trees of the heights, the
fieldfares busy in the berried holly, redwings flocking on
the bushes, nuts ripe in the hazel coppices. The bracken

was fading gold, and there were still flowers out on the gorse.

My horse, after his long rest, was fresh and eager, and we covered the first stretch of road at a fast canter. We met no one. Soon the road left the high crest of the limestone hills, and slanted downwards along a valley side. All along the lower reaches of the valley the slopes were crowded with trees in the flaming colours of autumn; beech, oak and chestnut, birch in its yellow gold, with everywhere the dark spires of the pine trees and the glossy green of holly. Through the trees I caught the glint of moving water. Down by the river, the innkeeper had told me, the way forked. The road itself held straight across the river, which here was paved in a shallow ford, and just beyond the water another way led off to the right, through the forest. This was a little-used track, and a rough one, which cut off a corner to rejoin the gravelled road some miles further towards the east.

This was the place I was making for. It was a full mile since I had seen any sort of dwelling; the ford was as private for our meeting as a midnight bedchamber. I dared not to go further to meet him. Whenever Arthur had to ride, he made all speed, and cut all corners. Not knowing the forest track, I could not count on his using it, so might miss him if I took one way or the other.

It was a good place to wait. Down in the hollow the sun shone warmly, and the air was mild but fresh. It smelled of pines. Two jays wrestled and scolded in a shaw of hollies, then flew low across the road with a flash of sky-blue in their wings. Distantly, in the woods to the south-east, I heard the long rasping noise that meant a woodpecker at work. The river whispered across the road, running gently, no more than a foot deep across the Roman setts of the ford.

I unsaddled my horse and slacked his bit, then unbuckled an end of the rein, tied it to a hazel stem, and left him to graze. There was a fallen pine a few paces from the river's edge, full in the sun. I set the saddle down by

the tree trunk, then sat down beside it to wait.

My timing had been good. I had waited there barely an hour when I caught the sound of hoofs on the gravel road. So, he had kept to the high road, not cutting the corner through the forest. He was not hurrying, but riding easily, no doubt resting his horse. Nor was he alone. Bedwyr, hard on his heels, had perhaps been allowed to come up with him.

I walked out in the road and stood waiting for him.

Three horsemen came trotting through the forest, and down the gentle slope leading to the far side of the ford. They were all strangers; moreover, they were a kind of man who nowadays was rare enough. In times past the roads, especially those in the wilder lands to the north and west, were rife with danger for the lonely traveller, but Ambrosius, and Arthur after him, had swept the main posting-roads clear of outlaws and masterless men. But not quite, it seemed. These three had been soldiers; they still wore the leather armour of their calling, and two of them sported battered metal caps. The youngest of them, sprucer than the others, had stuck a sprig of scarlet berries behind one ear. All three were unshaven, and armed with knives and short-swords. The oldest of them, with streaks of grey in a heavy brown beard, had an ugly-looking cudgel strapped to his saddle. Their horses were sturdy mountain cobs, cream, brown and black, their hides thick with dirt and damp, but well fed, and powerful. It did not need any prophet's instinct to know that here were three dangerous men.

They halted their horses at the river's brink and looked me over. I stood my ground and returned the look. I had the knife at my belt, but my sword was with the saddle-bags. And flight, with my horse stripped and tethered, was out of the question. If truth be told, I was still no more than faintly apprehensive; there had been a time when no one, however wild and desperate, would have dared lay a finger on Merlin; and I suppose that the confidence of power was still with me.

They looked at one another, and a message passed. It was danger, then. The leader, he with the greying beard and the black horse, walked the beast forward a pace, so that the water swirled past its fetlocks. Then he turned, grinning, to his fellows.

'Why, look you, here's a brave fellow, disputing the ford with us. Or are you the Hermes, come to wish us godspeed? I must say, you're not what one expects of the Herm.' This with a guffaw in which his fellows joined.

I moved aside from the centre of the road. 'I'm afraid I can't claim any of his talents, gentlemen. Nor do I mean to dispute the way with you. When I heard you coming I took you for the outriders of the troop that is due this way very soon. Did you see any sign of troopers on the road?'

Another glance. The youngest—he of the cream cob and the woodbine spray—set his horse at the water and came splashing out beside me. 'There was no one on the road,' he said. 'Troopers? What troopers would you be expecting? The High King himself, maybe?' He winked at his companions.

'The High King,' I said, equably, 'will be riding this way soon, by all accounts, and he likes the law of the roads looked to. So go your ways in peace, gentlemen, and let me go mine.'

They were all through the ford now, ranged round me. They looked relaxed and pleasant enough, good-tempered, even. Brown-beard said: 'Oh, we'll let you go, won't we, Red? Free as air to go, you'll be, good sir, free as air, and travelling light.'

'Light as a feather,' said Red, with a laugh. He was the one with the brown horse. He shifted the belt round from his thick thighs, so that the haft of his knife lay nearer to his hand. The youngest of the three was already moving towards the fallen pine where the saddle-bags lay.

I began to speak, but the leader kicked his horse in closer, dropped the reins on its withers, then suddenly

reached down, catching hold of me by the neck of my robe. He gathered the stuff in a choking grip, and half lifted me towards him. He was immensely strong.

'So, who were you waiting for, eh? A troop, was it? Was that the truth, or were you lying to scare us off?'

The second man, Red, thrust his horse near on the other side. There was no faintest chance of escaping them. The third one had dismounted, and, without troubling to undo them, had a long knife out and was slitting the leather of the saddle-bags. He had not even glanced over his shoulder to see what his fellows did.

Red had his knife in his hand. 'Of course he was lying,' he said roughly. 'There were no troops on the road. Nor any sign of them. And they wouldn't be coming by the forest track, Erec, you can be sure of that.'

Erec reached back with his free hand and slipped the knobbed cudgel from its moorings. 'Well, so it was a lie,' he said. 'You can do better than that, old man. Tell us who you are and where you're bound for. This troop you're talking about, where are they coming from?'

'If you let me go.' I said with difficulty, for he was half choking me, 'I will tell you. And tell your fellow to leave my things alone.'

'Why, here's high crowing from an old rooster!' But he relaxed his hold, and let me stand again. 'Give us the truth, then, and maybe do yourself a bit of good. Which way did you come, and where's this troop you were talking about? Who are you, and where are you bound?'

I began to straighten my clothes. My hands were shaking, but I managed to make my voice steady enough. I said: 'You will do well to loose me, and save yourselves. I am Merlinus Ambrosius, called Merlin, the King's cousin, and I am bound for Camelot. A message has gone before me, and a troop of knights is riding this way to meet me. They should be close behind you. If you go west now, quickly—'

A great guffaw of laughter cut me off. Erec rocked in his saddle. 'Hear that, Red? Balin, did you get it? This

is Merlin, Merlin himself, and he's bound for the court at Camelot!'

'Well, he might be, at that,' said Red, shaking with mirth. 'Looks a proper skeleton, don't he? Straight from the tomb, he is, and that's for sure.'

'And straight back to it.' Suddenly savage, Erec seized me again and shook me violently.

A shout from Balin gave him pause. 'Hey! Look here!' Both men turned. 'What have you got?'

'Enough gold to get us a month's food and good beds, and something to go in them, forby,' called Balin, cheerfully. He threw the saddle-bag down to the ground, and held up his hand. Two of the jewels glinted.

Erec drew in his breath. 'Well, whoever you are, our luck's in, it seems! Look in the other one, Balin. Come on, Red, let's see what he's got on him.'

'If you harm me,' I said, 'be sure that the King—'

I stopped, as if a hand had been laid across my mouth. I had been standing there, perforce, hemmed between the two horses, staring up at the bearded face bent down over me, with the high bright sky behind him. Now, across that sky, with the sun striking bronze from its black gloss, went a raven. Flying low, silent for once, tilting and sidling on the air, went the bird of Hermes the messenger, the bird of death.

It told me what I had to do. Till now, instinctively, I had been playing for time, as any man will play, to ward off death. But if I succeeded, if I made the murderers pause and hold their hands, then Arthur, riding alone, and on a weary horse, with nothing in his heart but the thought of meeting me, would come on them there, three to one, in this lonely place. In a fight, I could not help him. But I could still serve him. I owed God a death, and I could give Arthur another life. I must send these brutes on their way, and quickly. If he came across my murdered body here, he would go after them, no doubt of that; but he would know what he was doing, and he would have help.

So I said nothing. Balin started on the other saddle-bag. Erec seized me again, dragging me close. Red came behind me, tearing at the belt that held my wallet, with the rest of my gold stitched into its lining. Above me the knotted bludgeon swung high.

If I reached for my own weapon, they might kill me sooner. My hand went back for the knife in my belt. From behind Red's hard hand caught and held my wrist, and the knife spun to the ground. The bones of my hand ground together. He thrust his sweating face over my shoulder. He was grinning. 'Merlin, eh? A great enchanter like you could show us a thing or two, I'm sure. Go on then, save yourself, why don't you? Cast a spell and strike us dead.'

The horses broke apart. Something flashed and drove like light across the sky. The cudgel flew wide and fell. Erec's hand loosed me, so suddenly that I staggered, and fell forward against his horse. Bending above me still, the brown-bearded face wore a look of surprise. The eyes stared, fixed. The head, severed cleanly by that terrible, slashing blow, bounced on the horse's neck in a splatter of blood, then thudded to the ground. The body slumped slowly, almost gracefully, onto the cob's withers. A gush of blood, bright and steaming, flooded over the beast's shoulder and splashed down over me where I reeled, clinging to the breast-band. The horse screamed once, in terror, then reared and slashed out at the air, tore itself free, and bolted. The headless body bobbed and swayed for a bound or two before it pitched from the saddle to' the road, still spouting blood.

I was thrown hard down on the grass. The cool dampness struck up through my hands, steadying me. My heart thumped; the treacherous blackness threatened, then withdrew. The ground was thudding and shaking to the beat of hoofs. I looked up.

He was fighting the two of them. He had come alone, on his big grey horse. He had outstripped Bedwyr and the knights, but neither he nor the stallion showed any

trace of weariness. It was a wonder to me that the three murderers had not broken and fled at the very sight of him. He was lightly armed only—no shield, but a leather tunic stitched with metal phalerae, and a thick cloak twisted round his left arm. His head was bare. He had dropped the reins on the stallion's neck, and controlled him with knee and voice. The great horse reared and wheeled and struck like another battle-arm. And all around horse and King, like a shield of impenetrable light, whirled the flashing blade of the great sword that was mine and his; Caliburn, the King's sword of Britain.

Balin flung himself on his horse, and spurred, yelling, to his fellow's aid. A ribbon of leather flying from Arthur's tunic showed where one of them had slashed him from behind—while he was killing Brown-Beard, probably—but now, try as they might, they could not pass that deadly ring of shining metal, nor close in past the stallion's lashing hoofs.

'Out of the way,' said the King, curtly, to me. The horses plunged and circled. I started to drag myself to my feet. It seemed to take a long time. My hands were slimy with blood, and my body shook. I found that I could not stand, but crawled instead to the fallen pine, and sat there. The air shook and clashed with battle, and I sat there, helpless, shaking, old, while my boy fought for his life and mine, and I could not summon even the mortal strength of a man to help him.

Something glinted near my foot. My knife, lying where Red had struck it from my hand. I reached for it. I still could not stand, but threw it as hard as I could at Red's back. It was a feeble throw, and missed him. But the flash of its passing made the brown horse flinch and swerve, and sent its rider's blow wide. With the slither and whine of metal, Caliburn caught the blade and flung it wider, then Arthur drove the great stallion in and killed Red with a blow through the heart.

There was a moment when the sword jammed and

could not be withdrawn, and the body, falling, made a dead weight on the King's sword-arm. But the grey stallion knew about that, too. Balin, trying to wheel the cream cob to take the King in the rear, met teeth and armed hoofs. An upward slash laid the cream's shoulder open. It swerved, screaming, and turned against rein and spur to flee. But Balin—brave ruffian that he was— wrenched its head back by main force, just as the King dragged his sword clear of Red's body and wheeled back, right-handed, into fighting range.

I believe that, in that last moment, Balin recognised the King. But he was given no time to speak, much less beg for mercy. There was one more vicious, brief flurry, and Balin took Caliburn's point in his throat, and fell to the trampled and bloody grass. He writhed once, gasped, and drowned on a gush of blood. The cob, instead of running, now that it was no longer constrained, simply stood with head hanging and shaking legs, while the blood ran down its shoulder. The other horses had gone.

Arthur leaped down, wiped his sword on Balin's body, shook the folds of his cloak from his left arm, and came across to me, leading the grey. He touched my blood-stained shoulder.

'This blood. Is any of it yours?'

'No. And you?'

'Not a scratch,' he said, cheerfully. He was breathing only a little faster than usual. 'Though it wasn't quite a massacre. They were trained men, or so it seemed to me, when there was time to notice ... Sit quietly for a moment; I'll get you some water.'

He dropped the stallion's reins into my hand, reached to the pommel for the silver-mounted horn he carried there, then trod lightly towards the river. I heard his foot strike something. The quick stride stopped short, and he exclaimed. I turned my head. He was staring down at the wreck of one of my saddle-bags, where, in the scatter of spilled food and slashed leather, lay a strip of torn

velvet, heavily stitched with gold. One of the jewels that
Balin had torn from it lay winking beside it in the
grass.

Arthur swung round. He had gone quite white.

'By the Light! It's you!'

'Who else? I thought you knew.'

'*Merlin!*' Now he really was trying for breath. He came
back to stand over me. 'I thought—I hardly had time to
look—just those murdering rascals butchering an old
man—unarmed, I thought, and poor, by the look of the
horse and trappings ...' He went on both knees beside
me. 'Ah, Merlin, Merlin ...'

And the High King of all Britain laid his head down
on my knee, and was silent.

After a while he stirred and lifted his head.

'I got your token, and the message from the courier.
But I don't think I really quite believed him. When he
first spoke and showed me the Dragon it seemed right ...
I suppose I'd never thought you could really die, like
mortal men ... but on the way here, riding alone, with
nothing to do but think—well, it ceased to be real. I
don't know what I pictured; myself ending up again,
perhaps in front of that blocked cave-mouth, where we
buried you alive.' I felt a shiver go through him. 'Merlin,
what has happened? When we left you for dead, sealed
in the cave, it was the malady, of course, giving the appearance of death: I realise that now. But afterwards?
When you woke, alone and weighed down with your
own grave-clothes? God knows, that would be enough
to bring another death! What did you do? How survive,
locked alone in the hill? How escape? And when? You
must have known how sorely I was bereft. Where have
you been all this while?'

'Not so great a while. When I escaped, you were abroad.
They told me you had gone to Brittany. So I said nothing, and lodged with Stilicho, my old servant, who keeps
the mill near Maridunum, and waited for your return.

I'll tell you everything soon—if you will get me that drink of water.'

'Fool that I am, I was forgetting!' He jumped up and ran to the river. He filled the horn and brought it, then went down on one knee to hold it for me.

I shook my head and took it from him. 'Thank you, but I'm quite steady now. It's nothing. I was not hurt. I am ashamed to have been of so little help.'

'You gave me all I needed.'

'Which was not much,' I said, half laughing. 'I could almost feel sorry for those wretches, thinking they had an easy kill, and bringing Arthur himself down on them like a thunderbolt. I did warn them, but who could blame them for not believing me?'

'You mean to tell me they knew who you were? And still used you like that?'

'I told you, they didn't believe me. Why should they? Merlin was dead. And the only power I have now is in your name—and they didn't believe that, either. "An old man, unarmed and poor."' I quoted him, smiling. 'Why, you didn't know me yourself. Am I so much changed?'

He considered me. 'It's the beard, and, yes, you are quite grey now. But if I had once looked at your eyes ...' He took the horn from me and got to his feet. 'Oh, yes, it is you. In all that ever mattered, you are unchanged. Old? Yes, we must all grow old. Age is nothing but the sum of life. And you are alive, and back with me here. By the great God of heaven, I have you back with me. What should I fear now?'

He drained the horn, replaced it, and looked around him. 'I suppose I had better tidy up this mess. Are you really all right now? Could you tend my horse for me? I think he could be watered now.'

I led the stallion down to the water, and with it the cream cob, which was grazing quietly, and made no attempt to escape me. When they had drunk I tethered them, then got some salve from my pack and doctored

the cut on the cob's shoulder. It rolled an eye back at me, and the skin of its shoulder flickered, but it showed no sign of pain. The cut bled still, but sluggishly, and the beast was not walking lame. I loosed the girths of both horses, and left them grazing while I retrieved the scattered contents of my saddle-bag.

Arthur's way of clearing up the 'mess'—three men violently dead—was to haul the bodies by their heels to a decent hiding-place at the forest's edge. The severed head he picked up by the beard and slung it after. He was whistling while he did it, a gay little tune I recognised as one of the soldiers' marching songs, which was frank, not to say over-explicit, about the sexual prowess of their leader. Then he looked around him.

'The next rain will clear some of the blood away. And even if I had a spade or mattock, I'm damned if I'd spend the time and trouble in digging that carrion in. Let the ravens have them. Meanwhile, we might as well impound their horses; I see they've stopped to graze away up the road there. I'll have to wash the blood off first, or I'll never get near them. You'd better abandon that cloak of yours, it'll never be the same again. Here, you can wear mine. No, I insist. It's an order. Here.'

He dropped it over the pine log, then went down to the river and washed. While he remounted and went cantering up the road after the other horses, I stripped off my cloak, which was already stiffening with blood, and washed myself, then shook out Arthur's cloak of royal purple, and put it on. My own I rolled up and pitched after the dead men into the undergrowth.

Arthur came back at a trot, leading the thieves' horses. 'Now, where is the inn with the bush of holly?'

CHAPTER 8

The innkeeper's boy was out in the road watching for me. I suppose he had been posted there to give the goodwife warning of when the 'meal fit for the King's court' would be wanted. When he saw us coming, two men and five horses, he stood staring awhile, then went with a skip and a jump back into the inn. When we were still seventy paces short of the place, the innkeeper himself came out to see.

He recognised Arthur almost straight away. What drew his eye first was the quality of the King's horse. Then came a long, summing look at the rider, and the man was on his knee out on the road.

'Get up, man,' said the King, cheerfully. 'I've been hearing good things of the house you keep here, and I'm looking forward to trying your hospitality. There's been a little skirmish down by the ford—nothing deadly, just enough to get up a bit of an appetite. But that will have to wait a little. Look after my friend here first, will you, and if your goodwife can clean his clothes, and someone can tend to the horses, we'll cheerfully wait for the meal.' Then, as the man began to stammer something about the poverty of his house, and the lack of accommodation, 'As to that, man, I'm a soldier, and there've been times when any shelter from the weather could be counted a luxury. From what I've heard of your tavern, it's a haven indeed. And now, may we come in? Wine we cannot wait for, nor fire ...'

We had both in a very short time. The innkeeper, once he had recovered himself, came to terms quickly with the royal invasion, and very sensibly set all aside except the

immediate service that was needed. The boy came running to take the horses, and the innkeeper himself piled logs on the fire and brought wine, then helped me out of my soiled and blood-splashed robes, and brought hot water, and fresh clothes from my baggage roll. Then, at Arthur's bidding, he locked the inn door against casual passers-by, and got himself off to the kitchen, there, one imagined, to instil a panic frenzy into his excellent wife.

When I had changed, and Arthur had washed, and spread his cloak to the blaze, he poured wine for me, and took his place at the other side of the hearth. Though he had travelled fast and far, and with a fight at the end of it; he looked as fresh as if he had newly risen from his bed. His eyes were bright as a boy's, and colour sprang red in his cheeks. Between the joy of seeing me again, and the stimulus of the danger past, he seemed a youth again. When at length the goodwife and her husband came in with the food, making some ado about setting the board and carving the capons, he received them with gay affability, so easily that, by the time we had done, and they had withdrawn, the woman had so far forgotten his rank as to scream with laughter at one of his jests, and cap it herself. Then her husband pulled at her gown, and she ran out, but laughing still.

At last we were alone. The short afternoon drew in. Soon it would be lamp-lighting. We went back to our places one on either side of the blaze. I think we both felt tired, and sleepy, but neither of us could have rested until we had exchanged such news as could not be spoken of in front of our hosts. The King had, he told me, ridden the whole way with only a few hours' respite for sleep, and to rest his horse.

'For,' he said, 'if the courier's message, and the token he brought, told a true tale, then you were safe, and would wait for me. Bedwyr and the others came up with me, but they, too, stopped to rest. I told them to stay back, and give me a few hours' grace.'

'That could have cost you dear.'

'With that carrion?' He spoke contemptuously. 'If they hadn't caught you unarmed and unawares, you could have dealt with them yourself.'

And time was, I thought, when, without even a dagger in my hand, I could have dealt with them. If Arthur was thinking the same, he gave no sign of it. I said: 'It's true that they were hardly worth your sword. And talking of that, what have I been hearing about the theft of Caliburn? Some tale about your sister Morgan?'

He shook his head. 'That's over, so let it wait. What's more to the point now is that I should know what has been happening to you. Tell me. Tell me everything. Don't leave anything out.'

So I told my story. The day drew in, and beyond the small, deep-set windows the sky darkened to indigo, then to slate. The room was quiet, but for the crack and flutter of the flames. A cat crept from some corner and curled on the hearth, purring. It was a strange setting for the tale I had to tell, of death and costly burial, of fear and loneliness and desperate survival, of murder foiled and rescue finally accomplished. He listened as so many times before, intent, lost in the tale, frowning over some parts of it, but relaxed into the warmth and contentment of the evening. This was another of the times that comes vividly back to me in memory whenever I think of him; the quiet room, the King listening, the firelight moving red on his cheek and lighting the thick fall of dark hair, and the dark watching eyes, intent on the story I was telling him. But with a difference now: this was a man listening with a purpose; summing up what he was told, and judging, ready to act.

At the end he stirred. 'That fellow, the grave-robber— we must find him. It shouldn't be hard, if he's cadging drinks from that story all over Maridunum ... I wonder who it was who heard you the first time? And the miller, Stilicho; I've no doubt you'll want me to leave that to you?'

'Yes. But if you could ride over that way some time,

perhaps when you're next in Caerleon? Mai will die of terror and ecstasy, but Stilicho will take it as no more than his due, who served the great enchanter ... and then boast about it for the rest of his days.'

'Of course,' he said. 'I was thinking, while I was on the road; we'll go straight on from here to Caerleon now. I imagine you're not yet ready to go back to court—'

'Not now, or ever. Or to Applegarth. I have left that for good.' I did not add 'to Nimuë'; her name had not been mentioned by either of us. So carefully had we avoided it that it seemed to ring through every sentence that was spoken. I went on: 'I've no doubt you'll fight me to the death over this, but I want to go back to Bryn Myrddin. I'll be more than glad to stay with you in Caerleon until it can be made ready again.'

Of course he objected, and we argued for a while, but in the end he let me have my way, on the (very reasonable) condition that I did not live there alone, but was cared for by servants. 'And if you must have your precious solitude, then you shall have it. I shall build a place for the servants, out of your sight and below the cliff; but they must be there.'

' "And that is an order?" ' I quoted, smiling.

'Certainly ... There'll be time enough to see about it; I'll spend Christmas at Caerleon, and you with me. I take it you won't insist on going back there till the winter is past?'

'No.'

'Good. Now, there's something in your story that doesn't agree with the facts ... that business you described in Segontium.' He glanced up, smiling. 'So that was where you found Caliburn? In the soldiers' shrine of the Light? Well, it tallies. I remember that you told me, years ago, just before we left the Forest, that there were other treasures there still. You spoke of a grail. I still remember what you said. But the gift Morgause brought to me was no treasure of Macsen's. It was silver goods—cups and

brooches and torques, the sort of thing they fashion in the far north. Very handsome, but not as you described the treasure to me.'

'No. I did catch a glimpse of it, there in the vision. It was not Macsen's treasure. But the shepherd boy was certain that it was taken, and I believe him.'

'You don't know?'

'No. How could I, without power?'

'But you had this vision. You watched Morgause and the boys accost me at Camelot. You saw the silver treasure she gave me. You knew the courier had come, and that I was on my way to you.'

I shook my head. 'That was not power, not as you and I have known it. That is Sight only, and that, I think, I shall have until I die. Every village sibyl has it, in some degree or another. Power is more than that; it is doing and speaking with knowledge; it is bidding without thought, and knowing that one will be obeyed. That has gone. I don't repine now.' I hesitated. 'Nor, I hope, do you? I have heard tales of Nimuë, how she is the new Lady of the Lake, the mistress of the Island's shrine. I am told that men call her the King's enchantress, and that she has done you service?'

'Indeed, yes.' He looked away from me, leaning forward to adjust a log on the burning pile. 'It was she who dealt with the theft of Caliburn.'

I waited, but he left it there. I said at length: 'I understood she was still in the north. She is well?'

'Very well.' The log was burning to his satisfaction. He set his chin on a fist, and stared at the fire. 'So. If Morgause had the treasure with her when she embarked, it will be somewhere on the Island. My people saw to it that she did not go ashore between Segontium and her landing there. She lodged with Melwas, so it should not be beyond me to have it traced. Morgause is being held under guard until I get back. If she refuses to speak, the children will hardly be proof against questioning. The

younger ones are too innocent to see any harm in telling the truth. Children see everything; they will know where she left the treasure.'

'I understand that you're going to keep them?'

'You saw that? Yes. You would also see that your courier came just in time to save Morgause.'

I thought of my own effort to reach him with my dreaming will, when I thought she would use the stolen grail against him. 'You were going to kill her?'

'Certainly, for killing you.'

'Without proof?'

'I don't need proof to have a witch put to death.'

I raised a brow at him, and quoted what had been said at the opening of the Round Hall: ' "No man nor woman shall be harmed unjustly, or punished without trial or manifest proof of their trespass." '

He smiled. 'Well, all right. I did have proof. I had your own word that she tried to kill you.'

'So you said. I thought you said it to frighten her. I told you nothing.'

'I know. And why not? Why did you keep it secret from me that it was her poison that sent you to your death in the Wild Forest, and then left you with the sickness that was almost your death again?'

'You've answered that yourself. You would have killed her, after the Wild Forest. But she was the mother of those young sons, and heavy with another, and I knew that one day they would come to you, and become, in time, your faithful servants. So, I did not tell you. Who did?'

'Nimuë.'

'I see. And she knew, how? By divination?'

'No. From you. Something you said in your delirium.'

Everything, she had taken from me; every last secret. I said merely: 'Ah, yes ... And do I take it that she also found Mordred for you? Or did Morgause bring him into the open, once Lot and I were dead?'

'No. He was still hidden. I understand that he was

lodged somewhere in the Orkney Islands. Nimuë had
nothing to do with that. It was by the purest chance that
I heard of him. I got a letter. A goldsmith from York,
who had done work for Morgause before, travelled that
way with some jewels he hoped to sell her. These fellows,
as you know, get into every corner of the kingdom, and
see everything.'

'Not Beltane.'

His head came up, surprised. 'You know him?'

'Yes. He's as good as blind. He has to travel with a
servant—'

'Casso,' said the King, then, as I stared: 'I told you I
got a letter.'

'From *Casso*?'

'Yes. It seems he was in Dunpeldyr when—ah, I see,
that was when you met them? Then you will know they
were there on the night of the massacre. Casso, it appears,
saw and heard a good deal of what went on; people talk
in front of a slave, and he must have understood more
than he was meant to. His master could never be brought
to believe that Morgause had anything to do with events
so dreadful, so went up to Orkney to try his luck again.
Casso, being less credulous, watched and listened, and
managed at length to locate the child who went missing
on the night of the massacre. He sent a message straight
to me. As it happened, I had just heard from Nimuë that
it was Morgause who caused your death. I sent for her,
and saw to it that she brought Mordred with her. Why
are you looking so dumbfounded?'

'On two counts. What should make a slave—Casso was
a quarryman's labourer when I first found him—write
"straight to" the High King?'

'I forgot I had not told you; he served me once before.
Do you remember when I went north into Lothian to
attack Aguisel? And how hard it was to find some way of
destroying that dirty jackal without bringing Tydwal and
Urien down on my head, swearing vengeance? Some word
of this must have got around, because I got a message

from this same slave, evidence—with facts that could be proved — of something he had seen when he was in Aguisel's service. Aguisel had misused a page, one of Tydwal's young sons, and then murdered him. Casso told us where to find the body. We found it; and others besides. The child had been killed just as Casso had told us.'

'And afterwards,' I said drily, 'Aguisel cut out the tongues of the slaves who had witnessed it.'

'You mean the man is dumb? Well, that might account for the free way men seem to talk in front of him. Aguisel paid dearly for failing to make sure he could not read or write.'

'Neither he could. When I knew him in Dunpeldyr he was both dumb and helpless. It was I who, for a service he had done me—or rather, for no reason that I remember, except perhaps the prompting of the god—arranged to have him taught.'

Arthur, smiling, raised his cup to me. 'Did I call it "pure chance"? I should have remembered who I was talking to. I rewarded Casso after the Aguisel affair, of course, and told him where to send any other information. I believe he has been useful once or twice. Then, over this last thing, he sent straight to me.'

We spoke of it for a while longer, then I came back to present matters. 'What will you do with Morgause now?'

'I shall have to settle that, with your help, when I get back. Meanwhile I shall send orders that she is to be kept under guard, at the nunnery at Amesbury. The boys will stay with me, and I'll have them brought down to Caerleon for Christmas. Lot's sons will be no problem; they're young enough to find life at court exciting, and old enough now to do without Morgause. As for Mordred, he shall have his chance. I will do the same for him.'

I said nothing. In the pause, the cat purred, suddenly loud, and then stopped short on a sighing breath, and slept.

'Well,' said Arthur, 'what would you have me do? He is in my protection now, so—even if I could ever have

harmed him—I cannot kill him. I haven't had time to think this thing through, and there'll be time enough later to discuss it with you. But it has always seemed to me that, once the boy had survived Lot's murderous purge, I would sooner have him near me, and under my eye, than hidden somewhere in the kingdom, with the threat that that might entail. Say you agree with me.'

'I do. Yes.'

'So, if I keep him by me, and grant him the birthright that he must have thought he would never see—'

'I doubt if that has crossed his mind,' I said. 'I don't think she has told him who he is.'

'So? Then I shall tell him myself. Better still. He'll know that I needn't have accepted him. Merlin, it might be well. You and I both remember what it was like to live our youth out as unfathered bastards, and then to be told we were of Ambrosius' blood. And who am I to take on me yet again the wish for my son's death? Once was too much. God knows I paid for it.' He looked away again into the flames. There was a bitter line to his mouth. After a while he lifted a shoulder. 'You asked about Caliburn. It seems that my sister Morgan took herself a lover; he was one of my knights, a man called Accolon, a good fighter and a fine man—but one who could never say no to a woman. When King Urbgen was here with Morgan, she cast her eyes on Accolon, and soon had him at her girdle, like a greyhound fawning. Before she came south she had got some northern smith to make a copy of Caliburn, and while she was here in Camelot she managed to get Accolon to exchange this for the sword itself. She must have reckoned, in a time of peace, on getting herself free of the court and back to the north before the loss was discovered. I don't know what favours she granted Accolon, but certainly when she went north again with King Urbgen, Accolon took leave and went with them.'

'But why did she do this?'

His quick, surprised look made me realise how rarely

I had had to ask such a question. 'Oh, the usual reason: ambition. She had some idea of putting her husband on the high throne of Britain with herself as his queen. As for Accolon, I'm not sure what she promised him, but whatever it was, it cost him his life. It should have cost hers, too, but there was no proof, and she is Urbgen's wife. Her being my sister should not have helped her, but he knew nothing of the plot, and I cannot afford to have him as my enemy.'

'How did she hope to get away with it?'

'You had gone,' he said simply. 'She must have had word from Morgause that you were ailing, and she was making ready for her time of greatness. She reckoned that any man who held the sword could command a following, and if the King of Rheged were to raise it ... Before that, of course, I was to have been killed. Accolon tried. He picked a quarrel and fought me. It was the substitute sword, of course; the metal was brittle as glass. As soon as I tested it for use, I knew there was something wrong, but it was too late. At the first clash it broke off short below the hilt.'

'And?'

'Bedwyr and the rest were shouting "treachery", but they hardly needed to. I could see from Accolon's face that treachery was there. For all that his sword was still whole, and mine was broken, I think he was afraid. I drove the hilt into his face, and killed him with my dagger. I don't think he made any resistance. Perhaps he was a true man, after all. I like to think so.'

'And the true sword? How did you know where it was?'

'Nimuë,' he said. 'It was she who told me what had happened. Do you remember that day, at Applegarth, when she told me to beware Morgan and the sword?'

'Yes. I thought she must mean Morgause.'

'So did I. But she was right. All the time Morgan was at court, Nimuë hardly left her side. I wondered why, because it was obvious there was no love lost between them.' He gave a rueful little laugh. 'I'm afraid I took it

as a women's quarrel ... she's not overly fond of Guinevere, either ... but she was right about Morgan. The witch corrupted her when she was no more than a girl. How Nimuë got the sword back I don't know. She sent it down from Rheged with an armed escort. I haven't seen her since she went north.'

I started to ask something more, but he suddenly raised his head, listening.

'And here comes Bedwyr, if I'm not mistaken. We've had little enough time together, Merlin, but there will be other times. As God is good, there will be other times.' He got to his feet, put his hands down, and raised me. 'Now we have talked enough. You look exhausted. Will you go to your rest now, and leave me to face Bedwyr and the others, and give them the news? I warn you, it won't be a quiet party. They're likely to clean our good host out of anything drinkable he has in his cellars, and take the night to drink it ...'

But I stayed with him to receive the knights, and afterwards to drink with them. Nobody, all through the long, noisy celebration, mentioned Nimuë to me, and I did not ask again.

CHAPTER 9

We spent another full day resting at the 'Bush of Holly'. A party went back to the ford to bury the dead men, and from there on to Camelot with messages from the King. Another party was sent to Caerleon to give warning of the King's approach. Then, while I rested, the young men went hunting. Their day's sport provided an excellent dinner, and their servants and pages, who came up with us that day, helped the innkeeper and his wife cook and serve it. Where everyone slept that night, I have no idea; I suspect that the horses were turned out, and that the stable was even fuller than the inn. On the following day, to our hosts' evident regret, the royal party moved off for Caerleon.

Even after the building of Camelot, Caerleon had kept its status as Arthur's western stronghold. We rode in on a bright, windy day, with the Dragon standards snapping and rippling from the roofs, and the streets leading up to the fortress gates crowded with people. At my own insistence, I rode cloaked and hooded, and to the rear of the party, rather than beside the King. Arthur had finally been brought to accept my decision not to take my place near him again; one cannot go back on an abdication, and mine had been complete. He still had not mentioned Nimuë's part in that, though he must have been wondering (along with others, who also avoided mentioning her name to me) just how much of my power she had managed to assume. Of all people, she should have 'seen' that I was above ground again, and with the King; should have known, in fact, that I had been put still living into my tomb ...

But no one asked questions, and I was not prepared to supply what I believed to be the answers.

In Caerleon they had allotted royal chambers to me, next to Arthur's own. Two young pages, eyeing me with the liveliest curiosity, conducted me to the rooms through corridors crowded with bustling servants. Many of them knew me, and all had obviously heard some version of the strange story; some merely hurried past, making the sign against strong enchantment, but others came forward with greetings and offers of service. At last we reached my rooms, sumptuous apartments where a chamberlain awaited me, and showed me a splendid array of clothing sent by the King for me to choose from, with jewels from the royal coffers. A little to his disappointment I set aside the cloth of gold and silver, the peacock and the scarlet and the azure, and chose a warm robe of dark red wool, with a girdle of gilded leather, and sandals of the same. Then, saying, 'I will send light, my lord, and water for your washing,' he withdrew. A little to my surprise he signed to the two boys to leave the chamber with him, and left me there unattended.

It was already past the time of lamp-lighting. I went over to the window, where the sky was deepening slowly from red to purple, and sat down to wait for the pages to bring light.

I did not look round when the door opened. The flickering light of a cresset stole into the chamber, sending the evening sky receding, darkening beyond its weak young stars. The page moved softly round the room, touching lamp after lamp with flame, until the chamber glowed.

I felt tired after the ride, and heavy with reaction. It was time I roused myself, and let myself be made ready for the feasting tonight. The boy had gone out to set the cresset back in its iron bracket on the corridor wall. The chamber door was ajar.

I got to my feet. 'Thank you,' I began. 'Now, if of your goodness—'

I stopped. It was no page. It was Nimuë who came swiftly in, then stood backed against the door, watching me. She was clad in a long gown of grey, stitched with silver, and there was silver in her hair, which was loose, and flowing down over her shoulders. Her face was white, and her eyes wide and dark, and while I stood gazing, they suddenly brimmed over with tears.

Then she was across the room and had me fast in her arms, and was laughing and crying and kissing me, with words tumbling out that made no sense at all except the one, that I was alive, and that all the time she had been grieving for me as dead.

'Magic,' she kept saying, in a wondering, half-scared voice, 'it's magic, stronger than any I could ever know. And you told me you had given it all to me. I should have known. Ah, Merlin, Merlin ...'

Whatever had passed, whatever had kept her from me, or blinded her to the truth, none of it mattered. I found myself holding her close, with her head pressed against my breast, and my cheek on her hair, while she repeated over and over, like a child: 'It's you. It's really you. You've come back. It is magic. You must still be the greatest enchanter in all the world.'

'It was only the malady, Nimuë. It deceived you all. It was not magic. I gave all that to you.'

She lifted her head. Her face was tragic. 'Yes, and how you gave it! I only pray that you cannot remember! You had told me to learn all that you had to tell me. You had said that I must build on every detail of your life; that after your death I must be Merlin ... And you were leaving me, slipping from me in sleep ... I had to do it, hadn't I? Force the last of your power from you, even though with it I took the last of your strength? I did it by every means I knew—cajoled, stormed, threatened, gave you cordials and brought you back to answer me again and again—when what I should have done, had you been any other man, was to let you sleep, and go in peace. And because you were Merlin, and no

other man, you roused yourself in pain and answered me, and gave me all you had. So minute by minute I weakened you, when it seems to me now that I might have saved you.' She slid her hands up to my breast, and lifted swimming grey eyes. 'Will you tell me something truthfully? Swear by the god?'

'What is it?'

'Do you remember it, when I hung about you and tormented you to your death, like a spider sucking the life from a honey-bee?'

I put my hands up to cover hers. I looked straight into the beautiful eyes, and lied. 'My darling girl, I remember nothing of that time but words of love, and God taking me peacefully into his hand. I will swear it if you like.'

Relief swept into her face. But still she shook her head, refusing to be comforted. 'But then, even all the power and knowledge you gave me could not show me that we had buried you living, and send me back to get you out. Merlin, I should have known, I should have known! I dreamed again and again, but the dreams were full of confusion. I went back once to Bryn Myrddin, did you know? I went to the cave, but the door was blocked still, and I called and called, but there was no sound—'

'Hush, hush.' She was shivering. I pulled her closer, and bent my head and kissed her hair. 'It's over. I am here. When you came back for me, I must have been still in the trance. Nimuë, what happened was the will of the god. If he had wanted to save me from the tomb, he would have spoken to you. Now, he has brought me back in his own time, and for that, he saved me from being put quick into the ground, or given to the flames. You must accept it all, and thank him, as I do.'

She shivered again. 'That was what the High King wanted. He would give you, he said, a pyre as high as an emperor's, so that your death would be a beacon to the living the length and breadth of the land. He was wild with grief, Merlin. I could hardly make him listen to me. But I told him I had had a dream, and that you yourself

had said that you wished to be laid in your own hollow hill, and left in peace to become part of the land you loved.' She put a hand up to brush tears from her face. 'And it was true. I did have such a dream, one of many. But even so, I failed you. Who did what I should have done, and helped you to escape? What happened?'

'Come over here, to the fire, and I'll tell you. Your hands are cold. Come, we have a little time, I think, before we need go into the hall.'

'The King will stay for us,' she said. 'He knows I am here. He sent me to you.'

'Did he?' But I put that aside for the present. In a corner of the room a brazier burned red in front of a low couch covered with rugs and skins. We sat side by side in the warm glow, and, to her eager questions, I told my story yet again.

By the time I had finished her distress was gone, and a little colour had crept back into her cheeks. She sat close in my arm, with one of my hands held tightly in both her own. Magician or mortal man, there was no shadow of doubt in my mind that the joy she showed was as real as the glow of the brazier that warmed us both. Time had run back. But not quite: mortal man or magician, I could sense secrets still.

Meantime she listened and exclaimed, and held my hand tightly, and presently, when I had done, she took up the story.

'I told you about the dream I had. It made me uneasy; I began to wonder, even, if you had been truly dead when we left you in the cave. But there had seemed no doubt; you had lain so long without movement, and seemingly without breath, and then all the doctors declared you dead. So in the end we left you there. Then, when the dreams drove me back to the cave, all seemed normal. Then other dreams, other visions, came, which crowded that one out and confused it ...'

She had moved away from me while she was speaking, though she still held my hand between her own. She lay

back against the cushions at the end of the couch, looking away from me, into the heart of the glowing charcoal.

'Morgan,' I suggested, 'and the theft of the sword?'

She gave me a quick glance. 'I suppose the King told you about that? Yes. You heard how the sword was stolen. I had to leave Camelot, and follow Morgan, and take back the sword. Even there, the god was with me. While I was in Rheged a knight came there from the south; he was travelling to visit the queen, and at night, in Urbgen's hall, he told a strange tale. He was Bagdemagus—Morgan's kinsman, and Arthur's. You remember him?'

'Yes. His son was sick two summers back, and I treated him. He lived, but was left with an inflammation of the eyes.'

She nodded. 'You gave him some salve, and told him to use the same if the eyes troubled him again. You said it was blended with some herb you had at Bryn Myrddin.'

'Yes. It was wild clary, that I brought back from Italy. I had a supply at Bryn Myrddin. But how did he think he was going to get it?'

'He thought you meant that it grew there. He may have thought you had planted a garden, as we did at Applegarth. Of course he knew that you were buried there in the hill. He didn't admit to us that he was afraid, but I think he must have been. Well, he told us his story, how he had ridden across the hilltop, and heard music coming seemingly up out of the earth. But then his horse bolted in terror, and he didn't dare go back. He said he hadn't told anyone his story, because he was ashamed of his flight, and afraid of being laughed at; but then, he said, just before he came north, he had heard some tale in Maridunum about a fellow who had seen and spoken with your ghost ... Well, you know who that was, your grave-robber. Taken both together, and along with my persistent dreams, the story spoke aloud to me. You were alive, and in the cave. I would have left Luguvallium that night, but something else happened that forced me to stay.'

She glanced across at me, as if waiting for me to nod, knowing what was to come. But I said merely: 'Yes?'

There was the same brief flash of surprise that Arthur had shown, then she bit her lip, and explained.

'Morgause arrived, with the boys. All five. I was hardly a welcome guest, as you may guess, but Urbgen was civility itself, and Morgan was afraid of what she had done, and almost clung to me. I believe she thought, as long as I was there, that Urbgen's anger wouldn't be vented on her. And of course, I suppose she hoped that I might intercede with Arthur. But Morgause ...' She lifted her shoulders as if with cold.

'Did you see her?'

'Briefly. I could not stay there with her. I took my leave, and let them think I was going south, but I did not leave Luguvallium. I sent my page, secretly, to speak with Bagdemagus, and he came to see me at my lodgings. He's a good man, and he owed you his son's life. I did not tell him that I believed you were still living. I told him merely that Morgause had been your enemy, and your bane, and that Morgan had showed herself a witch also, and the enemy of the King. I begged him to spy, if he could, on their counsels, and report to me. You can be sure that I had already tried to reach Morgause's mind myself, and had failed. All I could hope for was that the sisters might talk together, and something could be learned from that about the drug that had been used on you. If my dream was right, and you still lived, the knowledge might help me save you yet. If not, I would have more evidence to give the King, and procure Morgause's death.' She lifted her hand to my cheek. Her eyes were sombre. 'I sat there in my lodgings waiting for him to come back, and knowing all the time that you might be dying, alone in the tomb. I tried to reach you, or even just to see, but whenever I tried to see you, and the hill, and the tomb, light would break across the vision and dash it aside, and there, moving down the light, floated a grail, clouded like a moon hidden in storm or mist. Then it would vanish,

and pain and loss would break through the dream till I
woke distracted, and crying, through the longing and the
sorrow, to dream again.'

'So you were warned of that? My poor child, left to
guard such a treasure ... Did Bagdemagus warn you
that Morgause had heard of it, and meant to steal it?'

'What?' She looked at me blankly. 'What do you mean?
What had Morgause to do with the grail? It would have
soiled the god himself if she had even looked at it. How
was she to know where to find it?'

'I don't know. But she took it. I was told so, by someone who watched her do it.'

'Then you were told a lie,' said Nimuë roundly. 'I took
it myself.'

'*It was you who took Macsen's treasure?*'

'Indeed it was.' She sat up, glowing. In her eyes two
little braziers, reflected, shone and glittered. The candid
grey eyes looked, with the red points of light, like cat's
eyes, or witch's. 'You told me yourself where it lay buried;
do you remember that? Or were you already gone into
your own mists, my dear?'

'I remember.'

She said soberly: 'You told me that power was a hard
master. It was the hardest thing I have ever done, to go
to Segontium, instead of travelling south again to Bryn
Myrddin. But in the end I knew I had been bidden to do
it, so I went. I took two of my servants, men I could
trust, and found the place. It had changed. The shrine
had gone, under a landslip, but I took the bearings you
had given me, and we dug there. It might have taken a
long time, but we had help.'

'A dirty little shepherd boy, who could hold a hazel
stick over the earth, and tell you where the treasure was
hidden.'

Her eyes danced. 'So, why do I trouble to tell you my
story? Yes. He came and showed us, and we dug down,
and took the box away. I went up into the fortress then,
and spoke with the Commandant. and slept there that

night, with a guard on my room. And during the night
as I lay in my bed, with that box beneath it, the visions
came teeming. I knew that you were alive, and free, and
that you would soon be with the King. So in the morning
I asked for an escort to take the treasure south, and set
off for Caerleon.'

'And so missed me by two days,' I said.

'Missed you? Where?'

'Did you think I "saw" the shepherd boy in the fire? No,
I was there.' I told her then, briefly, about my stay in
Segontium, and my visit to the vanished shrine. 'So when
the boy told me about you and your two servants, like a
fool I assumed it was Morgause. He didn't describe the
woman, except that she—' I paused, and looked across
at her with raised brows. 'He said she was a queen, and
the servants had royal badges. That was why I assumed—'

I stopped. Her hand, holding mine, had clenched suddenly. The laughter in her eyes died; she looked at me
fixedly, with a strange mixture of appeal and dread. It
did not need the Sight to guess the part of the story that
she had not told me, nor why Arthur and the rest had
avoided speaking of her to me. She had not usurped my
power, or had a hand in trying to destroy me: all she
had done, once the old enchanter had gone, was to take
a young man to her bed.

I seemed to have been expecting this moment for a
very long time. I smiled, and asked her, gently: 'Who is
he, the king of yours?'

The red rushed into her cheeks. I saw the tears sting
her eyes again. 'I should have told you straight away.
They said they hadn't told you. Merlin, I didn't dare.'

'Don't look like that, my dear. What we had, we had,
and one cannot drink the same draught of elixir twice.
If I had still been half a magician, I should have known
long ago. Who is he?'

'Pelleas.'

I knew him, a young prince, handsome and kind, with
a sort of gaiety about him that would help to offset the

haunted sombreness that sometimes hung around her. I spoke of him, commending him, and in a while she grew calmer, and began, with growing ease, to tell me about her marriage. I listened, and watched, and had time, now, to mark the changes in her; changes, I thought, due to the power that she had had so drastically to assume. My gentle Ninian had gone, with me into the mists. There was an edge to this Nimuë that had not been there before; something quietly formidable, a kind of honed brightness, like a weapon's edge. And in her voice, at times, sounded a subtle echo of the deeper tones that the god used, when, with authority and power, he descends to mortal speech. These attributes had once been mine. But I, accepting them, had taken no lover. I found myself hoping, for Pelleas' sake, that he was a strong-minded young man.

'Yes,' said Nimuë, 'he is.'

I started out of my thoughts. She was watching me, her head on one side, her eyes alight once more with laughter.

I laughed with her, then put out my arms. She came into them, and lifted her mouth. I kissed her, once with passion, and once with love, and then I let her go.

CHAPTER 10

Christmas at Caerleon. Pictures come crowding back to
me, sun and snow and torchlight, full of youth and
laughter, of bravery and fulfilment and time won back
from oblivion. I have only to shut my eyes; no, not even
that; I need only glance into the fire and they are here
with me, all of them.

Nimuë, bringing Pelleas, who treated me with deference, and her with love, but who was a king and a man.
'She belongs to the King,' he said, 'and then to me. And I
—well, it's the same, isn't it? I am his before ever I was
hers. Which of us, in the sight of God and King, is ever
his own man?'

Bedwyr, coming on me one evening down beside the
river, which slipped along, swollen and slate-grey, between its winter banks. A fleet of swans were proving the
mud at the water's edge among the reeds. Snow had
begun to fall, small and light, floating like swansdown
through the still air. 'They told me you had come this
way,' said Bedwyr. 'I came to take you back. The King
stays for you. Will you come now? It's cold, and will
get colder.' Then, as we walked back together: 'There's
news of Morgause,' he said. 'She has been sent north
into Lothian, to the nunnery at Caer Eidyn. Tydwal
will see to it that she's kept fast there. And
there's talk of Queen Morgan's being sent to join her.
They say that King Urbgen finds it hard to forgive
her attempt to embroil him in treachery, and he's afraid
that if he keeps her by him the taint will cling, to him
and to his sons. Besides, Accolon was her lover. So the
talk goes that Urbgen will put her away. He has sent

to Arthur for permission. He'll get it, too. I think Arthur will feel more comfortable with both his loving sisters safely shut up, and a good long way away. It was Nimuë's suggestion.' He laughed, looking at me sideways. 'Forgive me, Merlin, but now that the King's enemies are women, perhaps it is better that he has a woman to deal with them. And if you ask me, you'll be well out of it ...'

Guinevere, sitting at her loom one bright morning, with sun on the snow outside, and a caged bird singing on the sill beside her. Her hands lay idle among the coloured threads, and the lovely head turned to watch, down beside the moat, the boys at play. 'They might be my own sons,' she said. But I saw that her eyes did not follow the bright heads of Lot's children, but only the dark boy Mordred, who stood a little way apart from the others, watching them, not as an outcast might watch his more favoured brothers, but as a prince might watch his subjects.

Mordred himself. I never spoke with him. Mostly the boys were on the children's side of the palace, or in the care of the master-at-arms or those set to train them. But one afternoon, on a dark day drawing to dusk, I came on him, standing beside the arch of a garden gateway, as if waiting for someone. I paused, wondering how to greet him, and how he might receive his mother's enemy, when I saw his head turn, and he started forward. Arthur and Guinevere came together through the dead roses of the garden, and out through the archway. It was too far away for me to hear what was said, but I saw the Queen smile and reach out a hand, and the King spoke, with a kind look. Mordred answered him, then, in obedience to a gesture from Arthur, went with them as they moved off, walking between them.

And, finally, Arthur, one evening in the King's private chamber, when Nimuë brought the box to show him the treasure from Segontium.

The box lay on top of the big marble table that had been my father's. It was of metal, and heavy, its lid scored

and dented with the weight of the stuff that had fallen
on it when the shrine crumbled to ruin. The King laid
hands to it. For a few moments it resisted him, then
suddenly, light as a leaf, it lifted.

Inside were the things just as I remembered them.
Rotten canvas wrappings, and, gleaming through them,
the head of a lance. He drew it out, trying the edge with
a thumb, a gesture as natural as breathing.

'For ornament, I think,' he said, rubbing the jewels of
the binding with his hand, and laying it aside. Then came
a flattish dish, gold, with the rim crusted with gems. And
finally, out of a tumble of greyed linen fallen to dust, the
bowl.

It was the type of bowl they call sometimes a cauldron,
or a grail of the Greek fashion, wide and deep. It was of
gold, and from the way he handled it, very heavy. There
was chasing of some sort round the outside of the bowl,
and on the foot. The two handles were shaped like birds'
wings. On a band round it, out of the way of the drinker's
lips, were emeralds and sapphires. He turned and held
it out to me with both hands.

'Take it and see. It is the most precious thing I have
ever seen.'

I shook my head. 'It is not for me to touch.'

'Nor for me,' said Nimuë.

He looked at it for a moment longer, then he put it
back in the box with the lance and the dish, gently wrapping the things away in the linen which was worn thin,
like a veil. 'And you won't even tell me where to keep
such splendour, or what I am to do with it?'

Nimuë looked across at me, and was silent. When I
spoke, it was only a gentle echo of what I had said
before, long ago. 'It is not for you, either, Arthur. You do
not need it. You yourself will be the grail for your people,
and they will drink from you and be satisfied. You will
never fail them, nor ever leave them/quite. You do not
need the grail. Leave it for those who come after.'

'Then since it is neither mine nor yours,' said Arthur, 'Nimuë must take it, and with her enchantments hide it so that no one can find it except that they are fitted.'

'No one shall,' she said, and shut the lid on the treasure.

* * *

After that, another year dawned cold, and drew slowly into spring. I went home at April's end, with the wind turning warm, and the young lambs crying on the hill, and catkins shivering yellow in the copses.

The cave was swept and warm again, a place for living, and there was food there, with fresh bread and a crock of milk and a jar of honey. Outside, by the spring, were offerings left by the folk I knew, and all my belongings, with my books and medicines, my instruments and the great standing harp, had been brought from Applegarth.

My return to life had been easier than I had anticipated. It seems that, to the simple folk, as indeed to the people in distant parts of Britain, the tale of my return from death was accepted, not as plain truth, but as a legend. The Merlin they had known and feared was dead; a Merlin lived in the 'holy cave', working his minor magics, but only a ghost, as it were, of the enchanter they had known. It may be they thought that I, like so many pretenders of the past, was some small magician merely claiming Merlin's reputation and his place. In the court, and in the cities and the great places of the earth, people looked now to Nimuë for power and help. To me the local folk came to have their sores or their aches healed; to me Ban the shepherd brought the sickly lambs, and the children from the village their pet puppies.

So the year wore on, but so lightly that it seemed only like the evening of a quiet day. The days were golden, tranquil and sweet. There was no call of power, no great high clean wind, no pain in the heart or pricking of the flesh. The great doings of the kingdom seemed

no longer to trouble me. I did not hunger or ask after news, for when it came, it was brought by the King himself. Just as the boy Arthur, racing up to see me in the shrine of the Wild Forest, had poured out all the doings of every day at my feet, so did the High King of Britain bring me all his acts, his problems and his troubles, and spread them out there on the cave floor in the firelight, and talk to me. What I did for him I do not know; but always, after he had gone, I found myself sitting, drained and silent, in the stillness of complete content.

The god, who was God, had indeed dismissed his servant, and was letting him go in peace.

* * *

One day I drew the small harp to me, and set myself to make a new verse for a song sung many years ago.

> *Rest here, enchanter, while the fire dies.*
> *In a breath, in an eyelid's fall,*
> *You will see them, the dreams;*
> *The sword and the young king,*
> *The white horse and the running water,*
> *The lit lamp and the boy smiling.*
>
> *Dreams, dreams, enchanter! Gone*
> *With the harp's echo when the strings*
> *Fall mute; with the flame's shadow when the fire*
> *Dies. Be still, and listen.*
>
> *Far on the black air*
> *Blows the great wind, rises*
> *The running tide, flows the clear river.*
> *Listen, enchanter, hear*
> *Through the black air and the singing air*
> *The music …*

I had to leave the song there because a string broke. He

had promised to bring me new ones, next time he came.

* * *

He came again yesterday. Something had called him down to Caerleon, he said, so he had ridden up, just for an hour. When I asked him what the business was in Caerleon, he put the question aside, till I wondered—then dismissed it as absurd—if the journey had been made merely to see me. He brought gifts with him—he never came empty-handed—wine, a basket of cooked meats from his own kitchen, the promised harp-strings, and a blanket of soft new wool, woven, he told me, by the Queen's own women. He carried them in himself, like a servant, and put them away for me. He seemed in spirits. He told me of some young man who had recently come to court, a noble fighter, and a cousin of March of Cornwall. Then he spoke of a meeting he was planning with the Saxon 'king', Eosa's successor, Cerdic. We talked till the dark drew in, and his escort came jingling up the valley track for him.

Then he rose, lightly, and, as always now when he left me, stooped to kiss me. Usually he made me stay there, by the fire, while he went out into the night, but this time I got up and followed him to the cave entrance, and waited there to watch him go. The light was behind me, and my shadow stretched, thin and long, like the tall shadow of old, across the little lawn and almost to the grove of thorn trees where the escort waited below the cliff.

It was almost night, but over beyond Maridunum in the west, a lingering bar of light hinted at the dying sun. It threw a glint on the river skirting the palace wall where I was born, and touched a jewel spark on the distant sea. Near at hand the trees were bare with winter, and the ground crisp with the first frost. Arthur trod away from me across the grass, leaving ghost-prints in the frost. He reached the place where the track led down to the grove,

and half turned. I saw him raise a hand.

'Wait for me.' It was the same farewell always. 'Wait for me. I shall come back.'

And, as ever, I made the same reply:

'What else have I to do but wait for you? I shall be here, when you come again.'

The sound of the horses dwindled, faded, was gone. The winter's silence came back to the valley. The dark drew down.

A breath of the night slid, like a sigh, through the frost-hung trees. In its wake, faintly, like no sound but the ghost of a sound, came a faint, sweet ringing from the air. I lifted my head, remembering, once more, the child who had listened nightly for the music of the spheres, but had never heard it. Now here it was, all around me, a sweet, disembodied music, as if the hill itself was a harp to the high air.

Dark fell. Behind me the fire dimmed, and my shadow vanished. Still I stood listening, with the calmness over me of a great contentment. The sky, heavy with night, drew nearer the earth. The glimmer of the far sea moved, light and following shadow, like the slow arc of a sword sliding back to its sheath, or a barge dwindling under sail across the distant water.

It was quite dark. Quite still. A chill brushed my skin, like the cold touch of crystal.

I left the night, with its remote and singing stars, and came in, to the glow of the fire, and the chair where he had been sitting, and the unstrung harp.

THE LEGEND

When King Uther Pendragon lay close to death, Merlin approached him in the sight of all the lords and made him acknowledge his son Arthur as the new king. Which he did, and afterwards died, and was buried by the side of his brother Aurelius Ambrosius within the Giants' Dance.

Then Merlin had a great sword fashioned, and fixed by his magic art into a great stone shaped like an altar. There were gold letters on the sword which said: 'Whoso pulleth out this sword of this stone, is rightwise king born of all England.' When at length it was seen by all men that only Arthur could pull the sword from the stone, the people cried out: 'We will have Arthur unto our king, we will put him no more in delay, for we all see that it is God's will that he should be our king, and who that holdeth against it, we will slay him.' So Arthur was accepted by the people, high and low, and raised to be king. When he was crowned, he made Sir Kay the seneschal of England, and Sir Ulfius was made his chamberlain.

After this were many years of wars, and battles, but then came Merlin on a great black horse, and said to Arthur, 'Thou hast never done, hast thou not done enough? It is time to say Ho! And therefore withdraw you unto your lodging and rest you as soon as ye may, and reward your good knights with gold and with silver, for they have well deserved it.' 'It is well said,' quoth Arthur, 'and as thou hast devised, so it shall be done.' Then Merlin took his leave of Arthur, and travelled to see his master Blaise, that dwelt in Northumberland. So Blaise wrote the battles word by word, as Merlin told him.

Then one day King Arthur said to Merlin, 'My barons will let me have no rest, but needs I must take a wife.' 'It is well done,' said Merlin, 'that ye take a wife. Now is there any that ye love more than another?' 'Yea,' said King Arthur, 'I love Guinevere, the king's daughter, Leodegrance of the land of Cameliard, the which holdeth in his house the Table Round that ye told he had of my father Uther.' Then Merlin advised the King that Guinevere was not wholesome for him to take to wife, and warned him that Lancelot should love her, and she him again. In spite of this the King determined to wed Guinevere, and sent Sir Lancelot, the chief of his knights and his trusted friend, to bring her from her home.

On this journey Merlin's prophecy came to pass, and Lancelot and Guinevere loved one another. But they were helpless to realise their love, and in time Guinevere was married to the King. Her father, King Leodegrance, sent the Round Table to Arthur as a wedding gift.

Meanwhile Arthur's half-sister Morgause had borne her bastard son by the King. His name was Mordred. Merlin had prophesied that great danger should come to Arthur and his kingdom through this child, so when the King heard of the birth he sent for all the children born upon May-day, and they were put into a ship and set adrift. Some were four weeks old, some less. By chance the ship drove against a rock where stood a castle. The ship was destroyed, and all in it died except Mordred, who was found by a good man, and reared until he was fourteen years of age, when he was brought to the King.

Soon after the wedding of Arthur and Guinevere the King had to leave the court, and in his absence King Meleagant (Melwas) carried the Queen off into his kingdom from which, as men said, no traveller ever returned. The only way into her moated prison was by two very perilous paths. One of these was called 'the water bridge' because the bridge lay under water, invisible and very narrow. The other bridge was much more perilous, and had never been crossed by a man, made as it was of a

sharp sword. No one dared go after her but Lancelot, and he made his way through unknown country, until he came near Meleagant's lodge that had been built for the Queen. Then he crossed the sword bridge, and sustained grievous wounds therefrom, but he rescued the Queen, and later, in the presence of King Arthur and the court, he fought and killed Meleagant.

Then it befell that Merlin fell in a dotage on one of the damosels of the Lake, whose name was Nimuë, and Merlin would let her have no rest, but always he would be with her. He warned King Arthur that he should not be long above earth, but for all his craft he would be put alive into the earth, and he warned him also to keep his sword and the scabbard safely, for it would be stolen from him by a woman that he most trusted. 'Ah,' said the King, 'since ye know of your adventure, why do you not put it away by your magical arts, and prevent it?' 'That cannot be,' said Merlin. 'It is ordained that ye shall die a worshipful death, and I a shameful death.' Then he left the King. Shortly after this Nimuë, the damosel of the Lake, departed, and Merlin went with her wherever she went. They went over the sea to the land of Benwick, in Brittany, where King Ban was king, and Elaine his wife had with her the young child called Galahad. Merlin prophesied that one day Galahad should be the most man of worship in the world. Then after this Nimuë and Merlin left Benwick, and came into Cornwall. And the lady was afraid of him because he was a devil's son, and she did not know how to make away with him. Then it happened that Merlin showed her a cave in a rock which could be sealed with a great stone. So by her subtle working she made Merlin go under that stone to show her the magic that dwelt there, but she cast a spell on him so that he could not ever come out again. And she went away and left him there in the cave.

And anon a knight, a cousin of the King's called Bagdemagus, rode out from the court, to find a branch of an holy herb for healing. It happened that he rode by the

*rock where the Lady of the Lake had put Merlin under
the stone, and there he heard him lamenting. Sir Bagdemagus would have helped him, but when he went to
the stone to lift it, it was so heavy that an hundred men
could not have moved it. When Merlin knew he was there,
he told him to save his labour, for all was in vain. So
Bagdemagus went, and left him there.*

*Meantime it had happened as Merlin had foretold, and
Arthur's sister Morgan le Fay had stolen the sword of
Excalibur and its sheath. She gave these to Sir Accolon
with which to fight the King himself. And when the King
was armed for the fight there came a maiden from Morgan le Fay, and brought to Arthur a sword like Excalibur,
with its scabbard, and he thanked her. But she was false,
for the sword and the scabbard were counterfeits, and
brittle. So there was a battle between King Arthur and
Accolon. The Lady of the Lake came to this battle, for
she knew that Morgan le Fay wished ill to the King, and
she wanted to save him. King Arthur's sword broke in his
hand, and only after a grievous fight did he get his own
sword Excalibur back from Sir Accolon and defeat him.
Then Accolon confessed the treason of Morgan le Fay,
King Urien's wife, and the King granted mercy to him.*

*And after this the Lady of the Lake became the friend
and guardian of King Arthur, in the stead of Merlin the
enchanter.*

AUTHOR'S NOTE

According to legend, of which the main source is Malory's
Morte d'Arthur, *Merlin stayed above ground only a
short while after Arthur was crowned. The period of battles and tournaments that follows the coronation can
surely be taken to represent the actual battles fought by
the historic Arthur. All that we know of the real war-
leader, Arthur the Soldier* (dux bellorum), *is that he
fought twelve major battles before he could count Britain
safe from the Saxon enemy, and that eventually he died,
and Mordred with him, at the battle of Camlann. The
much-quoted account of the twelve battles occurs in the*
Historia Brittonum *written by the Welsh monk Nennius
in the ninth century.*

*Then Arthur fought against them in those days, with
the kings of the Britons, but he himself was the leader
of battles. The first battle was at the mouth of the
river which is called Glein. The second, third, fourth
and fifth, on another river, which is called Dubglas,
and is in the region of Linnuis. The sixth battle was on
the river which is called Bassas. The seventh was a
battle in the wood of Celidon, that is Cat Coit Celidon.
The eighth was the battle at Castellum Guinnion, in
which Arthur carried the image of Saint Mary, ever
Virgin, on his shoulders, and the pagans were put to
flight on that day and there was a great slaughter of
them through the power of our Lord Jesus Christ and
through the power of Saint Mary the Virgin, his mother.
The ninth battle was fought at the City of the Legions.
The tenth battle he fought on the river, which is*

called Tribuit. The eleventh occurred on the mountain, which is called Agned. The twelfth was the battle of Mount Badon, in which there fell together in one day 960 men in one onset of Arthur, and no one laid them low save himself alone. And in all the battles he remained victor.

Only two of these battles can be located with any kind of certainty; that in the Caledonian Forest—the Old Caledonian Forest that stretched down from Strathclyde into the modern Lake District—and the one at the City of Legions, which could be either Chester or Caerleon. I have contented myself with using Nennius' own place-names, and identifying only one other, the battle of the River Tribuit. It has been suggested that this is an early name of the River Ribble. There is a place where the old Roman road crosses the Ribble and heads towards the Aire Gap (the 'Pennine Gap'). This is called Nappa or Nappay Ford, and local tradition remembers a battle there. The nearby camp that I have called 'Tribuit' was at Long Preston; the other two in the Gap were of course Elslack and Ilkley. I also made use of a tradition that Arthur fought at High Rochester (Bremenium) in the Cheviots. Apart from these two 'battle sites' I have inserted none in the map.

Blaise. *According to Malory, Blaise 'wrote down Arthur's battles word for word', a chronicle which, if it ever existed, has vanished utterly. I took the liberty of building in a destructive agent in the person of Gildas, the young son of Caw of Strathclyde and brother of Heuil. These are historic personages. We are told that Arthur and Heuil hated one another. Gildas the monk, writing in about 540 A.D., refers to the victory of 'Mount Badon', but without mentioning Arthur by name. This has been interpreted as a sign, at the least, of disapproval of a leader who had shown himself no friend to the Church.*

Merlin's illness. *The episode in the Wild Forest is taken from the story of Merlin's madness as told in the* Vita Merlini, *a twelfth century Latin poem commonly ascribed to Geoffrey of Monmouth. This is in part a retelling of the older Celtic 'Lailoken' tale of the madman who roamed the Caledonian Forest. Merlin-Lailoken was present at the battle of Arfderydd (the modern Arthuret, near Carlisle) where his friend, the king, was killed. Driven mad by grief, he fled into the forest, where he eked out a wretched existence.*

There are two poems in The Black Book of Carmarthen *which are attributed to him. In one he describes the appletree that shelters and feeds him in the forest; in the other he addresses the piglet which is his sole companion.*

Guenever and Guinevere. *Tradition asserts that Arthur had two wives of the same name, or even three—though this was probably only a conveniently poetic round number. The rape of Guinevere by Melwas (or Meleagant) occurs in the mediæval romance* Lancelot *of Chrétien de Troyes. In Chrétien's story Lancelot has to cross a sword bridge leading to the hollow hill of faery—a version of the ancient rape fantasy that we find in the tales of Dis and Persephone, or Orpheus and Eurydice.*

Guinevere, according to the mediæval legends, suffered abduction from time to time as a matter of course, and equally as a matter of course was rescued by Lancelot. A modern reader can see how the stories rose around 'the much-abducted queen'. Mediæval singers found in 'King Arthur and his Court' a rich source of story-telling, and in time a long series of tales came to be hung around the central figures, much as the television series-writers hang their scripts today. Gradually, in the legends, Arthur himself fades into the background, and various new 'heroes' take the centre of the stage; Lancelot, Tristram, Gawain, Gereint. Lancelot, being purely fictional (and an invention some centuries later than the 'Arthurian fact'), is made to fill the role of the Queen's lover so essential to

the mediæval romancers and their convention of courtly love.

But it is tempting to believe that the first of the 'rape stories', the Queen's abduction by Melwas, was founded on fact. Certainly Melwas existed, and remains have been found of the right period that indicate strongholds on and near Glastonbury Tor. In my tale Bedwyr, whose name is linked with Arthur's long before 'Lancelot' ever appears, takes the Lancelot role. In the character of Guinevere, as here drawn, I believe I was influenced by Chaucer's treatment of the 'false' Criseyde.

Nimuë *(Niniane, Vivien). Nor is there any necessity to attribute the same sort of 'falseness' to Merlin's lover Nimuë. The 'betrayal' theme of this legend springs from the need to explain the death or disappearance of an all-powerful enchanter. My version of Merlin's end is based on a tradition which obtains still in parts of the 'Summer Country'. It was sent me many years ago by a Wiltshire correspondent. This version of the tale is that Merlin, with age drawing on, desired to hand on his magic powers to someone who could be Arthur's adviser after his death. For this he chose his pupil Nimuë, who showed herself adept. This tale not only allows the 'great enchanter' his dignity, and a measure of common sense, but also explains Nimuë's subsequent influence over Arthur. The King would hardly otherwise have kept her near him, or accepted her help against his enemies.*

Ninian. *The 'boy Ninian' episode was suggested by another incident found in the* Vita Merlini. *Here Merlin sees a youth buying shoes, and pieces of leather to repair them with to make them last longer. Merlin knows that the youth will have no need of the new shoes, as he will be drowned the same day.*

Cerdic Elesing. *The Anglo-Saxon Chronicle records that Cerdic and Cynric his son landed at Cerdices-ora with*

five ships. Cerdic was Elesing (the son of Elesa, or Eosa). The date given is 494 A.D.

Whatever doubt there may be about the dates of Cerdic's battles, or the locations of his first conquests (Cerdices-ora is thought to be Netley, near Southampton), all the chroniclers seem to agree that he was the founder of the first West Saxon monarchy from which Alfred was to claim descent. For Cerdic, and for the changing of the burial customs that Gereint suggests on page 103, see Hodgkin's History of the Anglo-Saxons, *Vol. 1, Section IV.*

Llud-Nuatha, or Nodens. *The shrine of Nodens is still to be seen, at Lydney in Gloucestershire.*

Merlin's song. *'He who is companionless' is based on the Anglo-Saxon poem 'The Wanderer'.*

Finally, for the many gaps in my knowledge of this enormous subject I can only beg forgiveness, and paraphrase what H. M. and N. K. Chadwick wrote in the preface to their Growth of English Literature: *'If I had read more widely I should never have completed this book.' More: if I had even known how much there was to read, I would never have dared to start to write at all. By the same token I cannot list all the authorities I have followed. But I can hope, in all humility, that my Merlin trilogy may be, for some new enthusiast, a beginning.*

Mary Stewart
Edinburgh 1975–1979

MARY STEWART

MADAM WILL YOU TALK?

'I stole a glance at his profile, with its expression of brooding bitterness, and the unpleasant set to the mouth. Then I remembered, with a queer cold little twist of the stomach, what Mrs. Palmer had said.

' "He must have been mad . . . they ought to have locked him up . . . *he must be mad* !" '

'Panic swept over me again, and at the same time a queer sense of unreality that I believe does come to people when they are in fantastic or terrifying situations.'

Charity's gay Provencal holiday turned into something very different, something both terrifying and precious. For in no time at all, she was enmeshed in the vile goings-on of a vicious gang of murderers, one of them a man with whom she was rapidly falling in love.

'The tension mounts steadily until it reaches breaking point . . . an excellent tale of mystery'
The Times

CORONET BOOKS

MARY STEWART
THE CRYSTAL CAVE

This is Mary Stewart's most triumphant bestseller – her magnificent novel of Merlin – the enigma in the days of King Arthur.

The Crystal Cave plunges the reader deep into Fifth Century Britain, a country in chaos and division after the Roman withdrawal, where minor kings plot and intrigue against each other in draughty, fog-bound settlements.

This is Merlin's world. The illegitimate son of a South Wales princess, his young life precariously in balance as the shifting tide of events wash over his homeland, he is aware at the earliest age of a great natural gift – the Sight.

Against a background of invasion and imprisonment, wars and conquest, we see his emergence into manhood equipped with learning and wisdom far in advance of his years and his time (which some were to call magic), and his dramatic role in the New Beginning – the coming of Arthur.

'Vivid, enthralling, absolutely first-class'

Daily Mail

CORONET BOOKS

'I asked if you were going to stay here till the crowning?'

'I think not. He may need me here for a while, if he's set on rebuilding. I'm hoping I shall have leave to go after Christmas, but I'll come back for the crowning.'

'If the Saxons give us leave to hold it.'

'As you say. To leave it till Pentecost would seem to be a little risky, but it's the bishops' choice, and the King would be wiser not to gainsay them.'

Valerius grunted. 'Maybe if they put their minds to it, and do some serious praying, God will hold the spring offensive back for them. Pentecost, eh? Do you suppose they're hoping for fire from heaven again ... theirs, this time, perhaps?' He eyed me sideways. 'What do you say?'

As it happened, I knew the legend to which he referred. Since the coming of the white fire into the Perilous Chapel, the Christians had been wont to refer to their own story, that once, at Pentecost, fire had fallen from heaven on their god's chosen servants. I saw no reason to quarrel with such an interpretation of what had happened at the Chapel: it was necessary that the Christians, with their growing power, should accept Arthur as their God-appointed leader. Besides, for all I knew, they were right.

Valerius was still waiting for me to answer. I smiled. 'Only that if they know from whose hand the fire falls, they know more than I do.'

'Oh, aye, that's likely.' His tone was faintly derisive. Valerius had been on garrison duty in Luguvallium on the night when Arthur lifted the sword from the fire in the Perilous Chapel, but, like everyone else, he had heard the tale. And, like everyone else, he shied away from what had happened there. 'So you're leaving us after Christmas? Are we to know where for?'

'I'm going home to Maridunum. It's five—no, six years since I was there. Too long. I'd like to see that all is well.'

'Then see that you do get back for the crowning. There will be great doings here at Pentecost. It would be a pity to miss them.'

By then, I thought, she would be near her time. I said

aloud: 'Oh, yes. With or without the Saxons, we shall have great doings at Pentecost.'

Then we spoke of other things until our quarters were reached, and we were bidden to join the King and his officers for meat.

* * *

Caerleon, the old Roman City of the Legions, had been rebuilt by Ambrosius, and since then kept garrisoned and in good repair. Arthur now set himself to enlarge it almost to its original capacity, and make it, besides, a king's stronghold and dwelling-place as well as a fortress. The old royal city of Winchester was reckoned now to be too near the borders of the Saxon federated territory, and too vulnerable, besides, to new invasion, situated as it is on the Itchen river where longboats had landed before now. London was still safely held by the British, nor had any Saxon attempted to thrust up into the Thames valley, but in Uther's time the longboats had penetrated as far as Vagniacae, and Rutupiae and the Isle of Thanet had long been securely in Saxon hands. The threat was felt to be there, and growing yearly, and since Uther's accession London had begun—imperceptibly at first, and then with increasing speed—to show decay. Now it was a city fallen on evil days; many of its buildings had collapsed through age and neglect; poverty showed itself everywhere, as markets moved away, and those who could afford to do so, left for safer places. It would never, men said, be a capital city again.

So, until his new stronghold should be ready to counter any serious invasion from the Saxon Shore, Arthur planned to make Caerleon his headquarters. It was the obvious choice. Within eight miles of it was Ynyr's capital of Guent, and the fortress itself, lying in a loop of the river but beyond the danger of flood, had mountains at its back, and was additionally protected on the east by marshes at the watersmeet of the Isca and the little Afon

Lwyd. Of course Caerleon's very strength restricted it; it could defend only a small portion of the territory under Arthur's shield. But for the present it could provide the headquarters for his policy of mobile defence.

I was with him all through that first winter. He did ask me once, with a smiling lift of the brows, if I was not going to leave him for my cave in the hills, but I said merely: 'Later,' and let it be.

I told him nothing about the dream I had had that night at Nodens' shrine. He had enough to think about, and I was only too thankful that he seemed to have forgotten the possible consequences of that night with Morgause. Time enough to talk to him when the news came from York about the wedding.

Which it did, in good time to stop the court's preparation to go north for the celebrations at Christmas. A long letter came first, from Queen Ygraine to the King; one came for me with the same courier, and was brought to me where I walked by the river. All morning I had been watching the laying of a conduit, but for the moment work had ceased, as the men went for their midday bread and wine. The troops drilling on the parade ground near the old amphitheatre had dispersed, and the winter day was still and bright, with a pearled mist.

I thanked the man, waiting, letter in hand, until he had gone. Then I broke the seal.

The dream had been a true one. Lot and Morgause were married. Before ever Queen Ygraine and her party reached York, the news had gone before them, that the lovers were handfast. Morgause—I was reading between the lines here—had ridden into the city with Lot, flushed with triumph and decked with his jewels, and the city, preparing for a royal wedding, with a sight of the High King himself, made the best of its disappointment, and, with northern thrift, held the wedding feast just the same. The King of Lothian, said Ygraine had borne himself meekly to her, and had made gifts to the chief men of the city, so his welcome had been warm enough. And Morgan

—I could read the relief in the plain words—Morgan had showed neither anger nor humiliation; she had laughed aloud, and then wept with what appeared to be sheer relief. She had gone to the feasting in a gay red gown, and no girl had been merrier, even though (finished Ygraine with the touch of acid that I remembered) Morgause had worn her new crown from rising to bedtime . . .

As for the Queen's own reaction, I thought that this, too, was one of relief. Morgause, understandably, had never been dear to her, whereas Morgan was the only child she had had by her to rear. It was clear that, while prepared to obey King Uther, both she and Morgan had disliked the marriage with the black northern wolf. I did, indeed, wonder if Morgan knew more about him than she had told her mother. It was even possible that Morgause, being what she was, had boasted that she and Lot had already lain together.

Ygraine herself showed no suspicion of this, nor of the bride's pregnancy as a possible reason for the hasty marriage. It was to be hoped that there was no hint, either, in the letter she had sent to Arthur. He had too much on his mind now: there would be time yet for the anger and the distress. He must be crowned first, and then be free to go about his formidable task of war without being shackled by what was women's business—and would, all too soon, be mine.

* * *

Arthur flung the letter down. He was angry, that was plain, but holding it on the rein.

'Well? I take it you know?'

'Yes.'

'How long have you known?'

'The Queen your mother wrote to me. I have just read the letter. I imagine it carries the same news as yours.'

'That is not what I asked you.'

I said mildly: 'If you are asking me, did I know this was going to happen, the answer is yes.'

The angry dark gaze kindled. '*You did?* Why did you not tell me?'

'For two reasons. Because you were occupied with things that matter more, and because I was not quite sure.'

'You? Not sure? Come, Merlin! This from you?'

'Arthur, all that I knew or suspected of this came to me in a dream, one night some weeks ago. It came, not like a dream of power, or divination, but like a nightmare brought on by too much wine, or by too much thinking about that hellcat and her works and ways. King Lot had been in my mind, and so had she. I dreamed I saw them together, and she was trying on his crown. Was that enough, do you think, for me to make you a report that would have set the court by the ears, and you, maybe, racing up to York to quarrel with him?'

'It would have been enough, once.' His mouth showed a stubborn and still angry line. I saw that the anger sprang from anxiety, striking at the wrong time about Lot's intentions.

'That,' I said, 'was when I was the King's prophet. No' —at his quick movement—'I belong to no man else. I am yours, as always. But I am a prophet no longer, Arthur. I thought you understood.'

'How could I? What do you mean?'

'I mean that the night at Luguvallium, when you drew the sword I had hidden for you in the fire, was the last time that the power visited me. You did not see the place afterwards, when the fire was gone and the chapel empty. It had broken the stone where the sword lay, and destroyed the sacred relics. Me, it did not destroy, but I think the power was burned out of me, perhaps for ever. Fires fade to ash, Arthur. I thought you must surely have guessed.'

'How could I?' he said again, but his tone had changed. It was no longer angry and abrupt, but slow and thinking. As I, after Luguvallium, had felt myself ageing, then

Arthur had, for good and all, left his boyhood. 'You've seemed the same as always. Clearheaded, and so sure of yourself that it's like asking advice of an oracle.'

I laughed. 'They were not always so clear, by all accounts! Old women, or witless girls mumbling in the smoke. If I've been sure of myself during these past weeks, it's because the advice I have been asked for concerns my professional skills, no more.'

' "No more?" Enough, one would think, for any king to call on, if that were all he had known from you ... But yes, I think I see. It's the same for you as for me; the dreams and visions have gone, and now we have a life to live by the rules of men. I should have understood. You did, when I went myself after Colgrim.' He walked over to the table where Ygraine's letter lay, and rested a fist on the marble. He leaned on it, frowning downwards, but seeing nothing. Then he looked up. 'And what of the years that are to come? The fighting will be bitter, and it will not be over this year, or the next. Are you telling me that I shall have nothing from you now? I'm not talking about your engines of war, or your knowledge of medicine; I'm asking you if I am not to have the "magic" that the soldiers tell me about, the help that you gave to Ambrosius and to my father?'

I smiled. 'That, surely.' He was thinking, I knew, of the effect my prophecies, and sometimes my presence, had had on the fighting troops. 'What the armies think of me now, they will go on thinking. And where is the need for further prophecies concerning the wars you are embarked on? Neither you nor your troops will need reminding at every turn. They know what I have said. Out there in the field, the length and width of Britain, there is glory for you, and for them. You will have success, and success again, and in the end—I do not know how far ahead— you will have victory. That is what I said to you, and it is still true. It is the work you were trained for: go and do it, and leave me to find a way to do mine.'

'Which is, now that you've flown your eagle chick, and

yourself stay earthborne? To wait for victory, then help me build again?'

'In time.' I indicated the crumpled letter. 'But more immediately, to deal with such things as this. After Pentecost, with your leave, I shall go north to Lothian.'

A moment of stillness, while I saw the flush of relief colour his face. He did not ask what I meant to do there, but said merely: 'I shall be glad. You know that. I doubt if we need to discuss why this happened?'

'No.'

'You were right before, of course. As ever. What she wanted was power, and it did not matter to her how she took it. Or indeed, where she looked for it. I can see that now. I can only be glad to feel myself absolved of any claim she might make on me.' A small movement of his hand brushed Morgause and her plots aside. 'But two things remain. The most important is that I still need Lot as an ally. You were right—again!—in not telling me of your dream. I would certainly have quarrelled with him. As it is—'

He paused, with a lift of the shoulders. I nodded.

'As it is you can accept Lot's marriage to your half-sister, and count it as sufficient alliance to hold him to your banner. Queen Ygraine, it seems, has acted wisely, and so has Morgan, your sister. This is, after all, the match that King Uther originally proposed. We may safely ignore the reasons for it now.'

'All the more easily,' he said, 'because it seems that Morgan is not ill pleased. If she had shown herself slighted ... That was the second problem I spoke of. But it seems to be no problem after all. Did the Queen tell you in her letter that Morgan showed nothing but relief?'

'Yes. And I have questioned the courier who brought the letters from York. He tells me that Urbgen of Rheged was at York for the wedding, and that Morgan hardly saw Lot for watching him.'

Urbgen was now King in Rheged, old King Coel having died soon after the battle at Luguvallium. The new King

was a man in his late forties, a notable warrior, and still a vigorous and handsome man. He had been widowed two or three years ago.

Arthur's look quickened with interest. 'Urbgen of Rheged? Now, that would be a match! It's the one I'd have preferred all along, but when the match was made with Lot, Urbgen's wife was still living. Urbgen, yes ... Along with Maelgon of Gwynedd, he's the best fighting man in the north, and there has never been any doubt of his loyalty. Between those two, the north would be held firmly ...'

I finished it for him. 'And let Lot and his queen do what they will?'

'Exactly. Would Urbgen take her, do you think?'

'He will count himself lucky. And I believe she will fare better than she could ever have done with the other. Depend upon it, you'll be receiving another courier soon. And that is an informed guess, not a prophecy.'

'Merlin, do you mind?'

It was the King who asked me, a man as old and wise as myself; a man who could see past his own crowding problems, and guess what it might mean to me, to walk in dead air where once the world had been a god-filled garden.

I thought for a little before I answered him. 'I'm not sure. There have been times like this before, passive times, ebb after flood; but never when we were still on the threshold of great events. I am not used to feeling helpless, and I own that I cannot like it. But if I have learned one thing during the years when the god has been with me, it is to trust him. I am old enough now to walk tranquilly, and when I look at you I know that I have been fulfilled. Why should I grieve? I shall sit on the hilltops and watch you doing the work for me. That is the guerdon of age.'

'Age? You talk as if you were a greybeard! What are you?'

'Old enough. I'm nearly forty.'

'Well, then, for God's sake—?'

And so, in laughter, we passed the narrow corner. He drew me then to the window table where my scale models of the new Caerleon stood, and plunged into a discussion of them. He did not speak of Morgause again, and I thought: I spoke of trust, what sort of trust is this? If I fail him, then I shall indeed be only a shadow and a name, and my hand on the sword of Britain was a mockery.

When I asked leave to go to Maridunum after Twelfth Night, he gave it half absently, his mind already on the next task to hand for the morning.

* * *

The cave I had inherited from Galapas the hermit lay some six miles east of Maridunum, the town that guards the mouth of the River Tywy. My grandfather, the King of Dyfed, had lived there, and I, brought up as a neglected bastard in the royal household, had been allowed by a lazy tutor to run wild. I had made friends with the wise old recluse who lived in the cave on Bryn Myrddin, a hill sacred to the sky-god Myrddin, he of the light and the wild air. Galapas had died long ago, but in time I made the place my home, and the folk still came to visit Myrddin's healing spring, and to receive treatment and remedies from me. Soon my skill as a doctor surpassed even the old man's, and with it my reputation for the power that men call magic, so now the place was known familiarly as Merlin's Hill. I believe that the simpler folk even thought that I was Myrddin himself, the guardian of the spring.

There is a mill set on the Tywy, just where the track for Bryn Myrddin leaves the road. When I reached it I found that a barge had come up-river, and was moored there. Its great bay horse grazed where it could on the winter herbage, while a young man unloaded sacks onto the wharf. He worked single-handed; the barge master must be withindoors slaking his thirst; but it was only one man's job to lift the half-score of grain sacks that had been sent up for grinding from some winter store. A child of

perhaps five years old trotted to and fro, hindering the work, and talking ceaselessly in a weird mixture of Welsh and some other tongue familiar but so distorted—and lisping besides—that I could not catch it. Then the young man answered in the same tongue, and I recognised it, and him. I drew rein.

'Stilicho!' I called. As he set the sack down and turned, I added in his own tongue: 'I should have let you know, but time was short, and I hardly expected to be here so soon. How are you?'

'My lord!' He stood amazed for a moment, then came running across the weedy yard to the road's edge, wiped his hands down his breeches, reached for my hand, and kissed it. I saw tears in his eyes, and was touched. He was a Sicilian who had been my slave on my travels abroad. In Constantinople I had freed him, but he had chosen to stay with me and return to Britain, and had been my servant while I had lived on Bryn Myrddin. When I went north he married the miller's daughter, Mai, and moved down the valley to live at the mill.

He was bidding me welcome, talking in the same excited, broken tongue as the child. What Welsh he had learned seemed to have deserted him for the moment. The child came up and stood, finger in mouth, staring.

'Yours?' I asked him. 'He's a fine boy.'

'My eldest,' he said with pride. 'They are all boys.'

'"All?"' I asked, raising a brow at him.

'Only three,' he said, with the limpid look I remembered, 'and another soon.'

I laughed and congratulated him, and hoped for another strong boy. These Sicilians breed like mice, and at least he would not, like his own father, be forced to sell children into slavery to buy food for the rest. Mai was the miller's only daughter, and would have a fat patrimony.

Had already, I found. The miller had died two years back; he had suffered from the stone, and would take neither care nor medicine. Now he was gone, and Stilicho was miller in his stead.

'But your home is cared for, my lord. Either I or the lad who works for me ride up every day to make sure all is well. There's no fear that anyone would dare go inside; you'll find your things just as you left them, and the place clean and aired ... but of course there'll be no food there. So if you were wanting to go up there now ...' He hesitated. I could see he was afraid of presuming. 'Will you not honour us, lord, by sleeping here for tonight? It'll be cold up yonder, and damp with it, for all that we've had the brazier lit every week through the winter, like you told me, to keep the books sweet. Let you stay here, my lord, and the lad will ride up now to light the brazier, and in the morning Mai and I can go up—'

'It's good of you,' I said, 'but I shan't feel the cold, and perhaps I can get the fires going myself ... more quickly, even, than your lad, perhaps?' I smiled at his expression; he had not forgotten some of the things he had seen when he served the enchanter. 'So thank you, but I'll not trouble Mai, except perhaps for some food? If I might rest here for a while, and talk to you, and see your family, then ride up into the hill before dark? I can carry all I shall need until tomorrow.'

'Of course, of course ... I'll tell Mai. She'll be honoured ... delighted ...' I had already caught a glimpse of a pale face and wide eyes at a window. She would be delighted, I knew, when the awesome Prince Merlin rode away again; but I was tired from the long ride, and had, besides, smelled the savoury stew cooking, which no doubt could easily be made to go one further. So much, indeed, Stilicho was naïvely explaining: 'There's a fat fowl on the boil now, so all will be well. Come you in, and warm yourself, and rest till supper time. Bran will see to your horse, while I get the last sacks off the barge, and it away back to town. So come your ways, lord, and welcome back to Bryn Myrddin.'

* * *

Of all the many times I had ridden up the high valley-side towards my home on Bryn Myrddin, I do not quite know why I should remember this one so clearly. There was nothing special to mark it; it was a home-coming, no more.

But up to this moment, so much later, when I write of it, every detail of that ride remains vivid. The hollow sound of the horse's hoofs on the iron ground of winter; the crunch of leaves underfoot, and snap of brittle twigs; the flight of a woodcock and the clap of a startled pigeon. Then the sun, falling ripe and level as it does just before candle-time, lighting the fallen oak-leaves where they lay in shadow, edged with rime like powdered diamond; the holly boughs rattling and ringing with the birds I disturbed from feeding on the fruit; the smell of damp juniper as my horse pushed through; the sight of a single spray of whin flowers struck to gold by the sunlight, with the night's frost already crisping the ground and making the air pure and thin as chiming crystal.

I stabled my horse in the shed below the cliff, and climbed the path to the little alp of turf before the cave. And there was the cave itself, with its silence, and the familiar scents, and the still air stirring only to the faint movement of velvet on velvet, where the bats in the high lantern of the rock heard my familiar step, and stayed where they were, waiting for the dark.

Stilicho had told me the truth; the place was well cared for, dry and aired, and, though it was colder by a cloak's thickness even than the frosty air outside, that would soon mend. The brazier stood ready for kindling, and fresh dry logs were set on the open hearth near the cave's entrance. There was tinder and flint on the usual shelf: in the past I had rarely troubled to use them, but this time I took them down, and soon had a flame going. It may be that, remembering a former, tragic home-coming, I was half-afraid to test (even in this tranquil after-time) the least of my powers: but I believe that the decision was made through caution rather than through fear. If I still

had power to call on, I would save it for greater things than the making of a flame to warm me. It is easier to call the storm from the empty sky, than to manipulate the heart of a man; and soon, if my bones did not lie to me, I should be needing all the power I could muster, to pit against a woman; and this is harder to do than anything concerning men, as air is harder to see than a mountain.

So I lit the brazier in my sleeping-chamber, and kindled the logs at the doorway, then unpacked my saddle-bags and went out with the pitcher to draw water from the spring. This trickled out of a ferny rock beside the cave-mouth, and lisped through the hanging lace of rime, to drip into a round stone basin. Above it, among the mosses, and crowned with icy glitter, stood the image of the god Myrddin, who keeps the roads of the sky. I poured a libation to him, then went in to look to my books and medicines.

Nothing had taken harm. Even the jars of herbs, sealed and tied as I had taught Stilicho to do it, seemed fresh and good. I uncovered the great harp that stood at the back of the cave, and carried it near the fire to tune it. Then, having made my bed ready, I mulled some wine and drank it, sitting by the leaping fire of logs. Finally, I unwrapped the small knee-harp that had been with me on all my travels, and carried it back to its place in the crystal cave. This was a small inner cave, with its opening set high in the rear wall of the main cavern, and so placed behind a jut of rock that in the normal way the shadows hid it from sight. When I was a boy it had been my gate of vision. Here, in the inner silence of the hill, folded deep in darkness and in solitude, no sense could play except the eye of the mind, and no sound come.

Except, as now, the murmur of the harp as I set it down. It was the one I had made as a boy, so finely strung that the very air could set it whispering. The sounds were weird and sometimes beautiful, but somehow outside the run of music as we know it, as the song of the grey seal on the rocks is beautiful, but is the sound of the wind and

the waves rather than of a beast. The harp sang to itself as I set it down, with a kind of slumbrous humming, like a cat purring to be back on its own hearthstone.

'Rest you there,' I told it, and at the sound of my voice running round the crystal walls it hummed again.

I went back to the bright fire, and the stars gemming the black sky outside. I lifted the great harp to me and—hesitating at first, and then more easily—made music.

> *Rest you here, enchanter, while the light fades.*
> *Vision narrows, and the far*
> *Sky-edge is gone with the sun.*
> *Be content with the small spark*
> *Of the coal, the smell*
> *Of food, and the breath*
> *Of frost beyond the shut door.*
> *Home is here, and familiar things;*
> *A cup, a wooden bowl, a blanket,*
> *Prayer, a gift for the god, and sleep.*
>
> *(And music, says the harp,*
> *And music.)*

CHAPTER 6

With the spring came, inevitably, trouble. Colgrim, sniffing his way cautiously back along the eastern coasts,
landed within the old federated territories, and set about
raising a new force to replace the one defeated at Luguvallium and the Glein.

I was back in Caerleon by that time, busy with Arthur's
plans for the establishment there of his new mobile cavalry
force.

The idea, though startling, was not altogether new.
With Saxon Federates already settled, and by treaty, in
the south-eastern districts of the island, and with the
whole eastern seaboard continually at risk, it was impossible to set up and effectively maintain a fixed line of
defence. There were, of course, certain defensive ramparts
already in existence, of which Ambrosius' Wall was the
greatest. (I omit Hadrian's Great Wall here; it was never
a purely defensive structure, and had been, even in the
Emperor Macsen's time, impossible to keep. Now it was
breached in a score of places; and besides, the enemy was
no longer the Celt from the wild country to the north;
he came from the sea. Or he was already, as I have explained, within the gates of south-east Britain.) The
others, Arthur set himself to extend and refurbish, not-
ably the Black Dyke of Northumbria, which protects
Rheged and Strathclyde, and the older Wall which the
Romans originally built across the high chalk downlands
south of the Sarum plain. The King planned to extend
this wall northward. The roads through it were to be
left open, but could be shut fast if any attempt was made
by the enemy to move towards the Summer Country to

the west. Other defensive works were planned, soon to be under way. Meanwhile, all the King could hope to do was fortify and man certain key positions, establish signal stations between these, and keep open the communicating roads. The kings and chiefs of the British would keep each his own territory, while the High King's work would be to maintain a fighting force that could be taken at need to help any of them, or be thrown into whatever breach was made in our defences. It was the old plan with which Rome had successfully defended her province for some time before the withdrawal of the legions: the Count of the Saxon Shore had commanded just such a mobile force, and indeed Ambrosius, more recently, had done the same.

But Arthur planned to go further. 'Caesar-speed', as he saw it, could be made ten time as speedy if the whole force were mounted. Nowadays, when one sees cavalry troops daily on the roads and in the parade grounds, this seems a normal enough thing; but then, when he first thought of it and put it to me, it came with all the force of the surprise attack he hoped to achieve with it. It would take time, of course; the beginnings, perforce, would be modest. Until enough of the troops were trained to fight from horseback, it would have to be a smallish, picked force drawn from among the officers and his own friends. This granted, the plan was feasible. But no such plan could be put into being without the right horses, and of these we could command relatively few. The cobby little native beasts, though hardy, were neither speedy enough nor big enough to carry an armed man into battle.

We talked it over for days and nights, going into every detail, before Arthur would put the idea before his commanders. There are those—the best, too, often among them—who are opposed to any kind of change; and unless every argument can be met, the waverers are drawn to cast with the noes. Between them Arthur and Cador, along with Gwilim of Dyfed and Ynyr from Caer Guent, hammered the thing out over the map-tables. I could contri-

bute little to the war-talk, but I did solve the problem of the horses.

There is a race of horses which are said to be the best in the world. Certainly they are the most beautiful. I had seen them in the East, where the men of the desert prize them more than their gold or their women; but they could be found, I knew, nearer than that. The Romans had brought some of these creatures back from North Africa into Iberia, where they interbred with the thicker-bodied horses from Europe. The result was a splendid animal, fast and fiery, but strong with it, and supple, and biddable as a war-horse should be. If Arthur would send across to see what might be bought, then as soon as the weather would allow safe transportation, the makings of a mounted force could be his by the following summer.

So when I got back to Caerleon in the spring, it was to put in motion the building of big new stable-blocks, while Bedwyr was dispatched overseas to do the horse-trading.

Caerleon was already transformed. Work on the fortress itself had gone quickly and well, and now other buildings were springing up nearby, of sufficient comfort and grandeur to grace a temporary capital. Though Arthur would use the commandant's house inside the walls as battle headquarters, another house (which the folk called 'the palace') was being built outside, in the lovely curve of the Isca River, by the Roman bridge. When finished this would be a large house, with several courtyards for guests and their servants. It was well built, of stone and brick-work, with painted plaster and carved pillars at the doors. Its roof was gilded, like that of the new Christian church, which was on the site of the old Mithras temple. Between these two buildings and the parade ground to the west of them, houses and shops were springing up, making a bustling township where before there had only been a small village settlement. The folk, proud of Arthur's choice of Caerleon, and willing to ignore the reasons for it, worked with a will to make the place worthy of a new reign, and a king who would bring peace.

He brought peace of a sort by Pentecost. Colgrim, with his new army, had broken bounds in the eastern regions. Arthur fought him twice, once not far south of the Humber, the second time nearer the Saxon boundary, in the reedy fields of Linnius. In the second of these battles Colgrim was killed. Then, with the Saxon Shore uneasily recoiling into quiet once more. Arthur came back to us, in time to meet Bedwyr disembarking with the first contingent of the promised horses.

Valerius, who had been to help disembark them, was enthusiastic.

'High as your breast, and strong with it, and as gentle as maidens. Some maidens, that is. And fast, they say, as greyhounds, though they're still stiff from the voyage, and it'll take some time before they get their land-legs again. And beautiful! There's many a maiden, gentle or otherwise, who'd sacrifice to Hecate for eyes as big and dark, or skins as silken ...'

'How many did he bring? Mares as well? When I was in the East they parted only with the stallions.'

'Mares as well. A hundred stallions in this first lot, and thirty mares. Better off than the army on campaign, but still fierce competition, eh?'

'You've been at war too long,' I told him.

He grinned and went, and I called my assistants and went up through the new cavalry lines to make sure that all would be ready to receive the horses, and to check yet again the new, light field-harness that the saddlers' workshops had made for them.

As I went, the bells began to ring from the gilded towers. The High King was home, and preparations for the crowning could begin.

* * *

Since I had watched Uther crowned I had travelled abroad, and seen splendours—in Rome, Antioch, Byzantium—beside which anything that Britain could do was

like the mumming of gaudy tumblers: but there was about the ceremony at Caerleon a young and springtime glory that none of the riches of the East could have procured. The bishops and priests were splendid in scarlet and purple and white, set off the more brilliantly by the browns and sables of the holy men and women who attended them. The kings, each with his following of nobles and fighting men, glittered with jewels and gilded arms. The walls of the fortress, crested with the shifting and craning heads of the people, stirred with bright hangings, and rang with cheering. The ladies of the court were gay as kingfishers: even Queen Ygraine, in a glow of pride and happiness, had put aside her mourning robes, and shone like the rest. Morgan, beside her, had certainly none of the air of a rejected bride; she was only a little less richly dressed than her mother, and showed the same smiling, royal composure. It was difficult to remember how young she was. The two royal ladies kept their places among the women, not coming to Arthur's side. I heard, here and there, murmurs among the ladies, and perhaps even more among the matrons, who had their eyes on the empty side of the throne; but to me it was fitting that there should be no one yet to share his glory. He stood alone in the centre of the church, with the light from the long windows kindling the rubies to a blaze, and laying panels of gold and sapphire along the white of his robe, and on the fur that trimmed the scarlet mantle.

I had wondered if Lot would come. Gossip had gathered, like a boil, to bursting-point before we knew; but come, in the end, he did. Perhaps he felt that he would lose more by staying away than by braving the King and Queen and his slighted princess, for, a few days before the ceremony, his spears were seen, along with those of Urien of Gore, and Aguisel of Bremenium, and Tydwal who kept Dunpeldyr for him, flouting the sky to the north-east. This train of northern lords stayed encamped together a little beyond the township, but they came crowding in to join the celebrations as if nothing unto-

ward had ever happened at Luguvallium or York. Lot himself showed a confidence too easy to be called bravado; he was relying, perhaps, on the fact that he was now hand-kin to Arthur. Arthur said as much, privately, to me; in public he received Lot's ceremonious courtesies blandly. I wondered, with fear, if Lot yet suspected that he had the King's unborn child at his mercy.

At least Morgause had not come. Knowing the lady as I did, I thought she might have come and faced even me, for the pleasure of flaunting her crown in front of Ygraine, and her swollen belly in front of Arthur and myself. But whether for fear of me, or whether Lot's nerve had failed him and he had forbidden it, she stayed away, with her pregnancy as the plea. I was beside Arthur when Lot gave his queen's excuses; there was no hint of any extra knowledge in his face or voice, and if he saw Arthur's sudden glance at me, or the slight paling of his cheeks, he gave no sign. Then the King had himself in hand again, and the moment passed.

So the day wore through its brilliant, exhausting hours. The bishops spared no touch of holy ceremonial, and, for the pagans present, the omens were good. I had seen signs other than that of the Cross being made in the street as the procession passed, and at the street corners fortunes were told with bones and dice and gazing, while pedlars did a brisk trade with every kind of charm and luck-piece. Black cockerels had been killed at dawning, and offerings made at ford and crossroads, where the old Herm used to wait for travellers' gifts. Outside the city, in mountain and valley and forest, the small dark folk of the upper hills would be watching their own omens and petitioning their own gods. But in the city centre, on church and palace and fortress alike, the Cross caught the sun. As for Arthur, he went through the long day with calm and pale-faced dignity, stiff with jewels and embroidery, and rigid with ceremony, a puppet for the priests to sanctify. If this was needed to declare his authority finally in the eyes of the people, then this was what he would do. But

I, who knew him, and who stood at his side all through
that endless day, could sense neither dedication or prayer
in that still composure. He was probably, I thought, planning the next fighting foray to the east. For him, as for
all who had seen it, the kingdom had been taken into his
hand when he lifted the great sword of Maximus from its
long oblivion, and made his vow to the listening forests.
The crown of Caerleon was only the public seal of what
he had held in his hand then, and would hold until he
died.

Then, after the ceremony, the feast. One feast is much
like another, and this one was remarkable only for the
fact that Arthur, who loved his food, ate very little, but
glanced about him from time to time as if he could hardly
wait for the feasting to stop, and the time of affairs to
come back.

He had told me that he would want to talk with me
that night, but he was kept till late, with the press of
people around him, so I saw Ygraine first. She retired
early from the feasting, and when her page came to me
with a whispered message, I caught a nod from Arthur,
and followed him.

Her rooms were in the King's house. Here, the sounds
of the revelry could be heard only faintly, against the
more distant noise of the town's rejoicing. The door was
opened to me by the same girl who had been with her at
Amesbury; she was slender in green, with pearls in the
light-brown hair, and eyes showing green as her gown:
not the gleaming witch-colour of Morgause, but a clear
grey-green, making one think of sunlight on a forest stream
reflecting the young leaves of spring. Her skin was flushed
with excitement and the feasting, and she smiled at me,
showing a dimple and excellent teeth, as she curtsied me
towards the Queen.

Ygraine gave me a hand. She looked tired, and the
magnificent gown of purple, with its shimmer of pearls
and silver, showed up her pallor, and the shadows at
mouth and eyes. But her manner, composed and cool as

always, betrayed no trace of fatigue.

She came straight to the point. 'So, he got her pregnant.'

Even as the knife-twist of fear went through me, I saw that she had no suspicion of the truth; she was referring to Lot, and to what she took to be the reason for his rejection of her daughter Morgan in favour of Morgause.

'It seems so.' I was equally blunt. 'At least it saves Morgan's face, which is all that need concern us.'

'It's the best thing that could have happened,' said Ygraine flatly. She smiled faintly at my look. 'I never liked that marriage. I favoured Uther's first idea, when he offered Morgause to Lot years ago. That would have been enough for him, and honour for her. But Lot was ambitious, one way or another, even then, and nothing would please him but Morgan herself. So Uther agreed. At that time he would have agreed to anything that sealed the northern kingdoms against the Saxons; but while for policy's sake I saw that it had to be done, I am too fond of my daughter to want her shackled to that wayward and greedy traitor.'

I put up my brows at her. 'Strong words, Madam.'

'Do you deny the facts?'

'Far from it. I was there at Luguvallium.'

'Then you will know how much, in loyalty, Lot's betrothal to Morgan bound him to Arthur, and how much marriage would have bound him, if profit pointed another way.'

'Yes. I agree. I'm only glad that you yourself see it like that. I was afraid that the slight to Morgan would anger you and distress her.'

'She was angry at first, rather than distressed. Lot is among the foremost of the petty kings, and, like him or not, she would have been queen of a wide realm, and her children would have had a great heritage. She could not like being displaced by a bastard, and one, besides, who has not shown her kindness.'

'And when the betrothal was first mooted, Urbgen of Rheged still had a wife.'

The long lids lifted, and her eyes studied my impassive face. 'Just so,' was all she said, without surprise. It was said as if at the end of a discussion, rather than the beginning.

It was no surprise that Ygraine had been thinking along the same lines as Arthur and myself. Like his father Coel, Urbgen had shown himself staunch to the High King. 'Rheged's' deeds in the past, and more recently at Luguvallium, were chronicled along with those of Ambrosius and Arthur, as the sky accepts the light of the setting and the rising sun.

Ygraine was saying thoughtfully: 'It might answer, at that. There's no need to ensure Urbgen's loyalty, of course, but for Morgan it would be power of the kind that I think she can manage, and for her sons ...' She paused 'Well, Urbgen has two already, both young men grown, and fighters like their sire. Who is to say that they will ever reach his crown? And the king of a realm as wide as Rheged cannot breed too many sons.'

'He is past his best years, and she is still very young.' I made it a statement, but she answered calmly:

'And so? I was not much older than Morgan, when Gorlois of Cornwall married me.'

For the moment, I believe, she had forgotten what that marriage had meant; the caging of a young creature avid to spread her wings and fly; the fatal passion of King Uther for Gorlois' lovely duchess; the death of the old duke, and then the new life, with all its love and pain.

'She will do her duty,' said Ygraine, and now I saw that she had remembered, but her eyes did not falter. 'If she was willing to accept Lot, whom she feared, she will take Urbgen willingly, should Arthur suggest it. It's a pity that Cador is too nearly related for her to have him. I would have liked to see her settled near to me in Cornwall.'

'They are not blood kin.' Cador was the son, by his first wife, of Ygraine's husband Gorlois.

'Too close,' said Ygraine. 'Men forget things too quickly, and there would be whispers of incest. It would not do,

even to hint at a crime so shocking.'

'No. I see that.' My voice sounded level and cool.

'And besides, Cador is to wed, come summer, when he gets back to Cornwall. The King approves.' She turned a hand over in her lap, admiring apparently the glint of the rings on it. 'So perhaps it would be as well to speak of Urbgen to the King, just as soon as some portion of his mind is free to think of his sister?'

'He has already thought of her. He discussed it with me. I believe he will send to Urbgen very soon.'

'Ah! And then—' For the first time a purely human and female satisfaction warmed her voice with something uncommonly like spite. 'And then we shall see Morgan take what is due to her in wealth and precedence over that red-haired witch, and may Lot of Lothian deserve the snares she set for him!'

'You think she trapped him deliberately?'

'How else? You know her. She wove her spells for this.'

'A very common kind of spell,' I said drily.

'Oh, yes. But Lot has never lacked women, and no one can deny that Morgan is the better match, and as pretty a lass besides. And for all the arts Morgause boasts, Morgan is better able to be queen of a great kingdom. She was bred for it, as the bastard was not.'

I watched her curiously. Beside her chair the brown-haired girl sat on her stool half asleep. Ygraine seemed careless of what she might overhear. 'Ygraine, what harm did Morgause ever do to you that makes you so bitter against her?'

The red came up in her face like a flag, and for a moment I thought she would try to set me down, but we were neither of us young any more, or needing the armour of self-love. She spoke simply: 'If you are thinking that I hated having a lovely young girl always near me, and near to Uther, with a right to him that went back beyond my own, it is true. But it was more than that. Even when she was a young girl, twelve, thirteen, no more, I thought of her as corrupt. That is one reason why I welcomed the

match with Lot. I wanted her away from the court.'

This was straighter than I had expected. 'Corrupt?' I asked.

The Queen's glance slid momentarily to the girl on the stool beside her. The brown head was nodding, the eyelids closed. Ygraine lowered her voice, but spoke clearly and carefully. 'I am not suggesting that there was anything evil in her relationship with the King, though she never behaved to him like a daughter; nor was she fond of him as a daughter should be; she cajoled favours from him, no more than that. When I called her corrupt, I spoke of her practice of witchcraft. She was drawn to it always, and haunted the wise women and the charlatans, and any talk of magic brought her staring awake like an owl at nighttime. And she tried to teach Morgan, when the princess was only a child. That is what I cannot forgive. I have no time for such things, and in the hands of such as Morgause...'

She broke off. Vehemence had made her raise her voice, and I saw that the girl, like the owl, was also staring awake. Ygraine, recollecting herself, bent her head, a touch of colour in her face again.

'Prince Merlin, you must pardon me. I meant no disrespect.'

I laughed. I saw, to my amusement, that the girl must have heard; she was laughing too, but silently, dimpling at me from beyond her mistress's shoulder. I said: 'I am too proud to think of myself in the same breath as girls dabbling with spells. I am sorry about Morgan. It is true that Morgause has power of a sort, and it is also true that such things can be dangerous. Any power is hard to hold, and power misused recoils on the user.'

'Perhaps some day, if you get the chance, you will tell Morgan so.' She smiled, trying for a lighter tone. 'She will listen to you, where she would shrug her shoulders at me.'

'Willingly.' I tried to sound willing, like a grandfather called in to lecture the young.

'It may be that when she finds herself a queen with real power, she will cease to hanker for another sort.' She turned the subject. 'So now that Lot has a daughter of Uther's, even if only a bastard, will he consider himself bound to Arthur's banner?'

'That I cannot tell you. But unless the Saxons make heavy enough gains to make it worth Lot's while to try another betrayal, I think he will keep what power he has, and fight for his own land, if not for the High King's sake. I see no trouble there.' I did not add. 'Not of that kind.' I finished merely: 'When you go back to Cornwall, Madam, I will send letters if you like.'

'I should be grateful. Your letters were a great comfort to me before, when my son was at Galava.'

We talked for a while longer, mainly of the day's events. When I would have asked after her health, she put the query aside with a smile that told me she knew as much as I, so I let it be, asking instead about Duke Cador's projected marriage. 'Arthur hasn't mentioned it. Who is it to be?'

'The daughter of Dinas. Did you know him? Her name is Mariona. The marriage was arranged, alas, when they were both children. Now Mariona is of age, so when the Duke is home again they will be wed.'

'I knew her father, yes. Why did you say "alas"?'

Ygraine looked, with a fond smile, at the girl by her chair. 'Because otherwise there would have been no difficulty in finding a match for my little Guenever.'

'I am sure,' I said, 'that that will prove more than easy.'

'But such a match,' said the Queen, and the girl made a smiling mouth and lowered her lashes.

'If I dared used divination in your presence, Madam,' I said, smiling, 'I would predict that one as splendid will present itself, and soon.'

I spoke lightly, in formal courtesy, and was startled to hear in my voice an echo, though faint and soon lost, of the cadences of prophecy.

Neither of them heard it. The Queen was holding a hand to me, bidding me good night, and the girl Guenever held the door for me, sinking, as I passed, into a smiling curtsy of humility and grace.

CHAPTER 7

'It's mine!' said Arthur, violently. 'You only have to
count! I heard the men talking about it in the guard-
room. They didn't know I was near enough to hear them.
They said she was big-bellied by Twelfth Night, and
lucky to catch Lot so early, they could pass it off as a seven-
month child. Merlin, you know as well as I do that he
never came near her at Luguvallium! He wasn't there
until the very night of the battle, and that night—that was
the night—' He stopped, choking on it, and turned with
a swirl of robes to pace the floor again.

It was well after midnight. The sounds of revelry from
the town were fainter now, muted with the chill of the
hour before dawn. In the King's room the candles had
burned low into a welter of honeyed wax. Their scent
mingled with the sharp smoke from a lamp that needed
trimming.

Arthur turned sharply on his heel and came back to
stand in front of me. He had taken off the crown and
jewelled chain, and laid his sword aside, but he still wore
the splendid coronation robe. The furred cloak lay across
the table like a stream of blood in the lamplight. Through
the open door of his bedchamber I could see the covers
turned back ready on the great bed, but, late though the
hour was, Arthur showed no sign of fatigue. His every
movement was infused with a kind of nervous fury.

He controlled it, speaking quietly. 'Merlin, when we
spoke that night of what had happened—' A breathing
pause, then he changed course with ferocious directness:
'When I lay incestuously with Morgause, I asked you what
would happen if she should conceive. I remember what

you said. I remember it well. Do you?'

'Yes,' I said, unwillingly, 'I remember it.'

'You said to me, "The gods are jealous, and they insure against too much glory. Every man carries the seeds of his own death, and there must come a term to every life. All that has happened tonight is that you yourself have set that term."'

I said nothing. He faced me with the straight, uncompromising look that I was to come to know so well.

'When you spoke to me like that, were you telling me the truth? Was the prophecy a sure one, or were you finding words of comfort for me, so that I could face what was to come next day?'

'It was the truth.'

'You meant that, if she bore a child to me, you could foresee that he—she?—would be my death?'

'Arthur,' I said, 'prophecy does not work like that. I neither knew, in the way most men think of "knowing", that Morgause would conceive, nor that the child would be a mortal danger for you. I only knew, all the time you were with the woman, that the birds of death were on my shoulders, weighing me down and stinking of carrion. My heart was heavy with dread, and I could see death, as I thought, linking the two of you together. Death and treachery. But how, I did not know. By the time I understood it, the thing was done, and all that was left was to await what the gods chose to send.'

He paced away from me again, over towards the bed-chamber door. He leaned there in silence, his shoulder to the jamb, his face away from me, then thrust himself off and turned. He crossed to the chair behind the big table, sat down, and regarded me, chin on fist. His movements were controlled and smooth, as always, but I, who knew him, could hear the curb-chain ring. He still spoke quietly. 'And now we know the carrion-birds were right. She did conceive. You told me something else that night, when I admitted my fault. You said I had sinned unknowingly, and was innocent. Is innocence, then, to be punished?'

'It's not uncommon.'

'The sins of the fathers?'

I recognised the phrase as a quotation from the Christian scriptures. 'Uther's sin,' I said, 'visited on you.'

'And mine, now, on the child?'

I said nothing. I did not like the way the interview was going. For the first time, talking with Arthur, I did not seem able to take control. I told myself I was weary, that I was still in the ebb-tide of power, that my time would come again; but the truth is I was feeling a little like the fisherman in the Eastern tale who unstoppered a bottle and let out a genie many times more powerful than himself.

'Very well,' said the King. 'My sin and hers must be visited on the child. It must not be allowed to live. You will go north and tell Morgause so. Or if you prefer, I shall give you a letter telling her so myself.'

I took breath, but he swept on without giving me time to speak.

'Quite apart from your forebodings—which God knows I would be a fool not to respect—can you not see how dangerous this thing could be now, if Lot should find out about it? It's plain enough what has happened. She feared she might be pregnant, and to save her shame she set herself to snare a husband. Who better than Lot? She had been offered to him before: for all we know she had wanted him, and now saw a chance to outshine her sister and give herself a place and a name, which she would lack after her father's death.' His lips thinned. 'And who knows better than I, that if she set herself to get a man, any man, he would go to her for the whistle?'

'Arthur, you talk of her "shame". You don't think you were the first she took to her bed, do you?'

He said, a little too quickly: 'I never did think so.'

'Then how do you know she had not lain with Lot before you? That she was not already pregnant to him, and took *you* in the hope of snaring some kind of power and favour to herself? She knew Uther was dying; she

feared that Lot, by his action at Luguvallium, had for-
feited the King's favour. If she could father Lot's child
on you ...'

'This is guesswork. This is not what you said that night.'

'No. But think back. It would fit the facts of my foreboding equally well.'

'But not the force of them,' he said sharply. 'If the
danger from this child is real, then what does it matter
who fathered it? Guesswork won't help us.'

'I'm not guessing when I tell you that she and Lot were
lovers before ever you went to her bed. I told you I had
had a dream that night at Nodens' shrine. I saw them
meet at a house some way off an ill-frequented road. It
must have been by pre-arrangement. They met like people
who have been lovers for a long time. This child may in
fact be Lot's, and not yours.'

'And we've got it the wrong way round? I was the one
she whistled up to save her shame?'

'It's possible. You had come from nowhere, eclipsing
Lot as you would soon eclipse Uther. She made her bid to
father Lot's child on you, but then had to abandon the
attempt, for fear of me.'

He was silent, thinking. 'Well,' he said at length, 'time
will tell us. But are we to wait for it? No matter whose
child this is, it is a danger; and it doesn't take a prophet
to see how that could be ... or a god to act on it. If Lot
ever knows—or believes—that his eldest child is fathered
by me, how long do you think this chary loyalty of his will
last? Lothian is a key point, you know that. I need that
loyalty; I have to have it. Even if he had wedded my own
sister Morgan, I could hardly have trusted him, whereas
now ...' He threw out a hand, palm up. 'Merlin, it's done
every day, in every village in the kingdom. Why not in
a king's house? Go north for me, and talk to Morgause.'

'You think she would listen? If she had not wanted the
child, she would not have scrupled to get rid of it long
since. She didn't take you for love, Arthur, and she bears
you no friendship for letting her be driven from court.

And to me'… I smiled sourly—'she bears a most emphatic
and justified ill-will. She would laugh in my face. More
than that: she would listen, and laugh at the power her
action had given her over us, and then she would do
whatever she thought would hurt us most.'

'But—'

'You thought she might have persuaded Lot into marriage merely for her own sake, or to score from her sister.
No. She took him because I foiled her plans to corrupt
and own you, and because at heart, whatever the time
may force him to do now, Lot is your enemy and mine, and
through him she may one day do you harm.'

A sharpening silence. 'Do you believe this?'

'Yes.'

He stirred. 'Then I am still right. She must not bear
the child.'

'What are you going to do? Pay someone to bake her
bread with ergot?'

'You will find some way. You will go—'

'I will do nothing in the matter.'

He came to his feet, like a bow snapping upright when
the string breaks. His eyes glittered in the candle-light.
'You told me you were my servant. You made me King,
you said by the god's wish. Now I am King, and you will
obey me.'

I was taller than he, by two fingers' breadth. I had
outfaced kings before, and he was very young. I gave it just
long enough, then said, gently:

'I am your servant, Arthur, but I serve the god first. Do
not make me choose. I have to let him work the way he
wills.'

He held my eyes a moment longer, then drew a long
breath, and released it as if it had been a weight he was
holding. 'To do this? To destroy, perhaps, the very kingdom you said he had sent me to build?'

'If he sent you to build it, then it will be built. Arthur,
I don't pretend to understand this. I can only tell you to
trust the time, as I do, and wait. Now, do as you did

before, put it aside and try to forget it. Leave it with me,'

'What will you do?'

'Go north.'

A moment of quickening stillness, then he said: 'To Lothian? But you said you would not go.'

'No. I said I would do nothing about killing the child. But I can watch Morgause, and perhaps, in time, judge better what we must do. I will send to tell you what happens.'

There was another silence. Then the tension went out of him, and he turned away, beginning to loosen the clasp of his belt. 'Very well.' He started to ask some question, then bit it back and smiled at me. Having shown the whip, it seemed that he was now concerned to retreat on the old trust and affection. 'But you will stay for the rest of the feasting? If the wars allow, I have to stay here myself for eight days before I can take horse again.'

'No. I think I must be gone. Better perhaps while Lot is still here with you. That way I can melt into the countryside before ever he gets home, and watch and wait, and take what action I can. With your leave, I'll go tomorrow morning.'

'Who goes with you?'

'Nobody. I can travel alone.'

'You must take someone. It's not like riding home to Maridunum. Besides, you may need a messenger.'

'I'll use your couriers.'

'All the same . . .' He had got the belt undone. He threw it over a chair. 'Ulfin!'

A sound from the next room, then discreet footsteps. Ulfin, carrying a long bedgown over one arm, came in from the bedchamber, stifling a yawn. 'My lord?'

'Have you been in there all the while?' I asked sharply.

Ulfin wooden-faced, reached to undo the clasps at the King's shoulder. He held the long outer robe as the King stepped out of it. 'I was asleep, my lord.'

Arthur sat down and thrust out a foot. Ulfin kneeled to

ease the shoe from it. 'Ulfin, my cousin Prince Merlin goes north tomorrow, on what may prove a long and hard journey. I shall dislike losing you, but I want you to go with him.'

Ulfin, shoe in hand, looked up at me and smiled. 'Willingly.'

'Should you not stay with the King?' I protested. 'This week of all weeks—'

'I do as he tells me,' said Ulfin simply, and stooped to the other foot.

As you do, in the end. Arthur did not say the words aloud, but they were there in the quick glance he gave me as he stood again for Ulfin to gird the bedgown round him.

I gave up. 'Very well. I shall be glad to have you. We leave tomorrow, and I should warn you that we may be away for some considerable time.' I gave him what instructions I could, then turned back to Arthur. 'Now, I had better go. I doubt if I shall see you before I set off. I'll send you word as soon as I can. No doubt I shall know where you are.'

'No doubt.' He sounded all at once grim, very much the war-leader. 'Can you spare a moment or two more? Thank you, Ulfin, leave us now. You'll have your own preparations to make ... Merlin, come and see my new toy.'

'Another?'

'Another? Oh, you're thinking about the cavalry. Have you seen the horses Bedwyr brought?'

'Not yet. Valerius told me about them.'

His eyes kindled. 'They are splendid! Fast, fiery, and gentle. I am told they can live on hard rations if they have to, and that their hearts are so high that they will gallop all day, and then fight with you to the death. Bedwyr brought grooms with them. If everything they say is true, then surely we shall have a cavalry force to conquer the world! There are two trained stallions, white ones, that are real beauties, even finer than my Canrith. Bedwyr

chose them especially for me. Over here ...' As he spoke
he led the way across the room towards a pillared archway
closed by a curtain. 'I haven't had time to try them yet,
but surely I can throw off my chains for an hour or two
tomorrow?'

His voice was that of a restive boy. I laughed. 'I hope
so. I am more fortunate than the King: I shall be on my
way.'

'On your old black gelding, no doubt.'

'Not even that. A mule.'

'A mule?—Ah, of course. You go disguised?'

'I must. I can hardly ride into Lothian's stronghold as
Prince Merlin.'

'Well, take care. You're certain you don't want an
escort, at least for the first part of the way?'

'Certain. I shall be safe. What's this you are going to
show me?'

'Only a map. Here.'

He pulled the curtain back. Beyond it was a kind of
anteroom, little more than a broad portico giving on a
small private courtyard. Torchlight winked on the spears
of the guards on duty there, but otherwise the place was
empty, bare even of furniture except for a huge table,
rough-adzed out of oak. It was a map-table, but instead
of the usual sand-tray it held, I saw, a map made of clay,
with mountains and valleys, coasts and rivers, modelled
by some clever sculptor, so that there, plain to see, lay
the land of Britain as a high-flying bird might view it
from the heavens.

Arthur was plainly delighted at my praise. 'I knew you
would be interested! They only finished setting it up
yesterday. Splendid, isn't it? Do you remember teaching
me to make maps in the dust? This is better than scraping
the sand into hills and valleys that change when you
breathe on them. Of course, it can still be remodelled
as we find out more. North of Strathclyde is anybody's
guess ... But then, by God's mercy, nothing north of
Strathclyde need concern me. Not yet, anyway.' He

fingered a peg, carved and coloured like a red dragon, that stood over 'Caerleon.' 'Now, which way do you plan to go tomorrow?'

'I thought, by the west road through Deva and Bremet. I have a call to make at Vindolanda.'

His finger followed the route northward till it reached Bremetennacum (which is commonly spoken of now as Bremet), and paused. 'Will you do something for me?'

'Willingly.'

'Go by the east. It's not so much further, and the road is better for most of the way. Here, see? If you turn off at Bremet, you'll take this road through the mountain gap.' His finger traced it out; east from Bremetennacum, up the old road following the Tribuit River, then over the pass and down through Olicana into the Vale of York. There Dere Street runs, a good, fast highway still, up through Corstopitum and the Wall and thence still north, right into Manau Guotodin, where lies Lot's capital of Dunpeldyr.

'You'll have to retrace your steps for Vindolanda,' said Arthur, 'but not far. You'll lose nothing in time, I believe. It's the road through the Pennine Gap that I want you to take. I've never been that way myself. I've had reports that it's quite feasible—you should have no difficulty, just the two of you— but it's too broken in places for a troop of cavalry. I shall be sending parties up to repair it. I shall have to fortify it, too ... You agree? With parts of the eastern seaboard so open to the enemy, if they should get a grip on the easterly plains this will be their way into our British heartland in the west. There are two forts there already; I am told they could be made good. I want you to look at them for me. Don't take time over it; I can get detailed reports from the surveyors; but if you can go that way, I would like to have your thoughts about it.'

'You shall have them.'

As he straightened from the map, a cock crowed outside somewhere. The courtyard was grey. He said quietly:

'For the other matter we spoke of, I am in your hands. God knows I should be thankful to be so.' He smiled. 'Now we had better get to our beds. You have a journey to face, and I another day of pleasure. I envy you! Goodnight, and God go with you.'

CHAPTER 8

Next day, furnished with food for two days' journey, and three good mules from one of the baggage trains, Ulfin and I set off on the journey northwards.

I had made journeys before in circumstances as dangerous as this, when to be recognised would be to court disaster, or even death. I had, perforce, become adept at disguise; this had given rise to yet another legend about 'the enchanter', that he could vanish at will into thin air to escape his enemies. I had certainly perfected the art of melting into a landscape: what I did in fact was assume the tools of some trade, and then frequent places where no one would expect a prince to be. Men's eyes are focused on what, not who a traveller is, who goes labelled with his skill. I had travelled as a singer, when I needed access to a prince's court as well as a humble tavern, but more often I went as a travelling physician or eye-doctor. This was the guise I liked best. It allowed me to practise my skill where it was most needed, among the poor, and it gave me access to any kind of house except the noblest.

This was the disguise I chose now. I took my small harp, but only for my private use; I dared not risk my skill as a singer earning me a summons to Lot's court. So the harp, muffled and wrapped into anonymity, hung on the baggage-mule's shabby saddle, while my boxes of unguents and roll of implements were carried plain to be seen.

The first part of our way I knew well, but after we reached Bremetennacum, and turned towards the Pennine Gap, the country was unfamiliar.

The Gap is formed by the valleys of three great rivers.

Two of these, the Wharfe and the Isara, spring from the limestone on the Pennine tops and flow, meandering, eastwards. The other, an important stream with countless smaller tributaries, lapses towards the west. It is called the Tribuit. Once through the Gap and into the valley of the Tribuit, an enemy's way would be clear to the west coast, and the last embattled corners of Britain.

Arthur had spoken of two forts lying within the Gap itself. I had gathered from seemingly idle questions put to local men in the tavern at Bremetennacum, that in times past there had been a third fort guarding the western mouth of the pass, where the Tribuit valley widens out towards the lowlands and the coast. It had been built by the Romans as a temporary marching camp, so much of the turf and timber structure would have decayed and vanished, but it occurred to me that the road serving it would stand a survey, and, if it were still in reasonable condition, could provide a quick corner-cut for cavalry coming down from Rheged to defend the Gap.

From Rheged to Olicana, and York. The road Morgause must have taken to meet with Lot.

That settled it. I would take the same road, the road of my dream at Nodens' shrine. If the dream had been a true one—and I had no doubt of it—there were things I wished to learn.

We left the main road just beyond Bremetennacum, and headed up the Tribuit valley on the gravel of a neglected Roman road. A day's ride brought us to the marching camp.

As I had suspected, little was left of it but the banks and ditches, and some rotting timber where the gateways had once stood. But like all such camps, it was cleverly placed, on a flank of moorland that looked in every direction over clear country. The hillside had a tributary stream at foot, and to the south the river flowed through flatlands towards the sea. Placed as the camp was, so far west, we might hope that it would not be needed for defence; but, as a staging-camp for cavalry, or as a tem-

porary base for a swift foray through the Gap it was ideal.

I had been unable to find anyone who knew its name. When I wrote my report to Arthur that night, I called it merely 'Tribuit'.

Next day we struck out across country towards the first of the forts of which Arthur had spoken. This lay in the arm of a marshy stream, near the beginning of the pass. The stream spread out beside it into a lake, from which the place took its name. Though ruinous, it could, I judged, be speedily brought into repair. There was abundant timber in the valley, and plenty of stone and deep moorland turf available.

We reached it towards late afternoon, and, the air being balmy and dry, and the fortress walls promising sufficient shelter, we made camp there. Next morning we began the climb across the ridge towards Olicana.

Well before midday we had climbed clear of the forest and onto heathland. It was a fine day, with mist drawing back from the sparkling sedges, and the song of water bubbling from every crevice in the rock, where the rills tumbled down to fill the young river. Rippling, too, with sound, was the morning sky, where curlews slanted down on ringing streams of song towards their nests in the grass. We saw a she-wolf, heavy with milk, slink across the road ahead, with a hare in her mouth. She gave us a brief indifferent glance, then slipped into the shelter of the mist.

It was a wild way, a Wolf Road such as the Old Ones love. I kept my eye on the rocks that crowned the screes, but saw no sign that I could recognise, of their remote and comfortless eyries. I had no doubt, though, that we were watched every step of the way. No doubt, either, that news had gone north on the winds, that Merlin the enchanter was on the road, and secretly. It did not trouble me. It is not possible to keep secrets from the Old Ones; they know all that comes or goes in forest and hill. They and I had come to an understanding long since, and Arthur had their trust.

We halted on the summit of the moor. I looked around

me. The mist had lifted now, dispersing under the steadily strengthening sun. All around us stretched the moor, broken with grey rock and bracken, with, in the distance, the still misty heights of fell and mountain. To the left of the road the ground fell away into the wide Isara valley, where water glinted among crowding trees.

It could not have looked more unlike the rain-dimmed vision of Nodens' shrine, but there was the milestone with its legend, OLICANA; and there, to the left, the track plunging steeply down towards the valley trees. Among them, only just visible through the leafage, showed the walls of a considerable house.

Ulfin, ranging his mule alongside mine, was pointing. 'If only we had known, we might have found better lodging there.'

I said, slowly: 'I doubt it. I think we were better under the sky.'

He shot me a curious glance. 'I thought you had never been this way, sir? Do you know the place?'

'Shall we say that I know of it? And would like to know more. Next time we pass a village, or if we see a shepherd on the hill, find out who owns that villa, will you?'

He threw me another look, but said no more, and we rode on.

Olicana, the second of Arthur's two forts, lay only ten miles or so to the east. To my surprise the road, heading steeply downward, then crossing a considerable stretch of boggy moorland, was in first-class condition. Ditches and embankments alike looked to have been recently repaired. There was a good timber bridge across the Isara itself, and the ford of the next tributary was cleared and paved. We made good speed in consequence, and came in the early evening into settled country. At Olicana there is a sizeable township. We found lodgings in a tavern that stood near the fortress walls, to serve the men of the garrison.

From what I had seen of the road, and the orderly appointments of the town's streets and square, it came as

no surprise that the walls of the fortress itself were in the same good order. Gates and bridges were sound and stout, and the ironwork looked fire-new. By carefully idle questions, and by listening to the talk in the tavern at suppertime, I was able to gather that a skeleton garrison had been placed here in Uther's time, to watch the road into the Gap, and to keep an eye on the signal towers to the east. It had been an emergency measure, taken hastily during the worst years of the Saxon Terror, but the same men were still here, despairing of recall, bored to distraction, but kept to a tingling pitch of efficiency by a garrison commander who deserved something better (one gathered) than this dismal outpost of inaction.

The simplest way to gather the information I needed was to make myself known to this officer, who could then see that my report was sent straight back to the King. Accordingly, leaving Ulfin in the tavern, I presented myself at the guard-room with the pass Arthur had supplied.

From the speed with which I was passed through, and the lack of surprise at my shabby appearance, and refusal even to state my name or my business to anyone but the commander himself, it could be judged that messengers were frequent here. Secret messengers, at that. If this really was a forgotten outpost (and admittedly nor I nor the King's advisers had known of it) then the only messengers who would come and go so assiduously were spies. I began to look forward all the more to meeting the commander.

I was searched before being taken in, which was only to be expected. Then a couple of the guards escorted me through the fort to the headquarters building. I looked about me. The place was well lighted, and as far as I could see, roads, courtyards, wells, exercise ground, workshops, barracks, were in mint repair. We passed carpenters' shops, harness-makers, smithies. From the padlocks on the granary doors, I deduced that barns were fully stocked. The place was not large but was still, I reckoned, under-manned. There could be accommodation for Arthur's

cavalry almost before the force could be formed.

My pass was taken through, then I was shown into the commander's room, and the guards withdrew, with a neatness that told its own story. This was where the spies came; and usually, I supposed, as late as this.

The commander received me standing; a tribute not to me, but to the King's seal. The first thing that struck me was his youth. He could not have been more than twenty-two. The second thing was that he was tired. Lines of strain were scored into his face: his youth, the solitary post up here, in charge of a bored and hardbitten contingent of men; the constant watchfulness as the tides of invasion flowed and ebbed along the eastern coasts; all this, winter and summer, without help and without backing. It seemed true that, after Uther had sent him here four years ago—four years—he had forgotten all about him.

'You have news for me?' The flat tone disguised no eagerness; that had long since been dissipated by frustration.

'I can give you what news there is when my main business is done. I have been sent, rather, to get information from you, if you will be good enough to supply it. I have a report to send to the High King. I would be glad if a messenger could take it to him as soon as it is completed.'

'That can be arranged. Now? A man can be ready within the half hour.'

'No. It's not so urgent. If we might talk first, please?'

He sat down, motioning me to a chair. For the first time a spark of interest showed. 'Do you mean that the report concerns Olicana? Am I to know why?'

'I shall tell you, of course. The King asked me to find out all I could about this place, and also about the ruined fortress in the pass, the one they call Lake Fort.'

He nodded. 'I know it. It's been a wreck for nearly two hundred years. It was destroyed in the Brigantian rebellion, and left to rot. This place suffered the same fate, but Ambrosius had it rebuilt. He had plans for Lake Fort,

too, so I have been told. If I had had a mandate, I might
have—' He checked himself. 'Ah, well ... You came from
Bremet? Then you'll know that a couple of miles north
of that road there is another fort—nothing there, only the
site—but I would have thought it equally vital to any
strategy involving the Gap. Ambrosius saw it so, they tell
me. He saw that the Gap could be a key point of his
strategy.' There was no perceptible emphasis on the 'he',
but the inference was clear. Uther had not only forgotten
the existence of Olicana and its garrison, he had either
ignored or misunderstood the importance of the road
through the Pennine Gap. As this young man, in his
helpless isolation, had not.

I said quickly: 'And now the new King sees it, too. He
wants to refortify the Gap, not only with a view to closing
and holding it against penetration from the east, if that
becomes necessary, but also to using the pass as a quick
line of attack. He has charged me to see what there is to
be done. I think you can expect the surveyors up after
my reports have been studied. This place is in a state of
readiness that I know the King did not expect. He will be
pleased.'

I told him something then about Arthur's plans for the
formation of the cavalry force. He listened eagerly, his
weary boredom forgotten, and the questions he put
showed that he knew a great deal about affairs on the
eastern seaboard. He assumed, besides, a surprisingly
intimate knowledge of Saxon movements and strategy.

I left that aside for the moment, and began to put my
own questions about Olicana's accommodation and supplies. After little more than a minute of it he got to his
feet, and, crossing to a chest locked with another of the
great padlocks, opened it and brought out tablets and
rolls on which, it transpired, were lists, fully detailed, of
all I wanted to know.

I studied these for a few minutes, then became conscious
that he was waiting, watching me, with other lists in his
hand.

'I think,' he began, then hesitated. In a moment he made up his mind to continue. 'I don't think that King Uther, in the last years, ever quite appreciated what the road through the Gap might mean in the coming struggle. When I was sent here—when I was young—I saw it as an outpost only, a place, you might say, to practise on. It was better than Lake Fort then, but only just ... It took quite a time to get it into working shape ... Well, you know what happened, sir. The war moved north and south; King Uther was sick, and the country divided; we seemed to be forgotten. I sent couriers from time to time, with information, but got no acknowledgment. So for my own instruction, and, I admit, entertainment, I began to send out men—not soldiers, but boys from the town mostly, with a taste for adventure—and gathered information. I am at fault, I know, but ...' He stopped.

'You kept it to yourself?' I prompted him.

'With no wrong motive,' he said hastily. 'I did send one courier, with some information I judged to be of value, but heard no more of him nor of the papers he carried. So I no longer wanted to commit anything to messengers who might not be received by the King.'

'I can assure you that anything I send to the King, has only to reach him safely to get his immediate attention.'

While we had been talking he had been studying me covertly, comparing, I suppose, my shabby appearance with the manner I had made no attempt, with him, to disguise. He said slowly, glancing down at the lists he held: 'I have the King's pass and seal, so I am to trust you. Am I to know your name?'

'If you wish. It is for you only. I have your promise?'

'Of course,' he said, a shade impatiently.

'Then I am Myrddin Emrys, commonly known as Merlin. As you will gather, I am on a private journey, so I am known as Emrys, a travelling doctor.'

'Sir—'

'No,' I said quickly, 'sit down again. I only told you so that you could be sure your information will reach the

King's ear, and quickly. May I see it now?'

He laid the lists down in front of me. I studied them.
More information; plans of fortified settlements, numbers
of troops and armaments; troop movements carefully
chronicled; supplies; ships ...

I looked up, startled. 'But these are plans of *Saxon*
dispositions?'

He nodded. 'Recent, too, sir. I had a stroke of fortune
last summer. I was put in touch—it doesn't matter how—
with a Saxon, a third-generation federate. Like a lot of
the old federates, he wants to keep to the old order. These
Saxons hold their pledged word sacred, and besides,' a
glimmer of a smile on the grim young mouth, 'they mistrust the incomers. Some of these new adventurers want
to displace the wealthy federates just as much as they
want to drive out the British.'

'And this information comes from him. Can you trust
it?'

'I think so. The parts I could check I have found to be
true. I don't know how good, or how recent the King's
own information is, but I think you should draw his
attention to the section—here—about Elesa, and Cerdic
Elesing. That means—'

'Elesa's son. Yes. Elesa being our old friend Eosa?'

'That's right, Horsa's son. You would know that after he
and his kinsman Octa escaped from Uther's prison, Octa
died, at Rutupiae, but Eosa made for Germany and
drummed up Octa's sons Colgrim and Badulf to make the
attack in the north ... Well, what you may not have
known was that, before he died, Octa was claiming the
title of "king" here in Britain. It didn't amount to much
more than the chieftainship he had had before, as Hengist's son: neither Colgrim nor Badulf seems to have set
much store by it; but now they are dead, too, and, as you
see ...'

'Eosa makes the same claim. Yes. With any more
success?'

'It seems so. King of the West Saxons, he calls himself,

and his young son Cerdic is known as "the Aetheling".
They claim descent from some far-back hero or demigod.
That's usual, of course, but the point is that his people
believe in it. You can see that this gives a new kind of
colour to the Saxon invasions.'

'It could alter what you were saying about the old-
established federates.'

'Indeed. Eosa and Cerdic have that sort of standing, you
see. This talk of a "kingdom" ... He's promising stability
—*and rights*—to the old federates, and a quick killing to
the incomers. He's genuine, too. I mean, he's shown himself to be more than a clever adventurer; he's established
the legend of a heroic kingship, he's accepted as a law-
giver, and powerful enough to enforce new customs.
Changed the grave-customs, even ... they don't burn
their dead now, I'm told, or even bury them with their
arms and grave-goods in the old way. According to Cerdic
the Aetheling, it's wasteful.' That grim little smile again.
'They get their priests to cleanse the dead man's weapons
ritually, and then they re-use them. They now believe that
a spear once used by a good fighter will make its next
owner as good, or better ... and a weapon taken from a
defeated warrior will fight the harder for being given a
second chance. I tell you, a dangerous man. The most
dangerous, perhaps, since Hengist himself.'

I was impressed, and said so. 'The King shall see this as
soon as I can get it to him. It will be brought to his attention straight away, I promise you that. You must know
how valuable it is. How soon can you have copies made?'

'I already have copies. These can go straight away.'

'Good. Now, if you'll allow me, I'll add a word to
your report, and put my own report on Lake Fort in with
them.'

He brought writing materials and set them in front of
me, then made for the door. 'I'll arrange for a courier.'

'Thank you. A moment, though—'

He paused. We had been speaking in Latin, but there
was something about his use of it that told me he came

from the West Country. I said: 'They told me in the tavern that your name was Gerontius. Do I hazard a guess that it was once Gereint?'

He smiled. It took years off him. 'It still is, sir.'

'It's a name that Arthur will be glad to know,' I said, and turned to my writing.

He stood still for a moment, then went to the door, opened it, and spoke with someone outside. He came back, and crossing to a table in the corner, poured wine and set a goblet by me. I heard him draw breath once, as if to speak, but he was silent.

At last I was finished. He went to the door again, and came back, followed this time by a man, a wiry fellow, looking as if he had just wakened up, but dressed ready for the road. He carried a leather pouch with a strong lock. He was ready to go, he said, putting away the packages Gereint handed to him; he would eat on the way.

Gerient's terse instructions to him showed once more how good his information was. 'You'll do best to go by Lindum. The King will have left Caerleon by now, and be heading back towards Linnuis. By the time you reach Lindum you'll get news of him.'

The man nodded briefly, and went. So, within a few hours of my reaching Olicana, my report, with how much more, was on its way back. Now I was free to turn my thoughts towards Dunpeldyr and what I would find there.

But first, to pay Gereint for his service. He poured more wine, and settled, with an eagerness that must have been foreign to him for a long time, to ply me with questions about Arthur's accession at Luguvallium, and the activities since then at Caerleon. He deserved good measure, and I gave it. Only when the midnight rounds were almost due did I get my own questions.

'Soon after Luguvallium, did Lot of Lothian ride this way?'

'Yes, but not through Olicana itself. There's a road— it's little more than a track now—that cuts aside from the main road, and leads due east. It's a bad road, and skirts

some dangerous bogland, so, though it's the quickest way for anyone heading north, it is very little used.'

'But Lot used it, even though he was heading south for York? To avoid being seen in Olicana, do you suppose?'

'That did not occur to me,' said Gereint. 'Not, that is, until later ... He has a house on that road. He would go there to lodge, rather than come into the town here.'

'His own house? I see. Yes, I saw it from the pass. A snug place, but lonely.'

'As to that,' he said, 'he uses it very little.'

'But you knew he was there?'

'I know most things that go on hereabouts.' A gesture at the padlocked chest. 'Like an old wife at the cottage door, I have little else to do but observe my neighbours.'

'I have reason to be grateful for it. Then you must know who met Lot at his house in the hills?'

His eyes held mine for a full ten seconds. Then he smiled. 'A certain semi-royal lady. They arrived separately, and they left separately, but they reached York together.' His brows lifted. 'But how did *you* know this, sir?'

'I have my own ways of spying.'

He said calmly: 'So I believe. Well, now all is settled and correct in the sight of God and mankind. The King of Lothian has gone with Arthur from Caerleon into Linnuis, while his new queen waits at Dunpeldyr to bear the child. You knew, of course, about the child?'

'Yes.'

'They have met here before,' said Gereint, with a nod that added, plainly, 'and now we see the results of that meeting.'

'Have they indeed? Often? And since when?'

'Since I came here, perhaps three or four times.' His tone was not that of one passing on tavern gossip, but merely briskly informative. 'Once they were here for as much as a month together, but they kept themselves close. It was a matter of report only; we saw nothing of them.'

I thought of the bedchamber with its regal crimson and gold. I had been right. Long-time lovers, indeed. If only

I could believe what I had suggested to Arthur, that the child could, in fact, be Lot's own. At least, from the neutral tone that Gereint had used, that was what most men assumed as yet.

'And now,' he said, 'love has had its way, in spite of policy. Is it presumptuous in me to ask if the High King is angry?'

He had earned an honest answer, so I gave him one.

'He was angry, naturally, at the way the marriage was made, but now he sees that it will serve as well as the other. Morgause is his half-sister, so the alliance with King Lot must still hold. And Morgan is free for whatever other marriage may suggest itself.'

'Rheged,' he said, immediately.

'Possibly.'

He smiled, and let the subject drop. We talked for a little longer, then I rose to go.

'Tell me something,' I asked him. 'Did your information run to a knowledge of Merlin's whereabouts?'

'No. Two travellers were reported, but there was no hint of who they might be.'

'Or where they were bound?'

'No, sir.'

I was satisfied. 'Need I insist that no one is to know who I am? You will not include this interview in your report.'

'That's understood. Sir—'

'What is it?'

'About this report of yours on Tribuit and Lake Fort. You said that surveyors would be coming up. It occurs to me that I could save them a good deal of time if I sent working parties over immediately. They could start on the preliminaries—clearing, gathering turf and timber, quarrying, digging the ditches ... If you would authorise the work?'

'I? I have no authority.'

'No authority?' He repeated, blankly, then began to laugh. 'No, I see. I can hardly start quoting Merlin's authority, or people might ask how it came my way. And

they might remember a certain humble traveller who peddled herbs and simples ... Well, since that same traveller brought me a letter from the High King, my own authority will doubtless suffice.'

'It's had to do so for long enough,' I agreed, and took my leave, well satisfied.

CHAPTER 9

So we journeyed north. Once we had joined the main
road north from York, the way they call Dere Street, going
was easy, and we made fair speed. Sometimes we lodged
in taverns, but, the weather being fine and hot, more often
than not we would ride on as long as the light lasted,
then make camp in some flowering brake near the road.
Then after supper I would make music for myself, and
Ulfin would listen, dreaming his own dreams while the
fire died to white ash, and the stars came out.

He was a good companion. We had known one another
since we were boys, I with Ambrosius in Brittany where
he gathered the army that was to conquer Vortigern and
take Britain. Ulfin as servant—slave-boy—to my tutor
Belasius. His life had been a hard one with that strange
and cruel man, but after Belasius' death Uther had taken
the boy into his service, and there Ulfin had soon risen
to a place of trust. He was now about five and thirty
years old, brown haired and grey eyed, very quiet, and
self-contained in the way of men who know they must
live their lives out alone, or as the companions of other
men. The years as Belasius' catamite had left their mark.

One evening I made a song, and sang it to the low hills
north of Vinovia, where the busy small rivers wind deep
in their forested valleys, but the great road strides across
the higher land, through leagues of whin and bracken,
and over the long heather moorlands where the only
trees are pine and alder and groves of silver birch.

We were camped in one such coppice, where the ground
was dry underfoot, and the slender birch boughs hung
still in the warm evening, tenting us with silk.

This was the song. I called it a song of exile, and I have

heard versions of it since, elaborated by some famous
Saxon singer, but the first was my own:

> He who is companionless
> Seeks oftentimes the mercy
> The grace
> Of the creator, God.
> Sad, sad the faithful man
> Who outlives his lord.
> He sees the world stand waste
> As a wall blown on by the wind,
> As an empty castle, where the snow
> Sifts through the window-frames,
> Drifts on the broken bed
> And the black hearth-stone.
>
> Alas, the bright cup!
> Alas, the hall of feasting!
> Alas the sword that kept
> The sheep-fold and the apple-orchard
> Safe from the claw of the wolf!
> The wolf-slayer is dead
> The law-giver, the law-upholder is dead,
> While the sad wolf's self, with the eagle,
> and the raven,
> Come as kings, instead.

I was lost in the music, and when at length I laid the
last note to rest and looked up, I was taken aback to see
two things; one that Ulfin, sitting on the other side of the
fire, was listening rapt, with tears on his face; the other,
that we had company. Neither Ulfin nor I, enclosed in
the music, had noticed the two travellers approaching us
over the soft mosses of the moorland way.

Ulfin saw them in the same moment that I did, and was
on his feet, knife ready. But it was obvious that there was
no harm in them, and the knife was back in its sheath
before I said, 'Put up,' or the foremost of the intruders

smiled, and showed a placating hand.

'No harm, masters, no harm. I've always been fond of a bit of music, and you've got quite a talent there, you have indeed.'

I thanked him, and, as if the words had been an invitation, he came nearer to the fire and sat, while the boy who was with him thankfully humped the packs off his shoulders and sank down likewise. He stayed in the background, away from the fire, though with the darkness of late evening a cool little breeze had sprung up, making the warmth of the burning logs welcome.

The newcomer was a smallish man, elderly, with a neat greying beard and unruly brows over myopic brown eyes. His dress was travel-worn but neat, the cloak of good cloth, the sandals and belt of soft-cured leather. Surprisingly, his belt buckle was of gold—or else thickly gilded—and worked in an elaborate pattern. His cloak was fastened with a heavy disk brooch, also gilded, with a design beautifully worked, a curling triskele set in filigree within a deeply fluted rim. The boy, whom at first I took to be his grandson, was similarly dressed, but his only jewel was something that looked like a charm worn on a thin chain at his neck. Then he reached forward to unroll the blankets for the night, and as his sleeve slid back I saw on his forearm the puckered scar of an old brand. A slave, then; and, from the way he stayed back from the fire's warmth, and silently busied himself unpacking the bags, he was one still. The old man was a man of property.

'You don't mind?' The latter was addressing me. Our own simple clothes and simpler way of life—the bedding rolls under the birches, the plain plates and drinking horns, and the worn saddlebags we used for pillows—had told him that here were travellers no more than his equals, if that. 'We got out of our way a few miles back, and were thankful to hear your singing and see the light of the fire. We guessed you might not be too far from the road, and now the boy tells me it lies just over yonder, thanks be to Vulcan's fires! The moorlands are all very well by

daylight, but after dark treacherous for man or beast ...'

He talked on; while Ulfin, at a nod from me, rose to fetch the wine flask, and offer it to him. But the newcomer demurred, with a hint of complacency.

'No, no. Thank you, my good sir, but we have food. We need not trouble you—except, if you will allow it, to share your fire and company for the night? My name is Beltane, and my servant here is called Ninian.'

'We are Emrys and Ulfin. Please be welcome. Will you not take wine? We carry enough.'

'I also. In fact, I shall take it ill if you don't both join me in a drink of it. Remarkable stuff, I hope you'll agree ...' Then, over his shoulder: 'Food, boy, quickly, and offer these gentlemen some of the wine that the commandant gave me.'

'Have you come far?' I asked him. The etiquette of the road does not allow you to ask a man directly where he has come from nor whither he is bound, but equally it is etiquette for him to tell you, even though his tale may be patently untrue.

Beltane answered without hesitation, through the chicken leg the boy handed him.

'From York. Spent the winter there. Usually get out before this onto the road, but waited there ... Town very full ...' He chewed and swallowed, adding, more clearly: 'It was a propitious time. Business was good, so I stayed on.'

'You came by Catraeth?' He had spoken in the British tongue, so, following suit, I gave the place its old name. The Romans called it Cataracta.

'No. By the road east of the plain. I do not advise it, sir. We were glad to turn onto the moor tracks to strike across for Dere Street at Vinovia. But this fool'—a hitch of a shoulder at the slave—'missed the milestone. I have to depend on him; my sight is poor, except for things as near to me as this bit of fowl. Well, Ninian was counting the clouds, as usual, instead of watching the way, and by duskfall we had no idea where we were, or if we had passed

the town already. Are we past it now? I fear we must be.'

'I'm afraid so, yes. We passed through it late in the afternoon. I'm sorry. You had business there?'

'My business lies in every town.'

He sounded remarkably unworried. I was glad of this, for the boy's sake. The latter was at my elbow with the wine-flask, pouring with grave concentration; Beltane, I judged, was all bark and bustle; Ninian showed no trace of fear. I thanked him, and he glanced up and smiled. I saw then that I had misjudged Beltane; his strictures, indeed, looked to be justified; it was obvious that the boy's thoughts, in spite of the seeming concentration on his tasks, were leagues away; the sweet, cloudy smile came from a dream that held him. His eyes, in the shadow-light of moon and fire, were grey, rimmed with darkness like smoke. Something about them, and about the absent grace of his movements, was surely familiar ... I felt the night air breathing on my back, and the hairs on my nape lifted like the fur of a night-prowling cat.

Then he had turned away without speaking, and was stooping beside Ulfin with the flask.

'Try it, sir,' Beltane urged me. 'It's good stuff. I got it from one of the garrison officers at Ebor ... God knows where *he* laid hands on it, but it's better not to ask, eh?' The ghost of a wink, as he chewed once more at his chicken.

The wine was certainly good, rich, smooth and dark, a rival to any I had tasted even in Gaul or Italy. I complimented Beltane on it, wondering as I spoke what service could have elicited payment like this.

'Aha!' he said, with that same complacency. 'You're wondering what I could have done to chisel stuff like this out of him, eh?'

'Well, yes, I was.' I admitted, smiling. 'Are you a magician, that you can read thoughts?'

He chuckled. 'Not that kind. But I know what you're thinking now, too.'

'Yes?'

'You're busy wondering if I'm the King's enchanter in disguise, I'll warrant! You'd think it might take his kind of magic to charm a wine like that out of Vitruvius ... And Merlin travels the roads the same as I do; a simple tradesman you'd take him for, they say, with maybe one slave for company, maybe not even that. Am I right?'

'About the wine, yes, indeed. I take it, then, that you are more than just a "simple tradesman"?'

'You could say so.' Nodding, self-important. 'But about Merlin, now. I hear he's left Caerleon. No one knew where he was bound, or on what errand, but that's always the way with him. They were saying in York that the High King would be back in Linnuis before the turn of the moon, but Merlin disappeared the day after the crowning.' He looked from me to Ulfin. 'Have you had any news of what's afoot?'

His curiosity was no more than the natural newsmon-gering of the travelling tradesman. Such folk are great bringers and exchangers of news: they are made welcome for it everywhere, and reckon on it as a valuable stock-in-trade.

Ulfin shook his head. His face was wooden. The boy Ninian was not even listening. His head was turned away towards the scented dark of the moorlands. I could hear the broken, bubbling call of some late bird stirring on its nest; joy came and went in the boy's face, a flying gleam as evanescent as starlight on the moving leaves above us. Ninian had his refuge, it seemed, from a garrulous master and the day's drudgery.

'We came from the west, yes, from Deva,' I said, giving Beltane the information he angled for. 'But what news I have is old. We travel slowly. I am a doctor, and can never move far without work.'

'So? Ah, well,' said Beltane, biting with relish into a barley bannock, 'no doubt we will hear something when we get to the Cor Bridge. You're bound that way, too? Good, good. But you needn't fear to travel with me! I'm no enchanter, in disguise or otherwise, and even if Queen

Morgause's men were to promise gold, or threaten death by fire, I could make shift to prove it!'

Ulfin looked up sharply, but I said merely: 'How?'

'By my trade. I have my own brand of magic, And for all they say Merlin is master of so much, mine is one skill you can't pretend to if you haven't had the training. And that'—with the same cheerful complacency—'takes a lifetime.'

'May we know what it is?' The question was mere courtesy. This, patently, was the moment of revelation he had been working for.

'I'll show you.' He swallowed the last crumb of bannock, wiped his mouth delicately, and took another drink of wine. 'Ninian! Ninian! You'll have time for your dreaming soon! Get the pack out, and feed the fire. We want light.'

Ulfin reached behind him and threw a fresh faggot on. The flames leaped high. The boy fetched a bulky roll of soft leather, and knelt beside me. He undid the ties, and unrolled the thing along the ground in the firelight.

It went with a flash and a shimmer. Gold caught the rich and dancing light, enamels in black and scarlet, pearly shell, garnet and blue glass—bedded or pinned along the kidskin were pieces of jewellery, beautifully made. I saw brooches, pins, necklaces, amulets, buckles for sandals or belts, and one little nest of enchanting silver acorns for a lady's girdle. The brooches were mostly of the round sort he was wearing, but one or two were of the old bow design, and I saw some animals, and one very elaborate curly dragonlike creature done with great skill in garnet set with cellwork and filigree.

I looked up to see Beltane watching me eagerly. I gave him what he wanted. 'This is splendid work. Beautiful. It is as fine as any I have seen.'

He glowed with simple pleasure. Now that I had placed him, I could let myself be easy. He was an artist, and artists live on praise as bees on nectar. Nor do they much concern themselves in anything beyond their own art; Beltane

had been barely interested in my own calling. His questions were harmless enough, a travelling salesman probing for news; and with the events at Luguvallium still a story for every fireside, what finer morsel of news could there be than some hint of Merlin's whereabouts? It was certain that he had no idea who he was talking to. I asked a few questions about the work; these out of genuine interest; I have always learned where I could about any man's skills. His answers soon showed me that he had certainly made the jewels himself; so the service for which the wine had been a reward was also explained.

'Your eyesight,' I said. 'You spoiled it with this work?'

'No, no. My eyesight is poor, but it is good for close work. In fact, it has been my blessing as an artist. Even now, when I am no longer young, I can see details very finely, but your face, my good sir, is by no means clear; and as for these trees around us, for such I take them to be ...' He smiled and shrugged. 'Hence my keeping this idle dreamer of a boy. He is my eyes. Without him I could hardly travel as I do, and indeed, I am lucky to have got here safely, even with his eyes, the little fool. This is no country to leave the roads and venture across bogland.'

His sharpness was a matter of routine. The boy Ninian ignored it; he had taken the chance of showing me the jewellery to stay near the fire.

'And now?' I asked the goldsmith. 'You have shown me work fit for king's courts. Too good, surely, for the marketplace? Where are you taking it?'

'Need you ask? To Dunpeldyr, in Lothian. With the king newly wed, and the queen as lovely as mayflowers and sorrel-buds, there will surely be trade for such as I.'

I stretched my hand to the warmth of the blaze. 'Ah, yes,' I said. 'He married Morgause in the end. Pledged to one princess and married to another. I heard something of that. You were there?'

'I was indeed. And small blame to King Lot, that's what everyone was saying. The Princess Morgan is fair

enough, and right enough a king's daughter, but the other one—well, you know how the talk goes. No man, let alone a man like Lot of Lothian, could come within arm's length of that lady, and not lust to bed her.'

'Your eyesight was good enough for that?' I asked him. I saw Ulfin smile.

'I didn't need eyesight.' He laughed robustly. 'I have ears, and I hear the talk that goes around, and once I got near enough to smell the scent she uses, and catch the colour of her hair in the sunlight, and hear her pretty voice. So I got my boy to tell me what she looked like, and I made this chain for her. Do you think her lord will buy it of me?'

I fingered the lovely thing, it was of gold, each link as delicate as floss, holding flowers of pearl and citrine set in filigree. 'He would be a fool if he did not. And if the lady sees it first, he certainly will.'

'I reckon on that,' he said, smiling. 'By the time I get to Dunpeldyr, she should be well again, and thinking of finery. You knew, did you? She was brought to bed two full weeks ago, before her time.'

Ulfin's sudden stillness made a pause of silence as loud as a shout. Ninian looked up. I felt my own nerves tighten. The goldsmith sensed the sharpening of the attention he was getting, and looked pleased. 'Had you not heard?'

'No. Since we passed Isurium we have not lodged in towns. Two weeks ago? This is certain?'

'Certain, sir. Too certain, maybe, for some folks' comfort.' He laughed. 'Never have I seen so many folk counting on their fingers that never counted before! And count as they may, with the best will in the world, they make it September for the child's conceiving. That,' said the little gossip, 'would be at Luguvallium, when King Uther died.'

'I suppose so,' I said, indifferently. 'And King Lot? The last I heard, he was gone to Linnuis, to join Arthur there.'

'He did, that's true. He'll hardly have got the news yet. We got it ourselves when we lay for a night at Elfete, on the east road. That was the way her courier took. He had

some tale of avoiding trouble by going that way, but it's my belief he'd been told to take his time. By the time King Lot gets news of the birthing, it'll be a more decent interval since the wedding day.'

'And the child?' I asked it idly. 'A boy?'

'Aye, and from all accounts a sickly one, so with all his haste, Lot still may not have got himself an heir.'

'Ah, well,' I said, 'he has time.' I turned the subject. 'Are you not afraid to travel as you do, with so much valuable cargo?'

'I confess I have had fears about it,' he admitted. 'Yes, yes, indeed. You must understand that commonly, when I shut my workshop, and take to the roads for summer, I carry with me only such stuff as the folks like to buy in the markets, or at best, gauds for merchants' wives. But luck was against me, and I could not get these jewels done in time to show them to Queen Morgause before she went north, so needs must I carry them after her. Now my luck is to fall in with an honest man like yourself; I don't need to be a Merlin to tell such things . . . I can see you're honest, and a gentleman like myself. Tell me, will my luck hold tomorrow? May we have your company, my good sir, as far as Cor Bridge?'

I had made up my mind already about that. 'As far as Dunpeldyr if you will. I'm bound there. And if you stop by the way to sell your wares, that suits me, too. I recently had a piece of news that tells me there is no haste for me to be there.'

He was delighted, and fortunately did not see Ulfin's look of surprise. I had already decided that the goldsmith might be useful to me. I judged that he would hardly have outstayed the spring weather in York, making up the rich jewels he had shown me, without some sort of assurance that Morgause would at least look at them. As he talked cheerfully on, needing very little encouragement to tell me more about the happenings in York, I found that I had been right. Somehow he had managed to engage the interest of Lind, Morgause's young hand-

maid, and had persuaded her, in return for a pretty trinket or two, to speak of his wares to the Queen. Beltane himself had not been sent for, but Lind had taken one or two of his pieces to show her mistress, and had assured the goldsmith of Morgause's interest. He told me all about it at some length. For a while I let him talk on, then said casually: 'You said something about Morgause and Merlin. Did I understand that she had soldiers out looking for him? Why?'

'No, you misunderstood me. I was speaking in jest. When I was in York, listening as I do to the talk of the place, I heard someone say that Merlin and she had quarrelled at Luguvallium, and that she spoke of him now with hatred, where before she had spoken with envy of his art. And lately, of course, everyone was wondering where he had gone. Queen or no, little harm could she do a man like that!'

And you, I thought, are luckily short of sight, otherwise I should have to be wary of a perceptive and garrulous little man. As it was, I was glad I had fallen in with him. I was still thinking about it, but idly, as finally even he decided it was time to sleep, and we let the fire go low and rolled ourselves in our blankets under the trees. His presence would give credence to my disguise, and he could be, if not my eyes, my ears and information at the court of Morgause. And Ninian, who acted as his 'eyes'? The cold breeze stirred my nape again, and my idle calculations dislimned like a shadow when the sun goes in. What was this? Foreknowledge, the half-forgotten stirring of a kind of power? But even that speculation died as the night breeze hushed through the delicate birch boughs and the last faggot sank to ash. The dreamless night closed in. About the sickly child at Dunpeldyr I would not think at all, except to hope that it would not thrive, and so leave me no problem.

But I knew that the hope was vain.

CHAPTER 10

It is barely thirty miles from Vinovia to the town at the Cor Bridge, but it took us six days' journeying. We did not keep to the road, but travelled by circuitous and sometimes rough ways, visiting every village and farmstead, however humble, that lay between us and the Bridge.

With no reason for haste, the journey passed pleasantly. Beltane obviously took great pleasure in our company, and Ninian's lot was made easier by the use of the mules to carry his awkward packs. The goldsmith was as garrulous as ever, but he was a good-hearted man, and moreover a meticulous and honest craftsman, which is something to respect. Our wandering progress was made slower than ever by the time he took over his work—repair-work, mostly, in the poorer places; in the bigger villages, or at taverns, he was of course occupied all the time.

So was the boy, but on the journeys between settlements, and in the evenings by the camp fire, we struck up a strange kind of friendship. He was always quiet, but after he found that I knew the ways of birds and beasts, that a detailed knowledge of plants went with my physician's skill, and that I could, at night, even read the map of the stars, he kept near me whenever he could, and even brought himself to question me. Music he loved, and his ear was true, so I began to teach him how to tune my harp. He could neither read nor write, but showed, once his interest was engaged, a ready intelligence that, given time and the right teacher, could be made to blossom. By the time we reached Cor Bridge I was beginning to wonder if I could be that teacher, and if Ninian could be brought —his master permitting—to serve me. With this in mind,

I kept my eyes open whenever we passed some quarry or farmstead, in case there might be some likely slave I could buy to serve Beltane, and persuade him to release the boy.

From time to time the small cloud oppressed me still, the hovering chill of some vague foreboding that made me restless and apprehensive; trouble was there at my whistle, looking for somewhere to strike. After a while I gave up trying to see where that stroke might fall. I was certain that it could not concern Arthur, and if it was to concern Morgause, then there would be time enough to let it worry me. Even in Dunpeldyr I thought I should be safe enough: Morgause would have other things on her mind, not least the return of her lord, who could count on his fingers as well as any man.

And the trouble might be no deep matter, but the trivial annoyance of a day, soon forgotten. It is hard to tell, when the gods trail the shadows of foreknowledge across the light, whether the cloud is one that will blot out a king's realm, or make a child cry in its sleep.

At length we came to Cor Bridge, in the rolling country just south of the Great Wall. In Roman times the place was called Corstopitum. There was a strong fort there, well placed where Dere Street, from the south, crossed the great east-west road of Agricola. In time a civilian settlement sprang up in this favoured spot, and soon became a thriving township, accepting all the traffic, civil and military, from the four quarters of Britain. Nowadays the fort is a tumbledown affair, much of its stone having been pillaged for new buildings, but west of it, on a curve of rising ground edged by the Cor Burn, the new town still grows and prospers, with houses, inns and shops, and a thriving market which is the liveliest relic of its prosperity in Roman times.

The fine Roman bridge, that gives the place its modern name, still stands, spanning the Tyne at the point where the Cor Burn runs into it from the north. There is a mill there, and the bridge's timbers groan all day under the loads of grain. Below the mill is a wharf where shallow-

draught barges can tie up. The Cor is little more than a stream, relying on its steep tumble of water to drive the mill wheel, but the great River Tyne is wide and fast, flowing here over bright shingle between its gracious banks of trees. Its valley is broad and fertile, full of fruit trees standing deep in growing corn. From this flowery and winding tract of green the land rises towards the north to rolling moorland, where, under the windy stretches of sky, sudden blue lakes wink in the sun. In winter it is a bleak country, where wolves and wild men roam the heights, and come sometimes over-close to the houses; but in summer it is a lovely land, with forests full of deer, and fleets of swans sailing the waters. The air over the moors sparkles with bird-song, and the valleys are alive with skimming swallows and the bright flash of kingfishers. And along the edge of the whinstone runs the Great Wall of the Emperor Hadrian, rising and dipping as the rock rises and dips. It commands the country from its long cliff-top, so that from any point of it fold upon fold of blue distance fades away east or westward, till the eye loses the land in the misty edge of the sky.

It was not country I had known before. I had come this way, as I had told Arthur, because I had a call to make. One of my father's secretaries, whom I had known first in Brittany, and thereafter in Winchester and Caerleon, had come north after Ambrosius' death, to retirement of a sort here in Northumbria. The pension he received from my father had let him buy a holding near Vindolanda, in a sheltered spot beside the Agricolan Road, with a couple of strong slaves to work it. There he had settled, growing rare plants in his favoured garden, and writing, so I had been told, a history of the times he had lived through. His name was Blaise.

We lodged in the old part of the town, at a tavern within the purlieus of the original fortress. Beltane, with sudden, immovable obstinacy, had refused to pay the toll exacted at the bridge, so we crossed at the ford some half mile down-stream, then turned along the river past the

forge, coming into the town by its old east gate.

Night was falling when we got there, so we put up at the first tavern we found. This was a respectable place not far from the main market square. Late though the hour was, there was still plenty of coming and going. Servants were gossiping at the cistern while they filled their water jars; through the laughter and talk came the cool splash of a fountain; in some house nearby a woman was singing a weaving-song. Beltane was in high glee at the prospects for trading on the morrow, and in fact started business that same night, when the tavern filled up after supper-time. I did not stay to see how he did. Ulfin reported a bath-house still in commission near the old west wall, so I spent the evening there and then retired, refreshed, to bed.

Next morning Ulfin and I breakfasted together in the shade of the huge plane tree which grew beside the inn. It promised to be a hot day.

Early as we were, Beltane and the boy were before us. The goldsmith had already set up his stall in a strategic place near the cistern; which meant merely that he, or rather Ninian, had spread some rush matting on the ground, and on that had laid out such gauds as might appeal to the eyes and purses of ordinary folk. The fine work was carefully hidden away in the lining of the bags.

Beltane was in his element, talking incessantly to any passer-by who paused even for a moment to look at the goods: a complete lesson in jewelcraft was given away, so to speak, with every piece. The boy, as usual, was silent. He patiently rearranged the items which had been handled and carelessly dropped back on the matting, and he took the money, or sometimes exchange-goods such as food or cloth. Between times he sat cross-legged, stitching at the frayed straps of his sandals, which had given a lot of trouble on the road.

'Or this one, madam?' Beltane was saying, to a round-faced woman with a basket of cakes on her arm. 'This we call cellwork, or inclosed work, very beautiful, isn't it?

I learned the art in Byzantium, and believe me, even in Byzantium itself you'd never see finer ... And this very same design, I've seen it done in gold, worn by the finest ladies in the land. This one? Why, it's copper, madam—and priced accordingly, but it's every bit as good—the same work in it, as you can well see ... Look at those colours. Hold it up to the light, Ninian. How bright and clear they are, and see how the bands of copper shine, holding the colours apart ... Yes, copper wire, very delicate; you have to lay it in pattern, and then you run the colours in, and the wire acts as a wall, you might say, to contain the pattern. Oh, no, madam, not jewels, not at that price! It's glass, but I'll warrant you've never seen jewels with colours finer. I make the glass myself, and very skilled work it is, too, in my little 'etna' there—that's what I call my smelting stove—but you've no time this morning, I can see that, madam. Show her the little hen, Ninian, or maybe you prefer the horse ... that's it, Ninian ... Now, madam, are the colours not beautiful? I doubt if anywhere in the length and breadth of the land you would find work to equal this, and all for a copper penny. Why, there's as much copper, nearly, in the brooch, as there is in the penny you'll give me for it ...'

Ulfin appeared then, leading the mules. It had been arranged that he and I would make the short journey to Vindolanda, and return on the morrow, while Beltane and the boy pursued their trade in the town. I paid for the breakfast, then, rising, went across to take leave of them.

'You're going now?' Beltane spoke without taking his eyes off the woman, who was turning a brooch over in her hand. 'Then a good journey to you, Master Emrys, and we hope to see you back tomorrow night ... No, no, madam, we have no need of your cakes, delicious though they look. A copper penny is the price today. Ah, I thank you. You will not regret it. Ninian, pin the brooch on for the lady ... Like a queen, madam, I do assure you. Indeed,

Queen Ygraine herself, that's the highest in the land, might envy you. Ninian'—this as the woman moved away, his voice changing to the habitual nagging tone he used to the boy—'don't stand there with your mouth watering! Take the penny now and get yourself a pair of new shoes. When we go north I cannot have you hobbling and lagging with flapping soles as you did all the way—'

'No!' I did not even realise that I had spoken, till I saw them staring. Even then I did not know what impelled me to add: 'Let the boy have his cakes, Beltane. The sandals will suffice, and see, he is hungry, and the sun is shining.'

The goldsmith's short-sighted eyes were puckered as he stared up at me against the light. At length, a little to my surprise, he nodded, with a gruff, 'All right, get along,' to the boy. Ninian gave me a shining look, then ran off into the crowd after the market-woman. I thought Beltane was going to question me, but he did not. He began to set the goods straight again, saying merely: 'You're right, I have no doubt. Boys are always starving, and he's a good lad and faithful. He can go barefoot if he has to, but at least let him have his belly full. It isn't often we get sweet stuff, and the cakes smelled like a feast, so they did.'

As we rode west along the river-side Ulfin asked, with sharp concern in his voice:

'What is it, my lord? Is something ailing you?'

I shook my head, and he said no more, but he must have known I was lying, because I myself could feel the tears cold on my cheeks in the summer wind.

*   *   *

Master Blaise received us in a snug little house of sand-coloured stone, built round a small courtyard with apple trees trained up the walls, and roses hiding the squared modern pillars.

The house had once, long ago, belonged to a miller; a stream ran past, its steep fall controlled by shallow water-

steps, its walled banks set with little ferns and flowers. Some hundred paces below the house, the stream vanished under a hanging canopy of beech and hazel. Above this woodland, on the steep slope behind the house, full in the sun, was the walled garden that held the old man's treasured plants.

He knew me straight away, though it was many years since we had met. He lived alone, but for his two gardeners and a woman who, with her daughter, cared for the house and cooked for him. She was bidden to get beds ready, and bustled off to do some scolding over the kitchen braziers. Ulfin went to see our mules stabled, and Blaise and I were free to talk.

Light lingers late in the north, so after supper we went out to the terrace over the stream. The warmth of the day breathed still from the stones, and the evening air smelled of cypress and rosemary. Here and there in the tree-hung shadows the pale shape of a statue glimmered. A thrush sang somewhere, a richer echo of the nightingale. At my elbow the old man (*magister artium*, as he now liked to style himself) was talking of the past, in a pure Roman Latin with no trace of accent. It was an evening borrowed from Italy: I might have been a young man again, on my youthful travels.

I said as much, and he beamed with pleasure.

'I like to think so. One tries to hold to the civilised values of one's prime. You knew I studied there as a young man, before I was privileged to enter your father's service? *Those* years, ah, yes, those were the great years, but as one grows older, perhaps one tends to look back too much, too much.'

I said something civil about this being of advantage to an historian, and asked if he would honour me with a reading from his work. I had noticed the lighted lamp standing on a stone table by the cypresses, and the rolls lying handily beside it.

'Would you really care to hear it?' He moved that way readily. 'Some parts of it, I am sure, would interest you

enormously. And it is a part that you can help me to add to, I believe. As it chances, I have it here with me, this roll, yes, this is the one ... Shall we sit? The stone is dry, and the evening tolerably mild. I think we shall come to no harm out here by the roses ...'

The section he chose to read was his account of the events after Ambrosius returned to Greater Britain; he had been close to my father for most of that time, while I had been involved elsewhere. After he had finished reading he put his questions, and I was able to supply details of the final battle with Hengist at Kaerconan and the subsequent siege of York, and the work of settlement and rebuilding that came after. I filled in for him, too, the campaign that Uther had waged against Gilloman in Ireland. I had gone with Uther, while Ambrosius stayed in Winchester; Blaise had been with him there, and it was to Blaise that I had owed the account of my father's death while I was overseas.

He told me about it again. 'I can still see it, that great bedchamber at Winchester, with the doctors, and the nobles standing there, and your father lying against the pillows, near to death, but sensible, and talking to you as if you were there in the room. I was beside him, ready to write down anything that was needed, and more than once I glanced down at the foot of the King's bed, half thinking to see you there. And all the while you were voyaging back from the Irish wars, bringing the great stone to lay on his grave.'

He fell to nodding then, as old men do, as if he would go back for ever to the stories of times gone by. I brought him back to the present. 'And how far have you gone, with your account of the times?'

'Oh, I try to set down all that passes. But now that I am out of the centre of affairs, and have to depend on the talk from the town, or on anyone who calls to see me, it is hard to know how much I miss. I have correspondents, but sometimes they are lax, yes, the young men are not what they were ... It's a great chance that brings you here,

Merlin, a great day for me. You will stay? As long as you wish, dear boy; you'll have seen that we live simply, but it's a good life, and there is still so much to talk about, so much ... And you must see my vines. Yes, a fine white grape, that ripens to a marvellous sweetness if the year is a good one. Figs do well here, and peaches, and I have even had some success with a pomegranate tree from Italy.'

'I can't stay this time, I'm afraid.' I spoke with genuine regret. 'I have to go north in the morning. But if I may, I'll come back before long—and with plenty to tell you, too, I promise you! There are great things afoot now, and you will be doing men a service if you will put them down. Meantime, if I can, would you like me to send letters from time to time? I hope to be back at Arthur's side before winter, and it will keep you in touch.'

His delight was patent. We talked for a little longer, then, as the night-flying insects began to crowd to the lamp, we carried it indoors, and parted for the night.

My bedchamber window looked out over the terrace where we had been sitting. For a long time before I lay down to sleep I leaned my elbows on the sill, looking out and breathing the night scents that came in wave after wave on the breeze. The thrush had stopped singing, and now the soft *hush* of falling water filled the night. A new moon lay on its back , and stars were out. Here, away from lights and sounds of town or village, the night was deep, the black sky stretching, fathomless, away between the spheres, to some unimaginable world where gods walked, and suns and moons showered down like petals falling. Some power there is that draws men's eyes and hearts up and outwards, beyond the heavy clay that fastens them to earth. Music can take them, and the moon's light, and, I suppose, love, though I had not known it then, except in worship.

The tears were there again, and I let them fall. I knew now what cloud it was that had lain over my horizon ever since that chance meeting on the moorland road. How, I did not know, but the boy Ninian, so young and

quiet, and with a grace in look and motion that gave the lie to the ugly slave-burn on his arm—he had had about him the mark of a coming death. This, once seeing, any man might have wept for, but I was weeping, too, for myself; for Merlin the enchanter, who saw, and could do nothing; who walked his own lonely heights where it seemed that none would ever come near to him. In the boy's still face and listening eyes, that night on the moor when the birds had called, I had caught a glimpse of what might have been. For the first time, since those days long ago when I had sat at Galapas' feet to learn the arts of magic, I had seen someone who might have learned worthily from me. Not as others had wanted to learn, for power or excitement, nor for the prosecution of some enmity or private greed; but because he had seen, darkly with a child's eyes, how the gods move with the winds and speak with the sea and sleep in the gentle herbs; and how God himself is the sum of all that is on the face of the lovely earth. Magic is the door through which mortal man may sometimes step, to find the gates in the hollow hills, and let himself through into the halls of that other world. I could, but for that shining edge of doom, have opened those gates for him, and, when I needed it no longer, have left him the key.

And now he was dead. I had known it, I think, after I had spoken in the market-place. My sharp, unthinking protest had been made for no reason that I knew: the knowledge came later. And always, when I spoke like that, men did unquestioningly as I bade them. So at least the boy had had his cakes, and the day's sunshine.

I turned away from the thin, brightening moon, and lay down.

* * *

'At least he had the cakes, and the day's sunshine.' Beltane the goldsmith told us about it as we shared supper at the town's tavern the next evening. He was unusually

silent, for him, and seemed stunned, clinging to our company as, in spite of his sharp tongue, he must have clung to the boy's.

'But—drowned.' Ulfin said it on a disbelieving note, but I caught a glance from him that told me he had begun to put events together and understand them. 'How did it happen?'

'That evening, at supper-time, he brought me back here and packed the things away. It had been a good day, and the take was heavy; we were sure of eating well. He had worked hard, and so when he saw some boys off down to bathe in the river, he asked if he might join them. He was a great one for washing himself ... and it had been a hot day, and people's feet kick up a lot of dust, and dung besides, in the market-places. I let him go. The next thing was the boys came back, running, with the story. He must have trodden into a hole, and slipped out of his depth. It's a bad river, they tell me ... How was I to know that? How could I know? When we came over yesterday the ford seemed so shallow, and so safe ...'

'The body?' asked Ulfin, after a pause when he could see that I was not going to speak.

'Gone. Gone downstream, the boys said, like a log on the flood. He came up half a league down-river, but none of them could come near him, and then he vanished. It's a bad death, a puppy's death. He should be found, and buried like a man.'

Ulfin said something kind, and after a while the little man's lamentations ran out, and the supper came, and he made shift to eat and drink, and was the better for it.

Next morning the sun shone again, and we went north, the three of us together, and four days later reached the country of the Votadini, which is called in the British tongue Manau Guotodin.

CHAPTER 11

Some ten days later, with due stops for trading, we reached Lot's city of Dunpeldyr. It was late afternoon of a cloudy day, and it was raining. We were lucky enough to find suitable lodgings in a tavern near the south gate.

The town was little more than a close huddle of houses and shops near the foot of a great crag on which the castle was built. In times past the crag had contained the whole stronghold, but now the houses crowd, haphazard, between cliffs and river, and on the slopes of the crag itself, right up to the castle wall. The river (another Tyne) curves round the roots of the cliff, then runs in a wide meander across a mile or so of flat land to its sandy estuary. Along its banks the houses cluster, and boats are pulled up on the shingle. There are two bridges, a heavy wooden one set on stone piers, that holds the road to the main castle gate above; and another narrow span of planking which leads to a steep path serving the side gate of the castle. There had been no road-building here; the place had grown without plan, and certainly without beauty or amenity. The town is a mean one, of mud brick houses with turfed roofs, and steep alleys which in stormy weather become torrents of foul water. The river, so fair only a short distance away, is here full of weed and debris. Between the crag and the river to the east is the market-place, where on the morrow Beltane would set out his wares.

One thing I knew I must do without delay. If, ironically enough, Beltane were to be my 'eyes' inside the castle, neither Ulfin nor I must be seen to go about with him; so, dependent as he was on a servant, someone must be

found to replace the drowned boy. Beltane had made no move to do this himself on our journey north, and now was only too grateful when I offered to do it for him.

A short way out of the town gates I had noticed a quarry; not much of a place, but still working. Next morning, carefully anonymous in a shabby cloak of rusty brown, I went there and sought out the quarry-master, a big genial-looking ruffian who was strolling around among the half-derelict workings, and the equally derelict workmen, like a lord taking the summer air in his country demesne.

He looked me up and down with a fine air of disdain. 'Able-bodied servants come expensive, my good sir.' I could see him assessing me as he spoke, and coming up with a poor enough answer. 'Nor have I one to spare. One gets all the riffraff in a place like this ... prisoners, criminals, the lot. No one who'd ever be a decent house slave, or be trusted on a farm, or with any kind of skilled job. And muscle comes expensive. You'd best wait for the fair. All sorts come then, hiring themselves and their families, or selling themselves or their brats for food—though, come to that, you'd have to wait for winter and sharp weather to get the cheap market.'

'I don't wish to wait. I can pay. I am travelling, and I need a man or a boy. He need have no skills, except to keep himself clean, and be faithful to his master, and have enough strength to travel even in winter, when the roads are foul.'

As I spoke his manner grew more civil, and the assessment moved up a notch or two. 'Travel? So, what is your business?'

I saw no reason to tell him that the servant was not for myself. 'I am a doctor.'

My answer had the effect it has nine times out of ten. He started eagerly to tell me of all his various ailments, of which, since he was more than forty years old, he had plenty.

'Well,' I said, when he had finished, 'I can help you, I

think, but it had better be mutual. If you have a likely
hand you can let me have as a servant—and he should
be cheap enough, since it's just the riffraff you get here—
then perhaps we can do a deal? One more thing. As you
will understand, in my trade there are secrets to be kept.
I want no blabbermouth; he must be sparing of speech.'

At that the rogue stared, then slapped his thigh and
laughed, as if at the greatest joke in the world. He turned
his head and bellowed a name. 'Casso! Come here!
Quickly, you oaf! Here's luck for you, lad, and a new
master, and a fine new life adventuring!'

A lanky youth detached himself from a gang which
was labouring on stone-breaking under an overhang that
looked to me to be ready to collapse. He straightened
slowly, and stared, before dropping his pick-helve and
starting towards us.

'I'll spare you this one, master doctor,' said the quarry-
master genially. 'He's everything you ask for.' And he went
off into fits of mirth once more.

The youth came up and stood, arms hanging, eyes on
the ground. At a guess, he was about eighteen or nineteen.
He looked strong enough—he would have to be, to survive
that life for more than six months—but stupid to the
point of idiocy.

'Casso?' I said. He looked up, and I saw that he was
merely exhausted. In a life without hope or pleasure there
was little point in spending energy on thought.

His master was laughing again. 'It's no use talking to
him. Anything you want to know you'll have to ask me,
or look for yourself.' He seized the lad's wrist and held up
the arm. 'See? Strong as a mule, and sound in wind and
limb. And discreet enough, even for you. Discreet as hell,
is our Casso. He's dumb.'

The youth noticed the handling no more than would a
mule, but at the last sentence he met my eyes again, briefly.
I had been wrong. There was thought there, and with it
hope; I saw the hope die.

'But not deaf with it, I gather?' I said. 'What caused it, do you know?'

'You might say his own silly tongue.' He started his great laugh again, caught my look, and cleared his throat instead. 'You'll make no cure there, master doctor, his tongue's out. I never got the rights of it, but he used to be in service down in Bremenium, and the way I heard it, he opened his mouth too wide once too often. Not one to have patience with insolence, isn't the Lord Aguisel ... Ah, well, but he's learned his lesson. I got him with a job lot of labour after the town bridges were repaired. He's given me no trouble. And for all I know it was house service he was in before, so you'll be getting a bargain with a fine, young—*Hey there!*'

While we had been talking his eye had gone, from time to time, to the gang at work on the stone. Now he started over that way, with some shouted abuse at the 'idle scum' who had seized the chance to work more slowly.

I looked thoughtfully at Casso. I had caught the look in his face, and the quick, involuntary shake of the head at the quarry-master's mention of 'insolence'. 'You were in Aguisel's household?' I asked him.

A nod.

'I see.' I thought I did, indeed. Aguisel was a man of evil reputation, a jackal to Lot's wolf, who laired in the hill-top remains of Bremenium fortress to the south. Things happened there which a decent man could only guess at. I had heard rumours of his trick of using dumb or blinded slaves.

'Am I right in thinking that you saw what you could not be allowed to report on?'

Another nod. This time his eyes remained fixed on me. It must have been long enough since anyone had tried even this sort of limited communication.

'I thought as much. I have heard stories, myself, of my lord Aguisel. Can you read or write, Casso?'

A shake of the head.

'Be thankful,' I said, drily. 'If you could, then by this time you would be dead.'

The quarry-master had got his gang working again to his satisfaction. He was on his way back to us. I thought quickly.

The youth's dumbness might be no disadvantage to Beltane, who was more than able to do his own talking; but I had been working on the assumption that the new slave must act as his master's 'eyes' while we were in Dunpeldyr. Now I saw that there was no need of this: whatever transpired in Lot's stronghold, Beltane was quite able to report on it himself. His sight was not strong, but his hearing was, and he could tell us what was said: what the place looked like would hardly matter. When we left Dunpeldyr, if the goldsmith needed a different servant, no doubt we could find one. But now time pressed, and here I could certainly purchase discretion, even if enforced, and, I thought, the loyalty that went with gratitude.

'Well?' asked the quarry-master.

I said: 'Anyone who has survived service in Bremenium is certainly strong enough for anything I might require. Very well. I'll take him.'

'Splendid, splendid!' The fellow waxed loud in his praise of my judgment and Casso's various excellences, so much so that I began to wonder if the slaves were in fact his own to dispose of, or if he was seeing a way to fill his own purse, and would perhaps report the youth's death to his employers. When he began to haggle about price, I sent Casso to collect whatever possessions he had, with instructions to wait for me on the road. I have never seen why, because a man is your captive, or a purchase, he should be stripped of an elementary self-respect. Even a horse or a hound works the better for retaining a pride in itself.

After he had gone I turned back to the quarry-master. 'Now, we agreed, if you remember, that I would pay some part of the price in medicines. You will find me at the

tavern by the south gate. If you come tonight, or send someone to ask for Master Emrys, I will have the medicines ready for you, and leave them to be picked up. And now, about the rest of the price ...'

In the end we were agreed, and, followed by my new purchase, I made my way back to the tavern.

Casso's face fell when he heard that he was not to serve me, but to go with Beltane; but by the time the evening was through, with the warmth and good food and the lively company that crowded into the tavern, he looked like a plant which, dying in darkness, has been plunged suddenly into sunlit water. Beltane was outspokenly grateful to me, and embarked almost straight away on a long and happy exposition of his craft for Casso's sake. The latter could hardly have found a place in which his mutilation would have mattered less. I suspected that, as the evening wore through, Beltane began to find it a positive advantage to have a dumb servant. Ninian had hardly spoken at all, but neither had he listened. Casso drank it all in, fingering the pieces with his calloused hands, his brain waking from the numbness of hopeless exhaustion, and expanding into pleasure as one watched.

The tavern was too small—and we were ostensibly too poor—to have a private chamber, but at the end of the hall, away from the fire, there was a deep alcove with a table and twin settles where we could be private enough. No one took much notice of us, and we stayed in our corner all evening, listening to the gossip that came into the tavern. Facts there were none, but there were plenty of rumours, the most important being that Arthur had fought and won two more engagements, and that the Saxons had accepted terms. The High King was to be in Linnuis for some time longer, but Lot, it was said, could be expected home any day now.

In fact he did not come for four more days.

I spent the days withindoors, writing to Ygraine and Arthur, and the evenings in familiarising myself with the town and its environment. The town was small, and did

not attract many strangers, so, since I wanted to avoid attention, I went out at dusk, when folk would mostly be at supper. For the same reason I did not advertise my trade: anyone who approached our party had his full attention claimed by Beltane, and did not think to look further. They took me, I imagine, for a poor scribe of some sort. Ulfin haunted the town gates, picking up what news he could, and waiting for tidings of Lot's approach. Beltane, innocent and unsuspicious, plied his trade. He set up his stove in the square near the tavern, and began to teach Casso the elements of the repairer's art. Inevitably, this drew interest, and then custom, and soon the goldsmith was doing a roaring trade.

This, on the third day, brought just the result we all hoped for. The girl Lind, passing through the market square one day and seeing Beltane, approached and made herself known. Beltane sent her back to her mistress with a message, and a new buckle for herself, and soon got his reward. Next day he was sent for to the castle, and went off triumphantly, with a laden Casso in his wake.

Even had he not been dumb, Casso could have reported nothing. When the two were passed in through the postern gate, Casso was detained to wait in the porter's kennel, while an upper servant conducted the goldsmith to the queen's chambers.

He came back to the tavern at dusk, bubbling with his news. For all his talk of great people, this was the first king's house he had been in, and Morgause the first queen who would wear his jewels. The admiration he had conceived for her in York had soared now to the point of worship; at close quarters, even on him, her rose and gold beauty acted like a drug. He poured his story out over supper, obviously never thinking for a moment that I would not be absorbed in any item of gossip he might retail. Casso and I (Ulfin was still out) were given a word by word account of all that was said, of her graces, her praise of his work, her generosity in buying three pieces and accepting a fourth; even of the scent she wore. He did

his best, too, with a description of her beauty, and of the splendours of the room where she received him, but here we were dealing with impressions only: the picture he conveyed was a perfumed haze of light and colour; the cool brightness from a window running along the sheen of an amber robe, and lighting the wonderful rose-gold hair; the rustle of silk and the glow and crackle of logs lit against the grey day. And music, too; a girl's voice whispering a lullaby.

'So the child was there?'

'Indeed. Asleep in a high cradle near the fire. I could see it, oh, clearly, outlined against the flames; and the girl rocking it and singing. The cradle was canopied with silk and gauze, with a little bell that chimed as she rocked it, and glinted in the firelight. A royal cradle. Such a pretty sight! I could have wished my old eyes different, for that alone.'

'And did you see the child itself?'

It appeared that he had not. The baby had woken once, and cried a little, and the nurse had hushed him without lifting him from the blankets. The queen had been trying a necklet at the time, and without looking round had taken the mirror from the girl's hand, and bidden her sing to the baby.

'A pretty voice,' said Beltane, 'but such a sad little song. And indeed, I would hardly have recognised the maiden herself, if she had not come to speak to me yesterday. So thin and creeping, like a mouse, and her voice gone thin, too, like something pining. Lind, her name is, did I tell you? A strange name for a maiden, surely? Does it not mean a snake?'

'I believe so. Did you hear the child's name?'

'They call him Mordred.'

Beltane showed a tendency, here, to go back to his description of the cradle, and of the pretty picture the girl had made, rocking it and singing, but I brought him back to the point.

'Was anything said about King Lot's coming home?'

Beltane, that single-minded artist, did not even see the implications of the question. They were expecting him, he told me cheerfully, at any time. The queen had seemed as excited as a young girl. Indeed, she could talk of nothing else. Would her lord like the necklet? Did the earrings make her eyes look brighter? Why, added Beltane, he owed half the sale to the king's coming.

'She did not seem afraid at all?'

'Afraid?' He looked blank. 'No. Why should she? She was happy and excited. "Just wait," she was saying to the ladies, just like any young mother with her lord away at the wars, "just wait till my lord sees the fine son I bore him, and as like his father as one wolf to another." And she laughed and laughed. It was a jest, you understand, Master Emrys. They call Lot the Wolf in these parts, and take pride in him, which is only natural among savage folks like these of the north. Only a jest. Why should she be afraid?'

'I was thinking of the rumours you spoke of once before. You told me of things you heard in York, and then, you said, there were looks and whispers here among the common folk in the market-place.'

'Oh, those, yes ... Well, but that was only talk. I know what you're getting at, Master Emrys, the wicked stories that have been going about. You know that always happens when a birth comes before its time, and there's bound to be more talk in a king's house, because, you might say, more hangs on it.'

'So it was before its time?'

'Yes, so they say. It took them all by surprise. It was born before even the king's own doctors could get there, that were sent north from the army to tend to the queen. It was the women delivered her, but safely, by God's mercy. You remember we were told it was a sickly child? And indeed, I could tell as much from the way he cried. But now he thrives and puts on weight. The maid Lind told me so, when I spoke to her on the way back to the gate. "And it is true he's the image of King Lot?" I said to her.

She gives me a look, as much as to say, that will silence the gossip, but all she says aloud is, "Yes, as like as can be." '

He leaned across the table, nodding with cheerful emphasis. 'So you see it was all lies, Master Emrys. And indeed, one only has to talk to her. That pretty creature deceive her lord? Why, she was like a bride again at the thought of him coming home. And she would laugh that pretty laugh, like the silver bell on the cradle. Oh, yes, you can be sure the stories were all lies. Put around in York, they would be, by those that had cause to be jealous ... You know who I mean, eh? And the child the image of him. They were all saying the same, "King Lot will see himself in a mirror, just as sure as you see yourself, Madam. Look at him, the image, the little lamb ..." You know how women talk, Master Emrys. "The very image of his royal father." '

So he talked on, while Casso, busying himself with polishing some cheap buckles, listened and smiled, and I, only a little less silent, let the talk go by me while I thought my own thoughts.

Like his father? Dark hair, dark eyes, the description could fit both Lot and Arthur. Was there some faintest chance that fate was on Arthur's side? That she had conceived by Lot, and then seduced Arthur in an attempt to shackle him to her?

Reluctantly, I put the hope aside. When, at Luguvallium, I had felt doom impending, it had been in a time of power. And it did not need even that to tell me to mistrust Morgause. I had come north to watch her, and now the new fragment of information I had just heard from Beltane might well have told me what to watch for.

Ulfin came in then, shaking a fine rain from his cloak. He looked across, saw us, and gave a barely perceptible sign to me. I got to my feet, and, with a word to Beltane, went over to him.

He spoke softly. 'There's news. The queen's messenger rode in just now. I saw him. The horse was hard ridden,

almost foundered. I told you I was on terms with one of the gatehouse guards? He says King Lot's on his way home. He's travelling fast. They're expecting him tonight or tomorrow.'

'Thank you,' I said. 'Now, you've been out all day. Get yourself into dry clothes, and get something to eat. I've just heard something from Beltane that persuades me that a watch on the postern gate might be profitable. I'll tell you about it later. When you've eaten, come down and join me. I'll find somewhere dry to wait, where we won't be seen.' We rejoined the others, and I asked: 'Beltane, can you spare Casso to me for half an hour?'

'Of course, of course. But I shall need him later on. I was bidden back there tomorrow, with this buckle mended for the chamberlain, and I need Casso's help for that.'

'I shan't keep him. Casso?'

The slave was already on his feet. Ulfin said, with a shade of apprehension: 'So you know what to do now?'

'I am guessing,' I said. 'I have no power in this, as I told you.' I spoke softly, and above the tavern's roar Beltane could not hear me, but Casso did, and looked quickly from me to Ulfin and back again. I smiled at him. 'Don't let it concern you. Ulfin and I have affairs here which will not touch you or your master. Come with me now.'

'I could come myself,' said Ulfin, quickly.

'No. Do as I told you, and eat first. It could be a long watch. Casso ...'

We went through the maze of dirty streets. The rain, steady now, made muddy puddles, and splashed the dung into stinking pools. Where lights showed at all in the houses, they were feeble, smoking glints of flame, curtained from the wet night by hides or sacking. Nothing interfered with our night-sight, and presently we could pick our way cleanly across the gleaming runnels. After a while the tree-banked slope of the castle rock loomed above us. A lantern hung high in the blackness, marking the postern gate.

Casso, who had been following me, touched my arm and

pointed where a narrow alley, little more than a funnel
for rainwater, led steeply downwards. It was not a way I
had been before. At the bottom I could hear, loud above
the steady hissing of the rain, the noise of the river.

'A short cut to the footbridge?' I asked.

He nodded vigorously.

We picked our way down over the filthy cobbles. The
roar of the river grew louder. I could see the white water
of the lasher, and against it the great wheel of a mill. Beyond this, outlined by the reflected glimmer of the foam,
was the footbridge.

No one was about. The mill was not running; the
miller probably lived above it, but he had locked his doors
and no light showed. A narrow path, deep in mud, led
past the shuttered mill and along the soaked grasses of the
river-side towards the bridge.

I wondered, half irritably, why Casso had chosen this
way. He must have grasped some need for secrecy, though
the main street was, surely, in this weather and at this
time, deserted. But then voices and the swinging light of
a lantern brought me up short in the shelter of the miller's
doorway.

Three men were coming down the street. They were
hurrying, talking together in undertones. I saw a bottle
passed from hand to hand. Castle servants, no doubt, on
their way back from the tavern. They stopped at the end
of the bridge and looked back. Now something furtive
could be seen in their movements. One of them said something, and there was a laugh, quickly stifled. They moved
on, but not before I had seen them, clearly enough, in the
lantern's glow: they were armed, and they were sober.

Casso was close beside me, pressed back in the dark
doorway. The men had not glanced our way. They went
quickly across the bridge, their footsteps sounding hollow
on the wet planks.

Something else the passing light had showed me. Just
beyond the mill, at the corner of the alley, another doorway stood open. From the pile of timber stocks and sawn

felloes outside in the weedy strip of yard, I took it to be
a wheelwright's shop. It was deserted for the night, but
inside the main shed the remains of a fire still glowed.
From that sheltering darkness I should be able to hear
and see all who approached the bridge.

Casso ran ahead of me into the warm cave of the shop,
and lifted a a couple of faggots. Taking them to the fire,
he made the motion of throwing them on the ashes.

'Only one,' I said softly. 'Good man. Now, if you will go
back and get Ulfin, and bring him here to me, you can
get yourself dried and warm, and then forget all about
us.'

A nod, then, smiling, a pantomime to show me that my
secret whatever it was, would be safe with him. God knew
what he thought I was doing; an assignation, perhaps,
or spy's work. Even at that, he knew about as much as I
knew myself.

'Casso. Would you like to learn to read and write?'

Stillness. The smile vanished. In the growing flicker of
the fire I saw him rigid, all eyes, unbelieving, like the
lost traveller who has the clue, against all hope, thrust
into his hand. He nodded, once, jerkily.

'I shall see that you are taught. Go now, and thanks.
Goodnight.'

He went, running as if the stinking alley were as light
as day. Halfway up it I saw him jump and spring, like a
young animal suddenly let out of its pen on a fine morning. I went quietly back into the shop, picking my way
past the wheel-pit and the heavy sledge left leaning by the
pile of spokes. Near the fireplace was the stool where the
boy sat who kept the bellows going. I sat down to wait,
spreading my wet cloak to the warmth of the fire.

Outside, drowning the soft sounds of the rain, the lasher
roared. A loose paddle of the great wheel, hammered by
the water, clacked and thudded. A pair of starving dogs
raced by, wrangling over something unspeakable from a
midden. The wheelwright's shop smelled of fresh wood,
and sap drying, and the knots of burning elm. The faint

tick of the fire was clearly audible in the warm darkness
against the water-noises outside. Time went by.

Once before I had sat like this, by a fire, alone, with my
mind on a birth-chamber, and a child's fate revealed to me
by the god. That had been a night of stars, with a wind
blowing over the clean sea, and the great king-star shining.
I had been young then, sure of myself, and of the god
who drove me. Now I was sure of nothing, save that I
had as much hope of diverting whatever evil Morgause
was planning, as a dry bough had of damming the force
of the lasher.

But what power there was in knowledge, I would have.
Human guesswork had brought me here, and we should
see if I had read the witch aright. And though my god had
deserted me, I still had more power than is granted to
common men: I had a king at my call.

And now here was Ulfin, to share this vigil with me as
he had shared it in Tintagel. I heard nothing, only saw
when his body blocked the dim sky in the doorway.

'Here,' I said, and he came in, groping his way over to
the glow.

'Nothing yet, my lord?'

'Nothing.'

'What are you expecting?'

'I'm not quite sure, but I think someone will come this
way tonight, from the queen.'

I felt him turn to peer at me in the darkness. 'Because
Lot is due home?'

'Yes. Is there any more news of that?'

'Only what I told you before. They expect him to press
hard for home. He could be here very soon.'

'I think so, too. In any case, Morgause will have to make
sure.'

'Sure of what, my lord?'

'Sure of the High King's son.'

A pause. 'You mean you think they will smuggle him
out, in case Lot believes the rumours and kills the child?
But in that case—'

'Yes? In that case?'

'Nothing, my lord. I wondered, that's all ... You think they will bring him this way?'

'No. I think they have already brought him.'

'*They have?* Did you see which way?'

'Not since I have been here. I meant that I am certain that the baby in the castle is not Arthur's child. They have exchanged it.'

A long breath beside me in the darkness. 'For fear of Lot?'

'Of course. Think about it, Ulfin. Whatever Morgause may tell Lot, he must have heard what everyone is saying, ever since it became known that she was with child. She has tried to persuade him that the child is his, but premature; and he may believe her. But do you think he will take the risk that she is lying, and that some other man's son, let alone Arthur's, lies there in that cradle, and will grow up heir to Lothian? Whatever he believes, there's a possibility that he may kill the boy. And Morgause knows it.'

'You think he has heard the rumours that it may be the High King's?'

'He could hardly help it. Arthur made no secret of his visit to Morgause that night, and nor did she. She wanted it so. Afterwards, when I forced her to change her plans, she might persuade or terrify her women into secrecy, but the guards saw him, and by morning every man in Luguvallium would know of it. So what can Lot do? He would not tolerate a bastard of any man's; but Arthur's could be dangerous.'

He was silent for a while. 'It puts me in mind of Tintagel. Not the night we took King Uther in, but the other time, when Queen Ygraine gave Arthur to you, to hide him out of King Uther's way.'

'Yes.'

'My lord, are you planning to take this child as well, to save him from Lot?'

His voice, softly pitched as it was, sounded thin with

some kind of strain. I hardly attended; far out somewhere
in the night, beyond the noise of the weir, I had heard a
beat of hoofs; not a sound, so much as a vibration under
our feet as the earth carried it. Then the faint pulse was
gone, and the water's roar came back.

'What did you say?'

'I wondered, my lord, how sure you were about the child
up at the castle.'

'Sure of what the facts say, no more. Look at them. She
lied about the date of birth, so that it could be put about
that the birth was premature. Very well; that could be a
face-saver, no more; it's done all the time. But look how
it was done. She contrived that no doctor was present, and
then alleged that the birth was unexpected, and so quick
that no witnesses could be called into the chamber, as is
the custom with a royal birthing. Only her women, who
are her creatures.'

'Well, why, my lord? What more was there to gain?'

'Only this, a child to show Lot that he could kill if he
would, while Arthur's son and hers goes scatheless.'

A gasp of silence. 'You mean—?'

'It fits, doesn't it? She could already have arranged an
exchange with some other woman due to bear at the same
time, some poor woman, who would take the money and
hold her tongue, and be glad of the chance to suckle the
royal baby. We can only guess what Morgause told her:
the woman can have no inkling that her own child might
be at risk. So the changeling lies there in the castle, while
Arthur's son, Morgause's tool of power, is hidden near
by. At my guess, not too far away. They will want news of
him from time to time.'

'And if what you say is true, then when Lot gets here—'

'Some move will be made. If he does harm the changeling, Morgause will have to see that the mother hears
nothing of it. She may even have to find another home
for Mordred.'

'But—'

'Ulfin, there is nothing we can do to save the changeling.

Only Morgause could save it, if she would. It's not even certain that it will be in danger; Lot is not quite a savage, after all. But you and I would only run on death ourselves, and the child with us.'

'I know. But what about all the talk up there in the castle? Beltane would tell you about it. He was talking while I got my supper. I mean, the baby being so like King Lot, the living image, they were all saying. Could this of yours just be a guess, sir? And the child be Lot's own, after all? The date could even have been right. They said it was a sickly child, and small.'

'It could be. I told you I was guessing. But we do know that Queen Morgause has no truth in her—and that she is Arthur's enemy. Her actions, and Lot's, bear watching. Arthur himself will have to know, beyond doubt, what the truth is.'

'Of course. I see that. One thing we could do, is find out who bore a male child at about the same time as the queen. I could ask around the place tomorrow. I've made a useful wine-friend or two already.'

'In a town this size it could be one of a score. And we have no time. Listen!'

Up through the ground, clear now, the beat of hoofs. A troop, riding hard. Then the sound of them, close and coming closer, clear above the river-noises, and, soon, the town noises as people crowded out to see. Men shouting; the crash of wood on stonework as the gates were flung open; the jingle of bits and the clash of armour, the snorting of hard-ridden horses. More shouting, and an echo from the castle rock high above us, then the sound of a trumpet.

The main bridge thundered. The heavy gates creaked and slammed. The sounds dwindled towards the inner courtyard, and were lost in the other, nearer noises.

I stood up and walked to the doorway of the wheelwright's shop, and looked up to where, beyond the mill roof, the castle towered against the clouded night. The rain had stopped. Lights were moving. Windows flared

and darkened as the king's servants lighted him through
the castle. To the west side were two windows bright with
soft light. The moving lights went there, and stayed.

'Lot comes home,' I said.

CHAPTER 12

Somewhere a bell clanged from the castle. Midnight. Leaning in the doorway of the wheelwright's shop I stretched shoulders aching with the damp of the night. Behind me, Ulfin fed another faggot to the fire, carefully, so that no spurt of flame should attract the attention of anyone who might be waking. The town, sunk back into its night-time stupor, was silent, but for the barking of curs and now and again the scritch of an owl among the trees on the steep crag-side.

I moved silently out from the door's shelter into the street near the end of the bridge. I looked up at the black bulk of the crag. The high windows of the castle still showed light, and light from the troopers' torches, red and smoking, moved behind the walls that masked the courtyard below.

Ulfin, at my elbow, drew breath for a question.

It was never asked. Someone, running chin on shoulder across the footbridge, ran headlong into me, gasped, gave a broken cry, and twisted to dodge past.

Equally startled, I was slow to react, but Ulfin jumped, grasped an arm, and clapped a hand tightly to stifle the next cry. The newcomer twisted and fought in his grip, but was held with ease.

'A girl,' said Ulfin surprised.

'Into the shop,' I said quickly, and led the way.

Once there, I threw another piece of elm on the fire. The flames leaped. Ulfin brought his captive, still writhing and kicking, into the light. The hood had fallen from her face and head, and I recognised her, with satisfaction.

'Lind.'

She stiffened in Ulfin's grip. I saw the gleam of frightened eyes staring at me above the stifling hand. Then they widened, and she went quite still, as a partridge does before a stoat. She knew me, too.

'Yes,' I said. 'I am Merlin. I was waiting for you, Lind. Now, if Ulfin looses you, you will make no sound.'

Her head moved, assenting. He took his hand from her mouth, but kept his grip on her arm.

'Let her go,' I said.

He obeyed me, moving back to get between her and the doorway, but he need not have troubled. As soon as he released her she ran towards me, and flung herself to her knees in the litter of shavings. She clung to my robe. Her body shook with her terrified weeping.

'Oh, my lord, my lord! Help me!'

'I am not here to harm you, or the child.' To calm her, I spoke coldly. 'The High King sent me here to get news of his son. You know I cannot come to the queen herself, so I waited here for you. What has happened up at the castle?'

But she would not speak. I think she could not. She clung, and shook, and cried.

I spoke more gently. 'Whatever has happened, Lind, I cannot help you if I do not know. Come near the fire, and compose yourself, and tell me.'

But when I tried to draw my robe from her clutches she clung the harder. Her sobs were violent. 'Don't keep me here, lord, let me go! Or else help me! You have the power—you are Arthur's man—you are not afraid of my lady—'

'I will help you if you will talk to me. I want news of King Arthur's son. Was that King Lot who arrived just now?'

'Yes. Oh, yes! He came home an hour ago. He is mad, mad, I tell you! And she did not even try to stop him. She laughed, and let him do it.'

'Let him do what?'

'Kill the baby.'

'He killed the child Morgause has at the castle?'

She was too distraught to see anything strange about the form of the question. 'Yes, yes!' She gulped. 'And all the while it was his own son, his very own son. I was there at the birth, and I swear it by my own hearth-gods. It was—'

'*What's that?*' This, sharply, from Ulfin, on watch in the doorway.

'Lind!' I stooped, pulled her to her feet, and held her steady. 'This is no time for riddles. Go on. Tell me all that happened.'

She pressed the back of one wrist to her mouth, and in a moment or two managed to speak with some sort of composure. 'When he came, he was angry. We had been expecting it, but nothing like this. He had heard what people were saying. that the High King had lain with her. You knew that, lord, you knew it was true ... So King Lot stormed and raved at her, calling her whore, adulteress ... We were all there, her women, but he cared nothing for that. And she—if she had talked sweetly to him, lied, even ...' She swallowed. 'It would have calmed him. He would have believed her. He never could resist her. That's what we all thought she would do, but she did not. She laughed in his face, and said, "But do you not see how like you he is? Do you really think a boy like Arthur could get such a son?" He said, "So it's true? You lay with him?" She said, "Why not? You would not wed me. You took that little honey-miss, Morgan, instead of me. I was not yours, not then." It made him angrier.' She shivered. 'If you had seen him then, even you would have been afraid.'

'No doubt. Was she?'

'No. She never moved, just sat there, with the green gown and jewels, and smiled. You would have thought she was trying to make him angry.'

'As she was,' I said. 'Go on, Lind, quickly.'

She had control of herself now. I loosed her, and she stood, still trembling, but with her arms crossed on her breast, the way women stand when grieving. 'He tore the

hangings off the cradle. The baby started to cry. He said, "Like me? The Pendragon brat is dark and I am dark. No more than that." Then he turned on us—the women—and sent us away. We ran. He looked like a mad wolf. The others ran away, but I hid behind the curtains in the outer chamber. I thought—I thought—'

'You thought?'

She shook her head. Tears splashed, glinting, in the firelight. 'That was when he did it. The baby stopped crying. There was a crash, as if the cradle fell over. The queen said, as calm as milk. "You should have believed me. It was your own, by some slut you tumbled in the town. I told you there was a likeness." And she laughed. He didn't speak for a bit. I could hear his breathing. Then he said, "Dark hair, eyes turning dark. The brat *his* slut threw would be the same. Where is he, then, this bastard?" She said, "He was a sickly child. He died." The king said, "You're lying still." Then she said, very slowly, "Yes, I am lying. I told the midwife to take him away, and find me a son I dared to show you. Perhaps I did wrong. I did it to save my name and your honour. I hated the child. How could I want to bear any man's child but yours? I had hoped it was your son, not his, but it was his. It is true that he was sickly. Let us hope that he is dead, too, by this." The king said, "Let us do more than that. Let us make sure."'

It was Ulfin this time who said quickly: 'Yes? Go on.'

The girl drew a shuddering breath. 'She waited a moment, then she said—in a light, slighting sort of way, the way you dare a man to do something dangerous— "And how could you do that, King of Lothian, except by killing every child born in this town since May-Day? I've told you I don't know where they took him." He didn't even stop to think. He was breathing hard, like someone running. He said, "Then that is just what I shall do. Yes, boys and girls alike. How else shall I know the truth of this accursed child-bed?" I would have run then, but I could not. The queen started to say something about the

people, but he put her aside and came to the door and shouted for his captains. They came running. He shouted it at them, the same. Just those orders, every young baby in the town ... I don't remember what was said. I thought I would faint, and fall, and they would see me. But I did hear the queen call out something in a weeping voice, something about orders from the High King, and how King Arthur would not brook the talk there had been since Luguvallium. Then the soldiers went. And the queen was not weeping at all, my lord, but laughing again, and she had her arms around King Lot. From the way she talked to him then, you would have thought he had done some noble deed. He began to laugh, too. He said, "Yes, let them say it of Arthur, not of me. It will blacken his name more surely than anything I could ever do." They went into her bedchamber then, and shut the door. I heard her call me, but I left her, and ran. She is evil, evil! I always hated her, but she is a witch, and she put me in fear.'

'Nobody will hold you to blame for what your mistress did,' I told her. 'And now you can redeem it. Take me to where the High King's son is hidden.'

She shrank and stared at that, with a wild look over her shoulder, as if she would run again.

'Come, Lind. If you feared Morgause, how much more should you fear me? You ran this way to protect him, did you not? You cannot do so alone. You cannot even protect yourself. But if you help me now, I shall protect you. You will need it. Listen.'

Above us, the main gates of the castle opened with a crash. Through the thick boughs could be seen the movement of torches, bobbing down towards the main bridge. With the torches came the beat and clatter of hoofs and the shouting of orders.

Ulfin said sharply: 'They're out. It's too late.'

'No!' cried the girl. 'Macha's cottage is the other way. They will come there last! I will show you, lord. This way.'

Without another word she made for the door, with

myself and Ulfin hard behind her.

Up the way we had come, across an open space, down another steep lane that twisted back towards the river, then along a river path deep in nettles where nothing moved but the rats a-scurry from the middens. It was very dark here, and we could not hurry, though the night breathed horror on the nape like a coursing hound. Behind us, away on the far side of the town, the sounds began. The barking of dogs first, the shouting of soldiers, the tramp of hoofs. Then doors slamming, women screaming, men shouting; and now and again the sharp clash of weapons. I have been in sacked cities but this was different.

'Here!' gasped Lind, and turned into another twisting lane that led away from the river. From beyond the houses the dreadful sounds still made the night foul. We ran along the slippery mud of the lane, then up a flight of broken steps and out again into a narrow street. Here, all was quiet still, though I saw the glimmer of a light where some scared householder had waked to wonder at the sounds. We ran out from the end of the street into the grass of a field where a donkey was tethered, past an orchard of tended trees and the gaping door of a smithy, and reached a decent cottage that stood away from the rest behind a quickthorn hedge, with a strip of garden in front, and a dovecote, and a kennel beside the door.

The cottage door was wide open and swinging. The dog, at the end of his chain, raved and leaped like a mad thing. The doves were out of the cote and winnowing the dim air. There was no light in the cottage; no sound at all.

Lind ran through the garden, and stopped in the black doorway, peering in.

'Macha? Macha?'

A lantern stood on a ledge beside the door. No time to search for flint and tinder. I put the girl gently aside. 'Take her outside,' I said to Ulfin, and, as he obeyed me, picked up the lantern and swung it high. The flame tore up hissing from the wick, vivid and alive. I heard Lind gasp,

then the sound caught in her throat. The brilliant light showed every corner of the cottage; the bed against the wall, the heavy table and bench; the crocks for food and oil; the stool, with the distaff flung down beside it and the wool unspinning; the clean hearth and the stone floor scrubbed white, except where the woman's body lay sprawled in the blood that had poured from her slit throat. The cradle by the bed was empty.

* * *

Lind and Ulfin waited at the edge of the orchard. The girl was silent now, shocked even out of her weeping; in the lantern's light her face showed blanched and sick. Ulfin had an arm round her, supporting her. He was very pale. The dog whined once, then sat back on his haunches and lifted his nose in a long, keening howl. It was echoed from the clashing, screaming darkness three streets away. And then again, nearer.

I shut the cottage door behind me. 'I'm sorry, Lind. There's nothing to be done here. We should go. You know the tavern at the south gate? Will you lead us there? Avoid the middle of the town where the noise is. Try not to be afraid; I said I would protect you, and I will. For the time being you had better stay with us. Come now.'

She did not move. 'They've taken him! The baby, they got the baby. And they killed Macha!' She turned blind-eyed to me. 'Why did they kill Macha? The king would never have ordered that. She was his leman!'

I looked at her thoughtfully. 'Why, indeed?' Then, briskly, taking her by the shoulder and giving her a gentle shake: 'Come now, child, we must not stay here. The men won't come this way again, but while you are in the streets you could be in danger. Take us to the south gate.'

'*She* must have told them the way!' cried Lind. I might not even have spoken. 'They came here first! I was too late! If you hadn't stopped me at the bridge—'

'Then you would be dead, too,' said Ulfin crisply. He sounded quite normal, as if the night's horrors touched him not at all. 'What could you have done, you and Macha? They'd have found you, and cut you down before you'd run to the end of the orchard yonder. Now, you'd best do as my lord says. That is, unless you want to go back to the queen and tell her what's happened here? You can depend on it, she's guessed where you went. They'll be looking for you soon.'

It was brutal, but it worked. At the mention of Morgause she came to herself. She threw a last look of horror at the cottage, then pulled her hood about her face; and started back through the orchard trees.

I paused by the grieving dog and stooped to lay a hand on him. The dreadful howling stopped. He sat shivering. I drew my dagger and cut through the rope collar that bound him. He did not move, and I left him there.

Some score of children were taken that night. Someone —wise-woman or midwife—must have told the troopers where to look. By the time we got back to the tavern, by a roundabout route through the deserted outskirts of the town, the horror was over, the troopers gone. No one accosted us, or even seemed to notice us. The streets were full and clamorous. People ran aimlessly about, or peered in terror from dark doorways. Crowds gathered here and there, centred on some wailing woman, and stunned or angry man. These were poor folk with no way of withstanding their king's will. His royal anger had swept through the town, and left them nothing to do but grieve.

And curse. I heard Lot's name: they had after all been his troopers. But with Lot's name came Arthur's. The lie was already at work, and with time, one could guess, would supersede the truth. Arthur was High King, and the mainspring of good and evil.

One thing they had been spared; there had been no holocaust of blood. Macha's was the only death. The soldiers had lifted the babies from their beds, and ridden

off with them into the darkness. Except for a broken head or two, where a father had resisted them, they had done no violence.

So Beltane told me, gasping it out. He met us in the tavern doorway, fully clothed and trembling with agitation. He seemed not even to notice Lind's presence. He seized me by the arm and poured out his story of the night's happenings. The clearest thing to emerge from it was that the troopers had not long ridden by with the infants.

'Alive still, and crying—you may imagine, Master Emrys!' He wrung his hands, lamenting. 'Terrible, terrible, these are savage times indeed. All the talk of Arthur's orders, who is to believe such a tale? But hush, say nothing! The sooner we are on the road, the better. This is no place for honest traders. I would have gone before this, Master Emrys, but I stayed for you. I thought you might have been called on to help, some of the men were hurt, they say. They will drown the children, did you know? Dear gods, and to think that only today ... Ah, Casso, good lad! I took the liberty of saddling your beasts, Master Emrys. I made sure you would agree with me. We should go now. I have paid the landlord, all's done, you may settle with me on the road ... And you'll see I bought mules for ourselves. I have meant to for so long, and today with the good fortune at the castle ... What a mercy, what a mercy! But that pretty lady, who could have thought—but no more of that here! Walls have ears, and these are dreadful times. Who is this?' He was peering short-sightedly at Lind, who clung to Ulfin's arm, half fainting. 'Why, surely—is it not the young damsel—?'

'Later,' I said quickly. 'No questions now. She is coming with us. Meantime, Master Beltane, thank you. You are a good friend. Yes, we should go without delay. Casso, shift the baggage, will you, please? The girl will ride on the pack-mule. Ulfin, you say you have a friend in the guard-house. Ride ahead, and talk us through. Find which way the troopers went. Bribe the guards if you have to.'

As it happened, there was no need. The gates were just being closed when we got there, but the guards made no difficulty about letting us through. Indeed, from the muttered talk that could be overheard, they were as shocked as the townspeople at what had happened, and found it quite understandable that peaceful traders should pack up hurriedly and leave the town in the middle of the night.

A short way down the road, out of earshot of the guard-house, I drew rein.

'Master Beltane, I have business to see to. No, not back in the town, so have no fear for me. I'll join you later. Do you ride on to the tavern we stayed at on our way north, the one with the bush of broom outside—remember? Wait for us there. Lind, you will be safe with these men. Don't be afraid, but you will do well to keep silent till I return. Do you understand?' She nodded dumbly. 'At the Bush of Broom, then, Master Beltane?'

'Of course, of course. I cannot say I understand, but perhaps in the morning—'

'In the morning, I hope, all will be made clear. For now, goodnight.'

They clattered off. I brought my mule's head up hard. 'Ulfin?'

'They took the east road, my lord.'

So by the east road we went.

*   *   *

Indifferently mounted as we were, we would not normally have expected to catch up with hard-riding troops. But our mounts were rested, while Lot's men must needs, I thought, still be using the poor beasts that had borne them from the battlefields in the south.

So when, after half an hour's riding, we caught no glimpse, nor heard any sound of them, I drew rein, and turned in the saddle.

'Ulfin. A word with you.'

He nudged his mule alongside. In that windy darkness I could not see his face, but something came from him that I could sense. He was afraid.

He had not been afraid before, even at Macha's cottage. And here there could only be one source of fear: myself.

I said to him: 'Why did you lie to me?'

'My lord—'

'The troopers did not come this way, did they?'

I heard him swallow. 'No, my lord.'

'Then which way?'

'To the sea. I think—it was thought they were going to put the children into a boat, and set it adrift. The king had said he would put them into God's hands so that the innocent ones—'

'Pah!' I said. "Lot speak of God's hands? He feared what the people might do if they saw the babies' throats cut, that is all. No doubt he'll have it put about that Arthur ordered the slaughter, but that he himself mitigated the sentence, and gave the babes their chance. The shore. Where?'

'I don't know.'

'Is that true?'

'Indeed, indeed it is. There are several ways. No one knew for sure. This is the truth, my lord.'

'Yes. If anyone had known. some of the menfolk might have tried to follow. So we go back and take the first road to the shore. We can ride along the beach to look for them. Come.'

But as I swung my mule's head round, his hand came down on the rein. It was something he would hardly have dared to do, except in desperation. 'My lord—forgive me. What are you going to do? After all this ... Are you still trying to find the child?'

'What do you think? Arthur's son?'

'But Arthur himself wants him dead!'

So that was it. I should have guessed long since. My mule jibbed as the reins jerked in my hands. 'So you were listening at Caerleon. You heard what he said to me that night.'

'Yes.' This time I could hardly hear him. 'To refuse to murder a child, lord, that is one thing. But when the murder is done for you—'

'There is no need to struggle to prevent it? Perhaps not. But since you were eavesdropping that night, you may also have heard me tell the King that I take orders from an authority beyond his own. And so far my gods have told or shown me nothing. Do you imagine they want us to emulate Lot, and his bitch of a queen? And you have heard the calumny they have thrown upon Arthur. For his honour's sake even just for his peace of mind, he has to know the truth. I am here for him, to watch and to report. Whatever is to be done, I shall do it. Now take your hand off my rein.'

He obeyed. I kicked the mule to a gallop. We pounded back along the road.

This was the way we had originally come to Dunpeldyr by daylight. I tried to remember what we had seen then of the coastline. It is a coast of high cliffs, with wide sandy bays between them. One great headland jutted out about a mile from the town, and even at low tide it seemed unlikely that a man could ride round it. But just beyond the headland was a track leading towards the sea. From there—and the tide, I reckoned, was well out now—we could ride the whole way back along the shore to the mouth of the Tyne.

Faintly, but perceptibly, the night was slackening towards dawn. It was possible to see our way.

Now a cairn of stones loomed on our right. On a flat slab at its base a bundle of feathers stirred in the wind, and the mules showed the whites of their eyes; I supposed they could smell the blood. And here was the track, leading off across rough grassland towards the sea. We swung into it. Presently the track sloped downhill, and there before us was the shore, and the grey murmur of the sea.

The vast headland loomed on our right; to the left the sand stretched level and grey. We turned that way, and struck once more to a gallop.

The tide was out, the rippled sand packed hard. To our right the sea threw a kind of grey light up to the cloudy sky. Some way to the north, set back in the midst of that luminous grey, was the mass of the great rock where the lighthouse stands. The light was red and steady. Soon, I thought, as our mules pounded along, we should be able to distinguish the looming shape of Dunpeldyr's crag to landward, and the level reaches of the bay where the river meets the sea.

Ahead of us a low headland jutted out, its seaward end black and broken, with the water whitening at its edge. We rounded it, the mules splashing fetlock deep through the creaming surf. Now we could see Dunpeldyr, a mile or two away inland, still alive with lights. Ahead of us lay the last stretch of sand. Shadowy trees marked the river's course, and the ashen glimmer where its waters spread out to meet the sea. And along the river's edge, where the sea-road ran, bobbed the torches of horsemen heading back at a steady canter for the town. The work was done.

My mule came willingly to a halt. Ulfin's stopped, blowing, half a length to the rear. Under their hoofs the ebbtide dragged at the grating sand.

After a while I spoke. 'You have your wish, it seems.'

'My lord, forgive me. All I could think of—'

'What do I forgive? Am I to bear you a grudge for serving your master rather than me?'

'I should have trusted you to know what you were doing.'

'When I have not known myself For all I know, you have been wiser than I. At least, since the thing is done, and it seems Arthur will bear some part of the blame for it, we can be forgiven for hoping that Morgause's child is dead with the rest.'

'How could any of them escape? Look, my lord.'

I swung round to where he pointed.

Away out to sea, beyond a low reef of rocks at the edge of the bay, a sail showed, a pale crescent, glimmering faintly in the sealight. Then it cleared the reef, and the

boat moved out to sea. The wind, steadily off-shore, filled the sail, taking the boat out with the speed of a gliding gull. Herod's mercy for the innocents lay there, in the movement of wind and sea, as the drifting boat dipped and skimmed, carrying its hapless cargo fast away from shore.

The sail melted into the grey and vanished. The sea sighed and murmured under the wind. The little waves lapped on the rock and dragged the sand and broken shells seaward past the mules' feet. On the ridge beside us the bent-grass whistled in the wind. Then, above these sounds, I heard it, very faintly carried to us over the water in a lull of the wind; a thin, keening wail, as unhuman as the song of the grey seals at their meeting-haunts. It dwindled as we listened; then suddenly came again, piercingly loud, straight over us, as if some soul, already leaving the doomed boat, had flown homing for the shore. Ulfin shied as if from a ghost, and made the sign against evil; but it was only a gull sweeping over us, high in the wind.

Ulfin did not speak again, and I sat my mule in silence. Something was there in the dark; something that weighed me down with grief. Not the children's fate only; certainly not the presumed death of Arthur's child. But the dim sight of that sail moving away over the grey water, and the sorrowful sounds that came out of the dark, found an echo somewhere in the very core of my soul.

I sat there without moving, while the wind dwindled to silence, and the water lapped on the rock, and on the sea the wailing died away.

Book II

CAMELOT

CHAPTER 1

Much as I would have liked to do so, I did not leave
Dunpeldyr straight away. Arthur was still in Linnuis, and
would want my report, not only on the massacre itself
but on what happened afterwards. Ulfin, I think, expected
to be dismissed, but, reckoning that to lodge in Dunpeldyr itself would hardly be safe, I stayed on at the Bush
of Broom, and so kept Ulfin with me to act as messenger
and connecting-file. Beltane, who had been understandably shaken by the night's events, went south straight away
with Casso. I kept my promise to the latter: it had been a
promise made on impulse, but I have found that such
impulses commonly have a source which should not be
denied. So I talked with the goldsmith, and easily persuaded him of the advantages of a servant who could read
and write; I made it clear, besides, that I was letting Casso
go to him for less than his cost to me on condition that
my wish was met. I found I had not needed to insist;
Beltane, that kindly man, promised with pleasure to teach
Casso himself, and then they both took leave of me and
went south, aiming once more for York. With them went
Lind, who, it seemed, had met a man in York who might
protect her; he was a small merchant, a respectable fellow
who had spoken of marriage, but whom, for fear of the
queen, she had rejected. I took leave of them, and settled
down to see what the next few days would bring.

Some two or three days after the terrible night of Lot's
return, the wreckage of the boat began to come ashore,
and with it the bodies. It was apparent that the boat had
driven on rock somewhere and had been broken up by the
tide. The poor women who went down to the beach fell

to a kind of dreadful squabbling as to which baby was which. The shore was haunted by these wretched women. They wept a great deal and said very little; it was apparent that they were accustomed, like beasts, to take what their lords handed out to them, whether alms or blows. It was also apparent to me, sitting in the alehouse shadows and listening, that, in spite of the tale about Arthur's responsibility for the massacre, most folk laid the blame squarely where it belonged, with Morgause, and with Lot, befooled and angry about it. And, because men are men everywhere, they were inclined not to blame their king overmuch for his hasty reaction to that anger. Any man, they were soon saying, would have done the same. Come home to find your wife delivered of another man's boy, and small blame to you if you lost your temper. And as for the wholesale slaughter, well, a king was a king, and had a throne to consider as well as his bed. And speaking of kings, had he not made kingly reparation? For this, wisely, Lot had done; and however much the women might still weep and mourn, the men on the whole accepted Lot's deed, along with the golden recompense that followed it, as the natural action of a wronged and angry king.

And Arthur? I put the question one evening, casually, into one such conversation. If the rumours that were being put about were true, of the High King's involvement in the killing, was not Arthur himself similarly justified? If the child Mordred was indeed his bastard by his halfsister, and a hostage to fortune with King Lot (who had not always been his keenest friend), surely it could be said that policy could justify the deed? What more likely way could Arthur find of keeping the great King of Lothian his friend, than to ensure the death of the cuckoo in the nest, and take the responsibility for its killing?

At this there were murmurs and head-shakings, which resolved at length into a sort of qualified assent. So I threw in another thought. Everyone knew that in matters like this of policy—and high and secret policy, with a great country like Lothian concerned—everyone knew it was

not the young Arthur who made the civil decisions; it was his chief adviser, Merlin. Depend upon it, this was the decision of a ruthless and tortuous mind, not of a brave young soldier who spent his every waking moment in the field against Britain's enemies, and who had little time for bedroom politics—except, naturally, those that every man could find time for . . .

So, like a seed of grass, the idea was sown, and as quickly as the grass it spread and grew; so that by the time the news came of Arthur's next victorious engagement the facts of the massacre had been accepted, and the guilt of it, whether of Merlin, Arthur or Lot, almost condoned. It was plain that the High King—may God preserve him against the enemy—had had little to do with it except see its necessity. Besides, the babies, most of them, would have died in infancy of one thing or another, and that without any gifts of gold such as Lot had handed to the bereaved fathers. Moreover, most of the women were soon bearing again, and had perforce to forget their tears.

The queen, also. King Lot was now seen to have behaved in a truly kingly fashion. He had swept home in anger, removed the bastard (whether by Arthur's orders or his own), then got a true heir in the dead boy's place, and ridden off again, his loyalty to the High King undiminished. Some of the bereaved fathers, being offered places in the troop, rode with him, confirmed in their own loyalty. Morgause herself, far from appearing cowed by her lord's violence, or apprehensive of the people's anger, looked (on the one or two occasions when I saw her riding out) sleek and pleased with herself. Whatever the people may have believed about her part in the massacre, she was safe from their illwill now that she was said to be carrying the kingdom's true heir.

If she grieved for her lost son, she gave no sign of it. It showed, the people said, that she had in truth been seduced by Arthur, and could never have wanted the bastard she had been made to bear. But to me, watching and waiting in drab anonymity, it began to mean something quite

different. I did not believe that the child Mordred had been in that boat-load of slaughtered innocents at all. I remembered the three armed men, sober and purposeful, who had gone back into the castle by the postern entrance just before Lot's return—and after the coming of Morgause's messenger from the south. The woman Macha, too, lying dead in her cottage beside the empty cradle with her throat cut. And Lind, running out into the dark without Morgause's knowledge or sanction, to warn Macha and take the child Mordred to safety.

Piecing it together, I thought I knew what had happened. Macha had been chosen to foster Mordred because she had borne Lot a bastard boy; it might even have pleased Morgause to watch the baby killed; she had laughed, Lind had told us. So, with Mordred safe, and the changeling ready for the slaughter, Morgause had waited for Lot's return. As soon as she had news of it, her men-at-arms had been sent with orders to dispatch Mordred to yet another safe foster-home, and to kill Macha, who, if her own baby were to suffer, might be tempted to betray the queen. And now Lot was pacified, the town was quiet, and somewhere, I was sure, the child who was Morgause's weapon of power, grew in safety.

After Lot had ridden to rejoin Arthur, I sent Ulfin south again, but myself stayed on in Lothian, watching and waiting. With Lot out of the way, I moved back into Dunpeldyr, and tried, in every way I could, to find some clue to where Mordred could now be hidden. What I would have done if I had found him, I do not know, but the god did not lay that burden on me. So I waited for fully four months in that squalid little town, and though I walked on the shore by starlight and sunlight and spoke to my god in every tongue and with every way I knew, I saw nothing, either by daylight or in dream, to guide me to Arthur's son.

In time I came to believe that I might have been wrong; that even Morgause could not be so evil, and that Mor-

dred had perished with the other innocents in that midnight sea.

So at length, as autumn slid into the first chills of winter, and news came that the fighting in Linnuis was done, and Lot would soon be on his way home once more, I thankfully left Dunpeldyr. Arthur would be at Caerleon for Christmas, and would look for me there. I paused only once on my journey, to spend a few nights with Blaise in Northumbria and give him the news, then I travelled south, to be there when the King came home.

* * *

He came back in the second week of December, with frost on the ground, and the children out gathering the holly and ivy for decking the Christmas feast. He barely waited to bathe and change from the ride before he sent for me. He received me in the room where we had talked before we parted. This time the door to the bedroom was shut, and he was alone.

He had changed a good deal in the months since Pentecost. Taller, yes, by half a head—it is an age when youths shoot up like barley-stalks—and with breadth to go with it, and the hard lean brownness got from the soldier's life he was leading. But this was not the real change. That was in authority. His manner showed now that he knew what he was doing and where he was going.

But for that, the interview might have been an echo of the one I had had with the younger Arthur, on the night of Mordred's begetting.

'They say that I ordered this abominable thing!' He had hardly troubled to greet me. He strode about the room, the same strong, light, lion's-prowl of a walk, but the strides were a hand-span longer. The room was a cage restraining him. 'When you know yourself how, in this very room, I said, no, leave it to the god. And now this!'

'It's what you wanted, isn't it?'

'All those deaths? Don't be a fool, would I have done it like that? Or would you?'

The question needed no reply, and got none. I said merely: 'Lot was never remarkable for his wisdom and restraint, and besides, he was in a rage. You might say the action was suggested to him, or at least encouraged, from without.'

He threw me a quick, smouldering look. 'By Morgause? So I understand.'

'I gather Ulfin has told you all the story? Did he also tell you of his own services in the matter?'

'That he tried to mislead you, and let fate overtake the children? Yes, he told me that.' A brief pause. 'It was wrong, and I said so, but it's hard to be angry at devotion. He thought—he knew that I would have been easy at the baby's death. But those other children ... Within a month of the vows I made to protect the people, and my name a hissing in the streets ...'

'I think you can comfort yourself. I doubt if many men believe that you had anything to do with it.'

'No matter.' He almost snapped it over his shoulder. 'Some will, and that is enough. As for Lot, he had an excuse of a kind; an excuse, that is, that common men can understand. But I? Can I publish it abroad that Merlin the prophet told me the child might be a danger to me, so I had it murdered, and others along with it for fear it should escape the net? What sort of king does this make of me? Lot's sort?'

'I can only repeat that I doubt if you are held to blame. Morgause's women were there within hearing, remember, and the guards knew where their orders came from. Lot's escort, too—they would know he was riding home bent on revenge, and I cannot imagine that Lot remained silent as to his intentions. I don't know what Ulfin has told you, but when I left Dunpeldyr most people were quoting Lot's orders as responsible for the massacre, and those who thought you ordered it, think you did so on my advice.'

'So?' he said. He really was very angry. 'I am the kind of

king who cannot even decide for myself? If there is to be blame allotted for this between us, then I should take it, and not you. You know that well enough. You remember as well as I do exactly what was said.'

There was no reply to that, either, and I made none. He prowled up the room and back again before he went on:

'Whoever gave the order, you can say if you like that I feel guilt in this. You would be right. But, by all the gods in heaven and hell, I would not have acted like that! This is the kind of thing that lives with you, and after you! I shall not be remembered as the king who beat the Saxons out of Britain, but as the man who played Herod in Dunpeldyr and murdered the children!' He stopped. 'What is there in that to smile at?'

'I doubt if you need trouble yourself about the name you will leave behind you.'

'So you say.'

'So I said.' The change in tense, or something about my tone, arrested him. I met his look, and held it. 'Yes, I, Merlin, said so. I said so when I had power, and it is true. You are right to be distressed at this abomination, and you are right, too, to take some of the blame to yourself. But if this thing goes down in story as your act, you will still be absolved of blame. You can believe me. What else is to come will absolve you of anything.'

The anger had died, and he was thinking. He spoke slowly. 'Do you mean that some danger will come of the child's birth and death? Something so terrible that men will see the murder as justified?'

'I did not mean that, no—'

'You made another prophecy, remember. You hinted to me—no, you told me—that Morgause's child might be a danger to me. Well, now the child is dead. Could this have been the danger? This smear on my name?' He paused, struck. 'Or perhaps some day one of the men whose sons were murdered will wait for me with a knife in the dark? Is that the kind of thing you had in mind?'

'I told you, I had nothing specific in mind. I did not say that the child "might" be a danger to you, Arthur. I said he would. And, if my word is to be trusted, directly so, and not by a knife in another man's hand.'

He was as still, now as he had been restless before. He scowled at me, intent. 'You mean that the massacre failed of its purpose? That the child—Mordred, did you say?—is still alive?'

'I have come to think so.'

He drew a quick breath. 'Then he was saved, somehow, from that wreck?'

'It's possible. Either he was saved by chance, and is living somewhere, unknowing and unknown, as you did through your childhood—in which case you may encounter him some day, as Laius did Oedipus, and fall to him in all ignorance.'

'I'll risk that. Everyone falls to someone, sometime. Or?'

'Or he was never in the boat at all.'

He gave a slow nod. 'Morgause, yes. It would fit. What do you know?'

I told him the little I knew, and the conclusions I had drawn. 'She must have known,' I finished, 'that Lot's reactions would be violent. We know she wanted to keep the child, and why. She would hardly have put her own child at risk on Lot's return. It's clear enough that she engineered the whole thing. Lind gave us more details later on. We know that she goaded Lot into the furious anger that dictated the massacre; we know, too, that she started the rumour that you were to blame. So what has she done? She has put Lot's fears to rest, and made her own position secure. And I believe, from watching her, and from what I know of her, that at the same time she has contrived—'

'To keep her hostage to fortune.' The flush had died from his skin. He looked cold, his eyes like slates with cold rain on them. This was an Arthur that other men had seen, but never I. How many Saxons had seen those eyes just before they died? He said, bitterly: 'I have been well

paid already for that night of lust. I wish you had let me kill her then. That is one lady who had better never come near me again, unless she comes on her knees, and in sackcloth.' His tone made a vow of it. Then it changed. 'When did you get back from the north?'

'Yesterday.'

'*Yesterday?* I thought ... I understood that this abomination took place months ago.'

'Yes. I stayed to watch events. Then after I began to make my guesses, I waited to see if Morgause might make some move to show me where the child was hidden. If Lind had been able to go back to her, and had dared to help me ... but that was impossible. So I stayed until the news came that you had left Linnuis, and that Lot would soon be on his way home again. I knew that once he came home I could do nothing, so I came away.'

'I see. All that way, and now I keep you on your feet and rail at you as if you were a guard caught sleeping on duty. Will you forgive me?'

'There's nothing to forgive. I have rested. But I should be glad to sit now. Thank you.'

This as he pulled a chair for me, and then sat himself in the big chair beyond the massive table. 'You've said nothing in your reports about this idea that Mordred was still alive. And Ulfin never mentioned it as a possibility.'

'I don't think it crossed his mind. It was mainly after he had gone, and I had time to think and watch, myself, that I thought back and reached my own conclusion. There's still no proof, of course, that I am right. And nothing but the memory of an old foreboding to tell me whether or not it matters. But I can tell you one thing; from the idle contentment that the King's prophet feels in his bones these days, any threat from Mordred, direct or otherwise, will not show itself for a long time to come.'

He gave me a look where no shadow of anger remained. A smile sparked deep in his eyes. 'So, I have time.'

'You have time. This was bad, and you were right to be angry; but it is already barely remembered, and soon

will be forgotten in the blaze of your victories. Concerning them, I hear talk of nothing else. So put this aside now, and think about the next. Time spent looking back in anger is time wasted.'

The tension broke up at last in the familiar smile. 'I know. A maker, never a breaker. How often have you told me? Well, I'm only mortal. I break first, to make room ... All right, I'll forget it. There is plenty to think about and plan for, without wasting time on what is done. In fact'—the smile deepened—'I heard that King Lot is planning a move northward to his kingdom there. Perhaps, in spite of laying the blame on me, he feels uncomfortable in Dunpeldyr ... ? The Orkneys are fertile islands, they tell me, and fine in the summer months, but tend to be cut off from the main all winter?'

'Unless the sea freezes.'

'And that,' he said, with most unkingly satisfaction, 'will surely be beyond even Morgause's powers. So distance will help us to forget Lot and his works ...'

His hand moved among the papers and tablets on the table. I was thinking that I should have looked further afield for Mordred: if Lot had told his queen his plans for taking the court northward, she might have made some arrangement for sending the child there. But Arthur was speaking again.

'Do you know anything about dreams?'

I was startled. 'Dreams? Well, I have had them.'

A glint of amusement. 'Yes, that was a foolish question, wasn't it? I meant, can you tell me what they mean, other men's dreams?'

'I doubt it. When my own mean something, they are clear beyond doubt. Why, has your sleep been troubled?'

'For many nights now.' He hesitated, shifting the things on the table. 'It seems a trivial thing to trouble over, but the dream is so vivid, and it's always the same ...'

'Tell me.'

'I am alone, and out hunting. No hounds, just myself

and my horse, hard on the track of a stag. This part varies a bit, but I always know that the chase has been going on for many hours. Then, just as we seem to be catching up with the stag, it leaps into a brake of trees and vanishes. At the same moment my horse falls dead beneath me. I am thrown to the turf. Sometimes I wake there, but when I go back to sleep again, I am still lying on the turf, by the bank of a stream, with the dead horse beside me. Then suddenly I hear hounds coming, a whole pack of them, and I sit up and look about me. Now, I have had the dream so many times that, even while dreaming, I know what to expect, and I am afraid ... It is not a pack of hounds that comes, but one beast—a strange beast, which, though I have seen it so many times, I can't describe. It comes crashing through the bracken and underbrush, and the noise it makes is like thirty couples of hounds quest-ing. It takes no heed of me or my horse, but stops at the stream and drinks, and then goes on and is lost in the forest.'

'Is that the end?' I asked, as he paused.

'No. The end varies, too, but always, after the questing beast, comes a knight, alone and on foot, who tells me that he, too, has killed a horse under him in the quest. Each time—each night it happens—I try to ask him what the beast is, and what the quest, but just as he is about to tell me, my groom comes up with a fresh horse for me, and the knight seizing it without courtesy, mounts and prepares to ride away. And I find myself laying hands on his rein to stop him, and begging him to let me undertake the quest, "for," I say, "I am the High King, and it is for me to undertake any quest of danger." But he strikes my hand aside, saying, "Later. Later, when you need to, you may find me here, and I shall answer for what I have done." And he rides away, leaving me alone in the forest. Then I wake, still with this sense of fear. Merlin, what does it mean?'

I shook my head. 'That I can't tell you. I might be

glib with you, and say that this was a lesson in humility: that even the High King does not need to take all responsibility—'

'You mean stand back and let you take the blame for the massacre? No, that's too clever by half, Merlin!'

'I said I was being glib, didn't I? I have no idea what your dream meant. Probably nothing more than a mixture of worry and indigestion. But one thing I can tell you, and it's the same one that I keep repeating; what dangers lie in front of you, you will surmount, and reach glory; and whatever has happened, whatever you have done, or will do, you will die a worshipful death. I shall fade and vanish like music when the harp is dead, and men will call my end shameful. But you will live on, in men's imagination and hearts. Meanwhile, you have years, and time enough. So tell me what happened in Linnuis.'

We talked for a long time. Eventually he came back to the immediate future:

'Until the ways open with spring, we can get on with the work here at Caerleon. You'll stay here for that. But in the spring I want you to start work on my new headquarters.' I looked a query, and he nodded. 'Yes, we spoke of this before. What was right in Vortigern's time, or even in Ambrosius', will not serve in a year or so from this. The picture is changing, over to the east. Come to the map and let me show you ... That man of yours now, Gereint, there's a find. I've sent for him. He's the kind of man I need by me. The information he sent to Linnuis was beyond price. He told you about Eosa and Cerdic? We're gathering what information we can, but I'm sure he is right. The latest news is that Eosa is back in Germany, and he's promising the sun, moon and stars, as well as a settled Saxon kingdom, to any who will join him ...'

For a while we discussed Gereint's information, and Arthur told me what had newly come from those sources. Then he went on: 'He's right about the Gap, too, of course. We started work up there as soon as I got your reports. I sent Torre up ... I believe the next push will

come from the north. I'm expecting word from Caw and
from Urbgen. But in the long run it will be here, in the
south-west, that we have to make the stand for good and
all. With Rutupiae as their base, and the Shore behind
them, call it 'kingdom' or not, the big threat must come
this way, here and here ...' His finger was moving on the
relief map of clay. 'We came back this way from Linnuis.
I got an idea of the lie of the land. But no more now,
Merlin. They're making new maps for me, and we can
sit over them later. Do you know the country thereabouts?'

'No. I have travelled that road, but my mind was on
other things.'

'There's little haste yet. If we can start in April, or May,
and you work your usual miracle, that should be soon
enough. Think about it for me, and then go and look
when the time comes. Will you do that?'

'Willingly. I have already looked ... No, I meant in my
mind. I've remembered something. There's a hill that
commands this whole tract of country here ... As far as
I remember, it's flat-topped, and big enough to house
an army, or a city, or whatever you want of it. And high
enough. You can see Ynys Witrin from it—the Isle of
Glass—and all the signal chain, and again clear for many
miles both to south and west.'

'Show me,' he said sharply.

'Somewhere here.' I placed a finger. 'I can't be exact,
and I don't think the map is, either. But I think this must
be the stream it lies on.'

'Its name?'

'I don't know its name. It's a hill with the stream curling round it, and the stream is called, I think, the Camel.
The hill was a fortress before the Romans ever came to
Britain, so even the early Britons must have seen it as a
strategic point. They held it against the Romans.'

'Who took it?'

'Eventually. Then they fortified it in their turn and held
it.'

'Ah. Then there is a road.'

'Surely. This one, perhaps, that runs past the Lake from the Glass Isle.'

So I showed him on the map, and he looked, and talked, and went on the prowl again, and then the servants brought supper and lights and he straightened, pushing the hair back out of his eyes, and came up out of his planning as a diver comes up out of water.

'Well, it will have to wait till Christmas is past. But go as soon as you can, Merlin, and tell me what you think. You shall have what help you need, you know that. And now sup with me, and I'll tell you all about the fight at the Blackwater. I've told it already so many times that it's grown till I hardly recognise it myself. But once more, to you, is not unseemly.'

'Obligatory. And I promise you that I shall believe every word.'

He laughed. 'I always knew I could rely on you.'

CHAPTER 2

It was on a sweet, still day of spring when I turned aside from the road and saw the hill called Camelot.

That was its name later; now it was known as Caer Camel, after the small stream that wound through the level lands surrounding it, and curved around near its base. It was, as I had told Arthur, a flat-topped hill, not high, but high enough over the surrounding flatlands to give a clear view on every hand, and steep-sided enough to allow for formidable defences. It was easy to see why the Celts, and after them the Romans, had chosen it as a stronghold. From its highest point the view in almost every direction is tremendous. To the east a few rolling hills block the vision, but to south and west the eye can travel for miles, and northwards, also, as far as the coast. On the north-west side the sea comes within eight miles or so, the tides spreading and filtering through the marshy flatlands that feed the great Lake where stands the Isle of Glass. This island, or group of islands, lies on its glassy water like a recumbent goddess; indeed it has from time immemorial been dedicated to the Goddess herself, and her shrine stands close beside the king's palace. Above it the great beacon top of the Tor it plainly visible, and, many miles beyond that, right on the coast of the Severn Channel, may be seen the next beacon point of Brent Knoll.

The hills of the Glass Isle, with the low and water-logged levels surrounding them, are known as the Summer Country. The king was a man called Melwas, young, and a staunch supporter of Arthur; he gave me lodging during my first surveys of Caer Camel, and seemed pleased

that the High King should plan to form his main strong-hold at the edge of his territory. He was deeply interested in the maps I showed him, and promised help of every kind, from the loan of local workmen to a pledge of defence, should that be needed, while the work was in progress.

King Melwas had offered to show me the place himself, but for my first survey I preferred to be alone, so managed to put him off with civilities of some kind. He and his young men rode with me for the first part of the way, then turned aside into a track that was little more than a causeway through the marshlands, and went cheerfully off to their day's sport. That is great country for hunting; it teems with wildfowl of every kind. I saw a lucky omen in the fact that, almost as soon as they left me, King Melwas flew his falcon at a flock of immigrant birds coming in from the south-east, and, within seconds, the hawk had killed cleanly and come straight back to the master's fist. Then, with shouting and laughter, the band of young men rode off among the willows, and I went on my way alone.

I had been right in supposing that a road would lead to the once-Roman fortress of Caer Camel. The road leaves Ynys Witrin by a causeway which skirts the base of the Tor, spans a narrow arm of the Lake, and reaches a strip of dry, hard land stretching towards the east. There it joins the old Fosse Way, then after a while turns south again for the village at the foot of Caer Camel. This had originally been a Celtic settlement, then the *vicus* to the Roman fortress, its occupants scraping some sort of living from the soil, and retiring uphill within walls in times of danger. Since the fortress had decayed, their lives had been hard indeed. As well as the ever-present danger to the south and east, they even had, in bad years, to beat off the people of the Summer Country, when the wetlands around Ynys Witrin ceased to provide anything but fish and marsh birds, and the young men craved excitement beyond the confines of their own territory. There was

little to be seen as I rode between the tumbledown huts with their rotting thatch; here and there eyes watched me from a dark doorway, or a woman's voice called shrilly to her child. My horse splashed through the mud and dung, forded the Camel knee-deep, then at last I turned him uphill through the trees, and took the steep curve of the chariot-way at a plunging canter.

Even though I knew what to expect, I was amazed at the size of the summit. I came up through the ruins of the south-west gateway into a great field, tilted to southward, but sloping sharply ahead of me towards a ridge with a high point west of centre. I walked my horse slowly up towards this. The field, or rather plateau, was scarred and pitted with the remains of buildings, and surrounded on all sides by deep ditching, and the relics of revetments and fortified walls. Whins and brambles matted the broken walls, and mole-hills had heaved up the cracked paving-stones. Stone lay everywhere, good Roman stone, squared in some local quarry. Beyond the ruined out-works the sides of the hill went down steeply, and on them trees, once lopped to ground level, had put out saplings and thickets of suckers. Between these the scarps were quilted with a winter network of bramble and thorn. A beaten pathway through sprouting fern and nettle led to a gap in the north wall. Following this, I could see where, half down the northern hillside, a spring lay deep among the trees. This must be the Lady's Well, the good spring dedicated to the Goddess. The other spring, the main water supply for the fortress, lay halfway up the steep road to the north-east gateway, at the hill's opposite corner from the chariot road I had taken. It seemed that cattle were still watered there: as I watched, I saw a herd, slow-moving, come up through the steep gap, and spread out to graze in the sunshine, with a faint, off-note chiming of bells. Their herdsman followed them, a slight figure whom at first I took for a boy, then saw, from the way he moved, using his staff to lean upon, that it was an old man.

I turned my horse's head that way, and walked him carefully through the tumble of stonework. A magpie got up and flew, scolding. The old man looked up. He stopped short, startled, and, I thought, apprehensive. I raised a hand to him in a sign of greeting. Something about the solitary and unarmed horseman must have reassured him, for after a moment he moved to a low wall that lay full in the sun, and sat down to wait for me.

I dismounted, letting my horse graze.

'Greetings, father.'

'And to you.' It was not much more than a mumble, in the strong burring accent of the district. He peered at me suspiciously, through eyes clouded with cataract. 'You're a stranger to these parts.'

'I come from the west.'

This was no reassurance. It seemed that the folk hereabouts had had too long a history of war. 'Why'd you leave the road, then? What do you want up here?'

'I came on the King's behalf, to look at the fortress walls.'

'Again?'

As I stared at him in surprise, he drove his stick into the turf, as if making a claim, and spoke with a kind of quavering anger. 'This was our land before the king came, and it's ours again in spite of him. Why don't 'ee let us keep it so?'

'I don't think—' I began, then stopped, on a sudden thought. 'You speak of a king. Which king?'

'I don't know his name.'

'Melwas? Or Arthur?'

'Maybe. I tell you I don't know. What do you want here?'

'I am the King's man. I come from him—'

'Aye. To raise the fortress walls again, then take away our cattle and kill our children and rape our women.'

'No. To build a stronghold here to protect your cattle and children and women.'

'It did not protect them before.'

There was silence. The old man's hand shook on his stick. The sun was hot on the grass. My horse grazed delicately round a thistle head growing low and circular, like a splayed wheel. An early butterfly alighted on a purple head of clover. A lark rose, singing.

'Old man,' I said gently, 'there has been no fortress here in your lifetime, nor in your father's. What walls stood here and looked south and north and westward over the waters? What king came to storm them?'

He looked at me for a few moments, his head shaking with the tremor of age. 'It's a story, only a story, master. My granda told it to me, how the folk lived here with cattle and goats and sweet grazing, and wove the cloth and tilled the high field, until the king came and drove them down through yon road into the valley bottom, and there was a grave for them all that day, as wide as a river and as deep as the hollow hill, where they laid the king himself to rest, and his time coming soon after.'

'Which hill was that? Ynys Witrin?'

'What? How should they carry him there? It's a foreign country there. They call it the Summer Country, for all it's a sheet of lake water all the year round save through the dry time of midsummer. No, they made a way into the cave and laid him there, and with him the ones who were drowned with him.' A sudden, high cackle. 'Drowned in the Lake, and the folk watched and made no move to save him. It was the Goddess took him, and his fine captains along with him. Who could have stopped her? They say it was three days before she gave him back, and then he came naked, without either crown or sword.' The cackling laugh again, as he nodded. 'Your king had best make his peace with her, tell him that.'

'He will. When did this happen?'

'A hundred years ago. Two hundred. How would I know?'

Another silence, while I assessed it. What I was hearing, I knew, was a folk memory that had come down tongue to tongue in a winter's tale by some peasant's hearth. But it

confirmed what I had been told. The place must have been fortified time out of mind. 'The king' could have been any one of the Celtic rulers, driven eventually from the hilltop by the Romans, or the Roman general himself who had stayed here to invest the captured strongpoint.

I said suddenly: 'Where is the way into the hill?'

'What way?'

'The door to the king's tomb, where they made the way for his grave.'

'How do I know? It's there, that's all I know. And sometimes, on a night, they ride out again. I have seen them. They come wi' the summer moon, and go back into the hill at dawning. And whiles, on a stormy night, when dawn surprises them, one comes late, and finds the gate shut. So he is doomed for the next moon to wander the hilltop alone, till ...' His voice faltered. He ducked his head fearfully, peering. 'A king's man, you said you were?'

I laughed. 'Don't be afraid of me, father. I'm not one of them. I'm a king's man, yes, but I have come for a living king, who will build the fortress up again, and take you and your cattle, and your children, and their children, into his hand, and keep you safely against the Saxon enemy from the south. And you will still get sweet grazing for your herd. I promise you this.'

He said nothing to that, but sat for a while, nid-nodding in the sun. I could see that he was simple. 'Why should I be afraid? There has always been a king here, and always will be. A king is no new thing.'

'This one will be.'

His attention was leaving me. He chirruped to the cows. 'Come up Blackberry, come up Dewdrop. A king, and tend the cattle for me? Do you take me for a fool? But the Goddess looks after her own. He'd best tend to the Goddess.' And he subsided, mumbling his stick, and muttering.

I gave him a silver coin, as one gives a singer the guerdon for his tale, then led my horse off towards the ridge that marked the summit of the plateau.

CHAPTER 3

Some days later the first party of surveyors arrived, to begin their measuring and pacing, while their leader was closeted with me in the temporary headquarters that had been made for us on the site.

Tremorinus, the master engineer who had taught me so much of his trade when I was a boy in Brittany, had died some time ago. Arthur's chief engineer now was a man called Derwen, whom I had first met years back, over the rebuilding of Caerleon in Ambrosius' time. He was a red-bearded, high-coloured man, but without the temper that often goes with that colouring; indeed, he was silent to the point of surliness, and could prove sullen as a mule when pressed. But I knew him to be competent and experienced, and he had the trick of getting men to work fast and willingly for him. Moreover, he had taken pains to be master himself of all trades, and was never above rolling up his sleeves and doing a heavy job himself if time demanded. Nor did he appear to mind taking direction from me. He seemed to hold my skills in the most flattering respect: this was not, I knew, because of any especial brilliance I had shown at Caerleon or Segontium —they were built to pattern on the Roman model, on lines laid down through time, and familiar to every builder—but Derwen had been an apprentice in Ireland when I had moved the massive king-stone of Killare, and subsequently at Amesbury, at the rebuilding of the Giants' Dance. So we got along tolerably well together, and understood each what the other was good for.

Arthur's forecast of trouble in the north had come true, and he had gone up in early March. But during the winter

months he and I, with Derwen, had spent many hours together over the plans for the new stronghold. Driven by my persistence, and Arthur's enthusiasm, Derwen had finally been brought to accept what he obviously thought of as my wild ideas about the rebuilding of Caer Camel. Strength and speed—I wanted the place ready for Arthur by the time the campaign in the north should near its close, and I also wanted it to last. Its size and force had to fit his state.

The size was there; the hill's summit was vast, some eight acres in area. But the strength ... I had had lists made of what material was already there, and, as best I could among the ruins, I had studied how the place had been built before, the Roman stonework on top of layer after layer of earlier Celtic wall and ditching. As I worked I kept in mind some of the fortifications I had seen on my travels abroad. strongpoints thrown up in wilder places than this, and on terrain as difficult. To rebuild on the Roman model would have been a formidable, if not impossible, task: even if Derwen's masons had had the knack of the Roman type of stonework, the sheer size of Caer Camel would have forbidden it. But the masons were all expert at their own dry-stone kind of building, and there was plenty of dressed stone to hand, and a quarry nearby. We had the oakwoods and the carpenters, and the sawyers' yards between Caer Camel and the Lake had been packed all winter with maturing timber. So I had made my final plans.

That they were carried out magnificently everyone can see. The steep, ditched sides of the place they now call Camelot stand crowned with massive walls of stone and timber. Sentries patrol the battlements, and stand guard over the great gates. To the northerly gate a waggon-road climbs between its guarded banks, while to the gate at the south-west corner—the one they call King's Gate—a chariot-way curves up, true-cambered to the fastest wheels, and wide enough for a galloping troop of horses.

Within those walls now, as well kept in these times of

peace as in the troubled days I built them for, a city has arisen, gay with gilding and the fluttering of banners, and fresh with gardens and orchard trees. On the paved terraces walk women in rich dresses, and children play in the gardens. The streets are crowded with folk, and full of talk and laughter, the chaffering of the market-place, the quick hoofs of Arthur's fleet and glossy horses, the shouts of the young men, and the clamour of the church bells. It has grown rich with peaceful commerce, and splendid with the arts of peace. Camelot is a marvellous sight, and one which is familiar now to travellers from the four corners of the world.

But then, on that raw hilltop, and among the mess of abandoned buildings, it was no more than an idea, and an idea sprung out of the hard necessities of war. We would start, of course, with the outer walls, and here I planned to use the broken stuff that lay about; tiles from the old hypocausts, flagstones, bedding from the floors, even from the old roadwork that had been laid in the Roman fortress. With these we would throw up a revetment of hard rubble which would retain the outer wall, and at the same time support a broad fighting platform laid along the inner side of the battlement. The wall itself would, on the outer side, rise straight out of the steep hillside, like a crown on a king's head. The hillside we stripped of its trees, and seamed with ditches, so that it became, in effect, a steep of breakneck minor crags, to be topped with a great wall faced with stone. For this we would use the dressed tufa found on site, along with materials quarried afresh by Melwas' masons and our own. Above this again I planned to set a massively smooth wall of wood, tied into the stonework and the rubble of the revetment by a strong timber frame. At the gateways, where the approach-roads ran uphill sunk between rocky banks, I designed a kind of tunnel which would pierce the fortified wall, and allow the fighting platform to run unbroken across, above the gates. These gated tunnels, high and wide enough to let horse-drawn traffic through,

or riders three abreast, would be hung with huge gates which could fold back against the oak-lined walls. To do this we would have to sink the roadways still further.

This, and much else besides, I had explained to Derwen. He had been sceptical at first, and only his respect for me had kept him, I could tell, from flat and mulish disagreement—especially about the gates, for which he could see no precedent; and most engineers and architects work, reasonably enough, from well-proved precedent, especially in matters of war and defence. At first he could see no reason to abandon the well-tried model of twin turrets and guard-rooms. But in time, sitting hour by hour over my plans, and conning the lists I had had drawn up of the materials already available on the site, he came to a qualified acceptance of my amalgam of stone and woodworking, and thence to a sort of guarded enthusiasm over all. He was enough of a professional to find excitement in new ideas, especially since any blame for failure would be mine and not his.

Not that blame was likely. Arthur, taking part in the planning sessions, was enthusiastic, but—as he pointed out when deferred to over some technical point—he knew his own business, and he would trust us to know ours. We all knew what the place's function would be; it was up to us to build it accordingly. Once we had built it (he concluded with the brevity of total and unconscious arrogance), he would know how to keep it.

Now, on site at last, and with good weather come early and looking settled, Derwen started work with keenness and despatch, and, before the old herdsman had called the cows home for the first evening's milking, the pegs were driven in, trenches had been started, and the first waggon-load of supplies was groaning uphill behind its straining oxen.

Caer Camel was rising again. The King was coming back.

*   *   *

He came on a bright day of June. He rode up from the village on his grey mare Amrei, accompanied by Bedwyr, and his foster-brother Cei, and perhaps a dozen others of his cavalry captains. These were now commonly known as the *equites* or knights: Arthur himself called them his 'companions'. They rode without armour, like a hunting-party. Arthur swung from his mare's back, threw the reins to Bedwyr, and while the others dismounted and let their horses graze, he trod up the slope of blowing grass alone.

He saw me, and lifted a hand, but did not hurry. He paused by the outer revetment, and spoke to the men working there, then walked out onto the planking that bridged a trench, while the labourers straightened from their tasks to answer his questions. I saw one of them point something out to him; he looked that way, and then all about him, before he left them to mount the central ridge where the foundations for his headquarters had been dug. From there, he could command the whole area, and make some sense, perhaps, out of the maze of trenching and foundations, half hidden as it was beneath the web of ropes and scaffolding.

He turned slowly on his heel, until he had taken in the full circle. Then he came swiftly over to where I stood, drawings in hand.

'Yes,' was all he said, but with a glowing satisfaction. And then: 'When?'

'There will be something here for you by winter.'

He sent his eyes round again, a look of pride and vision that could have been my own. I knew that he was seeing, as I could see, the finished walls, the proud towers, the stone and timber and iron that would enclose this space of golden summer air, and make it his first creation. It was the look, too, of a warrior who sees a strong weapon being offered to his hand. His eyes, full of this high and fierce satisfaction, came back to me.

'I told you to use a miracle, and I think you have. That is how I see it. Perhaps you are too much of a professional

to feel that way, when you see what was only a drawing on clay, or even a thought in your mind, being built into something real that will last for ever?' ·

'I believe all makers feel this way. I, certainly.'

'How fast it has moved! Did you build it with music, like the Giants' Dance?'

'I used the same miracle here. You can see it. The men.'

A quick glance at me, then his gaze went across the mess of churned ground and toiling labourers to where, as orderly as in an old, walled city, the workshops of the carpenters and smiths and masons rang with hammering and voices. His eyes took a faraway and yet inward look. He spoke softly. 'I'll remember that. God knows every commander should. I use the same miracle myself.' Then, back to me: 'And by next winter?'

'By next winter you shall have it complete inside, as well as safe to fight from. The place is everything we had hoped for. Later, when the wars are done, there will be space and time to build for other things, comfort and grace and splendour, worthy of you and your victories. We'll make you a veritable eagle's eyrie, hung on a lovely hill. A stronghold to hunt from in war, and a home to breed in in times of peace.'

He had half turned from me, to make a sign to the watching Bedwyr. The young men mounted, and Bedwyr approached us, leading Arthur's mare. Arthur swung back to me, brows up.

'So you know? I might have known I could keep no secrets from you.'

'Secrets? I know nothing. What secret were you trying to keep?'

'None. What would be the use? I would have told you straight away, but this came first ... Though she wouldn't like to hear me say so.' I must have gaped at him like a fool. His eyes danced. 'Yes, I'm sorry, Merlin. But I really was about to tell you. I am to marry. Come, don't be angry. That is something in which you could hardly guide me to my own satisfaction.'

'I am not angry. What right have I? This is one thing you must decide for yourself. It seems you have, and I'm glad. Is it concluded?'

'No, how could it be? I was waiting to talk to you first. So far it's only been a matter of letters between Queen Ygraine and myself. The suggestion came from her, and I suppose there'll be a lot of talking to do first. But I warn you—' a glint—'my mind is made up.' Bedwyr slipped from his saddle beside us, and Arthur took the mare's reins from him. I looked a query, and he nodded. 'Yes, Bedwyr knows.'

'Then will you tell me who she is?'

'Her father was March, who fought under Duke Cador and was killed in a skirmish on the Irish Shore. Her mother died at her birth, and, since her father's death, she has been under Queen Ygraine's protection. You must have seen her, but you would not notice her, I expect. She was in waiting at Amesbury, and then again at the crowning.'

'I remember her. Did I hear her name? I forget.'

'Guenever.'

A plover winged overhead, tumbling in the sun. Its shadow floated over the grass between us. Something plucked at the chords of memory; something from that other life of power and terror and bright vision. But it eluded me. The mood of tranquil achievement was unruffled as the Lake.

'What is it, Merlin?'

His voice was anxious, like a boy's who fears censure. I looked up. Bedwyr, beside him, was watching me with the same worried look.

'Nothing at all. She's a lovely girl, and bears a lovely name. Be sure the gods will bless the marriage when the time comes.'

The young faces relaxed. Bedwyr said something quick and teasing, then followed it with some excited comment about the building work, and the two of them plunged into a discussion in which marriage plans had no part. I

caught sight of Derwen over near the gateway, so we walked that way to talk with him. Then Arthur and Bedwyr took their leave, and mounted, and the other young men turned their fretting horses to ride downhill after their King towards the road.

They did not get far. As the little cavalcade entered the sunken gateway they came head on against Blackberry and Dewdrop and their sisters, making their slow way uphill. The old herdsman, tenacious as goosegrass, still clung to his grazing rights on Caer Camel, and brought the herd daily up towards the part of the field as yet unspoiled by the workings.

I saw the grey mare pause, veer, and start to curvet. The cattle, stolidly chewing, shouldered by, udders swinging. From somewhere among them as suddenly as a puff of smoke from the ground, the old man appeared, leaning on his staff. The mare reared, hoofs flailing. Arthur pulled her aside, and she turned back hard against the shoulder of Bedwyr's black colt, which promptly lashed out, missing Dewdrop by inches. Bedwyr was laughing, but Cei shouted out angrily:

'Make way, you old fool! Can't you see it's the King? And get your damned cattle out of the way. They've no business here now!'

'As good business as yourself, young master, if not better,' said the old man tartly. 'Getting the good of the land they are, which you and your likes can do nought but spoil! So it's you should take your horses off and get your hunting done in the Summer Country, and let honest folks be!'

Cei was never one to know when he should curb his anger, or even save his breath. He pushed his horse past Arthur's mare, and thrust his red face down towards the old man. 'Are you deaf, old fool, or just stupid? Hunting? We are the King's fighting captains, and this is the King!'

Arthur, half-laughing, began, 'Oh, leave it, Cei,' then had to control the mare sharply once more as the old

goblin bobbed up again at his bridle-hand. The dim eyes peered upwards.

'King? Nay, but you can't fool me, masters. 'Tis only a bit of a lad. The king's a man grown. Besides, 'tis not yet his time. He'll come at midsummer, wi' the full moon. Seen him, I have, with all his fighting men.' A gesture with his staff that set the horses' heads tossing again. 'These, fighting captains? Boys, that's all they be! Kings' fighting men have armour, and spears as long as ash trees, and plumes on them like the manes on their horses. Seen them, I have, alone here on a summer's night. Oh, aye, I know the King.'

Cei opened his mouth again, but Arthur put up a hand. He spoke as if he and the old man were alone in the field. 'A king who came here in the summer? What are you telling us, father? What men were they?'

Something in his manner, perhaps, got through to the other. He looked uncertain. Then he caught sight of me, and pointed. 'Told him, I did. Yes. King's man, he said he was, and spoke me soft. A king was coming, he said, who would tend my cows for me, and give me the grazing for them . . .' He looked about him, as if taking in for the first time the splendid horses and gay trappings, and the assured, laughing looks of the young men. His voice faltered, and he slid off into his mumbling. Arthur looked at me.

'Do you know what he's talking about?'

'A legend of the past, and a troop of ghosts that he says come riding out of their grave in the hill on a summer's midnight. It's my guess that he's telling an old tale of the Celtic rulers here, or the Romans, or maybe both. Nothing to trouble you.'

'Not trouble us?' said someone, sounding uneasy; I think it was Lamorak, a brave and high-strung gentleman who watched the stars for signs, and whose horse's trappings rang with charms. 'Ghosts, and not trouble us?'

'And he has seen them himself, on this very spot?' said

someone else. Then others, murmuring, 'Spears and horse-hair plumes? Why, they sound like Saxons.' And Lamorak again, fingering a piece of coral on his breast, 'Ghosts of dead men, killed here and buried under the very hill where you plan to build a stronghold and a safe city? Arthur, did you know?'

There are few men more superstitious than soldiers. They are, after all, the men who live closest to death. All laughter had vanished, quenched, and a shiver went across the bright day, as surely as if a cloud had passed between us and the sun.

Arthur was frowning. He was a soldier, too, but he was also a king, and, like the King his father before him, dealt in facts. He said, with noticeable briskness: 'And what of it? Show me any strong fortress as good as this which has not been defended by brave men, and founded on their blood! Are we children, to fear the ghosts of men who have died here before us, to keep this land? If they linger here at all, they will be on our side, gentlemen!' Then, to the herdsman: 'Well? Tell us your story, father. Who was this king?'

The old man hesitated, confused. Then he asked, suddenly: 'Did you ever hear of Merlin, the enchanter?'

'Merlin?' This was Bedwyr. 'Why, do you not know—?'

He caught my eye, and stopped. No one else spoke. Arthur, without a glance in my direction, asked, into the silence: 'What of Merlin?'

The filmed eyes went round as if they could see every man clearly, every listening face. Even the horses stood quiet. The herdsman seemed to take courage from the attentive silence. He became suddenly lucid. 'There was a king once, who set out to build a stronghold. And, like the kings of old, who were strong men and merciless, he looked for a hero, to kill and bury beneath the founda-tions, and hold them firm. So he caught and took Merlin, who was the greatest man in all Britain, and would have killed him; but Merlin called up his dragons, and flew away through the heavens, safely, and called a new king

into Britain, who burned the other one to ashes in his tower, and his queen with him. Had you heard that tale, master?'

'Yes.'

'And is it true that you are a king, and these your captains?'

'Yes.'

'Then ask Merlin. They say he still lives. Ask him what king should fear to have a hero's grave beneath his threshold. Don't you know what he did? He put the great Dragon King himself under the Hanging Stones, that he did, and called it the safe castle of all Britain. Or so they say.'

'They say the truth,' said Arthur. He looked about him, to see where relief had already overlaid uneasiness. He turned back to the herdsman. 'And the strong king who lies with his men within the hill?'

But here he got no further. When pressed, the old man became vague, and then unintelligible. A word could be caught here and there; helmets, plumes, round shields, and small horses, and yet again long spears 'like ash trees', and cloaks blowing in the wind 'when no wind blows'.

I said coolly, to interrupt these new ghostly visions: 'You should ask Merlin about that, too, my lord King. I believe I know what he would say.'

Arthur smiled. 'What, then?'

I turned to the old man. 'You told me that the Goddess slew this king and his men, and that they were buried here. You told me, too, that the new young king would have to make his peace with the Goddess, or she would reject him. Now see what she has done. He knew nothing of this story, but he has come here with her guidance, to build his stronghold on the very spot where the Goddess herself slew and buried a troop of strong fighters and their leader, to be the king-stone of his threshold. And she gave him the sword and the crown. So tell your people this, and tell them that the new king comes, with the Goddess's sanction, to build a fortress of his own, and to

protect you and your children, and let your cattle graze in peace.'

I heard Lamorak draw in his breath. 'By the Goddess herself, you have it, Merlin!'

'Merlin?' You would have thought the old man was hearing the name for the first time. 'Aye, that's what he would say ... and I've heard tell how he took the sword himself from the depths of the water and gave it to the King ...' For a few minutes then, as the others crowded close, talking again among themselves, relieved and smiling, he went back to his mumbling. But then, my final, incautious sentence having got through, he came suddenly, and with the utmost clarity of speech, back to the matter of his cows, and the iniquity of kings who interfered with their grazing. Arthur, with one swift, charged glance at me, listened gravely, while the young men held in their laughter, and the last wisps of trouble vanished in mirth. In the end, with gentle courtesy, the King promised to let him keep the grazing for as long as the sweet grass grew on Caer Camel, and when it did no longer, to find a pasture for him elsewhere.

'On my word as High King,' he finished.

It was not clear whether, even now, the old herdsman believed him. 'Well, call yourself king or not,' he said, 'for a lad you show some sort of sense. You listen to them that knows, not like some'—this with a malevolent glance in Cei's direction—'that's all noise and wind. Fighting men, indeed! Anyone who knows ought about fighting and the like, knows there's no man can fight with an empty belly. You give my cows the grass, and we'll fill your bellies for you.'

'I have said you shall have it.'

'And when yon builder'—this was myself—' has got Caer Camel spoiled, what land will you give me then?'

Arthur had perhaps not meant to be taken so quickly at his word, but he hesitated only for a moment. 'I saw good green stretches down by the river yonder, beyond the village. If I can—'

'That's no manner of good for beasts. Goats, maybe, and geese, but not cattle. That's sour grass, that is, and full of buttercups. That's poison to grazing.'

'Indeed? I didn't know that. Where would be good land, then?'

'Over to the badgers' hill. That's yonder.' He pointed. 'Buttercups!' He cackled. 'King or not, young master, however much folks know, there's always someone as knows more.'

Arthur said, gravely: 'That is something else I shall remember. Very well. If I can come by the badgers' hill, it shall be yours.'

Then he reined back to let the old man by, and, with a salute to me, rode away downhill, with his knights behind him. Derwen was waiting for me by the foundations of the south-west tower. I walked that way. A plover—the same, perhaps—tilted and side-slipped, calling, in the breezy air. Memory came back, halting me ...

... The Green Chapel above Galava. The same two young faces, Arthur's and Bedwyr's, watching me as I told them stories of battles and far-off places. And across the room, thrown by the lamplight, the shadow of a bird floating—the white owl that lived in the roof—*guen-hwyvar*, the white shadow, at whose name I had felt a creeping of the flesh, a moment of troubled prevision which now I could scarcely recall, except for the fear that the name Guenever was somehow a doom for him.

I had felt no such warning today. I did not expect it. I knew just what was left of the power I had once had to warn and to protect. Today I was no more than the old herdsman had called me, a builder.

'No more?' I recalled the pride and awe in the King's eyes as he surveyed the groundwork of the 'miracle' I was working for him now. I looked down at the plans in my hand, and felt the familiar, purely human excitement of the maker stir in me. The shadow fled and vanished into sunshine, and I hurried to meet Derwen. At least I still possessed skill enough to build my boy a safe stronghold.

CHAPTER 4

Three months later Arthur married Guenever at Caerleon. He had had no chance to see the bride again; indeed, I believe he had had no more speech with her than what slight formalities had passed between them at the crowning. He himself had to go north again early in July, so could spare no time to travel into Cornwall to escort her to Guent. In any case, since he was High King, it was proper that his bride should be brought to him. So he spared Bedwyr for one precious month to ride down to Tintagel and bring the bride to Caerleon.

All through that summer there was sporadic fighting in the north, mostly a business (in that forested hill country) of ambush and running skirmish, but late in July Arthur forced a battle by a crossing on the River Bassas. This he won so decisively as to create a welcome lull that prolonged itself into a truce through harvest-time, and allowed him at length to travel to Caerleon with a quiet mind. For all that, his was a garrison wedding; he could afford to sacrifice no sort of readiness, so the bridal was fitted in, so to speak, among his other preoccupations. The bride seemed to expect it, taking everything as happily as if it had been some great festive occasion in London, and there was as much gaiety and gorgeousness about the ceremony as I have ever seen on such occasions, even though men kept their spears stacked outside the hall of feasting, and their swords laid ready to lift, and the King himself spent every available moment in counsel with his officers, or out in the exercise grounds, or—late into the night sometimes—poring over his maps, with his spies' reports on the table beside him.

I left Caer Camel in the first week of September, and rode across country to Caerleon. The work on the fortress was going well, and could be left to Derwen to carry out. I went with a light heart. All I had been able to find out about the girl was in her favour; she was young, healthy, and of good stock, and it was time Arthur was married and thinking of getting himself sons. I thought about her no further than that.

I was in Caerleon in time to see the wedding party arrive. They did not use the ferry-crossing, but came riding up the road from Glevum, their horses gay with gilded leather and coloured tassels, and the women's litters bright with fresh paint. The younger of the ladies wore mantles of every colour, and had flowers plaited into their horses' manes.

The bride herself disdained a litter; she rode a pretty cream-coloured horse, a gift from Arthur's stables. Bedwyr, in a new cloak of russet, kept close by her bridle-hand, and on his other side rode the Princess Morgan, Arthur's sister. Her mount was as fiery as Guenever's was gentle, but she controlled it without effort. She appeared to be in excellent spirits, as excited, one gathered, over her own approaching marriage as over the other, more important wedding. Nor did she seem to grudge Guenever her central role in the festivities, or the deference she received for her new state. Morgan herself had state and to spare: she had come, in Ygraine's absence, to represent the Queen, and, with the Duke of Cornwall, to place Guenever's hand in that of the High King.

Arthur, being still ignorant of the seriousness of Ygraine's illness, had expected her to come. Bedwyr had a quiet word with him on arrival, and I saw a shadow touch the King's face, then he banished it to greet Guenever. His greeting was public and formal, but with a smile behind it that she answered with a demure dimple. The ladies rustled and cooed and eyed him, and the men looked on indulgently, the older ones approving her youth and freshness, their thoughts already turning towards an

heir to the kingdom. The young men watched with the same approval, coloured with simple envy.

Guenever was fifteen now. She was a shade taller than when I had last seen her, and more womanly, but she was still a little creature, with fresh skin and merry eyes, patently delighted with the fortune that had brought her out of Cornwall as bride of the land's darling, Arthur the young King.

She gave the Queen's excuses prettily, with no hint that Ygraine suffered from anything other than a passing ailment, and the King accepted them smoothly, then gave her his arm, and himself escorted her, with Morgan, to the house prepared for them and their ladies. This was the best of the town houses outside the fortress walls, where they could rest and make ready for the marriage.

He came back to his rooms soon after, and while he was still some way down the corridor I could hear him talking busily to Bedwyr. Nor was the talk of weddings and women. He came into the room already shedding his finery, and Ulfin, who knew his ways, was there ready to catch the splendid cloak as it was flung off, and to lift the heavy sword-belt and lay it aside. Arthur greeted me gaily.

'Well? What do you think? Has she not grown lovely?'

'She is very fair. She will be a match for you.'

'And she isn't shy or mim-mouthed, thank God. I've no time for that.'

I saw Bedwyr smiling. We both knew he meant it literally. He had no time to trouble with wooing a delicate bride; he wanted marriage and bedding, and then, with the elder nobles satisfied at last, and his own mind free, he could get back to the unfinished business in the north.

So much he was saying now, as he led the way into the anteroom where the map-table stood.

'But we'll talk of that in a moment, when the rest of the Council comes. I've sent for them. There was fresh news last night, by courier, Incidentally, Merlin, I told you, didn't I, that I was sending for your young man

Gereint, from Olicana? He got here last night—have you seen him yet? No? Well he'll be coming with the rest. I'm grateful to you; he's a find, and has proved his value already three times over. He brought news from Elmet ... But leave that now. Before they come, I want to ask you about Queen Ygraine. Bedwyr tells me there was no question of her coming north for the wedding. Did you know she was ill?'

'I knew at Amesbury that she was ailing, but she would not talk about it, then or later, and she never consulted me. Why, Bedwyr, what's the news of her now?'

'I'm no judge,' said Bedwyr, 'but she looked gravely ill to me. Even since the crowning I could see a change in her, thin as a ghost, and spending most of her time in bed. She sent a letter to Arthur, and she would have written to you, but it was beyond her strength. I was to give you her greetings, and to thank you for your letters, and your thought of her. She watches for them.'

Arthur looked at me. 'Did you suspect anything like this, when you saw her? Is this a mortal sickness?'

'I would guess so. When I saw her at Amesbury, the seeds of the sickness were already sown. And when I spoke to her again at the crowning, I think she knew herself to be failing. But to guess at how long ... Even had I been her own physician, I doubt if I could have judged of that.'

He might have been expected to ask why I had kept my suspicions from him, but the reasons were obvious enough so he wasted no breath on them. He merely nodded, looking troubled. 'I cannot ... You know that I must go north again as soon as this business is done.' He spoke as if the wedding were a Council, or a battle. 'I cannot go down into Cornwall. Ought I to send you?'

'It would be useless. Besides, her own physician is as good a man as you could wish for. I knew him when he was a young student in Pergamum.'

'Well,' he said, accepting it, and then again, 'Well ...'
But he moved restlessly, fidgeting with the pins that

were stuck here and there in the clay map. 'The trouble is, one always feels there is something one should be doing. I like to load the dice, not sit waiting for someone else to throw them. Oh, yes, I know what you will say—that the essence of wisdom is to know when to be doing, and when it is useless even to try. But I sometimes think I shall never be old enough to be wise.'

'Perhaps the best thing you can do, both for Queen Ygraine and for yourself, is to get this marriage consummated, and see your sister Morgan crowned Queen of Rheged,' I said, and Bedwyr nodded.

'I agree. From the way she spoke about it. I got the impression that she lives only to see both marriage-bonds safely tied.'

'That is what she says in her letter to me,' said the King. He turned his head. Faintly, from the corridor, came the sound of challenge and answer. 'Well, Merlin, I could ill have spared you for a journey into Cornwall. I want to send you north again. Can Derwen be left in charge at Caer Camel?'

'If you wish it, of course. He will do very well, though I should like to be back myself in good time for the spring weather.'

'There's no reason why you shouldn't be.'

'Is it Morgan's wedding? Or—perhaps I should have been more cautious? Is it Morgause again? ... I warn you, if it's a trip to Orkney, I shall refuse.'

He laughed. He certainly neither looked nor spoke as if Morgause or her bastard had been on his mind. 'I wouldn't put you at such risk, either from Morgause or the northern seas.. No, it is Morgan. I want you to take her to Rheged.'

'That will be a pleasure.' It would, indeed. The years I had spent in Rheged, in the Wild Forest which is part of the great tract of land they call the Caledonian Forest, had been the crest of my life; they had been the years when I had guided and taught Arthur as a boy. 'I trust I'll be able to see Ector?'

'Why not, once you've seen Morgan safely wedded? I must admit it will ease my mind, as well as the Queen's, to see her settled there in Rheged. It's possible that by spring-time there will be war in the north again.'

Put like that, it sounded strange, but in the context of those times it made sense. Those were years of winter weddings; men left home in spring to fight, and it was as well to leave a secure hearth behind them. For a man like Urbgen of Rheged, no longer young, lord of great domains, and a keen fighting man, it would be foolish to put off the proposed marriage any longer. I said: 'Of course I will take her there. How soon?'

'As soon as things are done here, and before winter sets in.'

'Will you be there?'

'If I can. We'll speak of this again. I'll give you messages, and of course you will carry my gifts to Urbgen.' He signed to Ulfin, who went to the door. The others came in then— his knights and the men of the Council and certain of the petty kings who had come to Caerleon for the wedding. Cador was there, and Gwilim, and others from Powys and Dyfed and Dumnonia, but no one from Elmet, or the north. This was understandable. It was a relief not to see Lot. Among the younger men I saw Gereint. He greeted me with a smiling gesture, but there was no time for talk. The King spoke, and we sat over our counsels until sunset, when food was brought in, and after that the company took their leave, and I with them.

As I made my way back to my own quarters, Bedwyr fell in beside me, and with him Gereint. The two young men seemed to know one another tolerably well. Gereint greeted me warmly. 'It was a good day for me,' he said, smiling, 'when that travelling doctor came to Olicana.'

'And, I believe, for Arthur,' I replied. 'How is the work going in the Gap?'

He told me about it. There was, it seemed, no immediate danger from the east. Arthur had made a clean sweep in Linnuis, and meantime the King of Elmet held watch

and ward for him. The road through the Gap had been rebuilt, right through from Olicana to Tribuit, and both the western forts had been brought to readiness. From talking about this he came to Caer Camel, and here Bedwyr joined him in plying me with questions. Presently we came to where our ways parted.

'I leave you here,' said Gereint. He glanced back the way we had come, towards the King's apartments. 'Behold,' he said, 'the half was not told me.' He spoke as if quoting from something, but it was something I had not heard. 'These are great days for us all.'

'And will be greater.'

Then we said goodnight, and Bedwyr and I walked on together. The boy with the torch was a few paces ahead. At first we talked, with lowered voices, about Ygraine. He was able to tell me more than he had said in front of Arthur. Her physician, not wishing to commit anything to writing, had entrusted Bedwyr with information for me, but nothing about it was new. The Queen was dying, waiting only—this was from Bedwyr himself—until the two young women, crowned and in due splendour, had taken their places, and thereafter it would be a strange thing (Melchior had said) if she lasted till Christmas. She had sent me a message of goodwill, and a token to be given to Arthur after her death. This latter was a brooch, finely made of gold and blue enamel, with an image of the mother-goddess of the Christians, and the name, MARIA, inscribed around the edge. She had already given jewels both to her daughter Morgan and to Guenever; these had come in the guise of wedding gifts, though Morgan already knew the truth. Guenever, it seemed, did not. The girl had been as dear, and lately almost dearer, to Ygraine than her own daughter, and the Queen had carefully instructed Bedwyr that nothing must spoil the marriage celebrations. Not that the Queen, said Bedwyr (who obviously held Ygraine in the greatest respect) had any illusions about Arthur's grief for her; she had sacrificed his love for that of Uther and the kingdom's future, and

she herself was resigned to death, secure in her faith; but she was aware how much the girl had come to love her.

'And Guenever herself?' I asked at length. 'You must have come to know her well on the journey. And you know Arthur, none better. How will they suit? What is she like?'

'Delightful. She's full of life—in her own way as full as he is—and she is clever. She plied me with questions about the wars, and they were not idle ones. She understands what he is doing, and has followed every move he has made. She was head over ears in love with him from the first moment she saw him in Amesbury ... in fact, it's my belief that she was in love with him even before that, like every other girl in Britain. But she has humour and sense with it, she's no greensick girl with a dream of a crown and a bedding; she knows where her duty will lie. I know that Queen Ygraine planned this and hoped for it. She has been schooling the girl all this while.'

'There could hardly be a better preceptress.'

'I agree. But Guenever has gentleness, and she is full of laughter, too. I am glad,' he finished simply.

We spoke of Morgan then, and the other marriage.

'Let us hope it suits as well,' I said. 'It's certainly what Arthur wants. And Morgan? She seems willing, even happy about it.'

'Oh, yes,' he said, and then, with a smiling shrug, 'you'd think it was a love-match, and that all the business with Lot had never been. You always say, Merlin, that you know nothing of women, and can't even guess at what moves them. Well, no more can I, and I'm not a born hermit, like you. I've known plenty, and now I've spent a month or so in daily attendance on them—and I still don't begin to understand them. They crave for marriage, which for them is a kind of slavery—and dangerous at that. You could understand it with those who have nothing of their own; but here's Morgan: she has wealth and position, and the freedom they give her, and she has the protection of the High King. Yet she would have gone

to Lot, whose reputation you know, and now goes, eagerly, to Urbgen of Rheged, who is more than three times her age, and whom she has hardly seen. Why?'

'I suspect because of Morgause.'

He shot me a look. 'That's possible. I spoke to Guenever about it. She says that, since news came of Morgause's latest lying-in, and her letters about the state she keeps—'

'In Orkney?'

'She says so. It does seem true that she rules the kingdom. Who else? Lot has been with Arthur ... Well, Guenever told me that lately Morgan's temper had been growing sharp, and she had begun to speak of Morgause with hatred. Also, she had begun to practise what the Queen called her "dark arts" again. Guenever seems afraid of them.' He hesitated. 'They speak of it as magic, Merlin, but it is nothing like your power. It is something smoky, in a closed room.'

'If Morgause taught her, then it must be dark indeed. Well, so the sooner Morgan is a queen in Rheged, with a family of her own, the better. And what of yourself, Bedwyr? Have you had thoughts of marriage?'

'None, yet,' he said, cheerfully. 'I have no time.'

On which we laughed, and went our ways.

* * *

So the next day, with a fine sun blazing, and all the pomp and music and revelry that a joyous crowd could conjure up, Arthur married Guenever. And after the feasting, when torches had burned low, and men and women had eaten and laughed and drunk deep, the bride was led away, and later, escorted by his companion knights, the bridegroom went to her.

That night I dreamed a dream. It was brief and cloudy, a glimmer only of something that might be true vision. There were curtains drawn and blowing, and a place full of cold shadows, and a woman lying in bed. I could not see her clearly, nor tell who she was. I thought at first that

it was Ygraine, then, with a shift of the blowing light, it might have been Guenever. And she lay as if she were dead, or as if she were sleeping soundly after a night of love.

CHAPTER 5

So once again I headed northward, keeping this time to the west road all the way to Luguvallium. It was truly a wedding journey. The good weather held all through that month, the lovely September month of gold that is best for travellers, since Hermes, the god of going, claims it for his own.

His hand was over us through all that journey. The road, Arthur's main way up the west, was repaired and sound, and even on the moors the land was dry, so that we did not need to time our journey to seek for stopping-places to suit the women. If, at sunset, no town or village was near, we made camp where we halted, and ate by some stream with trees for shelter, while plovers called in the dusk and the herons flapped overhead back from their fishing-grounds. For me, it would have been an idyllic journey, but for two things. The first was the memory of my last journey northward. Like all sensible men, I had put regret out of my mind, or thought I had; but when one night someone petitioned me to sing, and my servant brought the harp to me, it seemed suddenly as if I only had to look up from the strings to see them coming into the firelight, Beltane the goldsmith, smiling, with Ninian behind him. And after that the boy was there nightly, in memory or in dreams, and with him the most poignant of all sorrows, the regret for what might have been, and was gone for ever. It was more than simple grief for a disciple lost who might have done my work for me after I was gone. There was with it a wounding self-contempt for the helpless way I had let him go. Surely I should have known, in that moment of stinging, involuntary protest at Cor

Bridge, why the protest was made? The truth was, that the loss of the boy went far deeper than the failure to win an heir and a disciple: his loss was the very symbol of my own. Because I was no longer Merlin, Ninian had died.

The second wasp in the honey of that journey was Morgan herself.

I had never known her well. She had been born at Tintagel, and had grown up there through the years when I had lived in hiding in Rheged, watching over Arthur's boyhood. Since then I had only seen her twice, at her brother's crowning, and at his marriage, and had barely spoken to her on either occasion.

She resembled her brother in that she was tall for her age and dark-haired, with the dark eyes that came, I think, from the Spanish blood brought by the Emperor Maximus into the family of the Ambrosii, but in feature she resembled Ygraine, where Arthur favoured Uther. Her skin was pale, and she was as quiet as Arthur was ebullient. For all this I could sense in her something of the same kind of force, a power controlled, fire banked under cool ash. There was something, too, of the subtlety that Morgause, her half-sister, showed in such abundance, and Arthur not at all. But this is mostly a woman's quality; they all have it in some degree or another; it is too often their only weapon and their only shield.

Morgan refused to use the litter provided for her, and rode beside me for some part of each day. I suppose that when she was with the women, or among the younger men, the talk must have turned on the coming wedding, and the times to come; but when she was by me she spoke mostly of the past. Again and again she led me to talk of those of my deeds which had passed into legend, the story of the dragons at Dinas Emrys, the raising of the king-stone at Killare, the lifting of the sword of Macsen from the stone. I answered her questions willingly enough, keeping to the facts of the stories, and (remembering what I had learned of Morgan from her mother and Bedwyr) trying to convey to her something of what 'magic' meant.

As these girls see it, it is an affair of philtres, and whispers in darkened rooms, spells to bind a man's heart, or bring the vision of a lover on Midsummer Eve. Their main concern, understandably, is the aphrodisian lore—how to bring, or to prevent pregnancy. charms for safety in childbirth, predictions about the sex of a child. These matters, to do her justice, Morgan never broached with me; it was to be expected that she was versed in them already. Nor did she seem interested, as the young Morgause had been, in medicine and the healing arts. Her questions turned all on the greater power, and mainly as it had touched Arthur. All that had passed from Uther's first wooing of her mother, and Arthur's conception, to the raising of the great sword of Macsen, she was avid to know. I answered her civilly, and fully enough; she was, I reckoned, entitled to the facts, and (since she was going to be Queen of Rheged, and would almost certainly outlive her husband, and live to guide the future king of that powerful province) I tried to show her what Arthur's aims were for the settled times after the war, and to imbue her with the same ambitions.

It was hard to tell what sort of success I had. After a time I noticed that her talk turned more and more frequently to the hows and wherefores of the power I had owned. I put her questions aside, but she persisted, at length even suggesting, with an assurance as cool as Arthur's own, that I should show some demonstration of it, for all the world as if I were an old wife mixing spells and simples over the fire, or a soothsayer crystal-gazing on market day. At this last impertinence my answer was, I imagine, too cold for her to stomach. Soon afterwards she drew rein and let her palfrey lag back, and thereafter rode the rest of the way with the young people.

Like her sister, Morgan was rarely content with the company of women. Her most constant companion was one Accolon, a splendidly dressed, florid young man with a loud laugh and a high colour. She never let herself be alone with him more than was decent, though he made no

secret of his feelings; he followed her everywhere with his eyes, and, whenever he could, touched her hand, or brought his horse sidling so close to her that his thigh brushed hers, and their horses' manes tangled together. She never seemed to notice, and never once, that I could see, gave him other than the same cool looks and answers that she gave to everyone. I had, of course, a duty to bring her unharmed and virgin (if virgin she still was) to Urbgen's bed, but I could have no present fears for her honour. A lover would have been hard put to it to come to her on that journey, even if she had beckoned him. Most nights when we camped, Morgan was attended by all her ladies to her pavilion, which was shared by her two elderly waiting women, as well as her younger companions. She gave no hint that she wished it otherwise. She acted and spoke like any royal bride on her way to a welcome bride-bed, and if Accolon's handsome face and eager courtship moved her she made no sign.

We halted for the last time just short of the limits that are governed by Caer-luel, as the British call Luguvallium. Here we rested the horses, while the servants busied themselves over the burnishing of the harness and the washing of the painted litters, and—among the women—some furbishing of clothes and hair and complexions. Then the cavalcade re-formed, and we went on to meet the welcoming party, which met us well beyond the city limits.

It was headed by King Urbgen himself, on a splendid horse which had been a gift from Arthur, a bay stallion decked with crimson and cloth of gold. Beside it a servant led a white mare, bridled with silver and tasselled with blue, for the princess. Urbgen was as splendid as his steed, a vigorous man, broad-chested and strong-armed, and as active as any warrior half his age. He had been a sandy-coloured man, and now his hair and beard, as is the way with sand-fair men, had gone quite white, thick and fine. His face had been weathered by the summers of warfare and the winters of riding his cold marches. I knew

him for a strong man, a stout ally, and a clever ruler.

He greeted me as civilly as if I had been the High King himself, and then I presented Morgan. She had dressed herself in primrose and white, and plaited the long dark hair with gold. She gave him a hand, a deep curtsy, and a cool cheek to kiss, then mounted the white mare and rode on beside him, meeting the stares of his retinue, and his own assessing looks with unruffled composure. I saw Accolon drop back with a hot, sulky look, as Urbgen's party closed round the three of us, and we rode on at a gentle pace to the meeting of the three rivers where Luguvallium lay among the reddening trees of autumn.

* * *

The journey had been a good one, but its end was bad indeed, fulfilling the worst of my fears. Morgause came to the wedding.

Three days before the ceremony a messenger came galloping with the news that a ship had been sighted in the estuary, with the black sail and the badge of the Orcadians. King Urbgen rode to meet it at the harbour. I sent my own servant for news, and he was back with it, hot-foot, before the Orkney party could well have disembarked. King Lot was not there, he told me, but Queen Morgause had come, and in some state. I sent him south to Arthur with a warning; it would not be hard for him to find some excuse not to be present. Mercifully, I myself had no need to look far for a similar excuse: I had already arranged, at Urbgen's own request some days before, to ride out and inspect the signal stations along the estuary shore. With some dispatch, and perhaps a slight lack of dignity, I was gone from the city before Morgause's party arrived, nor did I return until the very eve of the wedding. Later I heard that Morgan, too, had avoided meeting her sister, but then it had hardly been expected of a bride so deep in preparations for a royal wedding.

So I was there to see the sisters meet, at the very gate of the church where, with the Christian rites, Morgan was to be married. Each of them, queen and princess, was splendidly dressed and magnificently attended. They met, spoke, and embraced, with smiles as pretty as pictures, and as fixedly painted on their mouths. Morgan, I thought, won the encounter, since she was dressed for her wedding, and shone as the bright centre-piece to the feast-day. Her gown was magnificent, with its train of purple sewn with silver. She wore a crown on her dark hair, and among the magnificent jewels that Urbgen had given her, I recognised some that Uther had given Ygraine in the early days of their passion. Her slim body was erect under the weight of her rich robes, her face pale and composed and very beautiful. To me she recalled the young Ygraine, full of power and grace. I hoped, with fervour, that the reports of the sisters' dislike of one another were true, and that Morgause would not manage to ingratiate herself, now that her sister stood on the threshold of position and power. But I was uneasy; I could see no other reason for the witch to have come to see her sister's triumph and be outshone by her both in consequence and beauty.

Nothing could take from Morgause the rose-gold beauty which, with her maturity, was, if anything, richer than ever. But it could be seen that she was once again with child, and she had brought with her, besides, another child, a boy. This was an infant, still in his nurse's arms. Lot's son; not the one for whom, half in hope, half in apprehension, I was looking.

Morgause had seen me looking. She smiled that little smile of hers as she made her reverence, then swept on into the church with her train. I, as Arthur's vicar in this, waited to present the bride. Obedient to my message, the High King was busying himself elsewhere.

Any hopes I had had of being able to avoid Morgause further were dashed at the wedding-feast. She and I, as the two princes nearest to the bride, were placed side by side at the high table. The hall was the same one where

Uther had held the victory feast that led to his death. In a room of this same castle she had lain with Arthur to conceive the child Mordred, and the next morning, in a bitter clash of wills, I had destroyed her hopes, and driven her away from Arthur's side. That, as far as she knew, had been our last encounter. She was still in ignorance—or so I hoped—of my journey to Dunpeldyr and my vigil there.

I saw her watching me sideways, under the long white lids. I wondered suddenly, with misgiving, if she could be aware of my lack of defence against her now. Last time we had met she had tried her witch's tricks on me, and I had felt their potency, closing on the mind like a limed web. But she could no more have harmed me then than a she-spider could have hoped to trap a falcon. I had turned her spells back on herself, bearing her fury down by the sheer authority of power. That, now, had left me. It was possible that she could gauge my weakness. I could not tell. I had never underrated Morgause, and would not now.

I spoke with smooth civility. 'You have a fine son, Morgause. What is he called?'

'Gawain.'

'He has a strong look of his father.'

Her lids drooped. 'Both my sons,' she said, gently, 'have a strong look of their father.'

'Both?'

'Come, Merlin, where is your art? Did you believe the dreadful news when you heard it? You must have known it was not true.'

'I knew it was not true that Arthur had ordered the killing, in spite of the calumny you laid on him.'

'I?' The lovely eyes were wide and innocent.

'Yes, you. The massacre may have been Lot's doing, the hot fool, and it was certainly Lot's men who threw the babies into the boat and sent them out with the tide. But who provoked him to it? It was your plan from the first, was it not, even to the murder of that poor child in the

cradle? And it was not Lot who killed Macha, and lifted the other child out of the blood and carried him into hiding.' I echoed her own half-mocking tone. 'Come, Morgause, where is your art? You should know better than to play the innocent with me.'

At the mention of Macha's name I saw fear, like a green spark, leap in her eyes, but she gave no other sign. She sat still and straight, one hand curved round the stem of her goblet, turning it gently, so that the gold burned in the hot torchlight. I could see the pulse beating fast in the hollow of her throat.

It was a sour satisfaction, at best. I had been right. Mordred was alive, hidden, I guessed, somewhere in the cluster of islands called the Orkneys, where Morgause's writ ran, and where I, without the Sight, had no power to find him. Or, I reminded myself, the mandate to kill him if found.

'You saw?' Her voice was low.

'Of course I saw. When could you hide things from me? You must know that everything is quite clear to me, and also, let me remind you, to the High King.'

She sat still, and apparently composed, except for that rapid beat under the creamy flesh. I wondered if I had managed to convince her that I was still someone to be feared. It had not occurred to her that Lind might have come to me; and why should she ever remember Beltane? The necklet he had made for her jumped and sparkled on her throat. She swallowed, and said, in a thin voice that hardly carried through the hubbub of the hall: 'Then you will know that, even though I saved him from Lot, I don't know where he is. Perhaps you will tell me?'

'Do you expect me to believe that?'

'You must believe it, because it is true. I don't know where he is.' She turned her head, looking full at me. 'Do you?'

I made no reply. I merely smiled, picked up my goblet, and drank from it. But, without looking at her, I sensed in her a sudden relaxation, and wondered, with a chill

creeping of the skin, if I had made a mistake.

'Even if I knew,' she said, 'how could I have him by me, and he as like to *his* father as one drop of wine to another?' She drank, set the goblet down, then sat back in her chair, folding her hands over her gown so that the thickening of her belly showed. She smiled at me, malice and hatred with no trace of fear. 'Prophesy about this, then, Merlin the enchanter, if you won't about the other. Will this be another son to take the place of the one I lost?'

'I have no doubt of it,' I said shortly, and she laughed aloud.

'I'm glad to hear it. I have no use for girls.' Her eyes went to the bride, sitting composed and straight beside Urbgen. He had drunk a good deal, and the red stood in his cheeks, but he kept his dignity, even though his eyes caressed his bride, and he leaned close to her chair. Morgause watched, then said with contempt: 'So my little sister got her king in the end. A kingdom, yes, and a fine city and wide lands. But an old man, rising fifty, with sons already ...' Her hand smoothed the front of her gown. 'Lot may be a hot fool, as you termed him, but he is a man.'

It was bait, but I did not rise to it. I said: 'Where is he, that he could not come to the wedding?'

To my surprise she answered quite normally, apparently abandoning the malicious game of chess. Lot, it seemed, had gone east again into Northumbria with Urien, his sister's husband, and was busying himself there overseeing the extension to the Black Dyke. I have written of this before. It runs inland from the northern sea, and provides some sort of defence against incursions along the north-eastern seaboard. Morgause spoke of it with knowledge, and in spite of myself I was interested, and in the talk that followed the atmosphere lightened; and then someone asked me a question about Arthur's wedding and the new young Queen, and Morgause laughed and said, quite naturally:

'What's the use of asking Merlin? He may know everything in the world, but ask him to describe a bridal, and I'll wager he doesn't even know the colour of the girl's hair or her gown!'

Then talk around us became general, with a lot of laughter, and speeches were made, and pledges given, and I must have drunk far more than I was accustomed to, because I well remember how the torchlight beat and swelled, bright and dark alternately, while talk and laughter surged and broke in gusts, and with it the woman's scent, a thick sweetness like honeysuckle, catching and trapping the sense as a limed twig holds a bee. The fumes of wine rose through it. A gold jug tilted, and my goblet brimmed again. Someone said, smiling, 'Drink, my lord.' There was a taste of apricots in my mouth, sweet and sharp; the skin had a texture like the fur of a bee, or a wasp dying in sunlight on a garden wall ... And all the while eyes watching me, in excitement and wary hope, then in contempt, and in triumph ... Then servants were beside me, helping me from my chair, and I saw that the bride had gone already, and King Urbgen, impatience barely held on a tight rein, was watching the door for the sign that it was time to follow her to bed.

The chair beside me was empty. Round my own the servants crowded, smiling, to help me back to my rooms.

CHAPTER 6

Next morning I had a headache as bad as anything that the aftermath of magic used to inflict on me. I kept to my rooms all day. On the day following I took leave of Urbgen and his queen. We had sat through a series of formal discussions before Morgause's arrival, and now I could leave the city—how thankfully, it may be guessed —and make my way south-west through the Wild Forest, at the heart of which stood Count Ector's castle of Galava. I took no leave of Morgause.

It was good to be out again, and this time with two companions only. Morgan's escort had been formed mainly of her own people from Cornwall, who had remained with her in Luguvallium. The two men who rode with me were deputed into my service by Urbgen; they would go with me as far as Galava, then return. It was vain for me to protest that I would rather go alone, and would be safe; King Urbgen merely repeated, smiling, that not even my magic would avail against wolves, or autumn fogs, or the sudden onslaught of early snow, which in that mountainous country can trap the traveller very quickly among the steep valley-passes, and bring him to his death. His words were a reminder to me that, armed as I was now with only the reputation of past power, and not the thing itself, I was as subject to outrage from thieves and desperate men as any solitary traveller in that wild country; so I accepted the escort with thanks, and in so doing I suppose I saved my life.

We rode out over the bridge, and along the pleasant green valley where the river winds, bordered with alder and willow. Though my headache had gone, and I felt

well enough, a certain lassitude still hung about me, and
I breathed the sweet, familiar air, full of pine scents and
bracken scents, with gratitude.

One small incident I remember. As we left the city gates,
and crossed the river bridge, I heard a shrill cry, which at
first I took to be a bird's, one of the gulls that wheeled
about the refuse on the river's banks. Then a movement
caught my eye, and I glanced down to see a woman, carrying a child, walking on the shingle by the river's edge
below the bridge. The child was crying, and she hushed
it. She saw me, and stood quite still, staring upward. I
recognised Morgause's nurse. Then my horse clattered off
the bridge, and the willows hid the woman and child
from view.

I thought nothing of the incident, and in a short while
had forgotten it. We rode on, through villages and farms
rich in grazing cattle. The willows were golden, and the
hazel groves a-scamper with squirrels. Late swallows
gathered along the rooftops, and as we approached that
nest of mountains and lakes that marks the southern
limits of the great forest, the lower hills flamed in the sun
with ripe bracken, rusty-gold between the rocks. Elsewhere
the forest, scattered oaks and pines, was gold and dark.
Soon we came to the edge of the Wild Forest itself, where
the trees crowd so thickly in the valleys that they shut
out the sun. Before long we crossed the track that led up
to the Green Chapel. I would have liked to revisit the
place, but this would have added some hours to the
journey, and besides, the visit could be made more easily
from Galava. So we held on our way, staying with the
road as far as Petrianae.

Today this hardly deserves the name of town, though
in Roman times it was a prosperous market centre. There
is still a market, where a few cattle and sheep and goods
exchange hands, but Petrianae itself is a poor cluster of
daub-and-wattle huts, its only shrine a mere shell of stonework holding a ruinous altar to Mars, in his person of the
local god Cocidius. I saw no offering there, except, on the

mossed step, a leathern sling, such as shepherds use, and a pile of sling-stones. I wondered what escape, from wolf or wild man, the shepherd was giving thanks for.

Beyond Petrianae we left the road and took to the hill tracks, which my escort knew well. We travelled at ease, enjoying the warmth of the late autumn sun. As we climbed higher the warmth still lingered, and the air was soft, with a tingle to it that meant the first frosts were not far away.

We stopped to rest the horses in one high, lonely corrie where a small tarn lay cupped in stony turf, and here we came across a shepherd, one of those hardy hillmen who lodge all summer out on the fell tops with the little blue-fleeced sheep of Rheged. Wars and battles may move and clash below them, but they look up, rather than down, for danger, and at the first onslaught of winter take to the caves, faring thinly on black bread and raisins, and meal-cakes made on a turf fire. They drive their flocks for safety into pens built between the rocky outcrops on the hillsides. Sometimes they do not hear another man's voice from lamb-time to clipping, and then on to autumn's end.

This lad was so little used to talking that he found speech hard, and what he did say came in an accent so thick that even the troopers, who were local men, could make nothing of it, and I, who have the gift of tongues, was hard put to it to understand him. He had, it seemed, had speech with the Old Ones, and was ready enough to pass on his news. It was negative, and none the worse for that. Arthur had stayed in Caerleon for almost a month after his wedding, then had ridden, with his knights, up through the Pennine Gap, heading apparently for Olicana and the Plain of York, where he would meet with the King of Elmet. This was hardly news to me, but at least it was confirmation that there had been no new war-move during the late autumn's peace. The shepherd had saved his best titbit till last. The High King (he called him 'young Emrys', with such a mixture of pride and familiarity that I guessed that Arthur's path must have crossed his in

times past) had left his queen with child. At this, the troopers were openly sceptical; maybe he had, was their verdict, but how, in a scant month, could anyone know for sure? I, when appealed to, was more credulous. As I have said, the Old Ones have ways of knowing that cannot be understood, but deserve to be respected. If the lad had heard this through them ... ?

He had. That was all he knew. Young Emrys had gone into Elmet, and the lass he'd wedded was with child. The word he used was 'yeaning', at which the troopers were disposed to be merry, but I thanked him and gave him a coin, and he turned back to his sheep well satisfied, with only a lingering look at me, half-recognising, I suppose, the hermit of the Green Chapel.

That night we were still well away from the roads, or any hope of a lodging, so when the dusk came down early and dim with mist, we made our camp under tall pines at the forest's edge, and the men cooked supper. I had been drinking water on the journey, as I like to do in mountain country where it is pure and good, but in celebration of the shepherd's news I broke open a new flask of the wine I had been supplied with from Urbgen's cellars. I planned to share this with my companions, but they refused, preferring their own thin ration-wine, which tasted of the skins they carried it in. So I ate and drank alone, and lay down to sleep.

* * *

I cannot write of what happened next. The Old Ones know the story, and it is possible that somewhere else some other man has set it down, but I remember it only dimly, as if I were watching a vision in a dark and smoking glass.

But it was no vision; they stay with me more vividly, even, than memory. This was a kind of madness that took me, brought on, as I now know, by some drug in the wine I had taken. Twice before, when Morgause and I

had come face to face, she had tried her witch's trick on me, but her novice's magic had glanced off me like a child's pebble off a rock. But this last time ... I was to recall how, at the wedding feast, the light thickened and beat around me, while the smell of honeysuckle loaded memory with treachery, and the taste of apricots brought back murder. And how I, who am frugal with food and wine, was carried drunken to bed. I remembered, too, the voice saying, 'Drink, my lord,' and the green, watching eyes. She must have tried her wiles again, and found that now her magic was strong enough to trap me in its sticky threads. It may be that the seeds of the madness were sown then, at the wedding feast, and left to develop later, when I was far enough away for there to be no blame cast on her. Her servant had been there at the river bridge to see me safely out of the city. Later, the witch had implemented the drug with some other poison, slipped into one of the flasks I carried. There she had been lucky. If I had not heard the news of Guinevere's pregnancy, I might never have broached the poisoned flask. As it was, we were well away from Luguvallium when I drank the poison. If the men with me had shared it, so much the worse for them. Morgause would have swept a hundred such aside, to harm Merlin her enemy. There was no need to look further for her motive in coming to her sister's marriage.

Whatever the poison, my frugal ways cheated her of my death. What happened after I had drunk and lain down I can only piece together from what I have since been told, and from the whirling fragments of memory.

It seems that the troopers, alarmed in the night by my groans, hurried to my bed-place, where they were horrified to find me obviously sick and in great pain, twisting on the ground, and moaning, apparently too far gone to be sensible. They did what they could, which was not much, but their rough help saved me as nothing could have done, had I been alone. They made me vomit, then brought their own blankets to augment mine, and wrapped me up warmly and made up the fire. Then one of them stayed

beside me while the other set off down the valley to find help or lodging. He was to send help back to us, and a guide, then ride on himself down to Galava with the news.

When he had gone the other fellow did what he could, and after an hour or two I sank into a sort of sleep. He hardly liked the look of it, but when at last he dared leave me, and took a step or two away among the trees to relieve himself, I neither moved nor made a sound, so he decided to take the chance to fetch water from the brook. This was a scant twenty paces off, downhill over silent mosses. Once there he bethought himself of the fire, which had burned low again, so he crossed the brook and went a bit further—thirty paces, no more, he swore it—to gather more wood. There was plenty lying about, and he was gone only a few minutes. When he got back to the camping-place I had vanished, and, scour the place as he might, he could find no trace of me. It was no blame to him that after an hour or so spent wandering and calling through the echoing darkness of the great forest, he took horse and galloped after his fellow. Merlin the enchanter had too many strange vanishings to his name to leave the simple trooper in any doubt as to what had happened.

The enchanter had disappeared, and all they could do was make their report, and wait for his return.

* * *

It was a long dream. I remember nothing about the beginning of it, but I suppose that, buoyed up by some kind of delirious strength, I crept from my bed-place and wandered off across the deep mosses of the forest, then lay, perhaps, where I fell, deep in some ditch or thicket where the trooper could not find me. I must have recovered in time to take shelter from the weather, and of course I must have found food, and possibly even made fire, during the weeks of storm that followed, but of this I remember nothing. All I can recall now is a series of pictures, a kind of bright and silent dream through which I moved like

a spirit, weightless and bodiless, borne up by the air as a heavy body is borne up by water. The pictures, though vivid, are diminished into an emotionless distance, as if I were looking on at a world that hardly concerns me. So, I sometimes imagine, must the bodiless dead watch over the world they have left.

So I drifted, deep in the autumn forest, unheeded as a wraith of the forest mist. Straining back now in memory, the pictures come to me. Deep aisles of beech, thick with mast, where the wild boar rooted, and the badger dug for food, and the stags clashed and wrestled, roaring, with never a glance at me. Wolves too; the way through those high woods is known as the Wolf Road, but though I would have been easy meat they had had a good summer, and let me be. Then, with the first real chill of winter, came the hoar glitter of icy mornings, with the reeds standing stiff and black out of curded ice, and the forest deserted, badger in lair and deer down in the valley-bottom, and the wild geese gone and the skies empty.

Then the snow. A brief vision this, of the silent, whirling air, warm after the frost; of the forest receding into mist, into dimness, breaking into whirling flakes of white and grey, and then a blinding, silent cold ...

A cave, with cave-smells, and turf burning, and the taste of cordial, and voices, gruffly uncouth in the harsh tongue of the Old Ones, speaking just out of hearing. The reek of badly cured wolf-skins, the hot itch of verminous wrappings, and, once, a nightmare of bound limbs and a weight holding me down ...

There is a long gap of darkness here, but afterwards sunlight, new green, the first bird-song, and a vision, sharp as a child's first sight of the spring, of a bank of celandines, glossy as licked gold. And life stirring again in the forest; the thin foxes padding out, the earth heaving in the badger-setts, stags trotting by unarmed and gentle, and the wild boar again, out foraging. And an absurd, dim dream of finding a pigling still with the stripes and long

silky hair of babyhood, that hobbled about on a broken leg, deserted by its kind.

Then suddenly, one grey dawn, the sound of horses galloping, filling the forest, and the clash of swords and the whirl of bright axes, the yelling and the screams of wounded beasts and men, and, like a flashing, intermittent dream of violence, a day-long storm of fighting that ended with a groaning quiet and the smell of blood and crushed bracken.

Silence then, and the scent of apple-trees, and the nightmare sense of grief that comes when a man wakes again to feel a loss he has forgotten in sleep.

CHAPTER 7

'Merlin!' said Arthur in my ear. *'Merlin!'*

I opened my eyes. I was lying in bed in a room which seemed to be built high up. The bright sunlight of early morning poured in, falling on dressed stone walls, with a curve in them that told of a tower. At the level of the sill I caught a glimpse of treetops moving against cloud. The air eddied, and was cool, but within the room a brazier burned, and I was snug in blankets, and good linen fragrant with cedarwood. Some sort of herb had been thrown into the charcoal of the brazier; the thin smoke smelled clean and resinous. There were no hangings on the walls, but thick slate-grey sheepskins lay on the floor, and there was a plain cross of olive-wood hanging on the wall facing the bed. A Christian household and, by the appointments, a wealthy one. Beside the bed, on a stand of gilded wood, stood a jug and a goblet of Samian ware, and a bowl of beaten silver. There was a cross-legged stool nearby, where a servant must have been sitting to watch me: now he was standing, backed up against the wall, with his eyes, not on me, but on the King.

Arthur let out a long breath, and some of the colour came back into his face. He looked as I had never seen him look before. His eyes were shadowed with fatigue, and the flesh had fallen in below his cheekbones. The last of his youth had vanished; here was a hard-living man, sustained by a will that daily pushed himself and his followers to their very limits and beyond.

He was kneeling beside the bed. As I moved my eyes to look at him, his hand fell across my wrist in a quick grip. I could feel the callouses on his palm.

'Merlin? Do you know me? Can you speak?'

I tried to form a word, but could not. My lips were cracked and dry. My mind felt clear enough, but my body would not obey me. The King's arm came round me, lifting me, and at a sign from him the servant came forward and filled the goblet. Arthur took it from him and held it to my mouth. The stuff was a cordial, sweet and strong. He took a napkin from the man, wiped my lips with it, and lowered me back against the pillows.

I smiled at him. It must have shown a little more than a faint movement of muscles. I tried his name, 'Emrys.' I could hear no sound. I fancy that it came as a breath, no more.

His hand came down again over mine. 'Don't try to speak. I was wrong to make you. You are alive, that's all that matters. Rest now.'

My eye, wandering, fell on something beyond him; my harp, set on a chair beside the wall. I said, still without a thread of sound. 'You found my harp,' and relief and joy went through me, as if, in some way, all must now be well.

He followed my glance. 'Yes, we found it. It's unharmed. Rest now, my dear. All is well. All is well, indeed ...'

I tried his name again, and failing, slid back into darkness. Faintly, like movements from the Otherworld of dream, I remember swift commands, softly spoken, the servants hurrying, slippered footsteps and the rustle of women's garments, cool hands, soft voices. Then the comfort of oblivion.

*   *   *

When I awoke again, it was to full consciousness, as if from a long, refreshing sleep. My brain was clear, my body very weak, but my own. I was conscious, gratefully, of hunger. I moved my head experimentally, then my hands. They felt stiff and heavy, but they belonged to me. Wherever I had been wandering. I had come back to my body. I had quitted the world of dream.

I could see, from the change in the light, that it was evening. A servant—a different one—waited near the door. But one thing was the same; Arthur was still there. He had pulled the stool forward, and was sitting by the bed. He turned his head and saw me watching him, and his face changed. He made a quick movement forward, and his hand came down on mine again, a gentle touch like a doctor's, feeling for the pulse in the wrist.

'By God,' he said, 'you frightened us! What happened? No, no, forget that. Later you'll tell us all you remember ... Now it's enough to know that you are safe, and living. You look better. How do you feel?'

'I have been dreaming.' My voice was not my own; it seemed to come from somewhere else, away in the air, almost outside my control. It was as feeble as the pigling's pipe when I mended its broken leg. 'I have been ill, I think.'

'Ill?' He gave a crack of laughter that held nothing of mirth. 'You have been stark crazy, my dear king's prophet. I thought you were gone clean out of your wits, and that we should never have you back with us again.'

'It must have been a fever of a kind. I hardly remember ...' I knitted my brows, thinking back. 'Yes. I was travelling to Galava with two of Urbgen's men. We made camp up near the Wolf Road, and ... Where am I now?'

'Galava itself. This is Ector's castle. You're home.'

It had been Arthur's home, rather than mine; for reasons of secrecy I had never lived in the castle myself, but had spent the hidden years in the forest, up at the Green Chapel. But as I turned my head and caught the familiar scents of pine forest and lake water, and the smell of the rich tilled soil of Drusilla's garden below the tower, reassurance came, like the sight of a known light through the fog.

'The battle I saw,' I said. 'Was that real, or did I imagine it?'

'Oh, that was real enough. But don't try to talk about

it yet. Take it from me, all is well. Now, you should rest again. How do you feel?'

'Hungry.'

This, of course, started up a new bustling. Servants brought broth, and bread, and more cordials, and the Countess Drusilla herself helped me to eat, and then, once more, disposed me for welcome and dreamless sleep.

* * *

Morning again, and the bright, clean light to which I had first woken. I felt weak still, but in command of myself. It seemed that the King had given orders that he was to be fetched as soon as I woke, but this I would not allow until I had been bathed and shaved and had eaten.

When he came at length he looked quite different. The strained look about his eyes had lessened, and there was colour in his face under the brown of weather. Something of his own especial quality had come back, too; the young strength that men could drink from, as at a spring, and be strengthened themselves.

I had to reassure him about my own recovery, before he would let me talk, but he eventually settled down to give me news. 'The last I heard,' I told him, 'was that you had gone into Elmet ... But that's past history now, it seems. I gather that the truce was broken? What was the battle I saw? It must have been up these parts, in the Caledonian Forest? Who was involved?'

He eyed me, I thought strangely, but answered readily enough. 'Urbgen called me in. The enemy broke across country into Strathclyde, and Caw didn't manage to hold them. They would have forced their way down through the Forest to the road. I came up with them, and broke them up and drove them back. The remnants fled south. I should have followed straight away, but then we found you, and I had to stay ... How could I leave again, till I knew you were home, and cared for?'

'So I really did see the fighting? I wondered if it was part of the dream.'

'You must have seen it all. We fought through the forest, along the river there. You know what it's like, good open ground with thin woodland, birch and alder, just the place for a surprise with fast cavalry. We had the hill at our backs, and took them as they reached the ford. The river was full; easy for horsemen, but for foot-soldiers a trap ... Afterwards, when we came back from the first pursuit, people came running to tell me that you were there. You'd been found wandering among the dead and wounded and giving directions to the doctors ... Nobody recognised you at first, but then the whispers started that Merlin's ghost was there.' A wry little smile. 'I gather that the ghost's advice was good, as often as not. But of course the whispers set up a scare, and some fools started throwing stones to drive you away. It was one of the orderlies, a man called Paulus, who recognised you, and put a stop to the ghost stories. He followed you back to where you were living, and then sent to me.'

'Paulus. Yes, of course. A good man. I've worked with him often. And where was I living?'

'In a ruined turret, with an ancient orchard round it. You don't remember that?'

'No. But something is coming back. A turret, yes, ruinous, all ivy and owls. And apple trees?'

'Yes. It was little more than a pile of stones, with bracken for bedding, and piles of apples rotting, and a store of nuts, and rags hung to dry on the apple boughs.' He paused to clear something from his throat. 'They thought at first you were one of those wild hermits, and indeed, when I first saw you myself ...' His smile twisted. 'You looked the part better than you ever looked it at the Green Chapel.'

'I can imagine that.' And so I could. My beard, before they had shaved me, had grown long and grey, and my hands, lying weakly on the bright blankets, looked thin and old, bones held together with a net of knotted veins.

'So we brought you here. I had to go south again soon after. We caught them up at Caer Guinnion, and fought a bloody engagement there. All went well, but then a messenger came down from Galava with more news of you. When we found you and brought you here, you were strong enough on your feet, but crazy; you didn't know anyone, and you talked about things that made no kind of sense; but once here, and in the women's care, you relapsed into sleep and silence. Well, the messenger came after the battle to tell me that you had never woken. You seemed to fall into a high fever, still talking in the same wild way, then finally lay so long unconscious that they took you for dead, and sent the courier to tell me. I came as soon as I could.'

I narrowed my eyes at him. The light from the window was strong. He saw this, and signed to the slave, who pulled a curtain across. 'Let me get this clear. After you had found me in the forest and brought me to Galava, you went south. And there was another battle? Arthur, how long have I been here?'

'It is three weeks since we found you. But it is fully seven months since you wandered off into the forest and lost yourself. You were gone all winter. Is it any wonder that we thought you were dead?'

'*Seven months?*' Often, as a doctor, I have had to give this kind of news to patients who have been long feverish, or lying in coma, and I always see the same sort of incredulous, groping shock. I felt it now, myself. To know that half a year had dropped out of time, and such a half year ... What, in those months, might not have happened to a country as torn and embattled as mine? And to her King? Other things, forgotten till now in the mists of illness, began to come back to me.

Looking at him, I saw again, with fear, the hollowed cheekbones and the smudge of sleepless nights beneath his eyes: Arthur, who ate like a young wolf and slept like a child; who was the creature of gaiety and strength. There had been no defeat in the field; his glory there had

not suffered even the smear of a shadow. Nor could his anxiety for me have brought him to this pass. There remained his home.

'Emrys, what has happened?'

Once more, in that place, the childhood name came naturally. I saw his face twist as if the memory were a pain. He bent his head and stared down at the blankets.

'My mother, the Queen. She died.'

Memory stirred. The woman lying in the great bed hung with rich stuffs? I had known, then. 'I am sorry,' I said.

'I heard just before we fought the battle at Caer Guinnion. Lucan brought the news, with the token you had left with him. You remember it, a brooch with the Christian symbol? Her death came as no surprise. We had expected it. But I believe that grief helped to hasten her death.'

'Grief? Why, has there been—?' I stopped dead. It had come back clearly now, the night in the forest, and the flask of wine I had opened to share with the troopers. And why. The vision stirred again, the moonlit chamber and the blowing curtains and the dead woman. Something closed my throat. I said, hardly: 'Guenever?'

He nodded, not looking up.

I asked, knowing the answer: 'And the child?'

He looked up quickly. 'You knew? Yes, of course you would ... It never came to term. They said she was with child, but shortly before Christmas she began to bleed, and then, at the New Year, died in great pain. If you had been there—' He stopped, swallowed, and was silent.

'I am sorry,' I said again.

He went on, in a voice so hard that it sounded angry: 'We thought you were dead, too. Then, after the battle, there you were, filthy and old and crazy, but the field surgeons said you might recover. That, at least, I have saved from the shambles of the winter ... Then I had to leave you to go to Caer Guinnion. I won it, yes, but lost some good men. Then on the heels of the action Ector's

courier came to tell me you were dead. When I got here at dawn yesterday I expected to find your body already burned or buried.'

He stopped, put his forehead hard down on a clenched fist, and stayed so. The servant, rigid by the window, caught my eye, and went, softly. In a moment or two Arthur raised his head and spoke in his normal voice.

'Forgive me. All the time I was riding north, I kept remembering what you said about dying a shameful death. It was hard to bear.'

'But here I am, clean and whole, with my wits clear, and ready to become clearer when you tell me all that has happened in the last six months. Now, of your kindness, pour me some of that wine, and go back, if you will, to your journey into Elmet.'

He obeyed me, and in a while talk became easier. He spoke of his journey through the Gap to Olicana, and what he had found there, and of his meeting with the King of Elmet. Then of his return to Caerleon, and of the Queen's miscarriage and death. This time, when I questioned him, he was able to answer me, and in the end I could give him the chilly comfort of knowing that my presence at court beside the young Queen could have been no help. Her doctors were skilled with drugs, and had saved her the worst of the pain; I could have done no more. The child was ill-conceived; nothing could have saved it, or its mother.

When he had heard what I had to tell him, he accepted this, and himself turned the subject. He was eager to hear what had happened to me, and impatient of the fact that I could remember little after the marriage feast at Luguvallium.

'Can you not remember anything of how you came to the turret where we found you?'

'A little. It comes clear bit by bit. I must have wandered about in the forest and kept myself alive somehow until winter. Then it seems to me as if some rude folk of the hill forest must have taken me in and cared for me. Without

that, I doubt if I could have survived the snow. I thought they might be some of Mab's people, the Old Ones of the mountain country, but if so, they would surely have sent word to you.'

'They did. Word came, but only after you had vanished again. As is usual, the Old Ones were snowed up in their high caves all winter, and you with them. They went hunting when the snow melted, and came back to their caves to find you gone. It was from them that I first heard that you had run mad. They had had to tie you, they said, but afterwards, at such times, you would be calm and very weak, and so it was at the time when they left you. When they got home, you had gone.'

'I remember being bound. Yes. So after that I must have made my way downhill, and ended up in the ruin near the ford. I suppose, in my crazed way, still making for Galava. It was spring; I remember a little of it. Then the battle must have overtaken me, and you found me there in the Forest. I recall nothing of that.'

He told me again how I had been found, thin and filthy and talking no kind of sense, hiding in the ruined turret, with a kind of squirrel's hoard of acorns and beech-nuts, and dried windfall apples put by, and a pigling with a splinted leg for company.

'So that part of it was real!' I said, smiling. 'I can remember finding the creature, and healing the leg, but not much else. If I was as sharp set as you say, it was good of me not to eat Master Piglet. What happened to it?'

'It's here in Ector's sties.' The first glimmer of humour touched his mouth. 'And marked, I think, for a long and dishonourable life. There's not one of the boys would dare lay a hand on the enchanter's personal pig, which looks like growing up into a good fighting boar, so it will end up as king of the sty, which is only proper. Merlin, you've told me all you can remember of what happened after making camp up there on the Wolf Road; what do you remember before that? What made you ill? Urbgen's men said it came on suddenly. They thought it was poison,

and so did I. I wondered if the witch had had you followed, after the wedding feast, and one of her creatures had dragged you from your bed that night while the trooper's back was turned. But if that had happened, surely they would have killed you? There was no suspicion of foul play from those two men; they were Urbgen's own, hand-picked.'

'None at all. They were good fellows, and I owe them my life.'

'They told me that you drank wine that night, from your own flask. They did not share it. They say, too, that you were drunk at the marriage feast. You? I have never seen you the worse for wine. And you sat beside Morgause. Have you any reason to believe that she drugged your wine?'

I opened my mouth to answer him, and to this day I swear that the word on my lips was 'Yes.' This, as far as I knew it, was the truth. But some god must have forestalled me. Instead of the 'Yes' that my mind had framed, my lips said, 'No.'

I must have spoken strangely, because I saw him staring, arrested with narrowed eyes. It was a discomforting look, and I found myself elaborating. 'How can I tell? But I don't think so. I have told you that I have no power now, but the witch would not know that. She is still afraid of me. She has tried before, not once but twice, to snare me with her woman's spells. Both times she failed, and I think she would not have dared try again.'

He was silent for a while. Then he said, shortly: 'When my Queen died, there was talk of poison. I wondered.'

At this I could protest truthfully. 'There always is, but I beg you will not regard it! From what you have told me, I am certain there was no such thing. Besides, how?' I added, as convincingly as I could: 'Believe me, Arthur. If she were guilty, can you see any reason why I should want to protect Morgause from you?'

He still looked doubtful, but did not pursue it further. 'Well,' was all he said. 'She'll find her wings clipped now

for a while. She is back in Orkney, and Lot is dead.'

I took this in silently. It was another shock. In these few months, how much had changed. 'How?' I asked him. 'And when?'

'In the Forest battle. I can't say that I mourn him, except that he had that rat Aguisel under his fist, and I believe that I shall have trouble there soon.'

I said slowly: 'I have remembered something else. During the fighting in the Forest I heard them calling to one another that the king was dead. It struck me with helpless grief. For me, there is only one king ... But they must have been speaking of Lot. Well, yes, at least Lot was a known evil. Now, I suppose, Urien will have it all his own way in the north-east, and Aguisel with him ... But there's time enough for that. Meanwhile, what of Morgause? She was carrying a child at Luguvallium, and should have been delivered by now. A boy?'

'Two. Twin sons, born at Dunpeldyr. She joined Lot there after Morgan's wedding. Witch or no witch,' he said, with a trace of bitterness, 'she is a good breeder of sons. By the time Lot rejoined us here in Rheged, he was bragging that he had left yet another in her before he quitted Dunpeldyr.' He looked down at his hands. 'You must have had speech with her at the wedding. Did you find anything out about the other boy?'

There was no need to ask which boy he meant. It seemed that he could not bring himself to say 'my son'.

'Only that he is alive.'

His eyes came up quickly to mine. There was a flash in them, suppressed instantly. But I was sure that it was one of joy. So short a time ago, and he had looked for the child only to kill it.

I said, schooling my voice to hide the pity I felt: 'She tells me that she does not know where he is to be found. She may be lying, I'm not sure of that. It must be true that she kept him hidden away from Lot. But she may bring him into the open now. What has she to fear, now that lot has gone? Except, perhaps, from you?'

He was looking at his hands again. 'She need not fear me now on that score,' he said, woodenly.

That is all I can remember of that interview. I heard someone saying, but the words seemed to go round the curved tower walls like a whispered echo, or like words in my head alone: 'She is the falsest lady at this time alive, but she must live to rear her four sons by the King of Orkney, for they will be your faithful servants, and the bravest of your Companions.'

I must have shut my eyes then, against the wave of exhaustion that broke over me, for when I opened them again it was dark, and Arthur had gone, and the servant knelt beside the bed, offering me a bowl of soup.

CHAPTER 8

I am a strong man, and heal fast. I was on my feet again soon after this, and, some two or three weeks later, thought myself fit enough to ride south in Arthur's wake. He had gone the next morning, riding down to Caerleon. Since then a courier had brought news that longships had been sighted in the Severn estuary, so it looked as if the King would soon have another battle on his hands.

I would have liked to stay a while longer at Galava, perhaps to pass the summer in that familiar country, and revisit my old haunts in the Forest. But after the courier's visit, though Ector and Drusilla tried to keep me, I thought it high time to be gone. The battle now imminent would be fought from Caerleon: indeed, it was possible (the dispatch had said) that the invaders were attempting in force to destroy the war-leader's main stronghold and supply centre. I had no doubt that Arthur would hold Caerleon, but it was time I got back to Caer Camel to see how Derwen had been doing in my absence.

It was high summer when I saw the place again, and Derwen's team had done wonders. There it stood on its steep, flat-topped hill, the vision made real. The outer works were complete, the great double wall, of dressed stone topped with timber, running along the rim of the slope to crown the whole crest of the hill. Piercing it at their two opposing corners, the vast gateways were finished, and impressive. Great double doors of oak, studded with iron, stood open, pulled back to wall the tunnels that led in through the thick rampart. Above them went the sentry-way behind its battlements.

Moreover, there were sentries there. Since winter, Der-

wen told me, the King had had the place invested, so that the work of finishing could proceed inside defended walls. And finished it soon would be. Arthur had sent word that, come July or August, he wanted to be there with the knights-companions and all his cavalry.

Derwen was all for pressing on with the headquarters buildings, and with the King's own rooms, but I knew Arthur's mind better than that. I had given instructions that the men's barracks, and the horse-lines, the kitchen and service quarters must be completed first, and this had been done. A good start had been made, too, on the central buildings: the King, certainly, must lodge under skins and temporary timber, as if he were still in the field, but his great hall was built and roofed, and carpenters were at work on the long tables and benches within.

There had been no lack of local help. The folk who lived nearby, thankful to see a strong place going up near their settlements, had come whenever they could to fetch and carry, or to lend their skills to our own workmen. With them came many who were willing, but too old or too young to labour. Derwen would have sent them away, but I set them to clearing the nettle-grown trenches of a site not far from headquarters where formerly there must have been a shrine. I did not know, and nor did they, to what god it had been consecrated; but I know soldiers, and all fighting men need some centre-point, with a light and an offering, to tempt their god down among them for a moment of communion, when strength can be received in return for hope and faith.

Similarly, the spring on the northern embankment, which was enclosed within the outer works of the fortification, I set the women to clearing. This they did eagerly, for it was known that, time out of mind, the spring had been dedicated to the Goddess herself. For many years now it had been neglected, and sunk in a tangle of thorny growth that prevented them from making their offerings and sending up the sort of prayers that women send. Now the woodmen had hacked the thickets

down, so I let the women make their own shrine. They sang as they worked; they had been afraid, I think, that their sacred place would be shut away in an enclave of men. I told them not so: when once the Saxon power was broken, it was the High King's plan that men and women should come and go in peace, and Caer Camel would be a fair city set on a hill, rather than a camp of fighting men.

Finally, on the lowest part of the field, near the northeast gate, we cleared a place for the people and their cattle, where they could take refuge, and live, if need be, till danger was past.

Then Arthur came. In the night the Tor flamed suddenly, and beyond the flame could be seen the point of light that was the beacon hill behind. In the early morning sunlight he came riding along the Lake's edge, at the head of his knights. White was still his colour; he rode his white war-horse; his banner was white, and his shield also, too proud for a device such as the others wore. He shone out of the misty landscape like a swan on the pearled reaches of the Lake. Then the cavalcade was lost to sight beyond the trees that crowded the base of the hill, and presently the beat of hoofs came steadily on, and up the new curling road to the King's Gate.

The double gates stood open to receive him. Inside them, lining the newly paved road, waited all those who had built the place for him. So for the first time Arthur, duke of battles, High King among the other kings of Britain, entered the stronghold which was to be his own fair city of Camelot.

*　　*　　*

Of course he was pleased with it, and that night a feast was held, to which everyone, man, woman or child, who had lent a hand to the work, was bidden. He and his knights, with Derwen and myself and a few others, sat in the hall, at the long table so newly sanded that the dust still hung in the air and made haloes round the torches.

It was a joyous occasion, without form or solemnity, like a feast on a victory field. He made some kind of speech of welcome—of which I now remember no single word—pitching his voice so that the people pressing outside the doors could hear him; then, once we in the hall had started eating, he left his place at the table's head, and, with a mutton bone in one hand and a goblet in the other, went the rounds of the place, sitting with this group or that, dipping into a pot with the masons or letting the carpenters ply him from the mead-barrel, all the time looking, questioning, praising, with all his old, shining way. In a short while, their awe of him melting, they pelted their questions like snowballs. What had happened at Caerleon? In Linnuis? In Rheged? When would he settle here? Was it likely that the Saxons could press this far and get across the downs? What was Eosa's strength? Were the stories—of this, that and the other thing—true? All of which he answered patiently: what men knew they must face, they would face: it was the fear of surprise and the arrow in the dark that unmanned the hardiest.

It was all in the style of the old Arthur, the young King I knew. His looks matched it, too. The fatigue and despair had gone; grief had been laid aside; this was once again the King who held all men's eyes, and whose strength they felt they could draw on for ever, and never weaken him. By morning there would be no one there who would not willingly die in his service. That he knew this, and was fully aware of the effect he made, did not detract one whit from his greatness.

As usually happened, we had a word together before sleep. He was housed simply, but better than in a field tent. A roof of leather had been stretched across the beams of his half-finished sleeping chamber, and rugs laid. His own camp bed had been put against a wall, with the table and reading lamp he worked with, and a pair of chairs and the clothes chest and the stand with the silver bowl and water-jug.

We had not spoken privately since Galava. He asked

after my health, and spoke of the work I had done at Caer Camel, and then of what still remained to do. What had happened in the Caerleon fighting I had heard already, in the talk at table. I said something about the change in him. He looked at me for a moment or two, then, apparently, came to a decision.

'There's something I wanted to say to you, Merlin. I don't know if I have any right, but I shall say it all the same. When you last saw me, at Galava, sick as you were, you must have seen something of what I was feeling. In fact, how could you help it? As usual, I laid all my troubles on you, regardless of whether you were fit to bear them, or not.'

'I don't remember that. We talked, yes. I asked you what had happened, and you told me.'

'I did indeed. Now I am asking you to bear with me again. This time, I hope, I am laying nothing on you, but ...' A brief pause, to gather his thoughts. He seemed oddly hesitant. I wondered what was coming. He went on: 'You once said to me that life divided itself into light and dark, just as time does into day and night. It's true. One misfortune seems to breed another; and so it was with me. That was a time of darkness—the first I had suffered. When I came to you I was half broken with weariness, and with the weight of losses coming one on the other, as if the world had turned sour, and my luck was dead. The loss of my mother, by itself, could be no great grief to me; you know my heart about that, and to tell you the truth, I would grieve more over Drusilla's death, or Ector's. But the death of my Queen, little Guenever ... It could have been a good marriage, Merlin. We could, I believe, have come to love. What made that grief so bitter was the loss of the child, and the waste of her young life in pain, and with it, besides, the fear that she had been murdered, and by my enemies. Added to that—and I can admit this to you—was the weary prospect of having to start all over again to look for a suitable match, and going once more through all the ritual of mating, when so much

else lies waiting for me to do.'

I said quickly: 'You surely do not still believe that she was murdered?'

'No. You have set my mind at rest there, as you have about your own sickness. I had the same fear about you, that your death had been my fault.' He paused, and then said flatly: 'And that was the worst. It came as the final loss, overtopping all the others.' A gesture, half shame-faced, half resigned. 'You have told me, not once but many times, that when I looked for you in need, you would be there. And always, until then, it was true. Then suddenly, at the dark time, you were gone. And with so much still to do. Caer Camel just begun, and more fighting expected, and after that, the settlements and the law-giving, and the making of civil order ... But you were gone—murdered. I thought, through my fault like my little Queen. I could not think past it. I did not kill the children at Dunpeldyr, but by God, I could have killed the Queen of Orkney, had she crossed my path during those months!'

'I understand this. I think I knew it. Go on.'

'You have heard, now, about my victories in the field during this time. To other men it must have seemed as if my fortunes were rising to their peak. But to me, mainly because of your loss, I felt life at its blackest depth. Not only for grief at the loss of what lies between us, the long friendship—guardianship—I would say love——but for a reason I don't have to remind you of again. You know that I have been used to turn to you for everything, except in matters of warfare.'

I waited, but he did not go on. I said: 'Well, that is my function. No one man, even a High King, can do it all. You are young still, Arthur. Even my father Ambrosius, with all his years behind him, took advice at every turn. There is no weakness in this. Forgive me, but it is a sign of youth to think so.'

'I know. I don't think it. This is not what I am trying to say. I want to tell you of something that happened

while you were sick. After the battle in Rheged, I took hostages. The Saxons fled in to a thick wood on a hill—above the turret where we found you just after. We surrounded the hill, and then drove in on all sides, killing, until the few who were left, surrendered. I believe they might have yielded sooner, but I gave them no chance. I wanted to kill. At the last, those few who were left threw down their arms and came out. We took them. One of them was Colgrim's former second-in-command, Cynewulf. I would have killed him then and there, but he had yielded his arms. I loosed him on the promise to take his ships and go; and I took hostages.'

'Yes? It was a wise try. We know it did not work.' I said it without expression. I guessed what was coming. I had heard the tale already, from others.

'Merlin, when I heard that, instead of going back to Germany, Cynewulf had turned in again to our coasts, and was burning villages, I had the hostages killed.'

'It was not your choice. Cynewulf knew. It was what he would have done.'

'He is a barbarian, and an outlander. I am not. Granted Cynewulf knew. He may have thought I would not carry out the threat. Some of them were no more than boys. The youngest was thirteen. younger than I was when I first fought. They were brought to me, and I ordered it.'

'Rightly. Now forget it.'

'How? They were brave. But I had threatened it and so I did it. You spoke of the change in me. You were right. I am not the man I was before this past winter-time. This was the first thing I have done in war that I knew to be evil.'

I thought of Ambrosius at Doward: of myself at Tintagel. I said: 'We have all done things that we would like to forget. It may be that war itself is evil.'

'How could it be?' He spoke impatiently. 'But I'm not telling you about it now because I want either your advice or your comfort.' I waited, at a loss. He went on, picking his words: 'It was the worst thing I have had to do. I

did it, and I will abide by it. What I have to say now is this: if you had been there, I would have turned to you, as always, and asked for your counsel. And though you have said that you no longer have the power of prophecy, I would still have hoped—been sure—that you could see what the future held, and would guide me in the path I ought to take.'

'But this time your prophet was dead, so you chose your own path?'

'Just so.'

'I understand. You offer me this as comfort, that both act and decision can be safely left to you, even though I am here again? Knowing, as we both do, that your "prophet" is still dead?'

'No.' He spoke quickly, strongly. 'You have mistaken me. I am offering you comfort, yes, but of a different kind. Do you think I don't know that it has been a dark time with you, too, ever since the raising of the sword? Forgive me if I am meddling in matters I don't understand, but looking back at what has passed, I think ... Merlin, what I am trying to tell you is this, that I believe your god is with you still.'

There was silence. Through it came the flutter of the flame in the bronze lamp, and, infinitely far away, the noises of the camp outside. We looked at one another, he still in early manhood, myself aged and (as I knew) sorely weakened by my recent sickness. And subtly, between us, the balance was changing; had, perhaps, already changed. He, to offer me strength and comfort. *Your god is with you still.* How could he think so? He had only to recall my lack of anything but the most trivial tricks of magic, my want of defence against Morgause, my inability to find out anything about Mordred. But he had spoken, not with the passionate conviction of youth, but with the calm certainty of a judge.

I thought back, for the first time pushing aside the apathy that, since my sickness, had succeeded the earlier mood of tranquil acceptance. I began to see which way

his thoughts had gone. One could say they were the thoughts of a general who can lift a victory out of a planned retreat. Or a leader of men who is able, with a word, to give or withhold confidence.

Your god is with you, he had said. With me, perhaps, in the poisoned cup, and the suffering months that had withdrawn me from Arthur's side, and forced him into solitary power? With me (though this he did not know) in the still whisper that had led me to deny the poisoning, and so save from his vengeance Morgause, the mother of those four sons ... ? With me in the losing of Mordred, whose survival had brought that glow of joy to Arthur's eye? As he would be with me, even, when at length I went to the living burial I feared, and left Arthur alone on middle-earth, with Mordred his fate still at large?

Like the first breath of living wind to the sailor becalmed and starving, I felt hope stir. It was, then, not enough to accept, to wait on the god's return in all his light and strength. In the dark ebbtide, as much as in the flow, could be felt the full power of the sea.

I bowed my head, like a man accepting a king's gift. There was no need to speak. We read one another's minds. He said, with an abrupt change of tone: 'How long before this place is complete?'

'In full fighting order, another month. It is virtually ready now.'

'So I judged. I can transfer now from Caerleon, foot, horse and baggage?'

'Whenever you please.'

'And then? What have you planned for yourself, until you are needed again to build for peace?'

'I've made no plans. Go home, perhaps.'

'No. Stay here.'

It sounded like an order. I raised my brows.

'Merlin, I mean it. I want you here. We need not split the High King's power in two before the time comes when we must. Do you understand me?'

'Yes.'

'Then stay. Make a place for yourself here, and stay away from your marvellous Welsh cave for a while longer.'

'For a while longer,' I promised him, smiling. 'But not here, Arthur. I need silence and solitude, things hard to come by within reach of such a city as this will become, once you are here as High King. May I look for a place, and build a house? By the time you are ready to hang your sword up on the wall over your chair of state, my marvellous cave will be here, near by, and the hermit installed, ready to join your counsels. If, by that time, you remember to need him.'

He laughed at that, and seemed content, and we went to our beds.

narrow causeway that led the road across, and here and there the boats of fishermen, or the barges of the marsh-dwellers.

From this shining sheet of water rose the hill called the Tor, shaped like a giant cone, as symmetrical as if hand-built by men. It was flanked by a gentler, rounded hill, and beyond that by another, a long, low ridge, like a limb drawn up in the water. Here lay the wharfs; one could see masts like reeds beyond a dip in the green. Beyond the Island's triple hill, stretching into the distance, was a great shining level of water, sown with sedge and bulrush and the clusters of reed thatch among the willows where the marsh-people lived. It was all one long, shifting, moving glimmer, as far as the sea. One could see why the Island was called Ynys Witrin, the Isle of Glass. Sometimes, now, men call it Avalon.

There were orchards everywhere on Ynys Witrin. The trees crowded so thickly along the harbour ridge and up the lower slopes of the Tor that only the plumes of woodsmoke, rising between the boughs, showed where the village lay. (King's capital though it was, it could earn no grander title.) A short way up the hill, above the trees, could be seen the cluster of huts, like hives, where the Christian hermits lived, and the holy women. Melwas left them alone; they even had their own church, built near the Goddess' shrine. The church was a humble affair made of wattle and mud, and roofed with thatch. It looked as if the first bad storm would blow it clean out of the ground.

Far different was the shrine of the Goddess. It was said that, with the centuries, the land itself had slowly grown up around it and possessed it, so that now it lay beneath the level of men's footing, like a crypt. I had never seen it. Men were not normally received within its precincts, but today the Lady herself, with the veiled and white-clad women and girls behind her, all bearing flowers, waited to welcome the High King. The old woman beside her, with the rich mantle, and the royal circlet on her

grey hair, must be Melwas' mother, the queen. Here, she took precedence of her son. Melwas himself stood off to one side, among his captains and young men. He was a thick-set, handsome fellow, with a curled cap of brown hair, and a glossy beard. He had never married: rumour had it that no woman had ever passed the test of his mother's judgment.

The Lady greeted Arthur, and two of the youngest maidens came forward and hung his neck with flowers. There was singing, all women's voices, high and sweet. The grey sky parted and let through a glint of sunlight. It was seen as an omen; people smiled and looked at one another, and the singing grew more joyous. The Lady turned, and, with her women, led the way down the long flight of shallow steps into the shrine. The old queen followed, and after her Arthur, with the rest of us. Lastly Melwas came, with his followers. The common folk stayed outside. All through the ceremony we could hear the muttering and shifting, as they waited to catch another look at the legendary Arthur of the nine battles.

The shrine was not large; our company filled it to capacity. It was dimly lit, with no more than half a dozen scented lamps, grouped to either side of the archway that led to the inner sanctuary. In the smoky light the white robes of the women shone ghostly. Veils hid their faces and covered their hair and floated, cloudy, to the ground. Of them all, only the Lady herself could be seen clearly: she stood full in the lamplight, stoled with silver, and wearing a diadem that caught what light there was. She was a queenly figure; one could well believe that she came of royal stock.

Veiled, too, was the inner sanctuary; no one save the initiated—not even the old queen herself—would ever see beyond that curtain. The ceremony that we saw (though it would not be seemly to write of it here) would not be the customary one sacred to the Goddess. It was certainly lengthy; we endured two hours of it, standing crowded together; but I suspect that the Lady wanted to

make the most of the occasion, and who was to blame her if thoughts of future patronage were in her mind? But it came to an end at last. The Lady accepted Arthur's gift, presented it with the appropriate prayer, and we emerged in due order into the daylight, to receive the shouts of the people.

It was a small incident, which might have left no mark in my memory, but for what came later. As it is, I can still recall the soft, lively feel of the day, the first drops of rain that blew in our faces as we left the shrine, and the thrush's song from the thorn tree standing deep in summer grass spiked with pale orchis and thick with the gold of the small flower they call Lady's Slipper. The way to Melwas' palace lay through precincts of summer lawn, where among the apple trees grew flowers that could not have come there in nature, all with their uses, as well I knew, in medicine or magic. The *ancillae* practised healing, and had planted the virtuous herbs. (I saw no other kind. The Goddess is not the same whose bloody knife was thrown, once, from the Green Chapel.) At least, I thought, if I have to live hereabouts, the country is a better garden for my plants than the open hillside at home.

With that, we came to the palace, and were welcomed by Melwas into his hall of feasting.

The feast was much like any other, except (as was natural in that place) for the excellence and variety of the fish dishes. The old queen occupied the central position at the high table, with Arthur to one side of her and Melwas to the other. None of the women from the shrine, not even the Lady herself, was present. What women there were, I noticed with some amusement, were far from being beauties, and were none of them young. Rumour had perhaps been right about the queen: I recalled a glance and a smile passing between Melwas and a girl in the crowd: well, the old woman could not watch him all the time. His other appetites were well enough; the food was plentiful and well cooked, though nothing fanciful, and

there was a singer with a pleasant voice. The wine, which was good, came (we were told) from a vineyard forty miles off, on the chalk. It had recently been destroyed by one of the sharp incursions of the Saxons, who had begun to come closer this summer.

Once this was said, it was inevitable which way the talk would go. Between dissection of the past, and discussion of the future, time passed quickly, with Arthur and Melwas in accord, which augured well.

We left before midnight. A moon coming towards the full gave a clear light. She hung low and close behind the beacon at the summit of the Tor, marking with sharp shadows the walls of Melwas' stronghold, a fort rebuilt on the site of some ancient hilltop fastness. It was a place for retreat in times of trouble: his palace, where we had been entertained, stood below, on the level near the water.

We were none too soon. A mist was rising from the Lake. Pale wreaths of it eddied across the grass, below the trees, smoking to our horses' knees. Soon the causeway would be hidden. Melwas, escorting us with his torch-bearers, guided us across the pale fog that was the Lake, and up into clear air, onto the ringing stone of the ridge. Then he made his farewells, and set off for home.

I drew rein, looking back. From here, of the three hills that made the island, only the Tor was visible, rising from a lake of cloud. From the shrouding mist near its foot could be seen the red torchlit glow of the palace, not yet quenched for the night. The moon had sailed clear of the Tor into a dark sky. Near the beacon tower, on the rising spiral of the road to the high fortress, a light flickered and moved.

My flesh crept, like a dog's at the sight of a spectre. A wisp of mist lay there, high, and across it a shadow strode, like a giant's. The Tor was a known gate to the Other-world; for a flash I wondered if, with the Sight come back to me, I was watching one of the guardians of the place, one of the fiery spirits who keep the gate. Then my sight cleared, and I saw that it was a man with a torch, running

up the steep of the Tor to light the beacon fire.

As I set spurs to my horse I heard Arthur's voice, lifted in quick command. A rider detached himself from the cavalcade and leaped forward at a stretched gallop. The others, silent all at once, followed him, fast but collected, while behind us the flames went up into the night, calling Arthur of the nine battles to yet another fight.

CHAPTER 10

The investing of Caer Camel saw the start of the new campaign. Four more years it took: siege and skirmish, flying attack and ambush—except during the midwinter months he was never at rest. And twice more, towards the end of that time, he triumphed over the enemy in a major engagement.

The first of these battles was joined in response to a call from Elmet. Eosa himself had landed from Germany, at the head of fresh Saxon war-bands, to be joined by the East Saxons already established north of the Thames. Cerdic added a third point to the spear with a force brought by longboat from Rutupiae. It was the worst threat since Luguvallium. The invaders came swarming in force up the Vale, and were threatening what Arthur had long foreseen, to break through the barrier of the mountains by the Gap. Surprised and (no doubt) disconcerted by the readiness of the fort at Olicana, they were checked and held there, while the message was sent flashing south for Arthur. The East Saxon force, which was considerable, was concentrated on Olicana; the King of Elmet held them there, but the others streamed westwards through the Gap. Arthur, heading fast up the west road, reached the Tribuit fort before them, and re-forming there in strength, caught them at Nappa Ford. He vanquished them there, in a bloody struggle, then threw his fast cavalry up through the Gap to Olicana, and, side by side with the King of Elmet, drove the enemy back into the Vale. From there a movement beyond countering, right back, east and south, until the old frontiers contained them, and the Saxon 'king', looking round on his

bleeding and depleted forces, admitted defeat.

A defeat, as it turned out, all but final. Such was Arthur's name now, that its very mention had come to mean victory, and 'the coming of Arthur' a synonym for salvation. The next time he was called for—it was the clearing-up operation of the long campaign—no sooner had the dreaded cavalry with the white horse at its head and the Dragon glinting over the helmets, showed in the mountain pass of Agned, than the enemy fell into the disarray of near panic, so that the action was a pursuit rather than a battle, a clearing of territory after the main action. Through all this fighting, Gereint (who knew every foot of the territory) was with the cavalry, with a command worthy of him. So Arthur rewarded service.

Eosa himself had received a wound in the fighting at Nappa. He never took the field again. It was the young Cerdic, the Aetheling, who led the Saxons at Agned, and did his best to hold them against the terror of Arthur's onslaught. It was said that afterwards, as he withdrew—in creditable order—to the waiting longboats, he made a vow that, when he next set foot on British territory, he would stay, and not even Arthur should prevent him.

For that, as I could have told him, he would have to wait till Arthur was no longer there.

*   *   *

It was never my intention here to give details of the years of battle. This is a chronicle of a different kind. Besides, everyone knows now about his campaign to free Britain and cleanse her shores of the Terror. It was all written down in that house up in Vindolanda, by Blaise, and the solemn, quiet clerk who came from time to time to help him. Here I will only repeat that never once during the years it took him to fight the Saxons to a standstill was I able to bring prophecy or magic to his aid. The story of those years is one of human bravery, of endurance and of dedication. It took twelve major engagements, and some

seven years' hard work, before the young King could count the country safe at last for husbandry and the arts of peace.

It is not true, as the poets and singers would have it, that Arthur drove all the Saxons from the shores of Britain. He had come to recognise, as Ambrosius did, that it was impossible to clear lands that stretched for miles of difficult country, and which had, moreover, the easy retreat of the seas behind. Since the time of Vortigern, who first invited the Saxons into Britain as his allies, the southeast shore of our country had been settled Saxon territory, with its own rulers and its own laws. There was some justification for Eosa's assumption of the title of king. Even had it been possible for Arthur to clear the Saxon Shore, he would have had to drive out settlers of perhaps the third generation, who had been born and bred within these shores, and make them take ship back to their grandfathers' country, where they might meet as harsh a welcome as here. Men fight desperately for their homes when the alternative is to be homeless. And, while it was one thing to win the great pitched battles, he knew that to drive men into the hills and forests and waste places, whence they could never be dislodged, or even pinned down and fought, was to invite a long war which could have no victory. He had before him the example of the Old Ones; they had been dispossessed by the Romans and had fled into the waste places of the hills; four hundred years later they were still there, in their remote mountain fastnesses, and the Romans themselves had gone. So, accepting the fact that there must be still Saxon kingdoms lodged within the shores of Britain, Arthur set himself to see that their boundaries were secure, and that for very fear their kings would hold to them.

So he passed his twentieth year. He came back to Camelot at the end of October, and plunged straight away into council. I was there, appealed to sometimes, but in the main watching and listening only: the counsel I gave him, I gave in private, behind closed doors. In the public sight, the decisions were his. Indeed, they were his as often as mine, and as time went on I was content to let his judgment have its way. He was impulsive sometimes, and in many matters still lacked experience or precedent; but he never let his judgment be ridden by impulse, and he maintained, in spite of the arrogance that success might be expected to bring with it, the habit of letting men talk their fill, so that when finally the King's decision was announced, each man thought that he had had a say in it.

One of the things that was brought up at length was the question of a new marriage. I could see he had not expected this; but he kept silent, and after a while grew easier, and listened to the older men. They were the ones who had names and pedigrees and land-claims by heart. It came to me also, watching, that they were the ones who, when Arthur was first proclaimed, would have nothing to do with the claim. Now not even his own companion knights could show more loyal. He had won the elders, as he had won all else. You would have thought each one of them had discovered him unknown in the Wild Forest, and handed him the sword of the Kingdom.

You would also have thought that each man was discussing the marriage of a favourite son. There was much beard-stroking and head-wagging, and names were suggested and discussed, and even wrangled over, but none met with general acclaim, until one day a man from Gwynedd, who had fought right through the wars with Arthur, and was a kinsman of Maelgon himself, got to his feet and made a speech about his home country.

Now when you get a black Welshman on his feet and ready to talk, it is like inviting a bard; the thing is done in order, in cadence, and at very great length: but such was this man's way, and such the beauty of his speaking voice, that after the first few minutes men settled back comfortably to listen, as they might have listened at a feast.

His subject seemed to be his country, the loveliness of its valleys and hills, the blue lakes, the creaming seas, the

deer and eagles and the small singing-birds, the bravery
of the men and the beauty of the women. Then we heard
of the poets and singers, the orchards and flowery
meadows, the riches of sheep and cattle and the veined
minerals in the rock. From this there followed the brave
history of the land, battles and victories, courage in
defeat, the tragedy of young death and the fecund beauty
of young love.

He was getting near his point. I saw Arthur stir in his
great chair.

And, said the speaker, the country's wealth and beauty
and bravery were all there invested in the family of its
kings, a family which (I had ceased to listen closely; I
was watching Arthur through the light of a badly flaring
lamp, and my head ached)—a family which seemed to
have a genealogy as ancient and twice as long as Noah's ...

There was, of course, a princess. Young, lovely, sprung
from a line of ancient Welsh kings joined with a noble
Roman clan. Arthur himself came from no higher stock
... And now one saw why the long-drawn panegyric, and
the eye slightly askance at the young King.

Her name, it seemed, was Guinevere.

* * *

I saw them again, the two of them. Bedwyr, dark and
eager, with eyes of love fixed on the other boy; Arthur-
Emrys, at twelve years old the leader, full of energy and
the high fire of living. And the white shadow of the owl
drifting overhead between them; the *guenhwyvar* of a
passion and a grief, of high endeavour and a quest that
would take Bedwyr into a world of spirit and leave
Arthur lonely, waiting there at the centre of glory to
become himself a legend and himself a grail ...

* * *

I came back to the hall. The pain in my head was fierce.

The fitful dazzling light struck like a spear against my eyes. I could feel the sweat trickling down beneath my robe. My hands slipped on the carved arms of the chair. I fought to steady my breathing, and the hammer-beat of my heart.

No one had noticed me. Time had passed. The formality of the council had broken up. Arthur was the centre now of a group, talking and laughing; about the table the older men sat still, relaxed and easy, chatting among themselves. Servants had come in, and wine was being poured. The talk was all around me, like water rising. In it could be heard the notes of triumph and release. It was done; there would be a new queen, and a new succession. The wars were over, and Britain, alone of Rome's old subject lands, was safe behind her royal ramparts for the next span of sunlit time.

Arthur turned his head and met my eyes. I neither moved nor spoke, but the laughter died out of his face, and he got to his feet. He came over as quickly as a spear starting for the mark, waving his companions back out of earshot.

'Merlin, what is it? This wedding? You cannot surely think that it—'

I shook my head. The pain went through it like a saw. I think I cried out. At the King's move there had been a hush; now there was complete silence in the hall. Silence, and eyes, and the unsteady dazzle of the flames.

He leaned forward, as if to take my hand. 'What is it? Are you ill? Merlin, can you speak?'

His voice swelled, echoed, was whirled away. It did not concern me. Nothing concerned me but the necessity of speech. The lamp flames were burning somewhere in my breast, their hot oil spilling in bubbles through my blood. Breath came thick and piercing, like smoke in the lungs. When I found words at last they surprised me. I had seen nothing beyond the chamber long ago in the Perilous Chapel, and the vision which might or might not have meant anything. What I heard myself saying, in a

harsh and ringing voice that brought Arthur up like a blow, and startled every man to his feet, had a very different burden.

'It is not over yet, King! Get you to horse, and ride! They have broken the peace, and soon they will be at Badon! Men and women are dying in their blood, and children cry, before they are spitted like chickens. There is no king near to protect them. Get you there now, duke of the kings! This is for you alone, when the people themselves cry out for you! Go with your Companions, and put a finish to this thing! For, by the Light, Arthur of Britain, this is the last time, and the last victory! Go now!'

The words went ringing into total silence. Those who had never before heard me speak with power were pale: all made the sign. My breathing was loud in the hush, like that of an old man fighting to stave off death.

Then from the crowd of younger men came sounds of disbelief, even scoffing. It was not to be wondered at. They had heard stories of my past deeds, but so many of these were patently poets' work, and all, having gone already into song, had taken the high colour of legend. Last time I had spoken so had been at Luguvallium, before the raising of the sword, and some of them had been children then. These knew me only as engineer and man of medicine, the quiet councillor whom the King favoured.

The muttering was all around me, wind in the trees.

'There has been no signal; what is he talking about? As if the High King could go off on his bare word, for a scare like this! Arthur has done enough, and so have we; the peace is settled, anyone can see that! Badon? Where is it? Well, but no Saxon would attack there, not now ... Yes, but if they did, there is no force there to hold them, he was right about that ... No, it's nonsense, the old man has lost his senses again. Remember, up there in the Forest, what he was like? Crazy, and that's the truth ... and now moon-mad again, with the same malady?'

Arthur had not taken his eyes off me. The whispers blew to and fro. Someone called for a doctor, and there

was coming and going in the hall. He ignored it. He and I were alone together. His hand came out and took me by the wrist. I felt, through the whirling pain, his young strength forcing me gently back into my chair. I had not even known I was standing. His other hand went out, and someone put a goblet into it. He held the wine to my lips.

I turned my head aside. 'No. Leave me. Go now. Trust me.'

'By all the gods there are,' he said, from the back of his throat. 'I trust you.' He swung on his heel, and spoke. 'You, and you, and you, give the orders. We ride now. See to it.'

Then back to me, but speaking so that all could hear: 'Victory, you said?'

'Victory. Can you doubt it?'

For a moment, through the stresses of pain, I saw his look; the look of the boy who had braved the white flame at my word, and lifted the enchanted sword. 'I doubt nothing,' said Arthur.

Then he laughed, leaned forward and kissed me on the cheek, and, with his Companions following, went swiftly out of the hall.

The pain lifted. I could breathe and see. I got up and walked after them, out into the air. Those left in the hall drew back and let me through. No one spoke to me, or dared to question. I mounted the rampart and looked outwards. The sentry on duty there moved away, not like a soldier, but sidling. The whites of his eyes showed. Word had gone round fast. I hunched my cloak against the wind and stayed where I was.

They had gone, so small a troop to throw against the might of the final Saxon bid for Britain. The gallop dwindled into the night and was gone. Somewhere in that darkness to the north the Tor was standing up into the black sky. No light, nothing. Beyond it, no light. Nor south, nor east; no light anywhere, or warning fires. Only my word.

A sound somewhere in the blowing darkness. For a moment I took it for an echo of that distant gallop; then, hearing in it, faintly, the cry and clash of armies, I thought that vision had returned to me. But my head was clear, and the night, with all its sounds and shadows, was mortal night.

Then the sounds wheeled closer, and went streaming overhead, high in the black air. It was the wild geese, the pack of heaven's hounds, the Wild Hunt that courses the skies with Llud, King of the Otherworld, in time of war and storm. They had risen from the Lake waters, and now came overhead, flighting the dark. Straight from the silent Tor they came, to wheel over Caer Camel, then back across the slumbering Island, the noise of their voices and the galloping wings lost at length down the reaches of the night towards Badon.

With the dawn, the beacon lights blazed across the land. But whoever led the Saxon hordes to Badon, must hardly have set foot on its bloody soil when, out of the dark, more swiftly even than birds could have flown or fire signalled, the High King Arthur and his own picked knights fell on them and destroyed them, smashing the barbarian power utterly, for his day, and for the rest of his generation.

So the god came back to me, Merlin his servant. Next day I left Caer Camel, and rode out to look for a place where I could build myself a house.